DERELICT

"Cohen has real talent with character development and interaction, and prickly, defensive Ro is a sympathetic and interesting heroine."

--Publishers Weekly

"LJ Cohen deftly weaves together realistic teenage characters, futuristic technology, and big stakes for a real page turner."

--Wen Spencer, Award winning SF&F novelist, author of the Ukiah Oregon and Elfhome series

"Get on board Derelict, and you'll take an edgy, nonstop flight into an audacious SF future with unremitting danger as your pilot -- and thrilling adventure your destination."

--Lynn Viehl, NYT best selling author of the Stardoc and Darkyn series

"Intricate plotting melded seamlessly with delightful characterizations kept me turning pages as fast as I could go in an attempt to keep up with the unfolding story. A cracking yarn set in a lush future I'm hoping we'll hear more of."

--Nathan Lowell, Creator of the Golden Age of the Solar Clipper and the Tanyth Fairport Adventures

THE BETWEEN

". . .a moving tale of heroism and compassion. . . Lydia is a young woman utterly unprepared for the world she's about to enter--but she learns fast. She's a character you'll want to meet again, from a writer you'll want to read again. Take good note: LJ Cohen is a new voice to follow."

--Jeffrey A. Carver, author of The Chaos Chronicles

DERELICT

Also by LJ Cohen

The Between
Future Tense
Stranger Worlds than These (short stories)

DERELICT
LJ Cohen

Interrobang Books
Newton, MA

Published by Interrobang Books
Newton, MA

www.interrobangbooks.com

First print edition: June, 2014

ISBN-10: 0984787089
ISBN-13: 978-0-9847870-8-1

To Neil, for always asking all the right questions

Chapter 1

ALL RO NEEDED was his signature.

She pressed back against the form-fitting surface of the chair and glanced at the door to her father's room. Once he signed, she'd be free. If he signed. With a quick gesture, she launched the heads-up mode on her micro and pulled up the scholarship application again, reviewing it for what felt like the hundredth time. There was nothing else she could add that she hadn't already sweated over for the past month. The rest was up to him.

After a final error-check, Ro signed and locked the document before collapsing the holographic display. All the color disappeared from the room, leaving behind bland standard-issue tan furniture and the glare of industrial lights reflecting off burnished metal walls.

The door opened, and she jerked upright, grabbing her micro as it tumbled off her lap. Her father strode into the common room and scowled when he saw her.

"I put on a fresh pot of coffee," Ro said, her voice rising as if she'd asked a question.

Unshaven and wearing the same rumpled coverall he'd had

on for days, he brushed past her to pour himself a cup.

Ro studied the set of his shoulders and waited until he finished drinking. "I pushed the consent form to your micro."

He slammed the empty cup on the counter. "You need to stop wasting my time."

"Will you just look at it?"

"I've already told you. It's impossible." Turning away, he dropped his cup in the sink.

She clenched her hands into tight fists and stood, looking for someone or something to hit, but her only satisfying targets were the metal door to their compartment and her father. Both were equally unyielding.

"It won't cost you anything," she said, forcing her hands to relax and her voice to stay level.

His ice-cold green eyes stared through her. "Maldonados don't accept charity."

"It's not charity. It's a chance at a scholarship. A merit scholarship." Ro hated herself for pleading. "You know I'm good enough."

"I don't have the funds to send you, and I won't be beholden to the Commonwealth." The conversation ended as most of them did—with her father walking away and Ro shaking with pent-up frustration.

Her hands trembled, and she slammed them on the galley's counter. "Then cut me loose. I'll figure it out on my own."

He turned at the door to the bedroom he had claimed as his workshop, his stare piercing. "No."

The blood pounded in her ears. He disappeared inside. She swore at the closed door and stormed out of their quarters. Nothing had changed. Ro squeezed her eyes shut on furious tears, cursing herself for hoping this time would be different.

She dried her face, pulled out her micro, and lodged another formal request with Commander Mendez. Her soft boots muffled the pounding of her feet as she stomped down the corridor. At the first airlock, she slammed her hand against the ident plate. The red light blinked, shifted to amber, and settled back on red, mocking her. "Piece of shit design," she muttered as she lightened her pressure and rested her whole hand on the metal until it deigned to register her metrics. She'd built better ones as a child out of the junk her father discarded from his workshop.

Ro counted to three, waiting for the station's tired AI to parse her request and decide to give her access. The round door irised in silence. Daedalus didn't even bother to acknowledge her. Wiggling her middle finger at the recessed ocular, she stepped through the opening into the central nexus. She needed to get as far away from her quarters and her father as she could despite the confines of the station.

"And then what?" Her shoulders slumping, she paused at the door that led to the command section and glared at another one of Daedalus' blinking red eyes. "No, I'm not talking to you, dumb-ass." Once again the AI didn't answer. A third door dilated. Ro jumped back as one of the station's doctors stepped through with her two sons.

Turning to the observation port, Ro stared out at the craggy surface of the asteroid the station called home. Sunlight glared off the pitted surface of the derelict transport ship that had crashed here decades before Daedalus had been built. A field of solar panels glinted in the harsh light outside. This side of the structure always faced its star, the other side showed the night sky. She, too, was trapped in a synchronous orbit on Daedalus, always subject to her father's gravity.

He'd moved them to Daedalus Station three years ago, only telling her he had voided his previous contract moments before dragging her onto the transport. Two years before that, he cut off her access to the Hub's Virtual School, insisting she had everything she needed and refusing to "waste" any more money on it. He'd yanked her from anything she had gotten comfortable with over the course of too many years and too many postings to count.

"Hey, Ro!"

She looked over her shoulder and shot the doctor's younger son a polite and not-in-the-mood-to-talk look. "Jem, Barre, Doctor Durbin."

Jem would hit escape velocity as soon as his test scores got transmitted off station. All the best Unis in the Hub, maybe even the ones on Earth, would be tripping over themselves for him.

He smiled up at her, teeth very white against dark skin, his brown eyes puppy-dog eager. "Didn't you see my message? I ran into a problem with the program I'm working on. Can I come by later and show you?"

Ro shrugged and didn't miss the frown that pursed the doctor's lips. The daughter of the station's engineer didn't reach anywhere near the Durbins' professional league. Everything about Leta Durbin came off as severe and elegant, from her sharp cheekbones to her close cropped tight black curls to the tailored bronze jumpsuit that brought out the highlights in her smooth, brown skin.

"Come on, Ro," Jem pleaded. "You're better at debugging than me, and you know it."

She glanced at Dr. Durbin and turned back to the slim boy. "I'll see if I have time later this week." He beamed up at her. She smirked as Dr. Durbin's frown deepened.

A syncopated tapping filled the silent nexus. Ro turned toward the noise. Jem's older brother Barre stared out the viewport, his gaze unfocused, his foot beating against the floor, his head bobbing to a rhythm no one else could hear. She and Barre were the same age, but Ro didn't think they'd ever said more than a few words to one another.

The two brothers had the same dark eyes, sculpted cheekbones and defined nose, courtesy of their mother. Barre had the woman's dark skin tone and hair, but sported dreads that hung past his shoulders. His unruly hair must have driven her mad. Jem kept his hair short and tight like his mother's, but his father's Afrikaner heritage gave the boy lighter skin and softer curls.

Dr. Durbin scowled at Barre. "Turn it off. Now."

Sighing, he shifted until he looked directly at Ro. She started before realizing he wasn't actually focusing on her but on a spot hanging in the air between them. His gaze shifted up and to the right before he blinked twice with deliberate slowness. Son of a bitch had a neural interface. They were pretty sweet and, if she could even hope for a chance at one, she would use it for a lot more than listening to music.

"Coming to dinner?" Jem asked. "We could go over my design, now."

"Sorry. Busy." Ever since Ro had made the mistake of answering one of Jem's endless questions about coding on the ed-list, he'd pestered her with more and more complex problems. Encouraging him only led to more questions. Despite herself, she grinned, convinced if he stayed on Daedalus long enough, he'd come up with one she couldn't answer.

The Durbins headed to the opposite airlock into the core and the communal dining room most of the transient staff preferred.

Alone again in the nexus, Ro stared out the viewport, seeing past the rocky ground covered with tilted solar panels and the pre-fab domes of the station's segments connected by lengths of shiny corridors. She imagined the field of stars beyond the asteroid and all the inhabited places she could reach if only she had her freedom.

Anywhere would be better than here. Anywhere she could escape her father would do. It didn't have to be Earth. Maybe she could hopscotch her way closer to the Hub. Ro stared out across the star field. There had to be jobs for someone like her.

*

Commander Mendez stood behind a completely clean desk with her back to Ro, studying her latest transfer request. Ro shifted her weight back and forth as the silence lengthened. Bare walls reflected the harsh lighting. Metal conference chairs lined the far side of the room like orderly soldiers. She brushed at the grime on her shirt, but there wasn't anything she could do about the oil stains and the frayed hem.

"Mediating family disputes is not part of my job description," Mendez said, without turning around.

Ro swore to herself.

"However," the commander continued, and this time she did face Ro, her dark eyes shadowed. "I am aware that Daedalus has taken advantage of your talents in addition to your father's."

In her crisp gray and silver uniform, her black hair cut in the severe standard military crop, she at least looked the part, even if the station was the last stand of the barely competent, or the first step for the desperately ambitious. After three years on Daedalus, Ro still couldn't figure out which Mendez was.

"Some compensation is owed you."

Screw compensation. There wasn't much to spend it on out here, and Ro doubted it would be enough to book passage anywhere, even if she could override her father's injunction. What she needed was transfer papers.

"Your father's contract runs two more standard years before he's up for review."

Ro turned away from another adult lecture on patience. So what? Two more years trapped here, and she'd still have nothing to show for it. Two more years for her father to skirt the edge of insubordination until he got fired again. Then he could find yet another dead end job he could claim was beneath him and paid him accordingly. The only difference two years would make is by then, she wouldn't need her father's permission for anything, ever again.

"I don't have the authority to give you a permanent station position, but in light of your work here, I can appoint you as an engineering intern."

She stared at Mendez.

"It comes with a small stipend."

"Thank you, Commander," Ro said, trying to keep the disappointment out of her voice.

Mendez's intense gaze never left Ro's face. "In a year, you will have earned the ability to apply for transfer. As a full citizen."

Ro's eyes snapped wide open. With a work history and

maybe even a recommendation, she could go anywhere. It was just a year. Ro could do anything for a year.

*

The nondescript food pocket clunked from the vending machine just as Ro's micro vibrated. She shoved the sandwich in her mouth and projected the display on the bulkhead wall. Mendez hadn't wasted any time getting her plugged into the system. Work orders scrolled faster than her eye could follow.

What the hell had her father been doing? No wonder the commander had been so happy to put her on the payroll. Well, the better Ro did her job, the sooner her work history would give her the advantage she needed and the ability to escape him and this rock.

She ordered the micro to reload the outstanding work. Climate control in the medical bay had been marked a priority. She bumped it to the bottom of the list—the Doctors Durbin were cold enough to keep a cryonics lab at subzero. Ro kept scrolling: broken beverage dispenser in the officers' break room, a clogged head in the residence section, and loose radiation shielding on the storage bay's roof. She put the beverage dispenser on her personal list. It was never a bad idea to keep the boss happy. Most of the issues were small nags instead of major system problems. No wonder her father had ignored them.

Whatever kept him up most nights, it certainly wasn't handling work orders.

She kept looking though the list, wondering what else she should prioritize. When an item near the end scrolled by, she stopped the display. Power draw in the derelict ship had spiked over baseline during the past few months and Daedalus was requesting authorization to re-balance the station's load. This was the AI's fourth request for the same problem, but her father had marked it as complete all four times.

Why would he risk falsifying station engineering records for something that should have been an easy fix? It didn't make any sense. That could get his contract terminated and permanently blacklist him.

If it was true and Ro could prove it, maybe Mendez would finally support her emancipation and award her the remainder of his contract.

She didn't even need to sneak around the station anymore. The commander had given her unrestricted access.

Sweet.

Chapter 2

MICAH GLANCED AROUND the generic space that had been their quarters for the past half year. It looked no different from any number of assigned living spaces scattered across dozens of sectors. A modular sofa with easily reconfigurable seating and a colorless nano-polymer cover took up most of the living area. Water rings overlapped the surface of the low table in interlocking circles. An empty glass sat at the table's edge exactly where it had been for the last three days.

He slipped into the corridor and headed to his lab in the cargo hold of the abandoned ship. It had taken him weeks of work, even with repair drones, and Mendez's tacit approval, but Micah had managed to clear out and power the forward storage bay, rig up full spectrum solars, and automate a weather loop for irrigation.

When he reached his green haven, Micah emerged into the full light of an artificial day, blinking until his vision adjusted to the brightness. The plants didn't care if their cycle matched the station, and he liked working at night better anyway. He looked up at the vaulting ceiling overhead. Enough moisture had condensed around the ceiling plates that it would probably rain later.

His seedlings looked healthy—long green leaves fanned out on each plant on five sides from a central stalk—but he'd gotten this far too many times before. It was make or break time. If none of his new crosses panned out, he'd be out of luck and out of business. The lovely, deep green foliage growing in neat rows up toward his artificial sun represented the last of his stolen seed cache.

"Botany for fun and profit," he said, as he logged the results of this trial. It was painstaking to manage so many variables, from hybrid pairs, to light levels, to water, and the trace elements in the soil. His work was a cross between old-fashioned Mendelian genetics and cutting-edge gene modification, except he didn't use pea plants and no lab in the Hub would risk crossing the drug cartels to support him.

He just needed to figure out what would give him plants that produced fertile seeds. Growing bittergreen itself was easy enough. It was a weed. Anyone could do it. That's what Micah counted on, if he could solve the seed problem. If. When. From behind the clear terraforming bubble wall, he watched the artificial rain and massaged the back of his neck trying to ease the stiffness.

"Nice setup."

Micah's legs tangled with the chair behind him and he hit the floor hard. He looked up into the face of the chief engineer's kid. At least it wasn't one of Mendez's security officers.

The girl leaned against the polished wall, her arms folded across her chest. She tapped one booted foot silently on the metallic floor. He scrambled to his feet and gave her a smile.

"You startled me." What was her name? Robyn? Raelin? His father could always remember names, drunk *or* sober.

"Really? Never would have guessed." Her muddy green eyes stared into his, and the only thing he could read was curiosity. She had the most open closed face he'd ever seen.

"Micah Rotherwood," he said, offering her his hand.

"I know who you are." She pushed off the wall, leaned down, and righted the chair. "The question is, why are you here?"

Micah lowered his hand, studying her reactions. "Commander Mendez let me have the space for my research." Her eyes, large and wide-set in an oval face gave her a childlike look. The restless intelligence behind those eyes was anything but childlike. Her lean body didn't have many curves, and she dressed in plain, utilitarian pants and short tunic. Her hair—blonde and long—was tied back into a tail that reached halfway down her spine. An interesting contradiction.

She nodded, but didn't respond.

He gave her his most charming smile. "I was just heading out for the night. Care to join me for some coffee?"

Her eyes brightened, and he felt his own expression shift to something more genuine.

"How quaint. Coffee. Especially when you have such a lovely supply of bittergreen."

Fuck. He wondered how long it would take him to erase any sign he'd been growing the drug here. "How did you find me?" Maybe she was bribable. He shook his head, the irony not lost on him, given his father's sorry history.

"You're not much of an engineer, are you?" she asked.

Damn, but her face was hard to read.

"Increased power draw on the station grid. You're lucky no

one came to investigate sooner."

"I really am studying to be a botanist."

"I really don't care."

Micah slumped against the desk. "You mean you're not going to shut me down?"

"Too much bother," she said, moving over to his computer. "But I do need to balance the power loading and mask your draw or someone will stumble in here to investigate."

"Someone like you?"

She gave him an odd look, pulled out her micro, and flung several rapid-fire gestures at it. "Yes. Exactly like me."

Micah's eyes widened as her micro's readout scrolled across the display on his computer screen. Damn. She'd just blown through all his security. How the hell had she done that? She set the micro on his desk. Bringing both hands up as if she was the conductor and the computer her orchestra, she controlled his machine using gestures faster than anyone he had ever seen. He recognized the signs for save and execute, but all the rest blurred in one continuous, graceful motion.

"Done," she said, slipping the micro back in her pocket. The computer returned to the Daedalus Station logo. "But I'd use a much better password in the future. Or maybe even some biometrics, though even those aren't infallible." She turned to go, leaving Micah sputtering.

"Wait. I don't understand. Why are you helping me?"

"There's plenty of room on this hulk. I might want to set up shop. And it's always good to get along with your neighbors." At the airlock, she paused to turn around. "And by the way, my name's Ro."

He didn't need to look at his reflection in the burnished

metal to know his face blazed red.

*

Ro clamped a hand over her mouth to stifle the laughter. What an idiot. It wasn't surprising, given his father. She couldn't give an empty airlock's worth of oxygen about the drugs. But the ship? The ship presented all kinds of possibilities.

Earning a journeyman's engineering rating was definitely better than being trapped in this dead-end place, but she wanted more than a series of lateral hops from job to job and subsistence living like her father. For that, she needed access to a solid Uni in the Hub. She looked down at herself and frowned at the grease stain on her shirt. An engineer's kid had about the same chance at one of the top schools as this wreck had to fly.

She stared at the scavenged ship. If her father had bothered to investigate the problem, he had to have discovered the bittergreen lab. But instead of reporting it to the commander or balancing the power draw, all he had done was bury the problem. Either he was working with Micah or he had some other reason for keeping prying eyes away from the ship.

That alone was reason enough for Ro to dig a little deeper.

The ship was essentially useless. They hadn't made this kind of freighter in decades, and even if the thing could be made to fly, the first gen models had been unstable buggers. AIs had come a long way since then.

An idea so crazy it might work danced through her mind. Accessing the ship would be simple given her new official status, and she had a program of AI enhancements she'd been dying to field test. If she could wow the admissions board—really wow them with something—she wouldn't need to apply for any scholarship.

Excitement bubbled through her like an oxygen high. She patted the hull. "You and me, baby, we could be something special." There was plenty of room to set up a little workshop. "Oh, yeah. This could totally work."

Ro pushed away from the corridor and paced as she schemed. Micah wouldn't risk making a fuss and besides, Ro's work wouldn't get in the way of his little greenhouse. Power might be an issue, but her mind was already churning on ways to find the additional resources she would need and how she could divert them. She stopped at the door seal that connected the ship with the now-permanent, temporary umbilical to Daedalus and tapped against the tarnished metal.

She needed an assistant—someone clever enough to follow her directions, be discreet, and keep the project moving while she knocked down Mendez's work list, but not so clever as to hijack her idea.

Micah wasn't smart enough to follow her lead in the programming and too clever and too sneaky by half to control. Besides, if he was working with her father in some way, he presented a security risk. No, she needed someone quite different. Smiling, she pulled out her micro. It was late, but he'd probably still be awake. "Message Durbin, Jem." Most likely he was still tinkering with the code he wanted her to look through.

"Ro! Did you get my message? I've been looking all over Daedalus for you."

She winced and dialed down the volume. If his incessant babbling didn't drive her mad, his unrelenting cheerfulness would.

"When you get a chance, patch that program directly through to my micro. I'll run it in protected mode and take a look."

"That's super! Thanks. It's not as elegant as your stuff, but it's still pretty cool. Look, I have this other idea—"

"Jem. Stop." She projected as much cold authority in her voice as she could.

"Oh. Sorry. I—"

"Shut up. Listen. No apologies. Just listen." She'd throttle him if he wasn't so damned smart and eager to please. "I have a job for you." That got his attention. "It's complex and probably doomed from the start. But I need your help—and you can't tell anyone about it. That includes the commander, my father, and your parents." She paused, enjoying the momentary silence.

"When do we start?"

First, she needed to do some investigating. "Check your syllabus in the morning. You've had a change in course require-ments."

Jem's low whistle pierced her ear. "Outstanding! You so need to give me those access codes."

"I think not," she said, laughing. There was no telling what Jem would do with that amount of unholy power. "Go to sleep. You'll need to be at your best tomorrow."

"Aren't I always?"

Ro snorted. "Go. Dream of perfect code."

"Oh, man, oh, man! This is gonna be great—"

She terminated the call mid-gush, not quite regretting her choice, but wondering how the hell she was going to keep Jem from making her crazy. "I guess it's time to head back to school," she said, tunneling into the ed database. Going directly against Daedalus would have been risky, but the teaching algorithm was a quasi-independent program only loosely connected to the station's AI, not too different from her own autonomic nervous system. Ro accessed Jem's coursework, replacing his syllabus with a new one, tailored to her needs.

Now she just needed to find out what her father knew.

Chapter 3

JEM BURST INTO his room with the intensity of an amp dialed way past distortion. Barre turned over and threw his arm over his eyes as his brother pushed the light levels up to mid-day. He flicked on his neural to check the time. 0700. "What the hell?"

"I'm working in the computer lab today. You wanted help with your advanced calc homework. Now or never."

Barre threw a pillow across the room. It missed Jem by half a meter.

"Come on. I have coffee for you."

He would need a lot more than coffee this morning. "I hate you."

Jem laughed.

"I'm up, I'm up. Now get the hell out and let me get dressed."

Jem sneaked in close to his bed and snatched his blanket, tossing it to where the pillow lay on the floor. "Not until you put your feet on the ground."

Barre shook the dreads out of his face and glared at his perfectly awake, perfect little brother as he walked out of the room. It wasn't Jem's fault he was their parents' darling, but it didn't make the sting any easier to take.

He accessed his music library and turned up the volume to drown out the self-pity party in his head. By the time Barre managed to get dressed, Jem probably would have invented a new language, discovered a rare element, and gotten three more acceptances to Uni. All Barre had was a blooming headache and the music burning through his mind.

When Barre emerged from his room, Jem, true to his word, handed him his coffee, fixed the way he liked it. "Black and sweet, just like you are," his brother said, smiling.

Barre scowled over the steaming mug. How could Jem be so freaky cheerful this early? He added it to the mental list of things that were unfair and not likely to change any time soon.

"Since when are you so eager for school?" Jem always hated the work anyone assigned him. Usually he tried to figure out ways to twist it to suit what he wanted to do. Maybe they weren't so different, after all.

"Doing a collab with Ro."

"I know, you only love her for her brain."

"Barre, it's not like that," Jem said, the skin on his cheeks brightening.

It was always so easy to fluster his little brother. At least some things in life were fair. "Do Mom and Dad know?"

Jem stared up at him, his eyes intense. "No. And they don't need to. I get my work done. I get good grades. What I do and who I do it with on my own time is none of their business."

"Whoa, kid." He swallowed the last of the coffee and set the cup down on the counter. "I'm not here to criticize." Barre had enough of his own secrets, including the packet of bittergreen in his back pocket. "Where are they, anyway?" he asked. Their

19

quarters were utterly silent except for the two of them.

"Station staff meeting. I waited until they left before coming to wake you."

"Thanks." And he meant it. The last thing Barre wanted was to spend another meal being picked apart by his disapproving parents.

"Can we go, yet?" Jem asked, just the barest hint of the whine in his voice that used to drive Barre crazy.

"Fine. Good. Whatever." Barre put his hands on Jem's shoulders and pressed down. "But we do the calc work first. Payback for waking me up."

"Deal," Jem said, slipping out from under his grip.

Other than a few night-shift staff heading to their quarters, the corridors were empty this early in the morning. The computer lab was empty, too, except for the AI's blinking red oculars. Barre logged into his syllabus, swallowing the resentment he always felt when he asked his little brother for help.

He remembered a time when Jem turned to him with questions. It hadn't lasted very long. Once Jem mastered the computer interface, he quickly pulled past him and never looked back.

Barre called up the module he struggled with and turned down the music. Conceptual math didn't get any easier with a soundtrack and Jem would be ticked if he thought Barre wasn't paying attention. He could compose complex pieces in his head for a fully tricked-out band even without the neural. If you needed it rewritten for an old-school orchestra, he could do that, no problem. Transposing was as simple for him as theoretical physics seemed to be for Jem.

But his parents only had room for Jem's talents in their lives.

The first time Barre had played something he wrote just for them, they nodded politely and couldn't be bothered to listen to the entire song.

"Focus, Barre."

He sighed. "Sorry."

Jem tapped the monitor. "Is this what you're having trouble with?"

For the moment, he couldn't find a sarcastic reply.

"Okay. Watch." Jem pushed away the ancient keyboard in favor of the holo display. Watching him use the heads-up module was like watching Judicious Monkey play the multi-synth. His hands moved in a blur and the equation danced in front of them. "Look here," Jem said, and exploded the view, showing the problem in three dimensions.

Barre stared, his mouth falling open as Jem built a representative construct, each piece linking to a part of the problem. Then he simplified the building, collapsing multiple layers of structure into a simple cube.

"You've got to be kidding me," Barre said.

"What do you mean? If you do it this way, you'll always get the right answer in the fewest steps."

There was no way he could ever replicate what Jem had just done. "I swear Mom and Dad bought you from Dynamic Machines and had you programmed by an evil genius."

"But Barre, it's simple. Just look—"

He cut his brother off before he could wipe the display clean and start again. "Wait. Listen." He linked his neural to the computer and played a few bars of the piece he'd been working on last night. "Now score it for twelve voices. And use a micro-tonal scale."

Jem stared at him open mouthed as the simple melody line played over and over. Part of Barre's mind had already started to create a counterpoint and a rhythm track.

"I can't. You know I can't."

Barre thrust his arm in the middle of Jem's display and sent fragments of equations flying around the room before the computer extinguished them. "But it's easy. Simple even. Since I can do it." He pulled up a reproduction of old-fashioned staff paper and with a few economical gestures, wrote the melody line out. "There, easier now?"

Jem glared at him, the anger in his expression a smaller reproduction of their mother's face.

"Never mind." Barre wiped his music away with an open-handed gesture and flicked off the playback. The room fell silent. "I need some space." He left Jem to the work he'd rather be doing anyway and stormed off into the corridors of Daedalus Station, trying to look like he had some specific destination in mind.

*

"Jerk," Jem said as the door slid shut, and turned back to the monitor. It wasn't his fault he was smart. Besides, he worked hard for his grades and opportunities. He shouldn't have to apologize for that. It wasn't fair. Every time he tried to help Barre, it ended badly, but Jem was the stupid one who kept trying.

He was done. He could be just as selfish as his older brother.

"Okay, Ro, what have you got for me?" he said, linking his micro to the AI and waiting for the revised syllabus to download.

His anger drained away as his new curriculum scrolled across the display: Cyber-neurolinguistics. AI interface design. A 3-d schema for the first-gen Dyn/Mac processor. Where the hell did she find that?

With shaking hands, he pulled up the schema and displayed it around him. "Wow," he whispered, blinking up at the AI source code. It was the most beautiful and terrifying thing he'd ever seen. Even the most basic of its subroutines had more complexity than any program he'd ever dared pull apart and rebuild. What did Ro think he could do with this?

"So, what do you think?"

He jumped, hearing Ro's voice behind him. She must have slipped in the room while he was drooling over the code.

"It's ..." He waved his hands at the holographic representation and fell silent, his gaze shifting from parts to the whole and back again as he tried to concentrate on the logic strings and numbers whirling through his mind. Dizzy, he grabbed the edge of the counter and looked up at Ro, trying to keep from losing his breakfast.

"Yeah. Me too," she said, a rare smile lighting up her face. "I was up all night playing. Here, this'll make it better." She turned to his interface and wriggled her fingers at it. Jem could have sworn she was tickling the computer, rather than sending it commands. Layers of code collapsed in on itself until what was left looked like a normal program. A massive program, yes, but something he could take in with one gulp.

How in the universe had she done that? He looked up at Ro, his mouth hanging open.

"Better?"

All Jem could do was nod, thinking of Barre and the massive

apology he owed his brother. "So what's the plan?" he asked, the squeak in his voice completely blowing the casual vibe he wanted. Now, he was glad he never got the chance to send Ro the code modifications he'd been working on.

"Don't worry. We don't have to deal with most of this." She waved her hand and more than half the program dimmed. "It's the interface I'm interested in, for now."

"Oh, that's all?" He grinned back at her. "What a relief."

She rubbed her hand along his head, brushing the short hair backwards. "You can handle it, small fry. I saw what you did with your interface mods."

His eyes widened.

"Yes, I peeked. Sorry."

But she wasn't sorry. He could see it in her smirk. Jem shrugged. He wasn't all that mad, even if she treated him like a kid brother instead of a colleague—even if she broke into his personal files. There probably wasn't another person on the station who could have. Jem looked back at her simplified schematic and swallowed hard. She thought he could handle it. "You want me to graft my interface onto this?"

"Hell, yeah," Ro said, waving her hands again and setting the program spinning like an old fashioned globe. She studied the dancing lines of code and stopped it with the gentlest press of her fingertip. "Isn't this just crying out for a little tweak?"

Jem pulled out his micro and called up his program. The massive AI code dwarfed it, even with Ro's simplification. "Do you really think so?"

She looked down at him, her changeable eyes squinting in concentration. Jem didn't know if she was scrutinizing him or his code. "Make it work. Then we can talk."

Make it work. He stared at the bewildering code. Make it work. The scale of what he thought she wanted was enough to make him feel slow and thick. "And if I can't?" Silence answered him. When he looked up, she was gone.

Chapter 4

Barre's anger and frustration drummed a pounding counterpoint to the music streaming through his head as he paced the circular corridors of Daedalus station. He owed Jem an apology, but he couldn't face going back to the computer lab.

He shook his head, the unruly dreads his mother and father both hated sweeping across his back. What he really needed was an acoustically perfect, sound-proofed room stocked with a multi-synth and the computer to augment it. Where his parents supplied Jem with the latest and greatest, along with access to research experts across the galaxy, Barre's consolation prize included a fast micro and a neural synaptic interface. They weren't the best tools for the job, but the neural was better than nothing, given how little they tolerated what they considered his hobby.

His hobby. He clenched his hands into tight fists and kept walking. The blood throbbing in his ears drowned out the music. He stopped short and someone barreled into him from behind.

"Watch it!"

Barre drew a breath to yell back when the officer glared at him and swept past. The silver stripes in his gray uniform matched the shine of the weapon holstered at his right hip. Barre swallowed his snippy response and watched the man's back until the curving corridor hid him. Plasma rifles were nasty. His parents insisted both Barre and Jem complete grueling advanced medic training, and the Doctors Durbin version of a first-aid class involved critically ill patients and gruesome injuries, including fatal ones. The mingled stench of flesh and plastic from treating plasma burns had clung to him for days.

A group of cadets jogged past him wearing full recon gear. They looked pretty stupid, their brown-and-tan patterned camo conspicuous against the shiny steel reflective walls. It was 0900 already. The station had a small fixed crew and an even smaller military presence, but anyone in the corridors was too many for Barre.

He tapped his back pocket, feeling for the reassuring shape of the small bag of bittergreen and headed back to the residence ring. Their family quarters were still empty. He grabbed a large mug, hit the dispenser for simmering water, and retreated into his room. The water needed to cool to just the right temperature before he shook the leaves over it: Too hot, and the trace elements that made the drug so effective would break down; too cold, and it would just be nasty. Either way would leave the tea useless, bitter, and undrinkable, without any of the high.

Barre eyed the small amount left, the last of his old supply from Hadria, and wondered if it still had enough of a kick to work its magic on his mood. He sprinkled a pinch over the mug and watched the leaves slowly uncurl and sink to the bottom. Five minutes and a few swallows later would let him cope with this bleak and silent place, at least for a little while.

With his parents and Jem out, Barre could crank up the music and turn his whole room into a surround-sound system. His headphones were the best commercially available, but he was old school. Hearing sound as it vibrated through the air and through his bones felt better. More than better, it felt right, almost as soothing as how his body felt after the bittergreen—alive, alert, and smooth.

Barre's shoulders dropped as the waves of sound washed over him. He reached for the tea, his nose wrinkling at the unexpected sour smell. Fresh bittergreen tea was sharp enough, but this tasted like dirty socks. It must be the old leaves starting to oxidize, but it was all he had, so he sipped it slowly and waited for his brain to settle. Closing his eyes, he concentrated on the melody he'd played for Jem in the lab. Even without a computer or a heads-up interface, he could represent each musical line as a sensory impulse in his oh-so-ordinary mind. Some sounds pulsed in colors, other burst through him as flavors or scents, some had details he couldn't even name, but felt in some dark recess of his consciousness. He tried to explain it once to his parents, and they were briefly interested in his expression of synesthesia until something more novel about Jem or some new disease or surgical technique snagged their attention.

It didn't matter. The music was more important.

A combination of sounds blasting through the speakers and the textures rolling through his mind played a counterpoint to all the harsh, reflective surfaces of Daedalus—the burnished walls, the uniforms, and the plasma guns. When Barre finished, he knew the composition would be like an auditory expression of his restlessness, the sound equivalent of one of the long-extinct hunting cats, something warm and alive and very dangerous.

*

Ro stood in front of her father's workshop door, her hands damp. After one last check on his location, she ran a service override on the door lock. It opened, silently retracting into the compartment's walls.

She hesitated at the threshold. If she turned around right now and sealed the door, he might never find out. But she'd never get her chance to escape. She swept the room with all the security subroutines she had. They all reported clean.

Swallowing the lump in her throat, she stepped inside. She paused, waiting for his angry voice or for an arm to grab her in the darkness. There were no sounds except for her heartbeat and harsh breathing.

"Lights up twenty percent," she whispered.

His work table was an explosion of computer components. Some were functional, some in various stages of repair, some clearly beyond even his help. Half-cleared notes on loose sheets of permapaper littered the floor.

She didn't even know what she was looking for, but she knew she didn't have a lot of time.

A large roll of archival perm took up most of the space across the desk. She unrolled the free edge, anchoring it down with a broken impeller. It was a schematic for an old class of freighter. The perm was marked up with her father's cramped writing and sketches. She peered closer, bringing her micro to illuminate the faint marks. The familiar connected block-and-tube outline of Daedalus station emerged, with the ship jutting out from one end.

Ro's heart raced. This was the wreck. Where had her father gotten its original engineering diagrams? And what was he doing with them?

"Daedalus, locate Maldonado, Alain," she whispered.

"Corridor delta seven."

Ro winced at the AI's loud voice. She turned back to her father's desk. The archival perm didn't have a standard interface, so she couldn't clone the data. But she could take screen captures and stitch the pieces together later. Unrolling sections of the schematic with trembling fingers, Ro snapped a picture of each one.

She re-rolled the perm and moved the impeller back to its spot on the desk. After a last quick glance around the room, she turned off the lights and shut the door behind her. Slipping her micro into a pocket, she headed for the galley. The door to their quarters opened. Ro tightened her hand on the mug she'd taken from the rack beside the sink full of dirty dishes.

"Rosalen."

Her father's gravelly voice made the hair on the back of her neck tingle.

"What are you doing?"

She turned, pressing her spine against the galley's edge. His eyes glittered in the low light. The galley's counter separated them, but there was no way for her to escape their quarters without passing within arm's reach of him.

"I was making coffee," she said, careful to keep her voice neutral. "Here," she said, sliding the mug across the counter to him.

Ro walked to the end of the galley and tried to slip past him, but he grabbed her upper arm and squeezed just hard enough to trap her. Keeping her body completely still, Ro fought to steady her breathing.

"Don't you have work to do?"

Mendez must have notified him. She lowered her gaze from his hard, green eyes, but carefully kept him in her peripheral vision.

Her father shook her softly and her gaze snapped to his face. Ro kept her tone bored, flat. "It's just an internship assignment. It won't interfere with my responsibilities here."

He let go of her arm. Ro stumbled back, resisting the impulse to rub where his fingers had been.

"I'll be in my workshop for several hours. I expect not to be disturbed."

Ro nodded.

Her father leaned over her to drop the mug into the nearly filled sink before returning to his workshop. He paused at the door.

Ro's heart hammered against her ribs.

"Just so you are aware, I'll be programming extra security measures. For your own protection."

The warning didn't have to be stated any more clearly. Well, he wasn't the only one here with a secret. "I have work to do."

"Best you get to it, then."

Ro frowned down at the mess of food archeology, her nose wrinkling at the smell. From now on, he could deal with his own meals. She would dine at the commissary with the other station staff. After all, she was one of them now. At least one of the Maldonados could start acting like it.

Striding down the corridors to the North nexus, Ro forced

her mind away from her father and back to the complex AI programming. It was one thing to identify a tiny piece of code and figure out how to tweak it, but to really understand the entirely of it? To figure out how badly damaged the ship's brain had been in the crash? Ro's doubts nearly sent her back to Mendez with her resignation in hand.

But that would leave Ro worse off than before. She squeezed into the crowded nexus, keeping her head down, waiting in line for the airlock.

"Good morning, Ro. Can I buy you that coffee, now?"

She glanced up into the smiling face of Micah Rotherwood, botanist, charmer, and aspiring drug distributor. He didn't seem the least bit flustered, nor did he look like she did after a late night of running code. His smooth face tanned from the time he spent under full spectrum plant lights, he reminded her of a younger, blonder, and less seedy version of his father. Even Ro knew enough of Senator Rotherwood's story to steer clear of him. She frowned, wondering if Micah had inherited more than just his good looks. "The coffee's free, and now that I officially work for Daedalus, so are my meals."

"Trust me, that's less of a bargain than you might think." The woman in line ahead of her turned and smiled. Elegant and slim, she had straight black hair that ended in a razor edge at her chin and warm brown eyes with more than a hint of some Asian ancestry.

"You're new," Ro said, trying not to think of the number of station personnel she had seen come and go in just the three years she'd been stuck on Daedalus.

"Konomi Nakamura. Call me Nomi. I'm communications. Night shift." She swallowed a yawn. "Sorry!"

The woman hardly looked like she'd been working all night, either. Ro glanced down at her usual rumpled clothes. That had to change.

"I'm heading for dinner. Can I join you?"

Instead of the polite excuse Ro expected, Micah smiled at Nomi, faint lines crinkling at the sides of his light blue eyes. "Oh, please do," he said. "Micah Rotherwood. Pleasure to meet you."

Ro had a sudden urge to warn Nomi about him, but didn't know what she would be warning her about. Neither of them were her business, but she stuck out her hand, getting between the two of them anyway. "Ro. Ro Maldonado."

Nomi turned, her expression thoughtful. "As in Chief Engineer Maldonado?"

Ro stared her down. "Yes, he's my father, and I got this job because I'm really good at what I do. If you have any questions, ask Mendez." This would get old quickly if she had to justify herself to every station employee.

"Hey, damp down the signal, Ro," Nomi said, shaking her head. "I wasn't implying anything. Do you think you could get him to look at the sound balance in comms? We're getting an intermittent cut-out at the high frequencies."

"I'll see what I can do," Ro said, adding it to her own personal list, partly out of guilt, but partly because Nomi's straightforward style was refreshing compared to Micah's manipulative charm.

"All channels clear, then? Excellent." Nomi's eyes lit up in unfeigned delight as she took Ro's arm. "Come on, I'm starving!"

She stiffened at the unexpected touch.

"It's nice to finally find some people to talk to," Nomi said. "It's hell being on nights. I hardly know anyone."

Ro knew everyone on the station, and it didn't make her any less lonely. "I've been stuck here nearly three years." Three years down, two more to go for her father's contract if she couldn't make good on Mendez's offer. At least this would be the last move she'd ever have to make for him.

"So why are you here?" Micah asked, slipping between them. "I figure you must know my family's history."

There weren't too many people in the Hub or beyond who didn't know the scandal involving the former Senator Rotherwood. He'd been indicted for money laundering, embezzlement, fraud, and bribery. While they never proved any of it, Rotherwood was probably responsible for propping up the biggest pyramid scheme in a century. Rumor said the cartel was still pulling his strings. The only reason the senator didn't see the inside of a dark cell was because he used his glib tongue to implicate a bunch of even more important men.

"You're surprisingly cheerful for the son of a man with death threats chasing him." Ro wondered why he stayed. Surely he could have sued for full citizenship and let his father fend for himself. She would have done so if she could. Better that than find yourself at the wrong end of an assassination attempt.

Micah shrugged. "It makes life interesting."

He was impossible to read.

Nomi laughed. "Much more interesting than my story, I'm afraid."

They moved through the commissary quickly as the line built up behind them. Nomi had been right about the morning offerings. Not a huge amount of variety, but the food was filling and nutritious enough. She selected some nondescript hot grain equivalent and black coffee. Ro chose the same and smirked, watching Micah purse his lips, shake his head, and dispense just a cup of coffee.

"Trust me, this isn't what the commander eats," he said.

Ro raised an eyebrow.

"It'll do," Nomi said, navigating easily through the now crowded room to an empty table in the corner. "So, Daedalus is my payback."

"What did you do to deserve us?" Micah asked, laughing.

Nomi took a sip of coffee and grimaced. "I can put up with almost anything except this." Sighing, she set the cup down and slid it away from her. "Just fulfilling my end of a bargain. My family didn't have the capital to send me to a Hub Uni, so I took a scholarship and signed on to give back one for one in an under-served posting."

"You agreed to come here for three years?" Ro asked.

Nomi's lips turned down into a pout. It made her face seem very young. "Four. Advanced degree."

Micah cocked his head. "Seriously? When did you start at Uni?"

"Before I turned fifteen."

"You have full citizenship?" Micah asked.

Nomi nodded.

Ro balled her hands into tight fists under the table as Micah whistled. She would have just about killed to get early admission somewhere, but her father had refused to sign her release papers during their last posting. Unless she figured out some way to attend Uni, Ro wouldn't even be eligible to take placement tests until she turned eighteen. And then she needed another two years of work experience to apply for citizenship. All to prove she wouldn't be a drain on society. She relaxed her hands and focused on Mendez's promise.

"But they didn't warn me about the coffee," Nomi said.

"I think I can help with that," Micah said.

"Oh, really?" Nomi's smile lit up her whole face.

"My father loves his coffee. Has it shuttled in special, direct from the Hub."

"I suspect your prices are above our pay grades," Ro said, looking at Nomi, trying to convey some kind of warning. What could Micah want from her?

"You have no idea," he said, laughing. "But not in this case. Besides, I think I owe you, Ro."

"All in an evening's work," she said. If he only knew what she planned for the ship, he'd figure a way to make her pay him. "Besides, how does giving Nomi coffee help me?"

"Well, it does if I share it with you," Nomi said, smiling, the light glinting in her eyes.

Ro felt her face get warm.

"See? You never know," Micah said, winking. "Just jumping it ahead."

"Look, I need to get going," Ro said, sliding her chair out. She leaned forward to pile all the dirty dishes onto her tray. When she reached for the half full cup in the center of the table, Nomi touched her lightly this time, just the press of her fingers on the back of Ro's hand. She wanted to curl her blocky fingers with their squared off nails and hide them behind her back.

"Hey, Ro, no static, yeah?"

Ro took a deep breath and let her hand relax. "Yeah."

"Time for bed." Nomi stifled a huge yawn. "See you around, Ro." She turned to Micah. "Nice meeting you."

"Right back at you," he said. After she left, Micah turned to

Ro and took the tray out of her hands. "Communications. Hmm. That could be useful."

She grabbed the tray back and banged it down by the recycler.

"What?" he asked, his expression the very pose of innocence.

"Go back to your little botany project," Ro said, through a tight jaw. *And leave me alone,* she thought.

"Hey, I only meant that it's good to have friends. And now I have one in engineering and one in communications."

"So I guess your father taught you everything he knows."

Anger flashed across his face. In a heartbeat, his power charm was back on full display. "No, not everything," he said, his voice light. The smile never reached his eyes.

Chapter 5

WHILE SHE SAT in the commissary waiting for the diagnostics to finish running on the medical bay temperature controls, Ro sneaked glances at the stolen schematics. Most of the tables stood empty, and the few station staff that stopped in for a late-afternoon snack ignored her.

Unwilling to risk using the holographic display, she squinted at the micro, coffee cooling at her side. The ship's design was simple enough that she memorized the basic configuration in a single glance. Its stubby body tapered down to a slim nose at one end and a blunt tail at the other. Two sets of wings, one larger and one smaller, jutted out from the sides in what was supposed to look like a dragonfly, but had been nicknamed the bumblebee almost from the beginning.

Her father's handwritten notes interested her even more than the design of the old transport ship. Tapping the engine compartment to enlarge it, she pondered his design mods, wondering if these were plans or completed work. There was only one way to find out.

The diagnostic finished running with a satisfied beep. At

least the Durbins wouldn't be able to complain about being too cold or too hot or too whatever in medical. She logged herself as working/unavailable/emergencies only and headed to the ship, a utility cart loaded with tools and supplies following behind her.

She tapped her micro. "Locate Rotherwood, Micah."

Daedalus's slightly nasal, bored voice responded. She guessed he figured he wouldn't be here long enough for him to personalize his message. "Habitation ring, 37/Beta."

That left her free to explore without his interference. She wound her way through the station proper, into the older, temporary corridors, and through the airlock into the ship.

Ro walked down the central corridor that linked the ship's nose to its tail. Once she got past Micah's lab, the lights dimmed. Halting her cart, she dug out a work-light and clipped it to the pocket of her coverall, leaving her hands free. It swept the area in front of her, illuminating a surprising lack of dust and debris.

The crew quarters had been transformed into large barracks, one on each side of the ship, temporary billets for soldiers on their way to deployments. The captain's quarters would probably be a better base of operations. She triggered the sensor. The door opened and she peered inside. A bare bunk frame with a desk beneath was anchored to the wall next to a chair bolted to the floor. That would do nicely. She would likely be able to scrounge all the spare computer parts she needed from the aft storage bays that had been used as Daedalus's scrap midden for years.

At the starboard bay, Ro waved her hand under the door sensor, but nothing happened. Frowning, she pulled out her micro. According to her read-out, there was power in all the basic sub-systems. Maybe the sensor had fried.

The port side bay door opened at her request and Ro slipped inside, playing her light against mounds of construction detritus, broken furniture, abandoned computers, and spare tools. There was more than enough to scavenge from. She piled what she thought she'd need on her cart before sealing the compartment again and heading aft.

The closed door nagged at her. All the other rooms on the ship had opened easily. Why not that one?

Leaving her utility cart in the corridor, Ro turned back to the starboard bay. She pulled out her micro and in an attempt to bypass the sensor, triggered an external override. The door still didn't open. "Hmmm," she mumbled, shining her light all around the door and looking for some sign of damage. There was no evidence of tampering, only normal wear that matched all the other surfaces on the ship.

Ro had never met a lock she couldn't coax, and she wasn't going to walk away from this one now. Studying the stolen schematic, she traced the door circuits, looking for the fail-safe. An electromagnetic kill switch ran in the ceiling conduits. She set her micro to flip its polarity.

With an audible click, the bay door opened. "Ha!" she cried and peered into the room. Her work-light splashed a cone of brightness a few meters in. Instead of the scrap she'd expected, the dim space was filled with row after row of boxes, piled at least a meter and a half high. She stiffened, rocking back on her heels. What was a hold full of sealed cargo doing behind a locked door? She turned the light off and stood in darkness, her heart pounding.

Frowning, she ran a security sweep. Silence pressed down on her. The back of her neck tingled with the sense of being watched. Ro stood her ground at the room's threshold.

Come on, come on, she thought, urging the micro to finish. If security had tagged her, she would have company soon. Having the full station access codes would at least give her plausible deniability as far as her presence here was concerned. She wasn't doing anything wrong, at least not yet. Micah would just have to fend for himself.

Time seemed to stretch out as she waited. Her own breathing echoed in the metallic space. Finally her micro gave a soft beep that also seemed loud in the silent storage bay. The sweep found no security threats. She exhaled, furrowed her brow, and turned her light back on.

Something was definitely out of true here: a sealed door, cargo where there should have been nothing but scrap, and no electronic security or tie in to Daedalus. Ro tapped her finger on the schematic's representation of the storage bay, thinking of her father. Her mind raced as the image enlarged and shrunk. If he needed to hide something, this would be the perfect place.

She stepped fully into the storage bay and the door slid shut behind her, silently. The vaulted ceiling swallowed her little light. As she moved, the shadows danced around her like living things. Unclipping the light, she gripped it in her hand, directing it into the room's corners. All she saw were rows of boxes. "Sorry, not leaving until I figure this out," she said aloud, as much to break the stillness as to convince herself. Even the cartons huddled close to each other, as if the darkness pressed in on them, too.

"All right, let's see what goodies we have here." Ro left the security of the solid door behind her, her light bouncing round the bay as she walked. There had to be hundreds of crates piled up. "A cargo manifest would be helpful," she muttered. Focusing the light on one of the boxes, she looked in vain for a label. "Yeah, why am I not surprised?"

Holding the light between her teeth, she grabbed the box on the top of the stack and carefully lowered it to the ground. When she saw the lid, Ro swore and the light tumbled from her mouth. She scrambled to pick it up and stared in horrified fascination.

These boxes had Hub Diplomatic Service seals. The most complex security in the Commonwealth, it came complete with a "phone home" feature and an anti-tamper subroutine. What the hell were diplomatic crates doing here? This couldn't be her father's doing–he'd never get access to this kind of cargo. And Daedalus wasn't a way-station from anywhere to anywhere.

Keeping her hands steady, she put the box back where she'd found it and backed out of the storage bay slowly. Somebody was hiding something. Whoever that somebody was would probably be coming through the ship to check on their stuff.

"Well, Micah, you're about to have company," she muttered. The cart followed her as she headed back to the ship's nose. Sharing his space wasn't ideal, but it also wouldn't advertise her presence. He'd be pissed, but by the time he returned, she'd have already set up her workstation.

A door whooshed open somewhere behind her. She froze, listening for footsteps. The seconds ticked by without a sound. It wasn't Micah. He had no reason to hide.

Ro crept along the corridor. The soft pad of footsteps moved away from her. She followed. For a supposedly abandoned place, the ship seemed to have a whole lot of traffic. Another door hissed open. The only hatch in this section led to the bridge. She reminded herself that she had the authorization to be here. Or at least access, which was almost the same thing.

Straightening to her full hundred and sixty two centimeter height, she triggered the door controls. It opened smoothly. The blood pounded in her ears. Ro's mouth fell open. Where the rest of the ship was mostly clean and well organized, the bridge looked like someone had dismantled it with lasers, crowbars, and hammers. The pilot and bridge crew consoles had been crumpled.

The large forward display had a jagged crack diagonally across the entire screen. She stepped carefully across the threshold, avoiding the sharp metal twisted and tortured all along the floor. What the hell happened here?

A blur of motion in the corner of her eye made Ro turn, her hands up and ready to defend herself.

"Ro! Isn't it amazing?"

Jem came up beside her, vibrating with excitement.

Tension spilled out of her body. She clenched her fists at her sides. "What the hell are you doing here?"

"I knew it. You really want to do this. I mean, it's not theoretical, right? The code you gave me matched the AIs used in the Bumblebee-class ships. And this is a Bumblebee." He stepped in front of her, his smile wide, his shining brown eyes large and bright.

"Why can't you just do what you're supposed to?" Now she was going to have to mask his tracks as well as her own, and she needed to figure out a way to keep him and Micah apart.

"Why? Do you?" He laughed and twirled around the bridge. "This! This is amazing. Do you really think you can wake the AI? I've been working with the interface for hours. Oh, wow, Ro, do you think can we make it fly again?"

Ro laughed, helpless to stay angry at his ridiculous enthusiasm. "I don't know, Jem. Someone did this place in pretty good." It didn't make a whole lot of sense, given the condition of the rest of the ship.

"But we're going to try, aren't we?"

She trailed a finger along the silent control panels and walked in a circle around the command chair. "Oh, yeah. Hell, yeah."

Chapter 6

JEM RAN BACK toward the habitation ring, images of the ship bursting through his mind. The ship he saw gleamed under starlight, its engine roaring, its wings trembling with an eagerness to fly again. If he could help Ro do this, his parents would have to understand. They'd have to.

But between now and his dream, more work waited than he could barely believe. A fierce grin stretched across his face. He could do this. He knew he could. Ro needed his help. Jem wove his way through the crowded corridors of the station, but no one really noticed him. At least there was some advantage to being small for his age. People who didn't know better always underestimated him.

He waited until Daedalus recognized him and opened the door to their quarters. Pounding music reverberated off the walls and vibrated through his chest. Well, that answered the question of whether his parents had gotten home. It also meant Barre was still pissed. Jem winced at the sound roaring through the place. This was his home, too, and he had to be able to work.

Smirking, he ran an environmental control subroutine he'd

been wanting to try out for a long time. It wouldn't make Barre any happier with him, but then again, he wasn't all that happy with Barre right now. The cacophony damped down in tiny steps until Jem could hear himself think. He started a silent countdown, figuring Barre would storm out of his room in ten seconds or less.

The program worked perfectly. Jem's ears rang in the blissful silence, but as ten seconds turned into several minutes, he frowned. Something didn't feel right. He hesitated at the sealed door. He frowned again, raised his fist, and pounded on the door. "I know you're in there. You want to sulk? Fine, but you're the one who owes me an apology."

Nothing.

The quiet unnerved Jem, and he wished Barre's music still blared through their quarters.

"Barre?"

Still nothing.

He signaled Daedalus. It would be just like Barre to set his music to ear-drum burst and then wander out. "Locate Durbin, Barre."

"Habitation ring, 05/Alpha."

That was their address.

"Barre, if you don't open this door right now, I'm hacking my way inside. You have ten seconds, and you know I can do it." Jem counted his own heartbeats, feeling them speed up as the seconds ticked by. The inner door locks lacked even the moderate sophistication of the external airlocks, and Jem had figured out how to hack those months ago. He reached up and tapped the override code and waited as the door slid open.

Barre lay sprawled face-down across his bed, his hair a wild mess spilling over the side. Jem frowned at the chaos of pillows, blankets, clothes, shoes, and permapapers scattered across the floor. How could he have fallen asleep with all that noise? And how did he not wake up when it stopped so suddenly?

Jem picked his way across the mine field of the room to the bed and shoved Barre in the side. "Hey. You're just lucky it was me and not Mom and Dad who came home first."

Barre didn't stir. Something cold coiled in the pit of Jem's stomach. He swallowed against a wave of nausea.

"Cut it out, this isn't funny." He shoved his brother again, harder this time. Barre's body rocked back and forth, his arm flopping off the bed. Jem watched, holding his breath as his brother's fingers brushed the floor like the sweep of a metronome. Leaning in close, Jem set a trembling hand on his brother's back. "Barre?" His voice squeaked in the small room.

He shut his eyes and concentrated on feeling for the rise and fall of Barre's breath, some logical part of his mind already going through the medical triage procedures his parents had drilled both of them in. Airway. Breathing. Circulation. The basics hadn't changed in centuries.

Okay, so Barre was breathing. Jem took a trembling breath of his own and rolled his brother over on his back, checking for his carotid pulse. It was thready but present. A quick sweep of his lanky torso and long arms and legs felt normal—nothing obviously broken, no bleeding. Jem peeled back one of Barre's eyelids and shuddered at the way his brother's eye rolled far in the back of his head.

"Daedalus—medical emergency, Durbin quarters."

"Medical responding," the bland voice responded.

His mother's voice overlapped the AI's, nearly as cold and

dispassionate. "This is medical. What is your emergency?"

"Mom—it's Barre. I can't get him to wake up!" Jem shook uncontrollably, his momentary calm evaporated.

"Does the patient have a pulse?"

"Mom, he needs help!"

"A team is on its way. Now, can you tell me if the patient has a pulse?"

"Yes. Barre has a pulse," Jem said, his voice tight.

"Good. Is he breathing?"

"Yes." Jem couldn't keep the fear out of his voice. Where was the response team?

How could she be so damned calm?

"Jem?"

"I don't know. I don't know. I just got home and found him like this. He's out. Out cold. He won't wake up. I did everything I was supposed to do. Now where are the damned medics?" Where was she?

"We're here, Jem." The front door swept open and his mother pushed inside, the crash team flanking her in well-practiced choreography.

Jem slid to the floor by his brother's side as the team swarmed the limp form on the bed. Their clinical shorthand blurred by him. Portable monitors played a strange medical percussion. Barre could probably write a song around it. Jem started laughing and couldn't catch his breath.

None of the medical team paused to give him a second glance. By the time the laughter finally died in Jem's throat, they had transferred Barre over to the waiting PCU, an oxygen mask covering most of his face, monitors communicating with the field sensors plastered on his forehead, throat, and chest, intravenous lines set.

A small plastic packet lay on the floor beside him and Jem slid it under his palm as they whisked his brother away.

"Jem?"

He jerked his head up. His mother stood, staring down at him. Jem tightened his hand with its secret inside.

"Did you notice anything at all strange when you came in here? Was Barre able to say anything to you? Do you know what he was doing?"

"No." The bittergreen ground to powder in his fist.

"Well, we'll figure it out when the tox comes back."

Bittergreen might be addictive and stupid, but it didn't do this.

His mother frowned, her gaze sweeping the room for clues. She didn't look worried. She looked furious.

Jem didn't want to be anywhere on Daedalus when they confronted Barre about whatever the hell he'd done this time.

*

Micah paced a tight triangle between his bed, the door, and his desk, furious with Ro for making him feel like he had to defend himself. She had no idea. She had no right. His micro buzzed. He waved at it.

"Micah, something's come up." His father's voice vibrated through the small speaker.

Flopping down on the narrow bed, he threw his arm over his face.

"We need to talk."

If Ro had lied to him and told his father about the

bittergreen ...

"Now would be a good time," his father said, and Micah could visualize the well-practiced look combining concern and amusement. That one look had always worked so well in his debates.

It was impossible to really avoid the man, not just because Daedalus only covered twenty thousand square meters, but because his intensity always eclipsed everything and everyone who stood near him. "I'll be right there."

Micah rolled off the bed and checked himself in the mirror. Appearances always counted with the senator.

He waited by Micah's door looking as if he'd just come by for an impromptu chat, dressed in the warm browns that contrasted so well with his still-thick blond hair. The only thing that spoiled his oh-so-casual stance was the slight frown. "Come on, let me buy you a cup of coffee."

Micah winced. He had asked Ro the same thing, in that exact same tone of voice earlier. "I'm fine, Dad."

He shrugged and walked into the galley. "Then I don't mind if I do," he said, pouring himself a cup. Instead of sugar, he flavored it with a generous slug of whiskey.

"I have work to do," Micah said, trying to keep the disapproval out of his voice.

"It can wait."

That was always the problem. Everyone else got to wait, even his mother, even when she so inconveniently got sick.

His father stared directly at Micah, his blue eyes cold and crystalline, an uncomfortable contrast with his high energy smile. "The Commonwealth Council has appointed me Ambassador to the Trest Consortium."

Micah clenched his jaw so hard his teeth ached. How had he managed to wrangle a posting even more remote than Daedalus? Ro had no idea what it cost him every time his father fucked up somehow and they had to flee again. Though a Council appointment meant he'd probably traded something in return for a post that had at least the trappings of political respectability.

It would be simpler if one of his father's enemies collected on the death bounty. Simpler, certainly, but he had promised his mother to take care of him and until Micah reached legal age, he would keep that promise, no matter what. "Trest?" He wondered how long they'd be there.

"Apparently they are seeking full admission to the Trade Exchange."

Micah burst out laughing. "And the Commonwealth wants to sabotage it so they're sending you."

His father frowned. Micah resisted pointing out that frown lines would mar his perfectly photogenic face.

"I've atoned for my actions and moved past them."

But what about all the people his father stole from? Micah was willing to bet they hadn't moved past what his father did to them. So they would be moving again. That made six times in less than three years. He'd hoped Daedalus would be the last stop on the humiliation shuttle, but clearly that wasn't the case. "How soon?"

"The advance team is negotiating our housing," he said, beaming at Micah. The heat of his father's approval made him turn away.

"Can I at least finish out the semester?"

He put his arm around Micah's shoulders. "Wait, is this the same Micah who described Daedalus as, and I quote, the ass end of the universe?" He laughed.

"I have a botany experiment running." Micah shrugged off his father's arm and paced the length of the galley. "If we leave now, I'll have to abort it and start all over. Six months of hard work wasted." He hated how whiny he sounded. No matter what he said, the chance of his father changing his mind or even flexing his plans was slim to none. He didn't even really know why he tried.

"I'm sorry, son."

He only called him son when trying to soften the impact of "no".

"Our transport has already been booked. Do what you can to finish up. Once we're on Tresthame, I'll be able to request whatever supplies you need for your work. I've been told they're quite sophisticated for an outlying colony." He paused. "Excuse me, former colony."

Micah imagined putting in a list that included bittergreen seeds, though given how self-absorbed his father was, sober or drunk, he'd probably never even notice. "When?"

"Two weeks."

"Two weeks," Micah echoed, his stomach churning.

His father topped off his coffee with the rest of the contents of the scotch bottle and raised the cup in a salute to him. "I knew I could count on you." He sauntered across the common room toward his sleeping quarters.

How could his father do this to him again? Whirling around, he swept the empty bottle from the counter. Jaw tightly clenched, he stared at his father as it crashed to the floor. Glass shards ricocheted across the room.

"If you need me," Micah said, his voice a growl in the back of his throat, "I'll be in my lab."

His father's hand trembled and the diluted coffee sloshed over the rim of the cup.

Chapter 7

JEM SAT ON his brother's bed and hung his head in his hands. There was nothing he could do for Barre in the infirmary. If he had used again, the blood screen would show it. And then what? How could Barre be so stupid?

He pulled out Barre's tiny bag of bittergreen and turned it over and over in his hand. "Daedalus, report on the medical condition of Durbin, Barre."

His mother's recorded voice answered. "Stable, unresponsive."

The answer hadn't changed from the last five times he asked. Fine—he'd stop asking. "Locate Maldonado, Rosalen."

"Working, leave a message."

Jem pushed up from the bed, slipped the bittergreen in his pocket, and went to find Ro. If he couldn't do anything for Barre, at least he could work on the AI interface. Maybe he could help her set up or something. Anything would be better than thinking of the slack expression on his brother's face and the glassy dark eyes that stared up at nothing when he'd peeled back his lids.

He slipped through the airlock from the station into the old-style corridor—the kind of structure they put up when a place first got terraformed. It was sort of a pop-up tent construction with interlocking umbilicals and habitation bubbles. This last umbilical remained.

The door to the ship sealed behind him. "Ro?" Her utility cart sat empty between the bridge and the forward cargo hold. Maybe she was still working on the bridge. "Ro?" he called again as the bridge door slid open. It looked as much of a wreck as it had a few hours ago but without Ro here, he had a hard time believing any of the main computer would ever work again.

Maybe she had realized that, too.

He picked his way around twisted, fused metal and melted polymers. Whatever destroyed this place had really done a job of it. The consoles and the monitoring stations were all ruined. Jem frowned at the untouched chairs. That made no sense. He couldn't imagine a pitched battle with weapons fire sparing the chairs.

Clearly Ro hadn't been spending her time here. He retreated, opened the cargo bay doors, and stepped inside. It looked like a battle had been waged between the forces of organization and chaos. Odds and ends of old computers lay scattered in random arrangement along a beat-up table. A monitoring station set on a bench wedged against a thickly fogged curved barrier made reassuring beeping sounds.

Jem walked close to the barrier. He placed a hand on its material and pushed gently. It had a little give, but was thicker and stronger than he expected. How had Ro set up an old terraforming bubble so quickly? And where in the cosmos had she even found it? He studied the length of the wall, looking for a way in. Metal uprights embedded in the glass formed the frame for a field-airlock. It wasn't pretty, but the design was effective in either keeping something in or something out, especially if that something was nasty and airborne.

What could Ro possibly need to wall out?

Jem slid the rudimentary lock open and stepped through. The inner door flashed red until he re-sealed the outer compartment. These things were rigged to do full air exchange or pressurization if need be. This one didn't seem set up for anything but a simple in and out. He slid the inner door open and stepped into instant dusk and the thick humidity of a rain forest.

Blinking, he tried to see past the thick clouds of fog and moisture condensing on every surface.

"Damn it, Ro, I thought we had an agreement."

Jem stiffened at the angry male voice shouting from the back of the bubble.

"Bad enough I have to share my space with you."

The voice came closer. Jem's pulse sped up double time and he glanced back at the airlock, ready for a quick retreat, when a light flickered in the corner of his eye and he caught a flash of green. The light strengthened and the mist cleared. A tall figure emerged out of the fog along with row after row of plants, all with the long, thin five-part leaves of bittergreen.

"What the hell?" Jem said, glaring up at Micah who stared back at him with narrowed eyes and his mouth a thin slash across his face. "What did you do to my brother?" he demanded. "I swear, if anything happens to him, I'll ruin you."

"Great. Just great. Not that it fucking matters anymore." He turned his back on Jem and walked down a row between planters, stopping to examine his crop.

Jem stood there, his mouth falling open, before digging out his brother's remaining dried bittergreen and stomping after Micah. "Don't you walk away from me!"

Micah turned and scowled, looking down at Jem. "You're the doctors' kid. Why are you here?"

"Really? You have no idea?" Jem squeezed the baggie in his fist and stared Micah down. It didn't matter that the senator's son had nearly a half meter and twenty-five kilos on him. "Or do you not give a shit that you're selling tainted bittergreen?"

"What in the Hub are you talking about?"

Jem gestured across the miniature drug farm. "So, you're going to tell me this isn't bittergreen? I may look like a little kid, but I'm not stupid." He nearly spit the words at Micah. "Barre is in the infirmary. He was using. I found his stash. And then look what I stumble into—your little secret garden."

"Look, kid, I have no idea what your brother is using, but it's not my bittergreen. So far, I haven't been able to bring a crop anywhere near to market. Trust me, I really want to. Besides, it's just bittergreen."

"Just bittergreen." The ghost of Barre's face and his limp arm swinging over the edge of the bed filled Jem's mind. "Something in this stuff took my brother down. If you really believe it's that harmless, then try some." Jem shoved the bag at him.

Micah backed away and the drugs fell to the floor. "Look, I had nothing to do with your brother. I'm sorry if he's sick or whatever."

"Pick it up," Jem said, his voice a hoarse, unfamiliar growl. "You pick it up and you figure out what did this to him."

"I don't have time for this." Micah started to walk away

again.

"The hell you don't," Jem said. His face blazed and pressure beat against his temples. He pulled out his micro. "Do it, or I'll video your little set-up directly to the commander. I think she'd be very interested in what you have going on here."

"Jem?"

He whirled around to find Ro standing behind him.

"This is your fault," Micah shouted, pointing at Ro.

"I guess I need to get working on some security for this place," she said, shrugging one shoulder.

Jem swiveled his head from Ro to Micah and back again. He didn't understand. Did Ro already know about the bittergreen? Was she part of it? His stomach clenched. Not Ro. It couldn't be Ro. She wouldn't want to hurt Barre, would she?

*

Micah shook his head. Jem's threats would almost be funny, except for the fact his father had just screwed up Micah's last, best chance to get this strain right. The hell with him. The hell with Ro and this kid, Jem. He'd already lost everything he cared about, starting with his mother.

"Those are not my drugs." He pointed down to the small packet of dried leaves at his feet. "And you," he glared at Ro. "You promised to leave me alone."

"I heard voices."

"Don't tell my parents that." Jem laughed and clamped his hand over his mouth.

"Jem, what happened?" Ro asked, softly.

"Ask him." He jabbed a finger at Micah.

"Damn it, I have no idea!" Micah shouted. "He starts raving at me like some lunatic about bittergreen and his brother. Like I'm the one who poisoned him or something. If he's sick, it's not because of me or the drug." Jem was so not convinced. Micah saw it in the set of his thin shoulders, vibrating with his anger and the dark, hooded eyes. "Why the hell do you think I chose the stuff to work with in the first place?" It was pretty benign and if his mother had had a sure supply of it, her last weeks wouldn't have been a nightmare of pain and despair.

The drug wasn't hard to grow, but the best strains were patented and completely controlled by the cartels. His attempts to get some for his mom were the beginning of the end for his father's political career and the start of Micah's botany experiments. He couldn't bring his mother back, but he could break the back of the cartels that ruined their lives.

"All I know is Barre is unconscious in the infirmary and I found that packet of bittergreen next to him." Jem shot a poisonous look at Micah before turning back to Ro. "You do the calculations."

Ro stepped forward to pick up the drugs. "Do you have what you need to analyze this?"

Jem looked as if he had tasted something sour.

Micah should have thought of that. If he hadn't been so angry, he probably would have. "Will you believe me if I show you the spectroscopic assays for the different strains?" He'd have to dry some of his new-growth leaves, but he should be able to prove his bittergreen had nothing to do with Jem's brother.

At least that was something he could accomplish. Forcing his crop to accelerate its growth would probably result in stressed-out plants that wouldn't be able to set buds. He didn't know why he bothered.

The small, dark-haired boy nodded and turned away.

"Now get the hell out of my lab."

Chapter 8

Ro placed her hand on Jem's shoulder and turned him away from Micah. "Come on." The tension in his body practically vibrated through her arm. "We'll only be in the way."

He stared up at her, his eyes wide and unblinking, and let her lead him out of the bubble. "Can you find out anything about Barre?"

"Maybe." That would mean getting dangerously close to Daedalus's primary processors. Skulking around the edges of its domain didn't raise any alarms, but trying to break into the infirmary systems might. "But first I need to ghost you."

At least something went according to plan. She and Micah were already ghosting. If anyone asked Daedalus for them, her program made it appear as if they were somewhere else, at the opposite side of the station from the querent, and occupied. If there was a second request within a specific amount of time, or by the same person, it would ping their micros, depending on the importance of the one asking. She hand-coded the authority algorithm specifically for each of them. "Anyone get priority except your parents?"

Jem winced. "Barre," he said. "Just Barre."

"I have to weight your folks in there, too, Jem. If they're looking for you and can't find you, they could get command involved. Too many people get curious and they'll find my little tweaks."

"Do what you need to do," he said, staring past her.

Guiding him over to her corner of Micah's lab, Ro pushed Jem into the only open chair. Every other possible surface was covered with her equipment. He sat heavily, staring past her, the muscles along his jaw bunched.

"Can you set up my terminal and access? Just the hard wiring. I'll do the config after."

He shrugged and stood, turning to organize the desk.

Ro pulled out her micro and added Jem to her ghost protocol. It wouldn't hold up to a full-on decontamination, but the innocuous little program didn't look like much to the casual observer. That's what people got wrong. They wanted the big hacks, the monster hacks. Ro prided herself on writing subtle code, code that never called attention to itself, modest code. She smirked.

Maybe that's why she'd been able to throw so many tweaks into Daedalus's systems over the years she'd been trapped here. Even it didn't seem to notice.

"You're good to go," Jem said. "Can you pull up Barre's medical file now?"

Directly hacking in to private records was probably next to impossible and it would take her time away from the AI code mods she'd started playing with. The program lived in her head and she couldn't wait to get it locked down and tested. "I don't know, Jem." She raked her fingers through her hair considering the risk. Frowning, she twisted it into a braid and snatched a spare wire tie from the floor to secure it out of her face. "Couldn't you just ask your parents?"

"No."

"Why don't you just go and see him for yourself? It's not like the chart's going to tell you a whole lot anyway." She could start work on the repair drones. They had a lot to do before tackling the AI proper anyway.

Jem stared at her, his face set in hard lines.

"Unless you're already a doc, too," Ro said, trying to lighten the mood.

The muscles in his face rippled as he clenched and relaxed his jaw. "I need access. It's the tox screen. I know Barre was using. They know Barre was using. But if they have the proof, this time they'll send him off-system to mandated rehab."

"Seriously? For bittergreen? Isn't that a little overkill?" They said mandated just rebooted the addiction centers, resetting the brain's neurotransmitters back to pre-drug exposure levels, but Ro knew a few kids who'd undergone treatment and came home more broken than when they left.

"You don't know my parents."

"No, I guess I don't," Ro said, thinking of her father and the times she wished she didn't know him.

"Look, if you won't do it, I will."

Crap, that's just what she needed—an amateur mucking about. Cleaning up after him would take even more time away from what she needed to do. "You're talking more than a hack and a look-see. Do you have any idea the kind of checksums they have around medical records?"

"I won't let them do that to my brother. He may be an idiot, but he doesn't deserve having his brain turned inside out. Do you have any idea what happens in places like that?"

Ro frowned, her hands on her hips. He didn't know what he was asking. If she got caught, it would be more than the end of her dreams. Tampering with personnel and medical records carried big-time penalties.

"They'll burn the music right out of him. Ro, please, it's all he's got." Jem's eyes got shiny.

Ro turned away, uncomfortable with his naked emotion. If someone tried to take away her ability to program, to see code as a living, breathing entity, she wasn't sure what she'd do. Even her father—who'd pretty much taken everything else from her—understood that. "All right. I'll do what I can."

Jem's smile blazed through the small room like an artificial sun.

"No guarantees. I have a few ideas, but if they don't work, it's a no go. Understand?"

He nodded, the fear back in his eyes.

Ro swept a pile of permapaper from a desk chair and sat down at the terminal. Jem pulled a second chair close and scooted in next to her. She tried to glare him away, but he didn't get the hint. Ignoring him, she set up her micro. This was going to take a degree of subtlety that a keyboard or even ordinary gestures wouldn't be able to capture and besides, this way there was little-to-no chance that Jem could figure out the access codes she used.

Going head to head with Daedalus would be monumentally stupid and suicidal as far as her future was concerned. She'd almost have better luck trying to access Mendez's personal logs than breaking directly into the medical records system. Looking over at Jem, Ro pursed her lips, thinking. Like Jem, Barre was still a student. The ed algorithm spidered through the entire AI and made its own webbing to the medical data.

All Ro had to do was follow the threads.

"Ro?"

"Hmm?"

"It won't help if they access the tox results before you get to them."

She threw him a dirty look and pointed to the door. "Out."

"It's my brother. I want to help."

Ro folded her hands in her lap. "You can't. And I won't lift a finger until you get the hell out from underfoot." The sooner this got done, the sooner she could get back to the AI.

Jem sputtered as Ro glared at him.

"I get it. Really." Well, not really. She'd never had any family to care about. Her mother got fed up with her father years ago and split, leaving Ro trapped like a tiny moon orbiting her father's universe. She didn't have any conscious memories of the woman and her father kept no holos. "I do need your help, just not with this. How good are you at drones?"

"What do you need?" he said, his thin shoulders slumped.

Rummaging through a pile of spare parts, she pulled out a few small components. "Grab whatever tools you need. Then find two drones and replace the phone-home chipsets with these."

Jem pressed his lips together.

"You do know how to put them in sleep mode, right?"

"That's grunt work," he said, snatching the tiny interrupts from her hand.

"Get used to it, grunt."

That surprised a wry grin from him.

"Do you think you can handle a basic code mod?"

He raised a single eyebrow for an answer, and Ro suppressed her own smile. At least this would keep him from brooding too much.

"Then set them to do a wide search pattern of the whole ship and transmit the images back to me in real time."

His eyes brightened.

"Now get out of here and let me get to that tox report." She turned back to her monitor before Jem left the room. Getting into Barre's ed file was the easy part. She projected the data in the space around her and spent a few minutes studying the basic coursework the algorithm programmed for him. Concepts he struggled with in mathematics, both the theoretical and the practical, Ro had mastered when she was far younger even than Jem. She collapsed his test scores. Poor bastard—even with his parents' money and connections, he'd never get to Uni.

It was no wonder he spent his time drowning his sorrows in music and bittergreen.

She found one math class—advanced pattern mapping and recognition—where Barre scored way off the charts, his work significantly past even graduate level students. Classes branched off from that one into auditory recall, history of composition, theory of tonal and atonal scales, and harmonic deconstruction, whatever that meant. Jem wasn't kidding when he said Barre's music was his life. Half his server space was filled with original compositions. Ro kept digging, looking for the thread that would lead her to Barre's med files. It had to be here.

At least a basic medical needed to be part of every student's profile and Daedalus didn't like to waste space or run the risk of multiple versions of the same data. It wouldn't create a duped copy when it could simply mirror it or link to it. Either would serve Ro's purpose if she could find it.

Something blinked in the corner of her eye. She called up the file. Barre had started to fill out an application for a music scholarship program off Daedalus. "Gotcha," she said to the empty room and the bright display. Paging through the application, she searched for the required medical information. At the very least, they would require proof of inoculations and a basic psych profile.

He'd attached a musical score to the file, along with the old fashioned convention of notating the song. The black dots scattered across the lined paper made absolutely no sense to her. If she had the time, she would've had the terminal play it for her, but if she could pull this off, she figured Barre owed her a live show.

"There you are." The medical info had been tucked into an addendum to the application. Now all Ro had to do was figure out how to follow the breadcrumbs back to where the original lived without Daedalus noticing.

Ro cleared everything in Barre's files except for the relevant addendum pages. Those she enhanced and enlarged, hanging them at her eye level like a piece of art. But she needed to see past the surface display. The language AIs used to render data evolved from the original source code of the old web. There were still simple applications that ran happily on historically accurate versions of HTML, C++, and Java, and a whole network of home-brew hobbyists who preferred them to the more complex languages that emerged later.

They reminded Ro of re-enactors, not programmers.

She gestured with her left hand and pulled up her toolbox, a collection of small custom subroutines she could use like building blocks to do practically anything she needed. This time, she wanted something quiet and patient to tiptoe through Daedalus's convoluted data-paths, that if discovered, would dissolve into harmless bits of junk code.

This is what Ro loved. The process was as much architecture as programming. She linked segments together by feel, looking at the resulting shape with approval. Now to reveal the display code. She pulled one small, elegant program out of the toolbox and tossed it toward the application. It latched on to the lower left hand corner of the page and pushed. The page spun around and around, each revolution a little slower than the one before, until it stopped, and flipped face down.

Line after line of simple code wrote itself across the page as Ro waited. Even with the advances in AI self-programming, it didn't take much to display a basic visual. She scanned down the commands looking for one specific tag.

"Your turn, Rover. Go!" She flicked the tracker program she'd designed toward the plain codes. It went burrowing in, found an opening almost immediately, and disappeared.

Now she just had to wait.

She turned to the AI mods, unwritten code burning in her mind's eye.

*

Locating the drones would probably be harder than doing the actual reprogramming. After poking through all of the ship's compartments, Jem found one sweeping a corner in the aft corridor. The stupid thing got itself tangled in a recursive loop banging between two adjacent walls. Jem grabbed the little all-purpose robot and hit the kill switch. It powered down with a soft whine.

Sitting cross-legged on the floor, Jem hunched over it, frustrated that Ro set him to waste his time on something even Barre could have done. He thought of their morning in the computer lab and grimaced. So what if Barre didn't care about what Jem loved? It didn't make his brother stupid.

Taking bittergreen did.

He grabbed his micro-loupes and dialed up the magnification. He hated busy work. Jem had been playing with dumb drones like this one from the time he could crawl. He should be in there with Ro, digging out Barre's records or working on the interface design she wanted, or at least keeping an eye on Micah, not sitting here flicking tiny switches on a control module.

A few lines of simple code and it would do what Ro wanted. He pulled out his micro, waiting as it paired with the newly installed chip before writing the commands to transfer its query path to Ro's computer. But she hadn't said that was all he should do. Smiling, Jem added a quick peek-a-boo subroutine. That way he would know what she was looking at.

He patted the top of the robot's "head" and sent it on its way before jumping up and brushing off his pants. Now for drone number two. They swept the station in what seemed like random patterns and asking Daedalus for their location would be logged as an unusual command. He looked at his little rogue robot. "How's about you find a brother or sister for me?" He sent a simple query through its rudimentary processor. It beeped softly and spun around back to the station.

Jem followed the drone through the familiar corridors of Daedalus. By the conventions of station time, it was afternoon and the second duty period would end in less than thirty minutes. He had the South nexus to himself, at least for a little while. The drone beeped again and bumped to a stop at the far airlock. When Jem didn't move, it backed up and hit the door again, beeping louder this time.

"Keep your cover on," Jem said, triggering the airlock door. A second drone waited, powered down in a charging alcove. As he bent down to snatch it, two angry voices filled the corridor. Jem froze, glancing up.

Ro's father strode toward him, the senator right at his heels. Jem shrunk back against the wall, curling up in the small niche.

"You have less than two weeks," Rotherwood said. "And then, no matter what, we need to move the cargo."

"And when will I get paid?" Maldonado asked, his voice low and cold.

"You'll get yours. You just have to trust me."

Maldonado snorted. "I'm not stupid, Senator."

"You just do your part," Senator Rotherwood said, nearly spitting the words out. "And we'll both—"

As Jem's heart beat triple time, they stepped past him, never even glancing down to see where he had hidden. He pulled out his micro and accessed the first drone's programming, sending it after them through the nexus. Nobody noticed work drones the same way nobody noticed him.

Jem grabbed the second drone and quickly did the mod, wondering what the senator and the chief engineer were arguing about. Clearly, Jem wasn't the only one with secrets on this station. Maybe his little eavesdropper would have some answers.

Eventually, it would dump the contents of its small memory to his micro. He ran his hands over his tight-clipped hair and watched the second drone head back to the ship to take the pictures Ro wanted.

She'd better have been able to intercept that tox report. Otherwise Barre's little mistake was about to get a whole lot bigger. He shoved his micro back in a pocket and headed to the infirmary.

Chapter 9

THE FULL ASSAY would take a few hours. Micah looked up at the plants craning their way toward their artificial sun. It wasn't as if he had anything else better to do with his time now. He waited in the terraforming bubble as the immature leaves flash-dried in the small dehydrator. This process wasn't optimal for concentrating the psycho-active compounds in bittergreen, but he wasn't looking for high-grade product here.

The scent of wet dirt and bruised herbs faded, replaced by a slight sharpness as the controlled heat drove all the moisture out of the green plant matter. That smell always brought back the dark room where his mother had spent her last days and the acrid sweat that overpowered the bittergreen tea he brewed for her.

He stood up from the uncomfortable chair and stretched his spine. The machine beeped and turned its heating coil and fan off. At least he'd be able to get viable DNA from his sample. Micah reached for the packet Jem had thrown at him, the isolation gloves snug around his hands. If the plant had been dried too quickly, or if the supplier used some of the commercial chemical methods, he wouldn't have a comparison and this would turn out to be a colossal waste of time.

Barre's bittergreen had a yellowish tinge to it. Micah opened the packet and an odd musty smell rose from the crumbly leaves.

Micah quickly lost himself in the routine: Weigh out ten micrograms of the dried sample. Add it and the extraction buffer to the test tube. Shake, warm, extract, chill. The familiar prep for the assay distracted him, at least a little, from his father. The hell of it was he loved the lab work and studying botany on the cellular level. His mother had been so proud when Micah got his early acceptance to Uni. She'd already started to show signs of the neural degeneration that would kill her eight months later, but Micah had been so absorbed in his schooling and his father in himself, that neither of them noticed. If his mother knew, she also knew there wasn't anything they could do about it.

The beep of a timer broke into his memories. He stripped off the gloves, grabbed the sample rack with two labeled test tubes, and headed through the rudimentary airlock back to what had been his office space before Ro had disrupted his only refuge. She, like his father, seemed to be able to wreck his life with as little thought to the consequences. What in the Hub was she doing here, anyway?

The heat and humidity faded as cool air from outside the bubble mixed in the airlock. The sweat chilled on Micah's skin, pimpling his arms in gooseflesh. The outer seal opened, and he stepped into the chaos of Ro's half of the room. She stood in front of the surplus counter that served as her desk, the holographic interface sparkling all around her.

Watching her manipulate the images and windows winking in and out of existence, he forgot his annoyance. She seemed more program than human, her whole body interacting with the display. Micah blinked, trying to keep her in focus. Her hair had slipped free of its usual tie back and whipped around her shoulders every time she moved her head. He couldn't look away.

By the time he realized what he had done, Micah was halfway across the room, standing just outside the colorful sphere surrounding her. His hands tightened around the test tube rack and the glass encased samples clanked against one another, startling him out of his trance. Ro's gaze flicked toward his face. He stared into her sometimes-brown, sometimes-green eyes before she shifted her glance away from him and back to a part of the program that scrolled so quickly, Micah couldn't make out more than a blurred letter or two.

He wasn't even sure she'd really seen him. Turning his back on her, he walked to his side of the room to load the centrifuge. Once the samples had been spun, he washed them gently in cold ethanol, shaking the test tube to collect as much of the material as he could. As long as he had to do this, he might as well do it right.

Out of the corner of his eye, he caught occasional blurs of movement. Ro still stood at her desk, manipulating something on the heads-up holo. She didn't try to talk to him. Working alongside someone who showed the same insane focus as he had, made the lab less lonely.

He turned back to the samples. The dried bittergreen had balled up nicely into tiny pellets he collected carefully and placed in a drying tray. He'd have to wait at least an hour until they could be loaded into the sequencer. For now, he could stretch the kinks out of his neck and shoulders.

Looking across the room, he caught Ro in a rare still moment. She stared into the display, her arms upraised, motionless, a frown adding lines to her forehead. Micah crossed to her side of the lab. One virtual window showed code more complex than he'd ever seen before. He squinted at it, but couldn't keep up with its scroll rate. A second displayed a full ship's schematic of the original freighter. A third window flickered with a barrage of lo res images Micah recognized from the ruined ship.

She pressed her lips together and swept her arm toward the third window. With fingers moving so fast, they practically blurred, Ro organized the images, overlapping some, discarding others, until she'd built a second ship to echo the schematic. She melded the images into a single fused picture and pulled it until it overlaid the middle one. Standing back, she stared through the photographic representation into the schematic beneath.

"What are you doing?" Micah asked.

She jerked, her hands jumping, the images spinning around the room. "Working," she said, before she swept her arm through the entire display and it folded in on itself, disappearing to a tiny point of light. "Did you finish the assay?"

"Waiting for the next phase."

"How about you wait somewhere else?"

Micah didn't know what annoyed him more—that she seemed immune to his Rotherwood charm, or that she was even more closed than he was. "I got here first."

"Tell you what, I won't snoop if you won't."

"That's hardly fair. You already know what I'm working on."

"And I don't care. Learn to cultivate a little disinterest, plant-boy."

A half smile twitched across her face. Fine. So Ro had secrets.

He excelled at uncovering secrets. Most people never looked past his surface. They saw the politician's son and little else. She wouldn't be the first to underestimate him.

Shrugging, he was glancing at the waiting gene sequencer across the room when an alert sounded. Ro stiffened and turned back to the terminal, ignoring Micah completely. He knew an opportunity when he saw it.

She pulled up what looked like a medical file. Micah added a few more degrees of difficulty to his self-appointed task. It was a good thing he liked a challenge. He leaned forward, squinting to make out Barre Durbin's blood tox results, the top right corner of the file flagged with a red virtual sticky note.

"You."

He jerked his head to face her, ready to retreat with an apology.

"How much do you know about biology? The breathing kind, not the plant kind."

Well, plants breathed too, but he knew that's not what she meant. "I'm good."

She frowned at him, probably wondering how much of a liar he was.

"What are we looking at?" He stepped beside her, and she moved over to give him room.

"I was hoping you'd tell me," she said.

"Well, it's a tox screen."

"That much I got, moron."

"Touchy, touchy," Micah said, smiling. He pointed to the information in the footnote. "That tells us they did a rapid assay with a limit of detection cutoff."

"And that's important why?"

"Because if the concentration of whatever they're digging for is below a certain threshold, it gets reported as negative, even if the drug is there. The absolute detection is more reliable, but it takes longer, and usually requires a bigger sample."

"Good."

Micah glanced over at her and raised an eyebrow before turning back to the report. "They tested for all the major metabolites. See?" The basic report was decent enough, but sloppy, scientifically. A real assay would have included the spectrophotometry curves and the absolutes.

"So he tested positive for bittergreen." Ro bracketed the results and blew them up.

"Yeah, but I still don't get how it's responsible for his symptoms." He gestured at the results, but nothing happened. "If you wouldn't mind?"

Ro flicked a finger and zoomed out to the full results.

"This doesn't make any sense." Part of him had hoped they'd find something other than the major metabolite for bittergreen. At least that might explain his collapse. "It's basically a borderline amount anyway." A few sips less or an hour later, and Barre's report would probably have shown up clean.

"Good. Then you have no scientific objections to doctoring the report."

"Look, there are things you don't screw with. This is probably one of them." What if it was something in the stuff? "I can't be responsible for this," he said, raising his hands and taking a step back.

Her laugh echoed back at him from all the hard surfaces in the storage bay. "Oh, that's rich, coming from a drug lord in the making."

Heat blazed to his face. "You don't play with someone's life."

"I'm not. I'm saving it." Ro turned her back on him.

"Fine. Do what you need to do." Micah strode back across the room to his corner. He would finish the comparative assay and be done. Done with this lab. Done with Daedalus. Done. He was smart. He was patient. He'd find another way to burn the cartel that destroyed his life.

*

Yawning again, Nomi glared at the clock display. Its blinking numbers glowed 1530. She should still be asleep. Groaning, she dropped her head back on the pillow, waiting for the alarm blare she'd set this morning when she stumbled into bed after leaving the commissary. Loneliness hit her worse than the terrible hours, the foul coffee, or the distant staff. Maybe that's why she took the risk at breakfast with Ro.

"Daedalus, ping Maldonado, Ro."

Ro's voice answered and brought a brief smile to Nomi's face, until she realized it was a personalized away message. "Working. Urgent calls only."

"And I got up early for that?" Maybe she could catch her at the end of her shift or something. "Okay then, locate Maldonado, Ro."

This time the AI's generic voice responded. "Common space. Reading room."

She hummed as she dressed, layering her crisp gray uniform over a deep red tank top. The rich color highlighted her eyes and her space-pale skin. She stopped to check herself in the mirror, making a face at her own reflection. Chances were whatever she felt for Ro wouldn't be reciprocated.

It didn't matter. If she didn't start meeting people, she'd end up going insane. Just six weeks apart from her family and friends and she already understood the depth of her mistake, but she had a debt to pay.

"Well, then," Nomi said to the empty room and utilitarian furniture. Even her old dorm room had more personality. "Let's go see what Ro's doing."

Striding through the station, Nomi forced herself to nod at the other personnel. At least the hallways showed some sign of life at this hour. By the time Nomi's shift started, she'd be lucky to interact with even a handful of people.

She kept walking until she stood outside the reading room, where she paused to tug her uniform top smooth. The door slid open and Mendez stepped out. "Commander," she said, startled.

Mendez frowned, reading her ident badge. "How are you settling in, Nakamura?"

"Well, thank you."

"Excellent." The commander's dark gaze took her in and dismissed her just as quickly. Nomi watched as she disappeared into the station before entering the reading room. "Ro?"

The small space had an old-fashioned holo-set vibe, as if someone researched historical libraries and recreated an ancient Victorian sitting room, complete with gloomy lighting, antique chairs, and shelves lined with reproduction paper books. The lights brightened as she stepped deeper inside. "Ro?"

Silence rang in the empty room.

"Daedalus, locate Maldonado, Ro."

The AI's voice echoed. "Engineering sub-level three."

That had to be wrong. There was no way Ro could have made

it from the reading room all the way across the station and down to engineering. Besides, they would have passed each other in the nexus. Was there some glitch in the AI's localization subroutine? "Locate Nakamura, Konomi."

The same bland voice answered her. "Common space, reading room."

"Huh." She swept her gaze around the empty library, wondering. "Ping Maldonado, Ro."

"Working, urgent calls only," the message repeated.

"Message Maldonado, Ro."

"Recording."

"Ro, this is Nomi Nakamura. I'd like to ask you a question when you're free. Please ping me at your convenience."

Maybe the senator's pretty-boy son would know where she was. "Daedalus, locate Rotherwood, Micah."

"Main cafeteria."

Maybe he'd have a line on that coffee he'd promised. She left the cluttered reading room behind and returned to the spartan station, happier than she'd been in a long while. It would be good to talk to someone—even Micah.

She strode down the corridor, looking up for a change and smiling at everyone she passed. Most smiled back. Maybe this wouldn't be such a terrible posting after all. They couldn't keep her on the overnight shift forever.

His attention glued to his micro, Micah Rotherwood brushed past her and ducked into the nexus. Nomi stared after him, frowning. She pulled out her micro and queried Daedalus in silent mode. The AI placed Micah in his quarters this time.

Nomi decided she didn't need to head to dinner just yet.

How well did she know either Ro or Micah, really? Were they

working together? One of them had hacked the AI. She would lay odds on it being Ro. But why would she mess with the localizations? What did she have to hide? She squeezed through a knot of people chatting in front of the nexus, apologized, and hurried after Micah, her curiosity even more powerful than her loneliness.

Chapter 10

Ro took a deep breath and copied the negative result for a narcotic metabolite and pasted it to the bittergreen, obliterating the flagged finding. Setting the report as unread, she saved and closed it. The file blinked red for official and unreported. She stepped away from the display, shaking out her fingers and getting ready for the next part of the hack.

Backing out of the medical file took Ro as much time and care as getting inside had, but no one would be able to trace her path through the system. She'd done as much as she could. What happened between Barre and his parents wouldn't be her concern anymore. Jem would owe her.

Ro erased the display, calling up the ship's data from her micro and the two drones' completed map. Someone had deliberately disguised recent structural repairs and Ro knew that someone had to be her father. That meant he was connected to the stolen cargo somehow. But how? She pulled her arms in close to her body, letting the holographic display collapse in on itself.

Now what?

Could this wreck even fly? Judging by his notes, her father seemed to think so, but she'd have to check every system aboard to see what he'd finished and what did and didn't work.

She folded her arms around herself, considered her options, and paced the room. Why wouldn't he let her leave? It would have cost him nothing to authorize her scholarship application. Now it was down to this: No AI, no scholarship, no escape. She couldn't do that, not and live with herself. She certainly couldn't continue living with him.

Ro stopped and called up the original AI core code. Letting it spiral around her in a wash of color and motion, she whistled in appreciation. No wonder her father left this for last. Even if the ship could take off, without a functioning AI, it couldn't do much more than orbit Daedalus or limp through interstitial space. No one would offer Ro a scholarship for that, unless she could troubleshoot its higher brain.

The original programming bootstrapped Dauber and May's self-learning, interactive, recursive, enhanced networks and the first gen AIs took it from there. The SIREN interface had revolutionized interstellar travel, simultaneously making the millions of tiny calculations needed to navigate in real time through interstitial space and mathematically mapping the unstable probability wells that let the next generation of crewed ships hopscotch through wormholes.

Without the AI, the ship was one very expensive, very stranded storage locker.

She squinted at the core code, wondering what the hell her father was planning. If the cargo was his, then he needed the ship to smuggle it off base. But if it could fly, blasting free of Daedalus station wouldn't exactly be subtle.

Right now it couldn't fly and he had left the AI for her. She was sure of it. For all his secrecy and the little confrontation they had this morning, it had been almost too easy to get into his workroom for the schematics.

What else had he done here? Frowning, Ro paced her corner of the storage room again. She had assumed the environmentals were running through Daedalus. Ro didn't like to make any assumptions where her father was concerned. At best they would be wrong. At worst, they could turn dangerous.

Turning back to her micro, Ro pulled up her toolbox again. She wasn't doing anything fancy this time, just basic system diagnostics, and if her search somehow did register with Daedalus, she would claim she was following up on the power drain. It disturbed her that she only spared a small twinge of guilt for throwing Micah under the afterburners. "Like father, like daughter."

Pairing her micro to the old standards took her a few minutes. The old computers didn't have the capability to access the holographic display, so she had to squint to make out the scrolling code on the micro's small screen.

"Son of a bitch." The underlying systems worked perfectly. Full autonomic functions were intact. While the environmentals still ran through the station, the ship could take over without a problem. Her father was a piece of work. Now all she had to do was heal the AI itself. Simple, right? She started to laugh, the sound harsh and mocking against the hard surfaces of the storage bay.

She opened a new virtual window, studying her code mods again. Every sim she ran came up five by five, which made her a little nervous. "Come on, Ro, get a grip." Slowing down the run-time, she started another test and watched it complete, matching the ideas in her head with the code she'd written.

Just like her hacking toolbox, her code mods stacked together like children's toys, small, stable modules, each individually tested to destruction, built into something elegant and robust. A tiny beep and a winking blue light pulled her attention back to the run window.

It passed every test she could think of.

She pulled her hands through her tangled hair. It was the tests she couldn't think of that drove her crazy. Nothing else remained but to try it live.

She shut the simulation down. Now what? Walk away because she could fail? Or because her father had manipulated her again? The code pulled at her and not just because of the challenge or the stakes. She wanted this. She needed to prove she could best him, even if it didn't lead anywhere. Whatever the hell he did with the ship afterward didn't matter. Maybe if she was lucky, he'd take off in it and never look back.

*

For someone with something to hide, Micah was surprisingly easy to follow. He kept his gaze glued to his micro, muttering to himself as he wound through Daedalus's corridors. Nomi kept him in her sight, partly amused, partly concerned when the AI kept listing him in different, random places in the habitation ring. When he branched off a service corridor, she paused, frowning. From here, he could get outside to the barely terraformed asteroid or into the wreck of the old ship.

Nomi could call in now and report what? A glitch in the

localization subroutine and a wandering resident? If she ever wanted to get assigned to a better shift, she'd better bring something more useful than that to Mendez. Besides, how did Ro figure into all of this? There had to be a logical explanation that wouldn't end up getting the engineer arrested.

At the next branch point, Nomi stopped again and listened. All was silent except for the slight whistle of the air handling system. She frowned, studying the external airlock. He could have gone outside here, but he would've needed an EVA suit. Besides, Daedalus monitored the airlocks closely. Air loss cost the station precious resources. Nomi bet Micah had gone to the ship.

If she was wrong, she could always request permission to leave the station and search after her shift. Of course, she'd need a decent reason. She'd worry about that after checking out the ship.

She snaked her way through the temporary corridors to the wreck, surprised by how intact it appeared. Neither the airlock nor the part of the hull she could see through the umbilicals showed evidence of any damage. The starboard side wings jutted out over the dusty rock of the asteroid.

Creeping forward, Nomi felt a prickle at the back of her neck, but she knew no one could be behind her. Micah was somewhere ahead, most likely in the ship, doing something.

This would be about the time her younger brother would leap out of an alcove and scare the crap out of her, but this was no horror vid and Daisuke and home were at least a dozen jumps away. She tapped out a distress call on her micro just in case, ready to trigger with either a touch or a voice command, shaking her head at the paranoia.

The airlock stood open in maintenance mode. She slipped inside and stopped again, one hand near her micro, ready to bolt. Her distorted reflection looked back at her in the metal walls. There wasn't any sign of damage on this side of the airlock, either.

She stepped through to the ship. An empty, silent corridor branched out on either side of her. Looking back and forth, Nomi had decided to head aft and work her way forward when raised voices from the front of the ship echoed harshly against the metal.

There were two distinct voices. One had to be Micah's. She didn't want the other to be Ro's. Her stomach roiled. Shifting her micro into recording mode, she crept forward, hoping they wouldn't be able to hear her above their own shouting.

Chapter 11

JEM HESITATED OUTSIDE the infirmary. If Ro messed up, he'd just made things much, much worse for Barre. But what the hell else was he supposed to do?

The infirmary gleamed in stainless steel efficiency. All the activity centered around one bay. "A slow day at the office," his father would joke, if it weren't Barre lying in a medi-bed. His mother stood, frowning at the complex display.

"This makes no sense," she said.

Jem jerked his head up to meet her gaze, but she wasn't talking to him. His father came up behind her to study the screen.

She slapped her hand against the wall. "Toxicology is negative. There's nothing in his blood work and unless he picked up some strange parasite or exotic infection between Hadria and Daedalus, he shouldn't be unconscious."

The lab techs looked away and avoided Barre's treatment bay. Jem's father placed his hands on his mother's shoulders. She closed her eyes and leaned back against him. Jem turned away from their unexpected intimacy.

"Jem."

He looked up into his mother's perfectly composed face.

"There's nothing you can do here. Barre is stable."

There was nothing in her expression or her piercing gaze that would have betrayed any frustration or concern. At least he knew how to deal with the cold, distant version of his mother.

"I know. I just wanted ..." Jem trailed off, gesturing at his quiet brother.

"Let him stay, Leta. It's his brother."

Jem nodded at his father, grateful for his intervention.

His mother walked away. Jem swallowed a lump in his throat and pulled a stool to Barre's cubicle, struggling with his conscience. Tampering with medical records was illegal, but what his parents would do to Barre if they found out he was using again was worse.

Jem leaned close to his silent brother and took his hand. "You can be such a jerk sometimes, you know?"

The soft beeping of monitors answered him. He watched the rhythmic rise and fall of Barre's breathing, wondering what kind of music his brother would write for it.

"If you can't find your way back from wherever you've wandered off to, I'll be alone with them."

The wail of an alarm made him twitch and he almost missed the gentle answering pressure against his fingers. A swarm of white-coated staff, led by his parents, displaced Jem from the bedside. He shrank back into a corner of the room, struggling to see what was happening.

Someone pushed an ampule of something clear and viscous through Barre's IV. His body arched away from the bed.

"Keep him still!" his mother shouted.

One brown arm shot up and yanked on a fistful of tubes and

wires.

"Shit. He's extubated himself!"

"Hold him!"

More alarms joined the jangle of the first. Jem couldn't see through the crush of bodies around Barre's bed. His mouth dried. What if he'd made the wrong choice? What if the drug had made his brother seriously sick? He'd have to tell his parents not only about Barre, but what he'd done to the records. He chewed on the side of his thumb until the cuticle bled.

"Get the fuck off me," Barre rasped, barely loud enough to be heard over the machinery.

"And he's back," his father said. Jem could hear the relief in his voice. "All right, team, give the boy some room."

Technicians scurried around, clearing machines and pulling all the tubes away from Barre's body. Jem took a few hesitant steps forward. His parents stood looking down at Barre, identical expressions of relief on their faces. That wouldn't last long.

"What am I doing here?" Barre asked.

Jem watched his mother's lips thin and her eyes narrow, the anger that was never far below the surface bubbling up. "I don't know what you took this time, but I know it was something and as soon as I prove it—"

"Mom, I don't—"

She leaned forward. "Don't you dare," she said, the deadly quiet in her voice sending chills down Jem's spine. He had definitely done the right thing. His mother whirled away from Barre, bright spots flushing her dark cheeks. His father shook his head and followed her. So everything was back to normal then and right on schedule.

Barre looked up into Jem's eyes and shrugged.

"Yeah, some things never change," Jem said.

"What am I doing here?"

Jem slid the stool back over to Barre's bedside and handed his brother a water bulb. "Really? You don't know?"

Barre sucked down the liquid and handed Jem back the empty container. "I was making music." He frowned, looked up, squinted at Jem. "My stash—"

"Don't," Jem warned, softly.

"You?"

"I have it."

Barre closed his eyes and exhaled heavily.

They sat in silence for a few minutes.

"I wouldn't do that to you," Barre said.

"Do what?"

"Leave you alone with them."

Jem nodded, not sure what else he could say. The silence stretched out. The normal buzz of conversations rose around them as the staff waited for the next emergency, or even the next routine call. A tech glanced at the monitor above Barre's bedside and walked away. Their parents didn't even look up from their desks.

"I guess I owe you one," Barre said.

"Well, you can bail me out the next time I'm an idiot."

"That's not fair."

"No?" Jem said, and struggled to lower his voice. "I can't believe you started using again. Especially after what they said they'd do after the last time." He jutted his chin toward his parents. "And you shouldn't trust Rotherwood."

Barre frowned. "The senator?"

"Don't play cute. Micah Rotherwood. Your source." Ro better

be watching him prepare that assay. If he did anything wrong in the process, Jem would make sure Micah would suffer.

"Keep your voice down!" Barre said in a fierce whisper. "And I don't know where you get your information, but for one thing, I didn't know Micah had access. So thank you."

Jem shot him a furious look.

"For another, I brought it from Hadria. Maybe it got contaminated or something." His gaze darted all around the room, but no one paid either of them the slightest attention now that it was clear Barre would live. "I know you won't believe me, but I tried to give it up. But Mom and Dad ... you have no idea what it's like not to be you."

"Don't you dare throw this on me!" Jem didn't realize he'd stood until he was leaning over Barre's bed, shouting. The monitors red-lined as Barre struggled to sit up, his face red, his eyebrows drawn over angry eyes. A technician tugged at Jem's arm. He struggled in the man's grasp. "You have choices, Barre, no matter what you tell yourself."

"I'm sorry, visiting hours are over," the tech said, his voice firm, his grip firmer.

"And they have nothing to do with me," Jem shouted. So much for his brother's gratitude. The hell with it. He didn't even care about Micah's assay anymore. What did it matter where Barre got the bittergreen? If he wanted to throw his life and his talent away, well, that was a choice too.

*

As far as Micah could tell, Ro hadn't moved from her spot standing in the middle of a personal 3-d show. He strode into his lab, unable to ignore her presence there, even when she stayed silent and focused on her own work. As much as sharing his space irritated him, Ro wasn't the cause of his anger, only the trigger.

Two weeks and another forced move to another posting that would start out full of promise and end horribly as either his father's enemies would find them, or his father would run afoul of some ethics rule. He glanced through the flexible wall to his plant nursery and cloned the assay data over to his micro.

Scanning through the comparison showed what Micah knew it would: Barre's bittergreen and his were separate cultivars. He superimposed the graphs of the two samples and highlighted the differences. It also showed him something he didn't expect. "Ro? I have Jem's proof."

She looked through her display at him with unseeing eyes. Soft brown in this light, they blinked, seeming to sharpen and turn more green as she focused on Micah. Stepping through the images, she held her hand out for his micro.

"Show me."

"You're welcome," Micah said. "See this?" He pointed out a spike in one of the graphs. "That's Barre's sample. It wasn't even the bittergreen that made him sick. It was mold. Mycotoxins. He must have had an allergic reaction."

She scanned up and down the micro's small screen. "You do good work."

"You sound surprised."

She shrugged.

"You left out the 'for a drug dealer' part," he said.

"No, I mean ... ," she started, but closed her mouth with an audible click before handing him back his micro and stepping back into her display. "Never mind."

That was it? She wasn't going to call Jem and show him his results? "You have no right to judge me. You look at me and see my father. Should I look at you and see yours?"

"That's not fair," she said, turning on him, red blotching her cheeks, eyes bright and glittering with anger.

"And what, exactly, are you doing here?" Micah gestured at the bright display. "I don't see this on any work order from Mendez."

"This has nothing to do with you."

He ignored her and walked into the center of her display. "That is *this* ship. Don't try to deny it."

She raised her arms. He stepped closer, getting up into her face.

"And this is the most convoluted programming I've ever seen. Do you want me to hazard a guess?"

Ro took a step back and lowered her arms, looking like she'd wanted to stare a hole through his forehead.

"That's the SIREN source code."

"So what if it is?" she said, the flush spreading down to her neck. "I'm not doing anything illegal."

If she thought a subtle threat would make him back down, then she didn't know him very well. "What's illegal about selective plant breeding and exo-botany?"

"You're growing bittergreen."

"It grows fast and hybridizes easily. Unless I plan to dry it and sell it, I haven't committed a crime." It wasn't the authorities he needed to worry about anyway. If they discovered a farm even as small as this one, they would just dust it with defoliant and move on. If the cartels found him, or even caught a rumor of what he was trying, Micah wouldn't have to worry about his plants anymore. They'd execute him. *Like father, like son,* he thought, flashing Ro a grim smile.

"Get the hell out of here before I call Mendez."

He couldn't even muster the anger to snap back at her. What did it matter anymore? "Fine," he said, turning his back on her and walking out of the display. "I don't care what you're doing. It doesn't involve me. Besides, I'm getting off this rock in two weeks. You can have the space all to yourself."

Ro didn't respond, but he could feel her staring at him.

"Do you have any idea what it's like to watch someone die in pain?" The words slipped out before Micah realized he'd said them, but once he started, he couldn't stop. Memories blasted through him like an ion storm.

"No," Ro whispered.

"What would you do if you knew there was one thing that could make it better? But that thing is illegal and when you buy it, the men you buy it from happily take your money. Then they discover who you are. Who your father is. And they threaten to cut off your supply unless he works for them." He squeezed his eyes shut, but the images of his father's face when the cartel chief hand-delivered his son along with a fresh week's dose of bittergreen for his dying wife would haunt him for a lifetime.

"I'm sorry."

Micah refused to turn around even when he felt Ro standing close behind him.

"Call Mendez or don't. I don't care." He gestured to the doomed plants, still happily growing under the more intense light. "This was my last shot to get back at the people who ruined my life."

"What do you mean?"

"What do you care?" he shot back. She didn't answer and after a long moment of uncomfortable silence, he turned to face her. "Go back to your work," he said. "I have to salvage what I can in the next two weeks."

"And then what?" This time he didn't hear any challenge in her voice.

"My father gets another chance to fuck up." And Micah would be right there with him.

Ro met his gaze with her own and he struggled not to flinch or look away.

"My father's been restoring this ship. I don't know for how long. Or why. Or even how far he's gotten, but he couldn't get the AI to work. I stole his plans. I'm going to wake it up." She continued to stare at him for several more minutes of silence before turning back to her work without another word.

"Wait," he called out, his heart beating with a possibility he was afraid to look at too closely. "This thing can fly?"

Ro paused, her arms upraised. "Not yet. But it will."

"And then what?" he asked, too softly for her to hear.

Chapter 12

WITH THE STATION so far from most of the major jump paths and most of the messages routed automatically by the AI, Nomi didn't have all that much to do. Alone in the communications relay, she stared up at the large heads-up display of all the sector's ansible nodes and listened to her recording of the conversation between Ro and Micah.

Could Ro really get the ship's AI back on line? Nomi whistled, the sharp sound piercing in the empty room. She still couldn't figure out what, if anything, she should tell Mendez. The ship was technically salvage. It didn't belong to Daedalus and if the Space Force hadn't claimed it by now, she was pretty sure they figured it a lost cause. Unless Ro had been given a direct order to stay off the ship, she wasn't breaking any station protocols.

The ghosting program was a problem and although simply growing bittergreen wasn't illegal, she was certain Mendez would shut Micah down.

Nomi bit her lower lip. Really, she should tell someone.

Something Micah said about Ro's father piqued her curiosity. Nomi accessed the station database for the publicly available CV's and contracts and read the scrolling data: Alain Maldonado. Chief Engineer, Daedalus Station. Age 41 standard. Contracted time on Daedalus Station: five years. Time to date: three years. Dependents: one.

She clicked through to see his previous postings and whistled. For the past 22 years, Alain Maldonado hadn't moved up at all in the Engineering Guild ranks. He'd never held a job longer than a single posting, sometimes less. Even with no guild advancement, a string of broken contracts, and not one single commendation in his file, he kept getting jobs.

Poor Ro had been dragged around the galaxy from one colony to another, from station to station, and even to one fleet designation. Nomi had lived her entire life in one place, with her parents and her younger brother. Her own childhood had been considered odd enough by her friends' standards. She couldn't imagine moving every few years for her whole life.

Now that Ro had an employee posting, her information would be searchable as well. Nomi glanced up at the silent communications array and then back to her micro, hesitating. Ro didn't strike her as the kind of person who'd take kindly to being snooped on.

A loud buzz vibrated in the still room. Nomi jerked her head up to the ansible display before she recognized her micro's message alert.

"Nomi. Are you still having trouble with the sound balance?"

Her heart beat faster at the sound of Ro's voice.

"Yeah, it definitely cuts out. But Ro, what are you doing awake at this insane hour?"

"Can I come up now?"

Nomi reached for the controls that would put Daedalus fully in charge of incoming communications for the next fifteen minutes so she could talk with Ro. From her perspective, there was little Daedalus couldn't do that a human in the relay room could, but station protocols stated otherwise. "All set. It's quiet up here. It'll be nice to have the company." Nomi liked it up here at night. The ansible nodes glittered like stars and with the interior lights dialed down, she felt like she hovered in space.

It would be lovely to share it with someone.

"On my way."

Nomi was glad she'd chosen the red tank beneath her uniform. She cleared the search from her micro. This would be much better than trolling through the database.

The relay room's doors slid open and Ro stood for a moment, back-lit in the corridor's brightness. Nomi blinked, her vision used to the dim interior. All she could make out was Ro's blonde hair, free of its usual tie back, a soft corona of light framing her face. "Welcome to my quiet world," Nomi said, smiling.

Ro stepped forward and the doors slid shut behind her. As Nomi's eyes readjusted to darkness, she noticed the frown on Ro's face and her smile faltered. "Is there something wrong?" she asked.

Ro shook her head and scanned the room with her micro.

"What are you doing?"

"Making sure of something." Ro's voice held none of the wry humor it had the other morning.

"I really appreciate you coming up tonight. I've reported the problem pretty much since I started here. But I guess it wasn't in anybody's queue." She glanced up at Ro, hoping this was more than just a conscientious engineering intern trying to impress the commander.

She didn't answer and Nomi cursed herself for being so eager for a friend that she'd totally misread signs that weren't there.

"Here. You can pair your micro to any of the consoles." She pointed to the ring of empty workstations around the raised dais where she sat. If there was ever a need, they could have six comms people fielding signals, but Nomi couldn't imagine Daedalus ever being that overrun by ansible traffic.

Ro took the station at the edge of the ring and sat half-facing Nomi and the door to comms, completely ignoring the twinkling display.

"Don't you ever sleep?" Nomi asked.

"Is it just the high frequencies?"

"Yes." The silence of the relay room usually comforted Nomi, but now she wanted to fill it with chatter. Even an ansible call would help. She sneaked glances at Ro as she worked with a focused intensity, the holographic display brightening the space around her head.

"I need a test signal. Push something from the logs through."

Nomi sat back at her station, slipped on her headset, and took control back from Daedalus. "Here," she said, calling up some of the traffic comms had passed during the last shift. "Try it now." As she waited for the messages to play back through the system, she thought again about what she'd overheard. Should she inform Mendez? Call security? Did Ro know she'd been on the ship?

Sound burst through her headset. Wincing, she turned down the volume. Standard traffic reports and worm-hole status updates chased away the awkward, nearly one-sided conversation.

"How's that sound?"

"Fine. Better." Nomi wondered where Ro's smile had gone. "Thank you."

Ro collapsed the display and slipped her micro in a pocket

before pushing back from the console and staring at Nomi, her eyes cold. "You kept looking for me and Micah this afternoon. Why?"

Crap. Ro must have captured all her queries somehow. "I—I left you a message. I wanted to talk to you," she said, her lips suddenly dry.

Ro took a step forward, her dark brows angry slashes across her forehead. Nomi shrunk back against her console.

"About what?"

The anger in Ro's eyes sent a chill down Nomi's spine.

"Did Mendez send you to spy on me? Did my father?"

"Ro—I—no," she stammered. "I just wanted—I thought we could be friends." She should have reported them when she had the chance.

A tense silence flooded the room. Nomi's hand stretched out toward the emergency call beacon on her console.

"You're scaring me, Ro."

Silence locked them both in place, Ro studying Nomi's face with a fierce intensity, Nomi's hand trembling over the alarm.

Ro squeezed her eyes shut, and let her shoulders slump. "What am I doing? I'm turning into my father. Shit." She spun on her heel and the door opened again. "I'm sorry."

Nomi stood alone in the empty room, her heart pounding, the ansible network's imitation starlight twinkling all around her.

*

Ro stormed through her room, gathering a change of clothes, not even bothering to mask the noise. She couldn't live with her father any longer. It didn't matter what happened next. An image of Nomi, her hands shaking, her face pale, and her dark eyes dilated, rose in her mind. She didn't deserve Ro's anger.

If the crew head on the ship worked, she'd move in there for the duration. If not, she could use the fitness room's facilities. Ro shoved her clothes and toiletries into a bag before pausing to look around the room she'd slept in for the past three years. There was little to show that a person actually lived there. Personalizing her quarters only made the inevitable packing and moving more difficult. Other than the quilt she inherited from her mother and had restored, there was nothing she couldn't walk away from. She folded the patchwork blanket carefully and slipped it inside her bag. Her micro had everything else she needed.

With one last glance at the closed door to her father's room, she quickly enabled the ghost subroutine. If someone was looking for her while she was officially off duty, Daedalus would place her in her quarters. No one would risk having to deal with her father in order to find her.

She didn't look back as she strode through the quiet station to her corner of Micah's workshop and the sleeping AI.

*

Jem couldn't block out the shouting. His parents argued late into the night, their raised voices penetrating two sets of doors in their quarters. He curled around a pillow and tried to sleep.

He didn't need to make out the words to know they were furious with Barre. But it wasn't really even about him. It was about them—about the Doctors Durbin and their selfless, dedicated, brilliant, perfect image.

A drug-addicted son marred their little fiction and now they were going to send him away.

Jem threw his useless pillow across the room and rolled out of bed. He pulled on pants and a shirt, grabbed his micro, and slipped out of their quarters.

Well, Barre had wanted their attention. He certainly got it this time.

Jem walked through the silent station towards the ship. If he couldn't sleep, he might as well work.

The soft whirring of the two reprogrammed drones greeted him as he stepped onto the bridge. He was going to have to see if the one he sent after the senator and Maldonado captured anything interesting, but for now, he really just wanted to lose himself in the code. As he slid into the pilot's command chair, his black mood evaporated. If only Ro could get the ship working again, then they could go anywhere.

Sighing, he pulled out his micro and configured it for wide angle heads-up display. He wasn't as skilled as Ro in managing the interface, but he could get the job done. He had to. Ro counted on him.

The AI code rose up all around him in its dazzling complexity. It would be easy to get lost, staring at it for hours and getting absolutely nothing done. He forced himself to focus. Jem found the small segment of the code that he needed to work on and expanded it until everything around it blurred away.

At right angles, he pulled up his mods. Until today, they'd just been theoretical models he'd played with for years, never dreaming he'd have a chance to actually test them. Jem licked dry lips, shut out the scurrying of the drones and the heap of scrap metal in the center of the bridge, and started to work.

"What are you doing awake?"

Jem whirled around to see Ro leaning against the ruined navigator's console. He shook out his hands and rubbed his eyes. "What time is it?"

"0-400."

"Wow." He'd been working for hours without a break. No wonder his eyes felt so gritty.

"Show me what you've got."

"Look, I have no way of knowing if this will work. Not until you get the AI back up." Now that Ro was here, his doubts returned about a thousand-fold.

She stepped over a drone to get a closer look at his display. "It's a solid idea. What's the worst that can happen? The AI's upper brain is already fried. Besides, there's no reason it shouldn't work."

Her confidence in him chased off the exhaustion. "Okay. See here?" He gestured at the corner where the two programs touched. "I needed a bridge. Something with enough of the AI's core code that it wouldn't reject the additions." It helped to think of this kind of work like an organ transplant. The body had to be tricked into accepting even the best artificial organs completely. "Sort of a shunt." He gestured to the left at a scrolling page of code.

She traced the lines of code while Jem fidgeted. What if he'd screwed up? What if she didn't think it would work now that she'd seen the full program? He was sure he must have overlooked something. A sour taste flooded his mouth and his stomach roiled.

"Oh, clever, clever boy," Ro said, smiling. "You *have* been busy."

Relief flooded through Jem. He sagged against the console, feeling the soreness in his neck and back for the first time since he sneaked in here. "I was just about to graft it on. If it works in the sandbox, then maybe we can try it for real."

Ro leaned forward, her eyes bright. "Nice!"

Jem stepped away from the display. "Do you want to do the honors?"

She raised her arms and zoomed through the code so quickly, Jem's vision blurred. He sighed and backed further away. Her project, her choice. At least he had the chance to work on it with her, even for this small piece.

The display flickered briefly. "Oh, no, this is your baby," she said, tucking her hands behind her back. "All yours."

"You sure?" His voice squeaked and Jem cleared his throat.

She nodded.

"This is outstanding!"

"Yes, yes it is," Ro said, staring at him hard. Jem shook out his hands. He could do this. He had to do this. It was just a trial run. It didn't have to be perfect.

"Okay," he said. "Here goes." First he had to prepare the AI program for the graft. Moving his hands carefully, he created a rough edge in the code representation. Then he did the same to his shunt. Theoretically, when he drew them together, the two programs should meld to each other and create a seamless whole. If it worked, then they should be able to use the holographic interface to pass commands to the AI. It would be much faster and more efficient than the original and very primitive voice command structure or console input as long as you were skilled in using it.

"What are you waiting for?" Ro asked, nudging him in the

ribs.

Jem put his arms down for a minute and rolled his shoulders before sending the final command to execute.

The display winked out as the new program compiled. The seconds ticked by. Jem waited, barely daring to breathe. Yes, this was only proof of concept, but unless it worked right out of the gate, he doubted Ro would trust him to continue with her.

Ro's breathing sounded harsh and ragged beside him. She clutched her micro so hard her knuckles had whitened. Jem smiled, glad she was just as nervous and excited as he was.

Red lights flared all over marred consoles, making the ruined polymers appear to be melting again. Jem sucked in his breath and turned to Ro, his eyes wide. "What the hell?"

"Oh, you brilliant boy," she said, her voice a husky whisper. "You did it."

Chapter 13

Ro gave a very startled Jem a bear hug and twirled him around in a circle before springing away and pairing her micro to the brilliant interface graft he'd just enabled.

"Ro, what did you do?" Jem said, a quaver in his voice.

She couldn't look away from her display. In one virtual window, she had the original program specs with her mods running. In another, one of her system tools coaxed the crippled AI to spool out its damaged code. "I knew it would work, so I yanked you out of the sandbox."

"Jesus, Ro, you could've told me!" Jem's voice cracked.

"Your code scanned five by five." It was a race between her and her father now and she needed Jem's interface if this was going to work.

"But I didn't get a chance to work out the bugs. What if—"

"Time to put on your big boy pants," Ro interrupted. You could 'what if' until the singularity. It was what she'd been doing, until now. "I aim to get this AI working. Help me or leave. What will it be?"

He didn't move and Ro smiled. "Good. Now watch and learn,

my young assistant," she said, sounding a hell of a lot more confident than she felt.

The strobing red lights cast distorted shadows across the bridge. Ro kept her gaze locked on her displays to keep from getting queasy. With Jem's code grafted on, she readied her modded program for full forced upload. The AI had too much damage to patch which was probably why her father gave up after getting the autonomic systems running. If this worked, it would have to build its personality subroutines from factory specs. It would take time, but it was better than the brain-dead mind that barely functioned.

"Ready?" She turned toward Jem. He stood just behind her, his arms hugged around his ribs, his gaze darting around the bridge before finally settling on her virtual display.

His interface hack had been brilliant. She wished she'd thought of it, but she didn't have the gene-mod background he did and if his genius was anything, it was his ability to create a code interpreter for a biological metaphor and make it work.

"No," he answered, softly. "But that's not going to change anything, is it?"

"No."

Jem's new holographic interface simplified the work of hand-feeding thousands of lines of code allowing her to build a virtual structure instead, something Ro was very, very good at. As she reviewed her schematics, she once again felt a familiar awe for Douber and May and what they might accomplish now, with something like this. She wondered what the two legendary programmers would make of her.

She quickly threw open another window and tossed it toward Jem. "Monitor the environmentals, okay? This could get a little messy."

"Messy?" Jem squeaked. "How?"

"Just keep us quiet, okay? I don't want Daedalus to get curious."

"Okay." He didn't sound comfortable, but Ro knew he'd have her back.

"Here we go," she said, and focused all of herself on the code. Jem would just have to cope without any hand-holding. If he couldn't, then she'd picked the wrong assistant.

With careful fingers, she pinched her program into a neat cube that lay sparkling in one palm. Her free hand pulled up one of her favorite subroutines. The auto-run sequencer was one of the first tools she'd built and she knew it so well she didn't even need to look at it.

"Okay, baby, she's all yours," Ro said, sending it spinning in the air towards the window where the ravaged code limped along. She regretted that she'd never get to meet the original AI. There was no hope for it, really, given how the code looked. Once the sequencer worked its magic, she should be able to force her program to override the damage and the AI would be able to create a new personality out of the ashes of the old.

Come on, Ro, you can do this, she thought, biting her lip. She had to. Her stomach cramped as she waited. Garish light washed through the bridge. "Who programmed these lights, anyway?"

"Sorry?" Jem said.

"Can't you do anything about it?" Red was a stupid color for emergencies.

"I'm on it."

She glanced up. The scrolling code stuttered to a stop. Ro held her breath, pulse pounding in her ears as the symbols slowly flashed, white lettering glowing in a smoky background. The background winked out, taking the letters with it. All her virtual windows crashed. The red wash of light abruptly cut out, leaving them blinking in near darkness.

"Fuck," she said, stiffening her arms so she wouldn't inadvertently send any commands.

A klaxon blared, the sound rising and falling in a painful wail that reverberated through the small space. Anyone even near the ship would hear them. "Jem!" she shouted over the cacophony.

"I'm on it!"

"Come on, come on," she urged. "Hurry." She needed to be able to see to send commands to the computer. Even the nauseating red light would be welcome. Her outstretched hands trembled, her prepared code waiting. She didn't dare move blind. And if the auto-run sequencer completely broke down the old program while she was immobilized, her new code wouldn't have anything to grab on to.

The damned siren made it impossible to concentrate. What the hell was taking Jem so long? Even if she could turn, she wouldn't be able to see him. "Now would be a good time," she said.

The sound cut out so suddenly, Ro nearly fell back. She risked turning her head. Jem stood hunched over his micro furiously inputting commands in its small display. Dim white lights rose up from the two drones in cone-shaped columns. "How's that?"

"Better."

"It wasn't my fault," Jem said in a small voice.

"Did I say it was?" Ro opened and closed her right hand, working the cramp out. The cube of her waiting program still hovered over her left.

"You overloaded the interface."

She gestured and new windows popped open all around her. "Yeah, I figured."

"You should've let me debug first."

Probably so, but that ship had jumped the wormhole. She studied the wrecked AI code and her helper utility. There was still time to make this work. Sweat dripped off her forehead and into one eye. Ro wished she had a hand free to push the hair out of her face.

"When you had me use the virtual window to interface with the emergency lights, everything crashed."

"I know. I know. Now will you shut up and let me work?" Damn but Jem was touchy. He started to talk, but Ro just kept right on going as if he hadn't said a thing. "Follow internal chatter from Daedalus. Let me know if it starts to ping the ship."

No sound from behind her. She could feel him sulking even without being able to see his face. Well, at least he was quiet.

Ro watched the code waver in the display. She had a narrow window. Too early, and the new program would bounce off the defenses of the old. Too late, and it wouldn't be able to anchor itself to the autonomic processes and form a unified AI. Even if she'd calculated everything perfectly, there was a solid chance the AI wouldn't coalesce and the programs would simply fragment, leaving a ship that could run basic environmentals but would never be able to fly.

No wonder her father hadn't even tried.

A flash of green caught her eye. Her hand steadied, holding the new code still. Without any conscious thought, she tossed the waiting cube underhand through the bridge towards the holo display. It sank through without a ripple and flattened, forming a large rectangle that bisected itself over and over, forming multiple sheets. Each represented a subroutine and each one folded into a complex three dimensional shape.

Each shape found a part of the program to fit itself into, seamlessly, before vanishing. She'd modeled the mechanism after the holographic version of old-style Tetris and the folding paper technique of origami. When all her pieces had seated themselves, instead of game over, it would be game just beginning.

Ro rolled her neck and squeezed her shoulders back. "Jem, you still with me?"

"Yeah."

She turned to him and spread her arms out. "Look, I should have told you. I'm sorry."

He shrugged as if he didn't really care, but Ro knew him well enough to know he was still pretty mad at her. "This is going to take some time." She gestured at the colorful shapes floating down through the broken code. "You should head to bed."

"I want to see this through."

Jem's eyes looked as red as a bittergreen user's.

"Oh, I have the assay results."

"And?"

"Micah was telling the truth. Look." She walked over to him and accessed her server space from his micro. The assay spooled out for them both to see. "It wasn't Micah's plants. The problem was with the stuff Barre used."

Jem stood silently for several minutes as her program continued to propagate through the old AI space. He frowned. "It doesn't matter. He's using again and he got sick. And I don't know what's going to happen to him."

"Well, isn't that his problem?"

Jem winced and Ro realized she'd crossed a line. That was something her father would say and it killed her to hear it coming out of her own mouth. He grabbed his micro and stomped out of the bridge before Ro had a chance to apologize.

"Shit."

In the display, her program continued to churn away. There was little Ro could do from here and chasing Jem through the station would only call attention to her and the ship. The program had stabilized itself enough to run on its own. It would take the time it took. She uncoupled her micro and left the bridge with one final look at the color and light display inside.

The rush of accomplishment never came. Instead, Ro clenched her jaw, thinking of her interactions with Nomi and Jem. If only people were as logical as programs, Ro could just debug them and everything would work.

Chapter 14

ALL NIGHT LONG, Micah stared up at the bare ceiling in his quarters. He shifted the lumpy pillow trying to get comfortable, but his mind continued to churn. He kept coming back to Ro and the ship. Could she really do it? Could she really get that thing to fly?

And why did Micah feel a surge of excitement every time he thought about it? Escape was a flat out impossible dream. He'd made a promise. It didn't matter that he'd made it years ago, before he could possibly have known the shape that promise would twist into.

Voices, slurred by anger and drinking, rose and fell in waves. Micah didn't want to know who his father was arguing with this time. It never mattered. It never changed the fact that he was trapped.

"You said you could manage it," his father said, his voice surprisingly clear for a moment. A second voice came through in an indistinct murmur.

Micah rolled out of bed slowly, gliding over to the door.

"We have less than two weeks. See to it."

He stiffened. What was his father planning?

"Keep your afterburners cool. She'll have it nailed down."

That was Alain Maldonado's voice. Micah drew his breath in and held it. He stood with his ear pressed against the cold surface of the door. There was no reason in the cosmos for Ro's father to be working with his father.

"We are already behind schedule. Your payment is contingent on delivery."

Shit. Micah had almost convinced himself that his father's new job meant a new start. He should have known better.

"Don't threaten me, Senator. You have as much to lose as I do."

His father laughed. Maldonado had no idea. The only thing Corwin Rotherwood had left was Micah and he wouldn't even have that for much longer. Either Micah's work would finally destroy the cartel and its hold on their lives, or he walked away when he earned his citizenship. Surely, the promise he'd made to his mother couldn't bind him beyond that.

Micah wanted to storm out into the common room and confront the two men, but that wouldn't accomplish much. He waited, hoping they would continue talking and that something they said would help him figure out what they were doing.

"The ship will be ready. Make sure you will be," Maldonado said.

Silence answered him and seemed to stretch until it filled the entire compartment.

Waiting until his legs had stiffened and his clenched jaw ached, Micah finally risked opening the door and stepping through to the living quarters. His father lay sprawled across the uncomfortable generic couch that furnished all the station's habitation ring, snoring, an empty bottle and a broken glass on the floor beside him.

There was a time when Micah would have struggled to drag his father to bed and clean up after him. Not anymore. He retreated to his room to wash and change, letting his father stew in his own alcoholic sweat. At least one of the Rotherwoods knew how to take care of himself.

He needed to talk to Ro, and this time, she couldn't dismiss him.

*

All shift long, Nomi replayed her interaction with Ro, trying to understand what had unsettled the engineer so badly. Unable to keep her focus tight-beamed, she went through the shift-change checklist on automatic pilot and handed over control of the array to her morning replacement. She yawned and glanced away from his ident, already forgetting the man's name.

"Anything interesting?" he asked, smiling.

"Just the usual field full of quiet," Nomi said.

"Night shift," he said, shaking his head. "Glad you came aboard. You saved me from another stint. How about I buy you dinner some night as a thank you?"

"Right now, all I want is to sleep." She yawned again, dramatically before turning away. It was rude, but she didn't want to chat with him. She certainly didn't want to flirt with him.

"See you around, Konomi."

"Later," she said and left the array, wondering how to find someone who didn't seem to want to be found.

"Nomi."

She whirled around, staring into Ro's face. Nomi felt her cheeks heat up. "I was just thinking about you."

Ro stared at her, without blinking, her eyes a muddy green and bloodshot. "I'm not very good with people and I owe you an apology. Is there somewhere we can talk?"

The dark circles beneath her eyes made her skin even paler in contrast and her usually neat braid unraveled into a hopeless tangle. "You look like you've been up all day and all night."

"I have."

"Look, it's okay. Why don't you head home and chill and we can meet later."

Ro shook her head and the rest of her hair slipped free of its tieback. Nomi resisted the urge to smooth it behind Ro's ear.

"I'm not going back. I'll get Mendez to issue me my own quarters."

Nomi frowned, wondering what it would be like to dislike her own parents so intensely. "When was the last time you ate anything?"

"I don't know. Breakfast?" Ro shook her head again. "It doesn't matter. I'm okay. I'll eat after I square things with you. Deal?"

"Deal," Nomi said. "We can talk in my quarters." Her face flushed again. "I mean, if you're comfortable with that." She forced herself not to look away. It wasn't like she was asking her out on a date. Nomi forced her shoulders to relax. What was wrong with her?

Ro flashed her a smile so brief it hardly eased the tension in her expression. "Five by five."

They walked toward the habitation ring through the

increasingly crowded morning shift. Nomi nodded to the few people she recognized. Ro scowled and kept her head down.

"Ro?"

She looked up, her gaze unfocused.

"We're here."

Nomi signaled for the door to open and waved Ro inside the standard single quarters that she'd done as much as she could to make home-like. A row of holos lined the wall of the short entryway. "Lights, morning scene." A pale pink glow softened the harsh metallic surfaces.

Ro stopped, studying the images of her family as if they were a rare biological specimen.

"My folks and my little brother, Daisuke."

"Traditionalists?"

"Not hardly, though you'd think so since my dad's big on old fashioned Japanese names." Nomi laughed, pointing at the image of her and her mother in kimonos. "That was the day Mom dragged us to the cultural fair. She made us dress up for the holo. 'Suke wanted to wear the shinobi costume, but Dad nixed that."

"You look happy." Ro frowned at the holo and then looked at her.

"It was a good day. Even with Daisuke complaining."

Ro turned to face her in the small entry space. "You miss them."

"They're my family."

"You're lucky," Ro said, and brushed past her into the main living quarters. Nomi's skin shivered at the touch.

Cut it out, Nomi thought, *she's probably not even into you.* "Make yourself comfortable." She was glad long force of habit made her stow the bed and organize the one room. Ro perched on the edge of the standard issue sofa. Nomi turned to the small galley kitchen. "What can I get you?"

"Coffee. Black."

"Any more caffeine and I think your head's going to explode."

"I'm a big girl, Konomi. I've been taking care of myself since I turned six."

Nomi turned around, the coffee carafe in her hand. "I'm sorry."

"Don't be. It's just the way things are." Ro raked her hands through her hair. "Can I use the head?"

"Through there."

Nomi busied herself making coffee and rummaging through her meager stores to put some food together. She cut up a few pieces of melon she'd splurged on from the commissary and cut off the rind from some left over cheese. A handful of crackers made the plate look more balanced. Her mother would have been able to put together a feast from the contents of an emergency ration kit, but this was the best Nomi could manage.

"You didn't have to do that," Ro said, startling her.

"You're welcome." Nomi handed her the plate.

Ro glanced away. "Thank you."

Nomi looked her up and down. She had re-braided her long, blonde hair, and seemed slightly less likely to collapse. "Sit. I'll get the coffee."

"Look, last night—I didn't mean to scare you," Ro said. "I'm not used to ... people."

Nomi set two cups of coffee down on the low table, black for Ro, lightened for herself. She pulled over a chair and sat across from the sofa, giving Ro some space, even though she'd rather have slipped in beside her. "What about friends?" Nomi asked, staring directly into her odd, changeable eyes.

"We never stayed anywhere long enough. Besides ... my father's ..." She trailed off, eyes unfocused. "Difficult."

"Is that all the family you have?" Her own folks could be considered traditionalists, at least in one sense: They worked hard to create an old-style biologic family, similar to what her great-grandparents might have had.

"If you could call a distant, emotionally stunted father family. Then yes."

"I'm sorry. I didn't mean to pry." She turned away.

Ro laughed, a thin, sad sound. "Probably he would have been happier without a child, grown or bred. But my mother had me with him the old-fashioned way. She was a closet tradie. Too bad for her, she picked the wrong man. I think he won custody just to spite her."

Nomi had to keep herself from leaning over to comfort Ro.

"But that's not the point. My father is a paranoid, angry man and he's molded me in his image." Her voice softened. "I was completely out of line with you in the comm array."

"It's okay," Nomi said, this time reaching her arm out.

Ro's lips thinned and she crossed her arms over her chest. Nomi pretended she'd been reaching for her coffee.

"This isn't your fault and it's not your issue. I appreciate the gesture." Ro indicated the coffee, as yet untouched, and the full plate. "But it's not necessary. I have work I need to do."

"If you keep pushing yourself like this, you're going to collapse."

"I don't need a babysitter," Ro said as she stood up.

"No, but you do need a friend." Nomi stood up as well,

glaring down at Ro from the advantage of a few more centimeters of height. "The ship's waited all these years. It can wait a few hours longer."

Ro's face blanched gray-white. The muscles of her jaw bunched and relaxed. "What do you know about the ship?"

Her brittle voice gave Nomi the chills and she couldn't help herself from stepping back. Where had that come from? She certainly hadn't meant to give away her snooping, but once you reached the wormhole, you had to make the jump. "I was trying to find you," she said, lifting her chin and staring across at Ro. "But I couldn't get through your away message and you weren't where Daedalus said you were. So I went looking for Micah. I found him, but he wasn't where Daedalus placed him either."

Ro opened and closed her mouth. No sound came out. Nomi pressed onward, wrapping her arms around herself.

"So I followed him. Right to the ship." She paused, swallowing. "And you."

"I don't know what you think, but I'm not doing anything wrong," she said, looking up at Nomi, her eyes pleading.

"I didn't say you were."

"Who have you told?" Ro exhaled and looked past Nomi toward the door.

She paused to take a deep breath. "You. Just you."

"Me," Ro whispered, slumping back onto the sofa. She pressed the heels of her hands to her eyes. "I don't understand."

"Are you that scrambled?" Nomi asked, shaking her head, a slow smile stretching across her face. If Ro wanted direct, Nomi could be direct too. "I like you, Ro. I didn't read you and Micah as a pair, so I figured I'd have a chance."

Nomi skirted the coffee table and sat next to her, hands

awkward in her lap. Ro hadn't rejected her, but she hadn't given her any other cues either. "Look, I get it. If you're not looking for anything more than a casual friend, I'm okay." She tried to catch Ro's gaze. "Hey, I'm not searching for a permanent contract here."

She didn't expect Ro's laughter, impossibly bright and loud. It burst through the room, shaking her shoulders.

"Well, you could just say you're not interested," Nomi said, trying not to laugh with her.

Ro wiped her eyes. "I'm sorry. Really. It's not you."

Nomi frowned. She hated that line and she'd just made a complete fool of herself.

"No, no, that's not what I meant," Ro said. "You don't under-stand." She looked up, her face strangely open and vulnerable. "I just figured you'd be a much better judge of character."

"I am," Nomi said.

"Trust me. You don't want to be my friend." Ro leaned forward, gathering her legs to stand.

Nomi stretched out her hand to her. "You really hate yourself that much?"

"I'm so tired. I don't know what to think."

"Look, I won't ask you for anything you're not willing to give. But you need to rest. Look at yourself. Will working to the point of exhaustion fix the ship any faster?"

"No." Ro dropped her head in her hands.

"Then stay. Sleep for a few hours. No one knows you're here, right?"

Ro glanced at her micro and back up at Nomi.

"You need to show me that ghosting program sometime."

"Four hours. No longer. Deal?"

Nomi let out the breath she didn't realize she'd been holding. "Deal." She tossed Ro the blanket folded behind the couch. Ro wrapped herself in it and stretched out, her head close to Nomi's lap.

"Thank you."

Hardly daring to move, Nomi sat as Ro's breathing settled and slowed. She waited until she was sure she was hard asleep and then waited even longer before reaching out a hand to smooth Ro's hair from her face.

Chapter 15

BARRE DRESSED BEHIND the privacy curtain around the medibed, glad to be free of the monitoring lines and being poked and prodded by a constant parade of medical staff. His mother pushed the curtain aside just as he tied his dreads in a knot so they draped down his back and out of his face.

"Your father will be here in a few moments." She stood, backlit by the bright exam lights and Barre was glad he couldn't see the expression on her face.

"I think I can find my way back to our quarters on my own," he said. "Besides, I feel fine."

"It's not about how you feel. And I know you're fine. I did your discharge eval myself." She stepped close to Barre and scowled, deep lines forming grooves between her eyebrows. "Just because I couldn't prove it, doesn't mean you weren't using."

His mother was as brutal and as blunt as ever. Barre shouldn't have expected anything different, but he couldn't ignore the pang of disappointment.

"And once I'm escorted home? Then what?" No one around

them in the surgery even looked their way. Partly that was because he kept his voice down and so did she and partly because no one wanted to risk getting in Leta Durbin's way. If only Barre could figure out how to avoid her.

"Then we'll talk."

Her voice had a chilly finality that terrified Barre more than any of her overt threats or endless disapproval. She looked him straight in the eye until he squirmed like a little kid caught out in a lie. Barre was the first to break away. For the thousandth time he wondered why they didn't just send him away. He wouldn't be the first child conveniently disposed of at any number of specialty boarding schools for under-performing scions of the upper class.

But then they would have to face their failure as parents.

His father walked in and settled his hand on Barre's shoulder like a clamp. "Ready?"

Barre swallowed and nodded. He glanced back at his mother, but she never looked up from her micro.

They headed back to their quarters in silence, his father walking beside him, frowning. The door opened. Barre stepped inside hoping he wouldn't have to deal with Jem. Even more, he hoped his father would let him be alone. What Barre needed most right now was his music.

With his mother working a full shift, it would be evening before he got double-teamed. Maybe he could find enough peace between now and then to get through it without blowing up. They couldn't prove anything. For whatever reason, they didn't find the bittergreen in him. Barre knew how lucky he was.

His father cleared his throat and Barre looked back at him. "Your door stays open."

"Dad!" Barre whined, hating the way his voice sounded. "You know I need to play."

"You have headphones. Use them." He turned away from Barre and settled onto the sofa, micro in hand. "I'll be sitting here if you need me."

Barre retreated to his room. Looking around, he cursed, not caring if his father heard. The bed had been freshly made, the sheets tightly tucked under the mattress. Permapapers lay in a neat pile on his otherwise empty desk. The floor was a bare expanse of burnished metal. Nothing was where he'd put it or where it should be. They must have turned the room practically inside out looking for drugs. Thank the cosmos for small favors or maybe just large irony that he hadn't been able to find a new supply on Daedalus.

Jem had the last of it now, but Barre wouldn't risk using any of what was left, even if he could convince his brother to give it back to him. He should have known by the smell and taste of that batch of tea that something was wrong. If he could get through the coming confrontation with his parents, then he'd have to find Micah Rotherwood. He just had to fill his mind with music and let his mother's rage flame over him without getting burned.

His headphones had been carefully hung off the pegboard he never used for anything except his dirty clothes. He snatched them, glaring through the open door at his father. Pairing his micro to the headphones and his neural interface, he searched for something loud and utterly consuming.

The last piece he'd worked on started pounding through his body, mimicking the beating of his heart and the thrum of tribal drums. High strings wailed his defiance, drowning out the uncertainty. The keyboard track echoed all of his disappointments.

It was the best thing he'd ever written and his parents wouldn't be able to appreciate it, even if he risked the rejection by sharing it with them. What a waste. Well, tonight would bring what it would bring.

He let the music spill through him.

*

Jem stood in the doorway watching Barre's dreadlocks sway as his head moved to music only he could hear. Their parents were going to send Barre to a place where his music wouldn't be able to follow. He shouldn't care. His brother made his own stupid choices.

Barre opened his eyes and focused on Jem. He slipped off his headphones and distorted music filled the room with drums and dissonance.

"Come on in." Barre shrugged, trying for a smile. "Door's open."

"Yeah, I see that." He looked back and forth between Barre and their father furiously typing away on his micro. What Jem had to say would only make the desperation in Barre's eyes worse.

Jem sat on the neatly made bed, creating wrinkles across its smooth surface. Barre met his gaze with an eyebrow lift. Without saying a word, they both grabbed pillows from their piled order by the wall and tossed them across the bed. Several landed on the floor, making the room feel a little more familiar.

"Here, give a listen. It's something I'm working on."

His brother had never shared his own compositions with Jem before. Barre slipped the headphones over his ears. Music surged and crashed against him. Jem shivered. This was what had been blaring through their quarters just before he'd found Barre unconscious.

"You wrote this?"

"Yes."

Jem drew in a breath and held it as he listened. His bones vibrated with the growl of engines. He closed his eyes, letting the complicated mix of drums, keyboards, and strings fill him. The music kept blurring and blending in strange ways and it was impossible to pick out each track. It triggered a memory of the colors flaring across the bridge when Ro grafted her repair to the AI.

Amid the clean brightness of starlight, the derelict ship rose around him in his mind.

More than that, Barre's song mirrored Jem's frustration and longing and became a soundtrack for a dream of escape—his, Barre's and Ro's.

The song ended, bringing a wash of quiet with it that was more than the absence of sound. "Wow."

Barre's smile drove away the simmering anger that always seemed to rise up between them. "Really?"

Jem smiled back. It was like a perfect piece of code—elegant and sharp; potentially dangerous. "Outstanding."

"Cool." Barre came over and sat next to Jem on the bed. "This is who I am. Can you get that?"

Jem nodded. He shot a glance back through the open door to his father who had slipped on his own headphones and never looked up from his micro. The echo of Barre's anthem surged through him. "You need to get out of here," he said, keeping his voice low.

"Yeah, no surprise there. What do you think I've been trying to do for the past few years?"

The fights just before they left for Daedalus had been particularly vicious. Jem didn't get why their folks wouldn't just let Barre go to follow his music. It wasn't like they had any hopes of him following in their footsteps. Jem looked up at his brother. His dark eyes were almost swallowed by the swollen skin beneath them, his dreads mashed flat from where he had lain motionless in the infirmary all night. "They're sending you to involuntary rehab."

The blood drained from Barre's face, graying the skin. "I don't ... they can't ..." He swallowed hard, the Adam's apple sharply visible in his throat. "Shit."

"They were arguing about it all night."

"Let me guess. It's for my own good, right?"

That's what their mother said. "You have to leave."

Barre laughed, a sharp bark of a sound that made Jem jump and turn to see if their father had heard. "And go where?" Barre asked, not even bothering to keep his voice down.

Jem looked around the room, looking at the guitars, horns, and drums lined up against the far wall. Barre could play any of them. But for how much longer? "I don't know. There has to be a freighter or a shuttle due here at some point, right? Just go. Anywhere." His voice cracked.

"Thanks for the warning, bro, but too little, too late, I think. The only ship due here is going to be the one that takes me away." He reached for his headphones. "Better play while I still can."

Jem grabbed his brother's muscular arm with both of his hands and shook as hard as he could. "Don't you dare give up!"

Barre looked down at him and pulled away with one quick jerk.

"You just told me music is who you are. If you let them do this, it'll be like killing you."

"You think I don't know that?" Barre glanced through the open door and pointed at their father. "You think they don't? It's not like I have any place to go. No matter where I try to hide, they'll find me. And if I miss this shuttle, they'll just send another one." He shrugged. "No expense spared for their first-born son, right?"

"There has to be something. I can't let them do this."

"Just be the good little son and everything will be fine," Barre said. His hands curled around the micro so tight, Jem saw the plastic warp.

"Wait. Ro can ghost you." He frowned, wondering what she was going to say about this, but she was already involved.

"What?"

He didn't have time to explain it. "Are you under like house arrest?"

"Mother set Father as my babysitter-slash-jailer. You'll need to take it up with him."

"I have an idea, but you're going to have to trust me."

"Do I have a choice?"

Jem looked around Barre's room again. "Sure. You could always let them burn out your music or try to kill yourself with another dose of that tainted bittergreen."

Barre opened his mouth to answer, but Jem didn't give him the chance.

"Or you could shut up and let me help you."

The snap of his closing jaw echoed in the room.

"I need to arrange some things. Sit tight. I'll be back as soon as I can."

"You know where to find me," Barre said, sweeping his arm around the room and glancing toward the open door.

*

Turning over, Ro fell off the sofa. Her legs tangled in an unfamiliar blanket. A light floral scent rose from it and she stiffened, remembering where she was. She freed herself from the stretchy fabric and stood up, rubbing her hip where it had hit the floor. Squinting in the dimness, she reached for her micro just as the lights flashed and the part of the room just over the sofa brightened. The soft chime of a wakeup call sounded after exactly four hours.

Outside the day shift would be in full swing. In here, the environmentals created a soft twilight. Ro stood up and stretched, looking around for Nomi in the quiet. She lay curled in the single bed that pulled out from a notch in the wall, her dark hair spiked up against the pillow, her face softened in sleep.

Ro exhaled. She owed her a thank you and probably more apologies, but didn't want to wake her. Working with live power or complex code didn't make Ro blink, but knowing what to say to a friend terrified her.

Rocking back and forth on her heels, Ro watched Nomi rest. Striking, sensual, and smart, Konomi Nakamura confused her. Ro looked down at her rumpled clothes and ran her fingers through sleep tangled hair. "I'm sorry. I'm not good friend material," she whispered, afraid to wake Nomi up even as part of her hoped the communications specialist would somehow hear her. "You deserve better."

She needed to check on the progress of the AI re-install and Nomi needed her sleep. Maybe Ro would figure out what to say to her later. For now, she retreated into the small head to try to clean up, at least enough so no one would stare as she moved through the busy corridors. She looked into the small mirror crammed into the compact bathroom. The commode doubled as a shower seat. Sheer waterproof curtains ran in a track along the ceiling and the floor drained and reclaimed the water. A shower would feel great, but Ro didn't have a change of clothes with her. She'd left everything on the ship.

Maybe Nomi would let her shower here later. Her cheeks blushed bright red in her reflection. Maybe that wasn't such a good idea.

Ro cleaned her face and swished some of Nomi's mouth rinse. Her hair tangled hopelessly. Without a brush, she had no way to properly braid it so she gathered it in a messy tail and tied it away from her face.

Her stomach gurgled as she stepped back into Nomi's living quarters. The last real meal she'd eaten was yesterday's breakfast, and it wasn't much of a meal. She looked back at Nomi and then towards the small galley kitchen. The plate she'd put together sat on the counter, wrapped in a clear seal with Ro's name written across it in an elegant script.

Taking the plate and leaving would be a poor thank you and an even poorer goodbye. Ro tiptoed to Nomi's bedside and looked down at her, marveling that she didn't wake up. If anyone loomed over Ro like that, she'd be up in a shot, ready to defend herself.

She hesitated for a moment before picking up Nomi's micro. Most people never bothered to disable the standard logons after enabling biometrics. It was a simple task to pair hers to Nomi's and exploit the little loophole using the peer-to-peer networking program she'd rebuilt and honed. Breaking into someone's personal computer was kind of stalkerish, but the tunneled line she installed would override the ghosting program and let Nomi always ping Ro directly.

She didn't know what scared her more—that she wanted Nomi to call or that she was completely rationalizing a hack.

Before now, Ro wouldn't think twice. If she needed access, she would take it.

Well, Nomi wanted to get to know her. This was part of the package. Grinning fiercely, she hacked into her friend's micro and added her phone-home utility. It would auto-run as soon as Nomi woke the micro. After a moment's hesitation, her stomach fluttering, Ro added a note.

She grabbed the food plate and slipped from Nomi's quarters feeling both acutely nauseated and exhilarated at the same time, her memory flashing to the first time she'd hacked past a security firewall. Somehow Nomi had figured a way past her own emotional ones. This must be what a computer felt like on the receiving end. The door closed behind her and Ro stood still, clutching the plate, feeling like an idiot.

Time to get to work.

Chapter 16

USUALLY MICAH LIKED the quiet of his plants, the soft whistle of the water pumps, and the gentle hiss of the rain, but today his restlessness drove him to pace the small work area. He wouldn't even mind Jem's company. A good argument might clear his mind, give him a target for his uneasiness.

Piecing together a conspiracy from a few overheard bits of a conversation was a chancy business, but he knew his father all too well. If there was an angle to play or money to be made, his father would be in the center of it. Micah guessed he and Ro had more things in common than either of them probably wanted to admit.

Even though he was waiting for her, he still flinched when the door opened and Ro slipped inside his lab space. She flinched, too, nearly dropping the plate she carried.

Her expression immediately soured and she turned away from him, walking toward her desk.

"Glad to see you too," Micah said.

She didn't respond.

"I have something you need to know."

Ro turned around and glared at him.

"Your father is conspiring with mine to use this ship."

She turned away, checking something on her micro.

"Hey! Did you just hear what I said?"

"Yes." Her voice was cold, distant.

Micah whirled toward the door. Fine. How could he ever have thought she would help him escape? "Whatever. He knows you're here working on the AI."

Ro didn't acknowledge him, but her body stiffened and Micah knew she was listening.

"Your father. He's manipulating you."

"How do you know?" she asked.

Swallowing a bitter laugh, he said, "I overheard them talking this morning before my father passed out in another of his famous alcoholic stupors."

She turned to face him, fatigue in the lines of her face and the slump of her shoulders. "What do you want from me? So you have father issues. Welcome to my world."

He did laugh this time. "You really are a piece of work. You're welcome," he said, nearly spitting out the words before heading for the door.

"It doesn't change anything, Rotherwood," she shouted.

He paused at the threshold. "You're right. So why bother with this?" He gestured at the ship around them. "Why not just walk away?"

"I can't."

"Well, that's the difference between you and me. I know a lost cause when I see one."

"Wait."

Micah stopped. He leaned against the door frame, his eyes

closed.

"What do they want with the ship?"

"How the hell should I know?"

"They're smuggling something," Jem said.

Micah's eyelids snapped open. "What?" Jem stood in the corridor in front of him, glaring, his hands balled into fists.

"Shit," Ro said, nearly simultaneously.

"I can prove it. Here." Jem pulled out his micro and his fingers flew across the interface.

"You have less than two weeks. And then, no matter what, we need to move the cargo."

"And when will I get paid?"

Ro gasped, hearing her father's voice.

"You'll get yours. You just have to trust me."

"I'm not stupid, Senator."

"You just do your part and we'll both get what we want."

The playback was scratchy, but Micah had no problem identifying his father's famous most persuasive and dangerous tone.

"Don't you always?"

The recording cut out.

"How did you get this?" Micah asked, his voice a low rasp.

Ro kicked over the stool by her desk and stormed out of the room, pushing her way through Micah and Jem, stomping off toward the aft compartments. They followed Ro down the corridor.

Jem had to practically run to keep up with his longer strides, but Micah didn't slow down. Ro owed him answers and he was going to get them. They caught up with her at the open doorway to the aft starboard storage bay.

"What in the cosmos is going on?" Jem asked, a little out of breath.

Ro whirled on Micah, fury burning in her eyes. "What's he smuggling?"

"How should I know?"

"Your bittergreen?" she asked, ignoring his answer and barreling through the doorway. "How about I crack one of these seals and we see who shows up?" Grabbing a box off the nearest stack, she reached for a utility knife hanging off her belt.

"Shit, those are diplomatic seals," Micah said.

"Want to bet?" Ro smiled a fierce challenge at him.

Before he could answer, before he could reach her arm to stop her, she slashed underneath the face of the seal.

"Ro, stop! Wait!" Jem shouted, diving back into the hallway.

"Fuck!" Micah cringed, backing away from the stacked cargo, waiting for the wail of an alarm and the splash of a nano-dye packet. The small amount of distance he put between himself and the box wouldn't matter. The nano-particles were so small and so well aerosolized as to be practically invisible and impossible to fully remove. Ro stood up, directly in front of the box, laughing, as if daring the seal to react.

"Are you insane?" Micah said, wanting to grab her by the shoulders and shake her, but she was still gripping the knife, holding it high in the air like a threat. The seconds ticked by. "Wait ..." Nothing happened. He shifted his gaze between Ro and the box. Nothing happened. "How the hell did you know?"

She stopped laughing and stepped back, flicked her knife closed, and slapped it back on her belt. "That they were forgeries? I didn't for sure until just now."

Micah swallowed hard and opened his mouth but no words

came out.

"I thought it was worth the risk."

"To you, maybe," Micah said, stepping away from her as if she were as explosive as the seals.

"Jem, it's safe to come out now. The big, bad wolf is gone." She turned back to the unsealed carton. "Shall we see what our fathers are smuggling?"

Micah struggled between curiosity and a deep loathing to get tangled up in anything his father plotted. He should have just left earlier when he had the chance, but he'd let Ro reel him back in. How had this gotten so complicated? A few days ago, the ship was his, and his biggest problem was getting his plants to seed. A theoretical problem. A safe problem, at least until he solved it.

He took several reluctant steps closer to Ro and the opened carton. Jem pushed past him and leaned over, staring, his eyes so wide, the whites showed all around the dark brown.

All the mirth and defiance drained out of her. She stepped back, giving Micah room to see.

His pulse pounding and his mouth dry, Micah looked inside. Rows of plasma rifles lay nestled in multi-gee cushions, neatly packed under a fake diplomatic seal. The room tilted around him. Micah had to lean against Jem to avoid crashing to the floor. "Seal it back. Now."

"What's your problem? What part of counterfeit did you not understand?" Ro asked.

"You have less than two weeks. And then, no matter what, we need to move the cargo." His father's angry words reverberated through his mind. The assignment to Tresthame was at best a cover. Maybe that's where these weapons were bound. It didn't matter. The clock was ticking. "You have to put everything back

the way it was."

When Ro didn't move, Micah knelt next to the carton and pulled the cover closed. He only hoped that she hadn't damaged the seal too badly. Maybe they could shift this carton to the bottom of a stack.

"What are you doing?" Ro demanded.

"Hiding our tracks, you idiot! If you can't get this ship to fly, my father is going to try to get these guns delivered sometime before we leave for Tresthame—probably as part of our housing cargo and within the next two weeks."

"Ro, what did you drag me into?" Jem's voice shook. He retreated to the relative safety of the doorway and disappeared.

"I didn't know anything about the guns! I swear!" Ro whirled on Micah. "Do you think my father does?"

"Does it matter?"

She stared at him for a long moment. "No, not really. Here, let me." She smoothed down the counterfeit seal. It stuck and the edges of the carton disappeared where it had been opened. "Quality work."

"My father doesn't do sloppy." He wasn't even a sloppy drunk. Micah covered his face with his hands, wondering what his mother would think if she were alive to see this.

"Come on," Ro said, dropping a hand on Micah's shoulder. "You're right. We need to put this away."

Micah flinched away from Ro's touch. "I got it. Go deal with Jem."

*

Jerking her hand back, Ro glanced at the empty doorway. Jem

was gone. "Shit." Would he tell anyone? Where the hell would he go? "Rotherwood—we're not done with this," she said, as she spun from the cargo bay and down the corridor after Jem.

She raced to the outer umbilical, hoping to head him off from returning to Daedalus, but either he'd had too much of a head start, or he was still on the ship. For all their sakes, she hoped it was the latter.

Where was Jem? She eyed all the sealed doors and potential hiding spaces on the ship and frowned. A physical search would take way too long. What if the senator or her father decided to check on their cargo and found them here? Ro jogged back to Micah's workroom. She snatched her micro. Asking Daedalus would only give her Jem's ghost, but there wasn't a programmer in the Hub or beyond who didn't add a back door to their code.

She figured Jem had to know that, which meant he wasn't really hiding from her.

"Jem," she called softly at the entry to the bridge. "We need to talk."

The room was bathed in darkness, but Ro didn't bother to turn up the lights. She stepped in and let the door close behind her. "I swear I didn't know." Well, she'd known about the cargo and even figured her father was involved somehow, but she wouldn't ever have pegged him as a gun-runner. It smacked of politics and the only politics her dad cared about were the politics of his own paranoid self-interest.

"I can't do this," Jem said, his voice floating toward her from somewhere to her right.

"I'm sorry." She should never have involved him. He was just a kid, no matter how bright. "Go home, Jem. Forget you were ever here."

"It's not that easy, Ro."

The suspicions her father schooled her in from the time she was a child lit a fire deep inside. What did Jem want from her? He was the one with options and with a future. "Sure it is. You stand up, you walk out, and you go back to your perfect little life."

A strange choking sound rose up from the darkness. It took her a few seconds to realize Jem was crying. "Look, I said I was sorry. You did great work."

Jem hiccupped softly in the silence. "I need your ghost program."

"Fine." If Ro's father were here, he would give her his variant of told-you-so. If that was the price of his silence and his safety, she'd gladly pay it.

His indrawn breath seemed to fill the room. "I'm sorry, Ro."

"So am I."

She accessed the environmental controls and turned the lights on. The drones had continued their work, oblivious to the drama unfolding around them. The bridge floor had been completely cleared of debris and so had the consoles. "Give me your micro," Ro said, not even looking over at him.

He walked toward her and handed it over, neither of them exchanging a word.

She paired the devices and pushed over the code. It beeped once, softly. Jem took his micro back and walked out, his head and shoulders slumped. Ro frowned at the door, long after he'd gone.

Chapter 17

HE HELD BACK tears as he left the broken ship, knowing his brother would never know what it cost Jem to help him. Ro didn't understand and he wondered if he would ever be able to explain it to her.

Could he even believe her anymore? Threading his way between crowded corridors and waiting for his turn in the nexus, all he could think about was the guns. If all those crates contained weapons, the contents of that cargo bay could support a small war. He shuddered, calculating the plasma energy all those guns represented.

It was easier to focus on the simple math problem than to think about the destruction waiting in that room to be unleashed.

Jem slipped back into their quarters. His father had kicked off his shoes and leaned back in the chaise, micro on his lap, his eyes closed. Barre lay sprawled across his bed, headphones leaking music. For a moment, Jem thought he had walked back in time and he had to blink, clearing away the memory of finding Barre, his body in a similar position, unresponsive. He grabbed his brother's ankle hard, harder than he meant to judging by how fast Barre leaped out of bed, ripping the headphones from his head, and cursing.

"Shh!" Jem warned, glancing towards their father. He didn't stir.

"So what's the plan, little brother?" Barre's bleary eyes could have been the after-effects of bittergreen, but Jem knew defeat when he saw it.

"What can't you live without?" Jem asked, looking around the room. A fortune in instruments and audio equipment lined the room. There was no way Barre could take it with him.

Barre frowned as he searched the small space. He must have made the same calculation, because he grabbed the headphones, his micro, and a few changes of clothes. "You don't really think this is going to work, right? Where am I going to hide where they can't find me?"

"We just need a few days until they call off the search." Jem set his micro on Barre's desk and opened Ro's ghost program. "Damn, she's good," he said, drawing his lips into a thin line. "Damn."

"Something wrong?"

Nothing he would tell Barre. "I can confuse Daedalus and make it think you're somewhere you're not."

Barre whistled his appreciation. "I could have used that on Hadria."

"If we were still on Hadria you wouldn't be in this mess." Jem couldn't help snapping at his brother, even if it wasn't really him he was furious with.

"Point taken," Barre said quietly. "Where did you get the program?"

"It doesn't matter." He turned to the display, pulling up a station plan. If he set Daedalus to ping Barre in any specific place, once his parents didn't find him, they would know something was wrong with the localization programming. Scanning Ro's interface, he found the option to set up a moving target and have the program shuffle among random locations.

"Damn," he said. That wouldn't work either. The more shifts, the higher the chance of Daedalus reporting ghost-Barre in a crowded location that would be too easy to double-check.

"Jem?"

"Shh." He kept his concentration on the display.

"Look, I appreciate your willingness to help. I just don't see this working."

Why couldn't his brother just shut up? "Go jump out an airlock," Jem muttered, his gaze shifting from one side of the station schematic to the other. "Airlock. Wait." Looking up, he smiled at Barre. "I've got it."

Jem found the station exit the furthest away from the derelict ship. It was a simple matter to get the door to log an unauthorized egress for one Durbin, Barre. "If anyone tries to look for you, Daedalus will report you as out of range, off station."

Barre's eyes widened. "How'd you ... never mind." He whistled softly. "You're something else, you know?"

"Not me. Ro," Jem said, a sour taste in his mouth. "We should go now. Before Mom shows up and while Dad's still out cold."

"So you've bought me some time. Then what?"

"I'm not sure. But maybe some time is all they'll need to come around."

Barre quirked his lips into a wry smile. "Do you really believe that?"

"No," he said, not looking he brother in the eye. "But it's worth a try."

"Whatever happens," Barre said, pausing to look around his room, "I owe you."

Jem waited as Barre slipped a bag across his chest. He hadn't even asked where Jem was taking him, not that it mattered. If their parents couldn't let Barre have his music, then maybe there was a way off Daedalus. Fixing Barre's ident to make him an adult wouldn't be easy or legal but neither was this. Not really. And then there were the guns in the hold of the ship. "Ready?"

"Not much choice even if I'm not."

"No."

Barre put his hand on Jem's shoulder and squeezed it lightly. They walked out of their quarters, past their sleeping father and into the station's corridors. Jem could feel the skin on his back crawling and struggled to shake off the sense of being watched. Keeping his breathing even, he led Barre through the station. Hardly anyone noticed them, but then again, as far as anyone on Daedalus knew, there was nothing unusual about the Durbin brothers. All their discord stayed behind sealed doors.

His brother remained silent until they reached the deserted corridor that led to the ship. "You've got to be kidding," Barre said. "Does it even have air?"

"Would you rather camp out on the bare rock?" Jem lifted his chin towards the external airlock. "We're not the only ones here, so you need to stay out of sight. I can bring you some food later."

"Others? Who?"

"Rotherwood and Ro." Jem winced. He wouldn't be on either of their short lists.

"The senator?"

"No. Micah."

"I guess I owe Ro a thank you, too."

"Well, she didn't do it for you," Jem said, nearly spitting out the words. "And if she finds you're here, she'll report you, so stay out of sight."

"Whoa, cool your afterburners," Barre said. "I though you and Ro were friends."

Jem frowned and looked at the floor. So did he. "I need to check something before I get you settled," he said, pulling out his micro, accessing his link to the drones. He exhaled, letting his shoulders relax. Ro hadn't shut him out. Driving the little robot like it was his avatar in a 3-d game, he had the drone scout out the ship's main corridor.

He parked it at the junction that led to the bridge and the forward storage area so it could warn him if either Ro or Micah entered the corridor. "All clear. Let's go." Jem led Barre down the ship's central corridor and into what had been crew barracks.

"You've got to be kidding me," Barre said, standing just inside the room.

The rectangular space might have been the size of Jem's and Barre's rooms put together, but it looked like it was meant to house twenty-one. The walls were lined with metal bunks, stacked three high, each covered with a thin mattress. The material had been some kind of white foam in its past life. Flecks of it coated the floor like artificial snow. A small metal box hung on the end of each frame; otherwise the room was utterly bare.

"So sorry. Would you rather go back to the comforts of house arrest?" Jem bit his lip to keep from apologizing for real. He wasn't the one who screwed up. "Look, I'll try to bring you a blanket or something, okay?"

"No, it's fine. It's just for a few days anyway."

"At least there's light. And oxygen."

"Oh, joy," Barre said. "What about a head?"

"Must be one here somewhere." Jem looked around and spied a door on the far side of the room. "It should be there," he said. "If it works."

"Great."

"Don't worry, I'll bring you a bucket."

Barre wrinkled his nose. "You're all heart, Jem."

*

Micah walked back to the forward hold. When had his father turned into someone who could run guns without even a twinge of conscience? *You're growing drugs, man,* he thought, *how different are the two of you?*

"Different enough," he said aloud to his silent lab. Bitter-green didn't kill, even if the cartel would. The door opened. Micah didn't bother to turn around. "Did you find him?"

"Yes." Ro sighed. "He's gone."

Micah logged into his terminal. Whatever data could be saved, he'd save. Ro drifted to stand behind him.

"What are you doing?"

"Shutting it down."

"Then what?"

Why couldn't she'd leave him alone? "Pack and get ready to move again."

"I could use your help."

"That's funny," Micah said, pivoting in his chair to face her. "I thought you didn't want anything to do with me." He flashed her a wry smile. "It's mutual, by the way."

"So you're just going to let your father disintegrate your life all over again?"

Micah's mind flashed on the image of all those guns. Anger pulsed through his chest, a pounding wave of heat that rose though his throat and into his face. "No."

"Then help me," she begged, a desperation in her voice that he'd never heard before.

He barked out a harsh laugh. If their fathers could work together, he guessed the two of them could, too. And if anyone could sabotage the ship, it would be Ro Maldonado.

He canceled the commands to end the artificial climate program. At least for a few more weeks he would let his plants have a chance to live and keep growing. If they were successful in keeping the ship grounded, maybe he'd buy himself a little more time. Would that be enough to keep his father from delivering the weapons? Would he and Ro have to go further? The thought of getting his father arrested made him queasy, but letting those guns out was worse. His mother would have been horrified.

"So, what do we disassemble first?"

*

"What are you talking about?" Ro asked, staring at him.

"What do you mean, what am I talking about? We have to keep this ship from ever taking off."

His expression was as open and as intensely focused as she'd ever seen.

"She won't fly until the AI is fixed and my father isn't capable of doing that." She might not be, either, but she wouldn't know for sure until she could check on the progress of her program. Without Jem, the work would be harder. Micah was no eager assistant, but he was competent. With his help, maybe they could get the ship fully functional again before her father and the senator needed to finish their deadly transaction.

"Then it's okay." Micah met her gaze, looking as earnest and as naïve as Jem. "If they can't take the guns off station, we have a chance to figure out what to do."

Ro laughed, an uncomfortable echo of her father's mockery in her mind. "This ship represents simple convenience for our fathers. Do you doubt they would find another way?"

"Then what are we going to do?"

"I'm going to take control of the ship. Figure out a way to lock them out." She turned to her monitor. The guns weren't her concern; the AI was. If she wanted to finally escape her father, she had no other options. In a weird way, the guns and his partnership with the senator helped her. Getting the AI on line would give her powerful leverage.

"You can't be serious."

Micah grabbed her forearm, trying to turn her around. Her arm burned with the memory of her father's hand pressing into the same place. Heat burst up from the pit of her stomach. She twisted until Micah's arm torqued and his fingers sprang open. "Don't ever touch me again," she warned.

He raised his hands and stepped back. "We ... I can't let my father do this."

"If you're not going to help me, figure out a way to delay him and leave me to my work."

"Damn it, what do you want me to do? Tell Mendez?"

"And what happens when she sees your little farm?" Maybe they'd do a two-fer deal—a father and son special.

"Fuck the bittergreen, Ro, this is serious."

The guns frightened her, too. How could she explain to him that her way was the only way she knew to fight back? "Do what you have to do."

Chapter 18

JEM GRABBED A few blankets from central supply, charging them to his parents' account. By the time they looked at their bill, he hoped this would be long over. Food would be more problematic. Walking around with meals to go would definitely raise suspicions. Barre would have to be grateful for the protein bars Jem nicked from the commissary. Not very tasty and with a texture that could crack teeth, they would sustain him for a few days.

He checked with his snooping drone again and sneaked back onto the ship.

*

The room's illumination slowly warmed from darkness to twilight to full daylight. Nomi blinked awake and reached for her micro. She had an hour before her shift. "Ro?" she called, not really expecting an answer.

Standing, she stretched, letting her blanket pool to the floor, her bare skin shivering in the cool air. "Daedalus, set temperature to twenty-one degrees, please." The room heated quickly and she walked around the bed toward the empty sitting area.

The pillow and blanket she'd given Ro were neatly folded on the sofa. Nomi leaned down and picked up the blanket, raising it to breathe in Ro's scent. Well, it was a start, she thought.

Humming to herself, she washed up and dressed for work, wondering what Ro was doing. Maybe they could meet for breakfast when her shift was done.

*

Barre paced the empty barracks, his footfalls making percussive sounds against the hard floor. The metallic surfaces made the space extremely live. It would create some interesting overlapping echoes. Even now, the possibility of music was everywhere. How could his parents do this to him?

Sitting down on the thin bunk pad, the metal frame pressing into his spine, Barre wondered when Jem would return. He wished he could believe this little stunt of his would change anything. As smart as Jem was, he was pretty stupid about their parents. Barre closed his eyes and picked his favorite play-list. He stretched out on the rigid bed letting the music flood his brain.

*

Micah strode through the ship's corridor toward Daedalus, trying to sort out who he was more furious at—his father or Ro. Right now, they were pretty even in the polling. If Ro wasn't going to help him, he had to figure out how to stop his father on his own.

The real question remained—what was he willing to risk? How much would the commander believe? He frowned, wondering how his father even got those fake diplomatic seals. He didn't have the skills to counterfeit them. The penalties for that were probably more severe than even smuggling the weapons.

At the ship's airlock, he froze. *The seals.* He needed Mendez to find one of those seals—preferably in his father's possession. Micah smiled and headed back to the storage bay.

*

"Good riddance," Ro said, to Micah's rigid spine. She wasn't surprised when he didn't turn back. First Jem and now Micah. Relying on anyone other than herself had been a mistake. Her father was right.

An image of Nomi's sleek, dark hair and her expressive almond-shaped eyes flitted through her mind and she pushed it away. Friends meant liabilities and compromises that led to disappointment and loss.

Ro grabbed her micro. Her program had terminated several hours ago and if the AI hadn't been utterly fried, it should be starting to re-integrate itself by now. With one last look at Micah's lab, she headed to the bridge.

The door slid open at her touch. Soft red down-lights glowed from the walls to illuminate the smashed displays. The rest of the space lay in shadow. A drone's small white light blinked from the floor across the room.

She accessed Jem's interface, hating the fact he was so good at this. With a few casual waves of her hand, her micro paired easily with the autonomics and she manually shifted the illumination from night vision to daylight mode. The room brightened steadily until the entire bridge was bathed in an even, white light.

It looked like all the environmentals worked fine.

As Ro scanned Jem's code again, something in his programming snagged her eye. "Huh," she said, her voice loud in the empty room. He had side-loaded a sophisticated voice module.

The environmentals were controlled by the autonomic subroutines, but just like in humans, the cortex could override them, at least to some degree. If the AI could parse a voice command and send it on to be processed, she would know the sensory input modules functioned.

"Illumination—night vision."

The brightness wavered. Ro held her breath, waiting. Nearly imperceptibly, the lights began to dim. Ro blinked and the shadows deepened. Shivering with anticipation, she stared, grinning as a red glow replaced the harsh white.

She opened her mouth to start another voice-command sequence when her micro beeped.

"Ro?" Nomi's voice warmed the harsh room, bringing an unexpected smile to Ro's face.

"I'm here," Ro said. The red lights deepened as she tried to figure out what else to say.

"I found your hack. Well, that's pretty obvious, right?"

"I'm sorry. I probably shouldn't have broken into your micro."

Nomi laughed. "Serves me right for not locking out the

defaults."

Ro could imagine her shrugging one slender shoulder. If someone had hacked her stuff, she would have been supremely pissed. "No static?"

"Five by five," Nomi said. "You free for breakfast?"

She glanced at the time on her micro. "You just got on shift. It's hours until breakfast."

"Yeah, but I don't want you making other plans."

The lights started shifting between night-vision red and daylight white. That wasn't supposed to happen.

"Ro? You still there?"

"Hang on a minute. Tracking down a glitch." Maybe it was the voice integration. Ro shifted back to her micro's heads-up display and found the manual illumination settings. "Let's try this again." She set the light levels back to daylight mode. Harsh white light dazzled her vision, as bright as a lightening flash. "Shit." It washed out her display.

"Ro?"

"Working on something." Nomi would have to wait. "Illumination—night vision," she said again, trying to override the stutter and get the environmentals to reset. The room glowed red. Ro's sight cleared and her displays returned to focus. Setting two additional windows, she called up her program in one and the live code in another. They should have been identical. The AI should have reverted to a factory reset with Jem's interface and Ro's tweaks enabled.

She opened her toolbox and pulled out a compare and contrast module. Given the complexity of the code involved, it would likely take hours to run.

"Yeah, breakfast sounds great, Nomi," Ro said, surprising

even herself, as she superimposed the two windows and flicked the assessment module over. Maybe she could even get a few hours of real sleep first.

The program tumbled end over end, a complex cube shape of glowing colors. It struck both windows and winked out, like a flame extinguished in a flood of water. "Huh," Ro said. That wasn't supposed to happen. "Nomi, can I catch you later?"

The bridge vibrated beneath Ro's feet, long dead engines growling like recently uncaged and hungry animals. Red lights pulsed. The wail of emergency sirens deafened her. The ship leaped up and Ro fell to the floor, her hands clasped over her ears. A giant's fist pressed her to the ground, her leg twisted at an awkward angle nature never intended. She screamed as her ankle broke beneath her, the sound swallowed by the klaxon and the angry engines.

Chapter 19

THE COMMUNICATIONS ARRAY seemed a lot less lonely and boring knowing Ro was on the other end of Nomi's micro, even if she was busy tinkering with something. The sound of a rumbling engine filled the array, even through the micro's tinny speaker.

"Ro, what are you working on?"

The whining increased until Nomi could practically feel the vibration through her bones.

"What the ... ?" The whole communications room shook. Her micro trembled on the edge of the console before tumbling to the ground. An alarm Nomi had never heard outside of her orientation training dopplered through the station. She could hear it from the corridor, slightly out of pitch and out of phase from the array's own alarm.

Commander Mendez's voice boomed through the communication system. "Alert level alpha. Emergency crew to stations. All non-essential personnel to quarters. This is not a drill."

"Ro!"

Even if she did answer, Nomi couldn't have heard it over the wailing siren. Lights flashed red all over her console. Her chair, bolted down for the vanishingly small chance of a station-level impact, shivered beneath her. She pressed her knees against where the armrests molded into the seat and leaned her torso against the console to keep from being dumped to the floor.

Red lights strobed through the room, dazzling Nomi's eyes. The room lurched beneath her and a new alarm added to the cacophony. That sound she knew. It was the warning of an airlock breach.

Her chair gave one more violent shake and then the motion stopped. All Nomi could feel was the wild pounding of her heart. She checked the air pressure. Wherever the breach happened, this room was tight. Closing her eyes, she struggled to think, alarms still ringing in her ears. What the hell just happened? She scrambled for her fallen micro. "Ro? Are you okay? Ro!"

The klaxons quieted to an irritating alert. "Bridge to communications, report!" Commander Mendez's voice cut through Nomi's confusion like a bucket of ice water down her spine. She dropped the micro into her lap.

Snapping upright in her chair, Nomi she studied the ansible display. "No indications of any large scale communications disruption, Commander."

"Damage assessment?"

Nomi scanned her console, running a manual check on the array. All the indicator lights extinguished before the system rebooted. One by one, green lights winked on all over her panel. She held her breath, waiting as several of them flashed amber before holding on steady red. Still, most of the panel glowed green.

"Short range communications intact. Unknown damage to the long range antenna and receiving array." The familiar routine of monitoring her equipment quieted her pulse and pushed her fear for Ro aside. "External sensors off line. Visual inspection needed for full assessment and repair options."

"Continue monitoring all frequencies. Report any unusual communications. Mendez out."

Red lights continued to wash across the room. Nomi leaned back in the chair and stared into the display. What the hell just happened?

The adrenaline washed out of Nomi's body, leaving her trembling and dry-mouthed. She looked down at her micro, triggering the private communications tunnel Ro had programmed, her hands shaking.

*

The ship surged beneath him and Jem struggled to keep his balance. He slammed into the corridor. Bright pain burst in his shoulder and slid down to his fingers. The blankets slipped from his stinging hands. He didn't even have enough time to curse before something flattened him to the floor, squeezing his chest so tight, he couldn't breathe.

Darkness swarmed his vision, dulling the shiny metal surfaces. A high-pitched whine sounded from a long distance away. Jem's pulse thudded in his throat.

The ship.

Ro got the ship to fly.

What the hell was she doing?

She was going to rip the station to pieces. Jem struggled to stand against the shuddering and the press of the acceleration, managing to push up onto his hands and knees. He felt like he massed about a hundred kilos of dead weight. Gritting his teeth, he reached his left arm up, grabbed onto one of the small handles set into the corridor for low-gee navigation, and dragged himself to standing. His right arm hung useless at his side, the pain a strange combination of sharp tingling and numbness.

The engines continued to growl, gravity fighting his every step as he struggled toward the bridge. He growled back, an angry sound, deep in his throat. She could have killed him. She could have killed them all. Jem glanced toward the crew quarters. There were no acceleration couches, no tethers, and no way to check on Barre.

The scant few meters between the main corridor and the bridge felt more like a hard uphill climb of ten klicks. The ship lurched sideways and surged upward. The violent shift ripped his hand from the grab bar and bounced him around the corridor. His head smashed against the wall before he fell again, his shoulder collapsing under his weight.

He had to reach the bridge. Why wasn't Ro doing anything? Why was the ship still accelerating?

A warm wetness slid down his forehead. Jem blinked the blood out of his eyes and reached his left hand up to his scalp. He winced, finding the cut and pressed his hand to it until the blood slowed down to a thin trickle.

His vision refused to come into focus. Dizziness made standing utterly impossible so Jem crawled, wincing whenever he had to take weight on his right shoulder. He ignored it. He also ignored the throbbing in his head.

Muttering to himself and leaving a trail of bloody hand-prints, he half-dragged himself toward the bridge. The door stretched above him, distorted by double vision. Jem tried to blink it away and struggled to stand, reaching his hand toward the manual release. The door slid open and he fell across the threshold onto the bridge, panting with the effort.

Jem's body felt like one big bruise, but he pulled himself further inside. Garish red lights washed across the damaged consoles.

"Ro?"

A string of curses answered him.

"Ro?" Jem called again.

"My ankle is broken." Her voice, low and husky with pain, came from the far side of the room.

"You have to stop the ship!"

"You think?" Ro laughed, a harsh sound.

Jem grabbed the edge of the nav station and levered himself up against the acceleration. The ship shuddered again. The impossible weight lifted. He overbalanced and slammed into a console, the impact jarring his head. Bile flooded his mouth as the room spun around him.

He leaned against the console waiting until the urge to retch passed. Glancing up, Jem sucked in a shocked breath. The main display flickered and jumped and he blinked several times again in a useless effort to clear his eyes. Stars streaked across the screen, interrupted by the crack that split it into two slightly misaligned halves. Daedalus station was nowhere in sight.

Now what? How far had they gone?

Steadying himself on the ruined consoles, he lurched over to where Ro lay curled on the floor, her face nearly colorless. Jem's mouth dried. He shook his head and nearly threw up from a fresh wave of dizziness. "What have you done?"

"Fucked up," she said. "Monumentally."

"You have to get us back," Jem said, unable to tear his gaze from the unfamiliar constellations.

"Right now, I'd settle for some painkillers and help standing."

He blinked and looked down. If her ankle was broken, she would need far more than that. Jem choked back a laugh. She needed the infirmary on Daedalus and his parents. He pressed the knuckles of his left hand to his mouth.

"You shouldn't be here, Jem," Ro said, as he picked his way closer to her. She shut her eyes briefly. "But I'm glad you are."

He sat down heavily beside her, cradling his right arm in his lap and waiting for the room to stop spinning. "Do you want the good news first or the bad?"

Ro winced. "Good."

"I can probably splint your ankle," he said, looking around the bridge. The drones had stacked piles of scrap in the corner.

"And the bad?"

"I'm not the only one you didn't count on." He took a deep breath. There was nothing he could do about it now. "Barre's here, too."

"Great. Just great." Ro squeezed her eyes shut. "I can't deal with that now. Help me with my ankle. I have to get control of the ship, first."

"What do you mean?" Jem's pulse raced, his head throbbing with every heartbeat. "You didn't do this? Where the hell are we? Oh my God, Barre." He could hear the high-pitched panic coloring his voice.

"Jem!" Ro's shout hit him like a slap across the face. "If you want to help your brother, get me on my feet. We're still moving and I have no idea where the ship is taking us."

He looked up at the display and swallowed hard. "How is that even possible?" he asked.

"Not sure that matters right now."

Keeping his head as still as possible, he went rummaging through the scrap piles for two slim uprights. "I only want to move you once."

Ro nodded.

"I dropped some blankets in the corridor. I need them for your splint. Okay?"

She nodded again. "Do what you need to."

Jem had to fight the urge to tell her not to go away. He couldn't move too quickly either. The tingling in his right arm remained, but at least he could use that hand. He steadied himself against the wall, leaving the bridge and the impossible star field on the forward display. They were flying. The hair prickled on the back of his neck.

This was crazy. He looked down the corridor toward the main airlock and where the station had been. Where it should be. "Barre?" he called, his voice swallowed up by the empty ship. Part of him wanted to leave Ro and find his brother, but his parents' training in triage took over: Treat the most serious injury in front of you first.

Barre would have to fend for himself, at least a bit longer. Jem snatched up the dropped blanket and limped back to the bridge.

*

The acceleration flattened Barre against the bunk, gasping for air. The padding compressed into a thin sheet of wrinkles that carved deep creases in his back. He struggled to get up, struggled to take more than a shallow sip of breath. The pressure was worse than the weight against his chest. What the hell had Jem done? Was he even aboard the ship?

The thought of being abandoned on a ghost ship sent shivers through him, distracting him from the pain. Someone had to be flying this thing. If not Jem then who? Time seemed to stretch thin as the ship kept hurtling on. What if it just kept accelerating? The human body could only survive a finite number of gravities. He couldn't help imagining himself flattened to the metal bunk to the point of organ collapse.

The terrible weight lifted so abruptly, Barre tumbled to the floor. Cursing, he limped over to the door. Staying hidden now made no sense. The whole station would have felt the impact of the ship taking off. No doubt, Mendez had already sent out chase boats. Who knew this old tub could even fly? This must have been what Jem had been working on with Ro.

At least no one would believe Barre had anything to do with it. Not fuck-up Barre with his just-adequate brain. Maybe Jem had done him a favor after all. Who would worry about some bittergreen when his brother had just stolen a fucking spaceship?

Out in the corridor, Barre squinted against the flashing red emergency lights and paused to orient himself. The bridge should be somewhere to the left, in the fore of the ship. That's where he would probably find Jem.

He struggled to keep his imagination in check as he walked through the too-empty ship. A low groaning echoed against the hard metallic surfaces. Barre froze, his pulse pounding. He peered down the poorly lit corridor but there was nothing to see but the wash of red shadows.

"Jem?"

A weak cough answered him.

"Shit." Barre sprinted down the long, narrow space, nearly stumbling on the body before he could stop. It wasn't Jem. He let his breath out in a long exhale. "Hey, are you all right?" he asked.

"Fuck, no," a hoarse male voice answered.

"Micah?" Barre reached out to his shoulder and looked down into the pain-lined face of Micah Rotherwood. "What are you doing here?"

He tried to laugh, but it turned into another cough. "Parts inventory. What do you think?" Micah wiggled his hands and feet and patted himself down. "Yup, all there. Help me up."

"You sure?" He didn't see any obvious signs of serious injury, but he could have internal bleeding or a concussion.

"No. But I'm not going to lie here all day."

Barre stood and offered Micah a hand up.

Micah glared at him. "What the hell did your brother do?"

He wasn't sure he liked the tone of Micah's accusation, even though it was what he had just been wondering. "That's what I was on my way to find out." His micro buzzed and Barre jumped, nearly hitting his head on the low ceiling.

"Going to answer that?" Micah asked, leaning against the corridor, smirking.

Barre tapped the micro through his pocket. Jem's voice poured through.

"Barre, Barre, are you all right?" Even through the small speaker, Barre could hear the panic in his brother's voice. He caught Micah's eye and shrugged.

"Where are you? What the fuck just happened?" Barre fired back.

"Thank the cosmos. I don't know what I would have done if. If—" Jem trailed off.

"Jem, pull yourself together. What did you do?"

"Barre, I swear ... I didn't ... I was just helping ... coding an interface. You have to believe me!"

"It's not your brother's fault," a soft voice interrupted. "I don't know exactly what happened, but it'll be better if you see it for yourself. Come to the bridge. Ro out."

"She sounds like crap," Micah said.

Barre thought she sounded more like Mendez or his mother taking charge, throwing orders around. "Let's go see how badly we're screwed."

"I'd say pretty well screwed." Micah took a few steps toward the fore section and stopped, wincing. "Don't walk too fast, okay?"

That suited Barre just fine. The two of them leaned against the bulkhead walls and used the grab rails for support. They paused at the main airlock to peer out the viewport. A remnant of flexible tubing trailed after them like a tentacle. It must have ripped clean away from the station. "What a mess," Barre muttered.

"At least the airlock was closed at both ends."

They would have had a short, messy trip otherwise.

At the bridge door, Micah paused. "After you. I insist."

Barre didn't know Micah all that well and wasn't sure how to take his sarcastic tone. He tapped the door panel, and decided to ignore him. The door opened onto a disaster area. All the control surfaces had been destroyed, turned into puddles of melted polymers and sculptures of twisted metal. Jem crouched on the floor at the far side of the room next to Ro.

"How the hell did you get this scrap heap to fly? And what were you thinking?" Barre winced at hearing the ghost of his parents' voices in his own. Jem frowned and looked away.

"Help me up," Ro said, glancing at Barre.

"Who elected you in charge?"

Jem struggled to stand between Barre and Ro, his hands clutching the twisted console. "Help her up or I will. Her ankle's broken. I just splinted it."

"Shit, Jem, your head." What Barre had thought dirt, was a patch of dried blood that covered most of his forehead and the right side of his face.

"I can't put any weight on my leg. I don't want Jem to hurt himself any further. That leaves you," Ro said, spitting each word out slowly. She pointed to the console opposite her. "I need to get to my micro so I can figure out what happened to the ship."

"What happened to the ship is that it blasted off Daedalus." Micah limped onto the bridge. "Congratulations, Ro, your father will be so proud of you."

Ro's face blanched white and then flushed bright red. Her hands clawed at the base of the console as she dragged herself upright, her jaw muscles bunching with the effort.

Barre looked back and forth between them, their obvious anger the only thing he understood. He glanced over at Jem, but his brother glared at Micah and wouldn't meet his gaze. "Well, now that we're all one big happy family, would someone mind telling me what the hell is going on?"

Chapter 20

"Ro?" NOMI WHISPERED even though she knew she was alone in the communications room. Silence answered her. She bit her lower lip and tried running the program again. Unless Ro were actively ignoring her or her micro was destroyed, she should get some kind of response. The outgoing query just kept returning an out-of-range message. It made no sense.

Nothing made a whole lot of sense. She shifted her display from the ansible network to the external viewer, following a team of repair personnel in EVA suits as they swarmed over the antenna array. Frowning, Nomi studied the topography of the asteroid trying to figure out why it looked wrong to her.

It took her several minutes to process what her eyes were telling her and even then, she wasn't sure. Manipulating the display, she looked past the array and to where the station bit into the rocky surface of the asteroid. Beyond, she could see taller outcrops of rock. Between the station and those rocks, the spot where the clunker ship should have been was scoured clean as if by a burn-blast.

Her throat constricted. "Ro, what have you done?" The

message on her micro flashed 'Out of range. Out of range'. That was no seismic event or large asteroid impact. The ship had gone, taking Ro with it. Nomi's hands shook as she flicked her screen back to the ansible network and its twinkling display that reminded her so much of space. Ro was somewhere out there, in the true cosmos, hurtling through a field of stars.

If the bumblebee survived its violent takeoff.

Cold washed through her body and she shut her eyes, muttering a prayer she hadn't said since childhood, in a language she didn't understand, to a deity no one in her family had worshiped for several generations. The alert tone nearly knocked Nomi from her seat.

"Attention, Daedalus Station." Commander Mendez's voice blared through the communications room. She could hear the echo of the station-wide announcement from the corridor. "Alert is canceled. Lock-down is lifted. We are secured." She paused while the echoes died away. "I repeat we are secured. Intra-station communications are on priority override, urgent only. Updates will be broadcast every quarter hour. Senior staff to conference room one. "

Ro was on that ship. Nomi knew it. Her hand hovered over the comm channel to command. How could she tell Mendez what she knew and how she knew it? She balled her hand into a fist. But if she kept her silence, precious time would be lost trying to account for all the station's personnel. What if Ro were hurt or in danger?

She opened her hand and punched the emergency channel.

"Mendez here."

"Commander Mendez, this is Konomi Nakamura, communications. I have some information that may be critical to the situation." At least her voice stayed steady and professional, even if her stomach did back-flips.

A moment of silence seemed to stretch an eternity.

"I'm sending your relief. As soon as he arrives, join the senior staff briefing in Conference One."

"Yes, Commander," Nomi said, swallowing the lump in her throat. She didn't wait long.

The laconic man who had tried to flirt with her the other day took over the balance of her shift with barely a word beyond what was needed for turn-over. Emergencies had a way of doing that, even here, in the back end of nowhere. She signed out her terminal, leaving him to silent duty monitoring an ansible network they couldn't currently reach.

Even in the middle of third shift, she had never seen the station so deserted. Two armed security personnel stood at attention monitoring access to command. She recognized both of them, but couldn't recall their names.

The woman on the right blocked Nomi's way. "Ident chip."

She frowned as she handed the guard her ID for more than the cursory scan she expected.

"Konomi Nakamura, you may proceed."

"Thank you." Nomi shivered at the strange formality. Would the guard have taken out her weapon if Nomi hadn't stopped?

"Come with me."

The guard escorted her into the conference room, gave a crisp salute to Mendez, and spun on her heel to return to her post. When had Daedalus become an active military base?

"Ensign Nakamura, report."

Nomi shivered at the unexpected harshness and at the use of her rank. Nominally, anyone placed through the Commonwealth of Planets belonged to the reserve force, but there hadn't been any active fighting since the war forty years ago and the commissions were just a formality.

She stood at attention about halfway down the long side of the large rectangular conference table, studying the assembly of senior staff, gathering her thoughts. Most of the hyper-alert station personnel sat upright around the table, most probably woken from their rest cycles and looking bleary-eyed and a little shell-shocked. Nomi's gaze was drawn to a formally dressed, distinguished looking blond man leaning back a little too casually in his chair.

What was Senator Rotherwood doing here?

"Ensign?"

Nomi cleared her throat. "Commander, I believe Rosalen Maldonado was aboard that ship when it broke free of Daedalus Station."

Rotherwood stirred, his bloodshot eyes suddenly laser focused on her. Mendez leaned forward, but otherwise gave no sign that this was or wasn't news. Nomi swallowed, deciding to ignore the senator for now.

"She informed me that she was tracking down some unusual power fluctuations coming from the derelict. I have been unable to raise her on comms, sir."

Mendez raised an eyebrow. "Was this before or after I ordered emergency communications only?"

Nomi forced herself to stand still. "Before, sir. We were speaking during my break." It wasn't exactly the full truth, but close enough for Mendez, she hoped.

"Daedalus—priority override. Locate Maldonado, Rosalen."

"Habitation Ring 21/Beta." Nomi jerked toward the speaker at the sound of Ro's impossible voice.

"Open a channel to the Maldonado residence."

The bland mechanized voice of the AI answered crisply. "Channel open."

"Maldonado, report!"

Silence rang in the room.

"Contact Maldonado, Alain."

A loud clang followed by a string of curses filled the room. "Whoever the hell you are, your problem isn't any more important than anyone else's. Get in line."

Several of the staff winced or shot curious glances at the commander. Her expression didn't change. "Chief Engineer," Mendez's voice rang out with easy authority. "When is the last time you saw your daughter?"

"Yesterday. Maldonado out."

Mendez tapped one finger on the desk. "Dispatch a security team to 21/Beta. Search the premises."

Nomi sighed. Mendez swiveled to stare at her. So did the rest of the senior staff and the senator. She stood up straighter. "I don't know why Daedalus pings her there. We were speaking ..." Nomi glanced up at the time display, shocked at how slow the minutes had passed. "We were speaking just a quarter hour ago. She was on board at the time. Just before the incident, I heard the sound of engines."

The senator sat up and smoothed his already immaculate shirt front. "I suggest we dispense with these formalities and send one of these fine officers after that ship."

Mendez stared him down with a look that could have melted permafrost. "And how would you suggest we track it down without a working comm array?" She turned to Nomi. "How long until it's functional?"

That was a question she could answer. "Once the external repair is done, the diagnostics and calibration can take two to three hours."

"In two to three hours, the ship could be anywhere!" Rotherwood stood and glared at her, his face bright red.

Nomi took a startled step away from the table. Was he here because of Micah? She chewed her lower lip wondering if she should say anything about what she heard on the ship. Did he even know his son was growing bittergreen? Did it matter?

"Commander, I am holding you personally responsible for the return—for the safety of my son."

What? Micah was aboard too?

"Ensign."

She swiveled around, relieved to face the stern Mendez. "Commander?"

"You have thirty minutes. Take what staff you need. I want to know the instant we have long range capability."

The senator stormed from the room. Nomi let out her breath. "Yes, Commander." Her voice came out in a high squeak. How in the cosmos was she going to get the comms up and running in half an hour?

*

Ro leaned on the console, stared up at Micah, and tried not to wince at the pain shooting up her leg when she put weight down on her foot. "Maybe if you would shut up, I could figure out what happened." She pointed at the senator's pretty-boy son. "Hand me my micro."

"I got it," Jem said, leaning over to pick up the small computer. The color leeched out of his face as he handed it to her, the dark skin turning ashy gray. He blinked slowly and pressed the heel of his hand to his forehead.

"Get him on the floor before he passes out," Ro ordered, glancing over at both Micah and Barre.

"I'm okay." Jem squinted up at the view-screen. "Let me help you."

Barre glared at Ro before stepping over to his brother. It wasn't her fault Jem was here. She clenched her teeth. None of them were supposed to be here. And none of this was supposed to happen. Ro sat down on an intact chair and tried to ignore the sound of Jem and Barre arguing.

"Where in the Hub are we?" Micah asked. He stood just inside the bridge, staring at the display, his blue eyes wide and unblinking.

Well, that was the problem. They weren't in the Hub or anywhere she recognized. "Working on it." At least the burn had stopped. If she could pair her micro with the ship's AI, maybe she could figure out their flight path or find some point of congruity with the star charts. If the AI would even respond.

She set the micro down on the console, triggering its holo display.

"Wait. Stop," Barre said.

Ro looked over at him. He'd gotten Jem to lie down with his legs propped up on some wreckage. At least a little color had flooded back into his face. She leaned into the console, feeling for the slight vibration of the ship. It shouldn't have happened. Even fully flight worthy, the ship should have stayed dormant without a specific launch command. "Look, we're still moving and every second we're getting further from Daedalus. I can't get us back until I know where we are. I can't even call for help until I can map us to the ansible network."

"I know that. I'm not stupid. But do you even know what the hell you're doing?"

"No," she whispered, closing her eyes briefly.

"Yes," Jem said, nearly simultaneously.

"So how'd you do it?" Micah asked.

"I didn't." Her diagnostics shouldn't have caused the ship to take off. Hell, without a fully functioning and responsive AI, the ship shouldn't have been able to take off. "I was working on the autonomic systems, tracking down a problem with the environmentals." She shrugged. "You know the rest."

Jem winced. "Would it have been something in my interface code?"

"No." Everything started to go to shit when she tried to use voice commands. But she'd been over every line of his code. Clean, elegant, it should have worked. That left her programming. But it checked out in every sim she ran and she'd been using her own diagnostics for years, so that couldn't have been it. None of what Ro did should have done anything but repair the damaged AI. And the AI shouldn't have torn the ship loose from Daedalus.

But here they were. She raised her hands again to the display.

"What if you're wrong?" Micah asked.

She looked around the broken bridge and at Jem, still pale and shaken. "It's not like we have much of a choice. The only way out of this is to figure out what happened to the AI. Unless you have a better idea."

"My brother needs help. We have to get him back to

Daedalus."

"Well then, you can all just shut up and let me do my work." She turned her back on them and focused on her micro, holding her breath as it paired to the autonomics. The normal low hum of a ship skimming through interstitial space didn't change. The lights didn't so much as flicker. Ro exhaled in relief. Dying of acute depressurization and vacuum wouldn't be pleasant.

"So what are you doing now?" Micah asked.

This is why she preferred working alone. "Just before the ship took off, I started a diagnostic on the AI repair in progress."

"And what, you just pushed the wrong button?"

Ro ignored Micah. "The compare routine encapsulates the program in safe mode. Even if something went wrong with my tool set, the AI was protected and so were we." If they hadn't skipped across a wormhole, they couldn't be all that far from Daedalus station. It would just be a matter of dimensional mapping.

"So why are we here?"

"If anyone can figure that out, it's Ro," Jem said. "How about you get out of her way?"

Ro flashed a grateful smile Jem's way, though she felt more than a little guilty about his support after their earlier fight. None of that mattered now. Focusing on her micro, she tuned out the three of them and got to work.

Programming had always been a game to Ro. Even when she hacked into Barre's medical records, it had been a challenge as much as anything, but this was different. They could die out here. She couldn't help a quick glance back at Jem. He could die out here.

Doing nothing wasn't an option. Ro raised her hands and

started with the autonomic systems. Readouts popped up for life support and basic systems: Atmosphere and pressure checked out Earth normal. Hull integrity stable. Propulsion steady at twenty percent standard. Holding her breath, Ro waited to see if anything changed. So far, so good.

She looked up at the external display, studying the blur of unfamiliar starlight. Frowning, she glanced back at Micah, Barre, and Jem before triggering her diagnostic. She hoped none of them were close enough to see her shaking hands.

As she listened for any change in engine vibration, two familiar windows stretched up in front of her, data scrolling as fast as she could scan. The bridge lighting remained steady. The ship's vibration didn't change. She wished that made her feel better.

Minimizing the live windows, she called up the program's first-pass analysis. With all the time in the world, she would study the raw code line by line, but they didn't have time.

"So what's the bad news?"

Ro swiveled around in the seat. Barre stood behind her looking up at the display.

"How about the good news first?" she asked.

He shrugged.

"The AI is functioning."

"We knew that, genius," Micah said from across the bridge, his arms folded across his chest.

Ro ignored him and focused on Barre. "It didn't freak out when I accessed the diagnostic."

"What's the bad news?" Jem's voice echoed his brother's.

Ro glanced over at him, wincing at the bruise spreading over his forehead. "There's definitely damage. I'm not sure how much or how bad. If I can get the AI to respond to direct commands, I might be able to figure it out." If the damage was distributed widely across the AI, chances were good that redundant systems would fill in for the missing functions. If the dead sectors clumped together in one critical area, say navigation, they could be seriously screwed.

"Or you could blow us all up or send us into the gravity well of a planet," Micah said.

"Lay off her. This isn't Ro's fault," Jem said, struggling to sit up.

Barre crossed back to his brother and pressed his hand on his chest, pushing him back to the floor. "Don't be stupid, Jem."

"The hell it's not," Micah said, ignoring Jem and Barre, picking his way over neat piles of wreckage to stand between Ro and the console, staring down at her, his blue eyes cold. "I told you your father was manipulating you. I warned you, and you still had to hack in to what you didn't understand."

Ro's face flushed. She sent her display spinning towards Micah. He shifted back a few steps. "Since you apparently know everything, Rotherwood, how about you get us back home."

"Cut it out. Let me up. I can help." Jem pushed against Barre's hold.

"You have a concussion, dumb ass. You want to make things worse?"

"That's enough," Ro shouted, struggling to her feet. "You." She pointed at Jem. "Lie still." Using the console as a crutch, she limped up to Micah, her ankle screaming with every step. "Here." She pushed the transparent window right up against his face. "You want to give it a try? Go right ahead."

His face paled and he shook his head.

"Fine. Then we can all stand around and wait for the air to run out. Or the ship to skip across an unmapped wormhole. Or we could just starve. I don't know about you, but I'd like to keep living."

"Ro?" Jem's small voice pierced the silence that fell after she stopped talking.

"What?" she snapped, not taking her eyes off Micah.

"Do you feel that?"

She didn't feel anything. "Shit." The soft whine of the engines had fallen silent. The faint stir of air died away. As she stared up at the programming window, its glow seemed to brighten until it was the only source of light on the bridge. "Shit," she said again, a whisper against the eerie quiet.

A red light blinked through the room. "Intruder alert, bridge. Security protocol alpha." The computer had a pleasant female voice with the same brief hesitation between phonemes as Daedalus.

"Guess they haven't made a whole lot of progress in voice synth in the past forty years."

"Ro, I think we're in trouble," Jem said, his voice wavering.

"Intruder alert, bridge. Security protocol alpha," the bland artificial voice repeated.

"Congratulations," Micah said. "You brought the AI back from the dead and it wants to kill us."

Chapter 21

"Ro?" from his spot on the floor, Jem struggled to be heard over his brother's and Micah's raised voices.

Micah slammed his hand on the main console and Jem jerked in surprise. His head hit the floor sending a fresh wave of pain into his eyes. He squeezed them shut. He had to concentrate. The AI had fallen silent, though the red emergency lights continued to blink in an extremely annoying and totally random pattern that by design was impossible to shut out and ignore even through Jem's closed lids.

It didn't do good things to his headache.

Micah and Barre both turned on Ro like a pair of well synchronized drones and continued yelling. She crossed her arms and stood her ground, refusing to say a word. Jem fought to clear his foggy brain and think. They had to get access to the AI's core, somehow, and before they ran out of air.

He took a larger breath and tried again. "Ro!"

Micah paused, mid-rant and turned to Jem. "What?"

Barre shut his mouth with an audible click and scurried over to him. "You okay? What's wrong?"

"Other than the fact that you're giving me a headache, the ship is drifting in space, and we have no life-support?" Jem's head pounded louder in the silence. He'd lived in ships or stations practically his whole life and the soft whoosh of an air handler was a familiar and ignored sound. Now his ears rang in the strange stillness. Barre looked on the verge of another outburst. "Stop it. We don't have time for this. Help me up."

"Jem, you're still bleeding," Ro said, glaring at Barre and Micah as she hobbled past the two of them to sit next to him.

"And Ro's foot's still broken. None of which is going to matter ..." Micah paused to glance at his micro. "In about an hour. More or less."

"Less," Ro said, wincing.

Barre glanced at Jem, his wordless question clear. Jem nodded. "Well that's just great," Barre said.

Jem ignored his brother and the seething Micah.

"I'm sorry." Ro laid her hand on his shoulder. "I should have been more up front with you. I just ..." Her head drooped practically to her chest. Her hair slid forward to cover her face. "Micah's right. It doesn't matter now."

"Ro!"

She flinched, but didn't lift her head.

"Look, I have an idea, but I can't do it myself."

This time Ro did look up, her eyes red-rimmed, her gaze unfocused.

"We need to pair our micros." Jem wasn't sure how much the damaged AI could parse from their conversation, but the less it heard, the better.

He pushed Ro's hand away and glared at his brother before sitting up against one of the consoles. His stomach flipped as if he were in free-fall, and the bridge spun wildly around him.

"Jem," Barre said, his tone eerily like his mother, "you have pretty bad nystagmus."

"Yeah, and I should be in the infirmary. Tell me something I don't know." Keeping his vision focused on anything was going to be hell. He pointed to his micro and held out his hand. Barre frowned and handed it to him. "Micah. Make yourself useful," Jem said, jutting his chin towards the console Ro had been working on.

Micah tossed him an ugly look, but threw Ro her micro.

She caught it and flipped it over and over between her hands, staring across the bridge.

"This is not a good time to decide your father was right," Jem said.

Ro whipped her head around to glare at him, her eyes narrow, her lips thin and bloodless, her hands clawed around her micro.

He held her gaze, refusing to back down, even through the nausea and the tendency of the room to spin. It hadn't been very long, but Jem could already taste the flatness in the air. If he thought about it, he could probably even calculate exactly how much time it would take before the O_2 pressure dropped sufficiently to render them all unconscious. He went over the variables: four bodies, small, sealed compartment, fixed air volume. They wouldn't have long.

Work with me, Ro, he begged, wordlessly.

She broke eye contact first and Jem let his shoulders relax and his eyes close briefly. He still felt as if he were spinning, a planet of one, orbiting his own misery. Even if they did regain control over the environmentals, they still had to get back to

Daedalus Station. The dizziness and the nystagmus were bad signs. But where a brain bleed might eventually kill him, lack of air would definitely kill them all.

"Okay," Ro said, her voice curiously flat in the dead air. "I'm ready."

Jem brought his micro up close to his face trying not to have to move his head. Tapping in commands one-handed would be slow, but using the holo interface would probably make him hurl. He turned off discoverability, set it to paranoid mode, and opened a private peer-to-peer link with Ro's micro, trusting that she'd figure out what he was doing without any explanation.

"Got it," she said and mirrored his commands.

"Jem?" Barre sat down next to him and put a hand on his shoulder.

"Working on it," he said, shrugging his brother's hand away.

"Anything I can do to help?"

"Yes. Shut up," Jem said. Barre stood and walked away. There would be plenty of time to worry about bruised feelings and tender egos if they survived this.

"Done," Ro said. Their micros pinged one another. He forced his eyes to focus on the split screen, his data on the left, hers on the right.

He opened a silent chat window, barely able to keep his eyes on the too-bright text. Left a back door.

Where?

Text only. Command line access. Ro would have to program on the fly and fast—not just because their air was running out, but if the AI caught them breaking in, it could decide to fly them all into an asteroid or depressurize the entire ship. Not that there was a whole lot of difference between actively dying and passively dying except the amount of time it took.

Show me.

He pushed the code over to her micro and closed his eyes while she scanned it.

"Jem."

He looked up at her and tried not to notice when she winced and slid her gaze away from his twitching eyes.

"If this doesn't work—"

"Make it work," he said, and slid back to the floor, trying not to add vomit to the smell of fear-sweat in the room.

*

Nomi paused just outside the communications room. The door slid open and she blinked at the flurry of activity inside. The man who had relieved her waved Nomi to the central console. She was certain he outranked her. A half dozen other men and women in their dark gray uniforms manned every station in the room, waiting. Mendez must have called every shift in at once.

"Nakamura—I hear you got put in the hot seat," her colleague said.

She read his name off his ident: Simon Marchand. "Wrong place, wrong time, I guess. Status on the external repair crew?"

"We should have signal momentarily." He looked up at the main screen. The display had been split in half. One side showed the asteroid surface and the anonymous crew members in their bulky EVA wear. The other displayed a schematic of the ansible network, network error messages overlaying each one.

Nomi leaned forward on her console, her head drooping. Transmitting through the ansible grid required pinpoint accuracy. Calibration from one relatively fixed point to any single satellite took skill. Bringing the station in resonance with all of them in half an hour? It was more than impossible, no matter how much staff got thrown at the task.

"So what's next, boss?" Marchand said.

Tugging her hands through her hair, Nomi struggled to think clearly. Mendez didn't want to hear what couldn't be done. The ship could be anywhere. Even with all the ansibles working, the chance of pinging it randomly was slim to none.

Leaning forward, she stared up at the silent ansibles. Marchand mirrored her pose, hands on the console and face upturned.

"Maybe we don't need them all," she said, pursing her lips. Well, eventually they would, for normal network traffic, but the priority was bouncing a signal to Ro. And Nomi would bet every last credit she owned that Ro would be trying to establish communication from her end. If she had survived. Nomi let her head droop again. Marchand placed a hand on her shoulder.

She stiffened. His hand slid away. This was her show. Mendez believed in her so she had better damn well believe in herself.

Movement on the viewer caught her eye. The repair crew filed toward the airlock. "Now it's up to us," Nomi said, meeting Marchand's worried look. "So we prioritize. Network traffic will have to wait a little while longer."

"This is like looking for a needle in a planet's worth of haystacks. Hell, a system's worth. That ship could be anywhere. How do we know which ansible stations to choose?"

"It doesn't matter." She snatched up a light pen and circled about a third of the communications satellites, hoping it didn't seem as random to him as it did to her. "We'll hopscotch around the network, establishing a low level see-you-see-me link with as many stations as we can, starting with these."

Marchand's brows furrowed and he rocked back and forth on the balls of his feet. "So we'll be able to get a basic ping-back. What good will that do? You can't transmit or transfer data at that level, and even if you could, you'd need to know where the ship is relative to an ansible quadrant." He gestured to the display. "Too many holes in the net."

"We're not trying to find them. We're not even trying to send them a message." She turned to the rest of the comms personnel waiting for her orders. A shiver worked its way down Nomi's back.

"Then what are we doing?" Marchand asked.

"Trying to make noise." She squared her shoulders and one at a time made eye contact with each member of the communications staff. "There are eight of us." Turning back to the display, Nomi carved up the screen into eight segments. "Each of you claim a sector. Get a ping and move on. We're not looking for accuracy."

Marchand frowned. His thick eyebrows jutted forward and shaded his eyes. "A sledgehammer solution. You're going to drown out whatever comm traffic is moving through the network."

"Can't be helped. Mendez wants that ship found. We don't have the resources to find it, but if Daedalus makes enough noise, the ship will be able to find us."

"That's assuming there's someone on the ship to listen."

If something had happened to Ro, it wouldn't matter even if they had full duplex. "I know." She met his gaze without blinking and held it for a moment before glancing up at the watching staff. "The clock is running, people." Squeezing her eyes closed briefly, Nomi held to an image of a delicate face framed by a soft curtain of long blond hair and filled with a driving, restless intelligence. Ro was listening for her. She had to be. "Free drinks at the commissary for whoever gets the most ping-backs."

*

Red light continued to stutter through the bridge. In the silence, Ro could hear all of her involuntary crew breathing too fast and too hard. It was easy to visualize them turning all the available oxygen into carbon dioxide. At least it made for a painless death. She glanced up at Barre and winced at the worry she read in his face. Even if she was good at the whole reassurance thing, she'd be lying if she told him Jem would be all right. There were more ways for them to die than to survive. Jem knew it. She wondered if Micah and Barre did.

Ro wrote across her micro and held it up for the two of them to see. Brace yourselves. Not waiting for their acknowledgment, she turned to Jem's elegant program. Damn but that kid could code.

There was really no way she could strap him in anywhere. She wedged herself against the command console, wincing as her foot twisted. If the ship accelerated again, they would all be flung around the room and things would get a lot worse, but there was no help for that.

She triggered Jem's interface override. The screen scrolled up, all the code vanishing, replaced by a single blinking old-school cursor. Ro held her breath as she typed in what she hoped would let her access the AI's core. The seconds stretched out. "Respond. Come on. Come on. Respond," she urged, setting the micro on her pants and wiping her damp hands across the thin fabric.

Words typed themselves across the small screen. SIREN version 1.7b. Initializing ...

Ro exhaled and picked up the micro. The series of scrolling dots stopped, replaced by another waiting cursor. Except for the rustling of fabric and the whistle of harsh breathing, there wasn't another sound in the room. Her fingers flew across the tiny virtual keyboard in an effort to convince the dumb machine underneath the complex AI to reboot and suspend the damaged brain.

There was no time to test her code. No time to even to look it over for the most basic of errors. It just had to work. She finished, lifting her hands from the micro, and let her head slump down to her chest, eyes closed.

"Ro?" Micah's voice echoed in the metallic space.

She ignored him.

"Ro!"

Snapping her head up, she glared at him. "What?"

"Look. The lights." The red emergency strobes stopped and white diffuse glow brightened the room. A tentative smile spread across his face, making him seem younger and a lot less like his father.

Ro took a welcome breath of air that tasted cool and crisp against her tongue. The hum of the air scrubbers filled her ears with a sound she swore never to take as given again. She met Micah's gaze before turning to Barre and Jem, the strange relief making her oddly grateful to her accidental companions.

Jem gave her a thumbs-up, and Barre nodded before settling back down next to his brother.

"Well, nice to know we won't asphyxiate," Micah said. His expression had closed down again. "We'll just die of starvation. Or boredom. I know—maybe if we're lucky, we'll be hit by an asteroid."

So much for the Ro Maldonado fan club.

"What's your next brilliant plan?" he asked. "Or do we wait here for a tow?"

"You're welcome," she said.

"Jem? Come on, you have to stay awake." Barre leaned over his brother and lifted a closed eyelid.

"What's the matter?" Ro asked, scooting closer to them.

"Closed head injury. I have no way of knowing how bad the damage is."

Barre stared directly into her eyes. He didn't have to say the "no thanks to you" part.

"He needs a head scan. Fluids. Probably a sedative if he gets restless and confused. That means getting back to Daedalus."

Ro glanced up at the viewport and the unmoving and unfamiliar star field. "We need the AI to navigate."

"Should have thought of that before you started fucking with the ship," Micah said, his voice ringing across the bridge from where he stood, leaning against the bulkhead, his arms crossed.

"You weren't supposed to be here. None of you." It was hard to feel any kind of moral authority when Ro had to look up at him from the floor.

"You couldn't leave well enough alone," Micah shouted. "Even after I told you about your father."

"My father? What about yours? Do you think those

diplomatic seals just faked themselves?"

Micah's face burned bright red against his blond hair. "This is your fault. You could have helped me ground the ship, ground their cargo, tell Mendez. But no, you had to be smarter than everyone else."

"That's enough!" Jem's soft croak commanded all their attention.

"Don't you dare try to get up!" Barre said, his hand on the center of his brother's chest, holding him down.

Jem stopped struggling and closed his eyes. "Fine. But my head hurts enough without you all screaming at each other. At least we have air. Ro will think of something."

Even after everything, he still had this blind, stubborn faith in her. If he wasn't already in such bad shape, she would shake some sense into him. "I don't know what to do." She winced, admitting her own helplessness. "We can't get home until we figure out where the hell we are. We can't get any sort of nav fix without the AI. And it's fried."

"Well thank you, Doctor Obvious," Micah said.

Doctor. They didn't have a doctor, but the ship had a medical bay. She grabbed Jem's micro and pulled up his copy of the ship's schematics, circling the infirmary. "Take this," she said, holding out the little computer to Micah and pointing out where he needed to go. "Inventory the medical bay. Text me what you find. I need to know what supplies are still there." The "if any," she kept to herself.

"Why me?"

"You know your way around biologicals and test equipment." She wasn't at all sure Barre would leave his brother and even if he would, Ro didn't want to deal with Micah. She pointed to her ankle. "And I'm grounded for the time being."

Micah held her gaze for a long minute as if looking for the right words to start up the fight with her again. Then he pushed away from the bulkhead and strode out of the bridge.

"My brother seems to trust you," Barre said.

Ro shrugged.

"For all of our sakes, I hope he's right."

Chapter 22

MICAH PUNCHED THE bulkhead next to the bridge door and swore at the pain. At least it cleared his head. And he'd be able to treat it if the medical bay was intact.

Ro's face burned in his mind. The arrogance reminded him far too easily of his father. He strode through the silent, empty corridor, past several rooms his map labeled barracks and a large mess hall, empty of everything except the tables and benches bolted to the floor, before reaching medical. A bare bones ship, everything had been stripped down for speed and efficiency. It was nothing like the elegant and lush vessels his family had traveled in during the years before his mother's death —and his father's disgrace.

At least while they had possession of this ship, his father couldn't deliver the crates full of weapons to whatever smoldering conflict had paid the most or for whomever owned him. Though he doubted that had been Ro's intent in triggering the cascade that woke the AI. Beware the unintended consequence was the story of his life.

Micah triggered the manual door release. Lights flickered on as he stepped over the threshold. For a craft abandoned for something over four decades, it was remarkably free of dust and dirt. Basic environmental tech had been pretty much perfected in the first interstellar wars, along with the artificial gravity that allowed soldiers to stay deployed long enough to reach the fight and still be able to return planet-side with enough bone stock and muscle mass to survive. That is if they survived the actual battles.

The med-tech had been designed with battlefield injuries in mind. Metal plinths with shock cradles lined the long wall, primitive scanner displays at the head of each. In the center of the room, a command chair with a clamp for a portable readout faced the row of patient beds. Along the right hand wall, a glassed in room had been carved out of the main medical bay. Micah peered through the window and the elaborate airlock entrance. A metal plinth sat in the middle of the room, retractable lighting over it. It could have been an isolation chamber or a morgue. Knowing the purpose of these ships, probably both.

Up along the ceiling of the entire bay, and lining the isolation room, high pressure nozzles faced down. He shivered from more than the cold, empty air. This was a place designed to be simple to disinfect, probably with an independent air supply and external overrides on the door. In the calculus of war, the lives of a half dozen or so soldiers and med staff meant little against the chance of some biological agent or alien virus getting loose. He glanced back, looking for the reassurance of the dimly lit hallway.

As long as they were drifting and the AI shut down, he knew he could get out, but knowing something and keeping his adrenals from reacting to the fear were different matters. He forced his shoulders to drop and his jaw to relax as he looked for supplies. The wall opposite the isolation room was lined with neatly labeled drawers. He opened a few at random.

Micah triggered Jem's micro and started typing.

Medical ?? operational. Scanners not powered. Likely tied into the AI. Place cleaned out except for what's bolted down.

He didn't wait for a reply before backing out of the sterile space, chills arcing between his shoulder blades.

Fuck. We need supplies. See what you can find.

Searching the ship gave Micah reason not to be in the same room as Ro, even if her giving him orders irked him.

He wandered along the central corridor. The barracks rooms all followed the same pattern: rows of metal bunk beds with an integrated storage bin bolted to the floor, handrails across the walls and ceiling, a small head, as bare and as utilitarian as the medical bay with nothing to salvage.

There was nothing useful here except what he'd brought on board for his plants. At least all his work would be good for something. Maybe they could salvage the cloth row cover for bandage material. They wouldn't die of thirst. His closed system contained nearly 200 liters of water. At the bare minimum of two liters per person, per day, it wasn't hard to do the math in his head. Worst case scenario, even if the recycling systems didn't work on the ship, raiding the water from his bittergreen plants would buy them a few weeks. Food was another matter.

How long would it take for Ro to get the AI working and get them back to Daedalus? No, that was the wrong question. The right question was how long it would take for his father to mobilize every resource he could to find the ship.

They needed to get back to the station before that happened.

Some of those questionable resources would view them as complications. Micah would be safe. No matter how low his father sank, he protected his son. But Ro, Barre, and Jem?

Micah bypassed the mess hall. Even from the doorway he could see it had nothing they needed. According to the map, the compartments aft of the mess contained access to the engines. They would probably yield nothing of value. The only other supplies on this old boat were the ones his father stowed here. They couldn't eat weapons or ammunition, but maybe some of the other cartons had more useful contents.

He triggered the door release. The utility lights along the floor and ceiling provided a dim illumination. He poked around Jem's micro and set it to flashlight mode.

The mound of silent cartons threw oddly shaped shadows across the cavernous hold as he walked around. Micah didn't have a knife, but he figured they didn't have to worry about keeping the seals intact anymore. He set Jem's micro down on the top of a box and pulled several boxes down from neighboring stacks.

"Damn it, Dad," he said, staring down at the diplomatic seals, his hands curled into tight fists.

He tore open one box after another, shoving the ones full of weapons aside. What would his father do if they just tossed them all out of the airlock? He certainly couldn't complain to Commander Mendez. As satisfying as that would be, it would also destroy all the proof and any leverage he might have. He paused at a fresh box, waiting for the guilt that always came at the thought of abandoning his father. All he saw when he closed his eyes was his mother's face, lined with pain and regret.

"At least you didn't live to see this," Micah said to the empty room. He turned back to the box at his feet and tore open the cover. "Jackpot!"

*

Barre paced the small area between the command console and the forward display. He was as useless here as he was on Daedalus or Hadria. Or any of the other postings their parents had dragged them through. He glanced down at his brother's face, gray in the harsh light, and wanted to punch something.

Ro hadn't looked up from her micro since Micah had gone. It would be convenient if he could blame this all on her, but it wasn't Ro's fault he was on the ship. It wasn't even Jem's. Barre had let his brother talk him into this. He could have refused, stood his ground with his parents.

He looked up and studied the unfamiliar star pattern on the display. If they died out here, at least he'd still be himself, with a head full of music. He drummed his fingers lightly against the console, enjoying the hard resonance of the room. It reminded him of the piece he was working on and he triggered his neural link to the micro stowed in his pocket.

Tuning out the drifting ship, he let the song sweep though his body, controlling the micro with directed pulses of different rhythms. It was something he'd figured out on his own, even if he wasn't as brilliant as Jem. Back on Daedalus, he could even use his micro and the neural to tune the environmentals of his room.

The lighting here was all wrong. It burned into the song, introducing discordant notes. Lost in the music, he reached out to dial down the brightness, his shoulders dropping and his jaw relaxing as the whole room softened.

The demands of his body fell away, too. Barre knew they would need to find food and water, but for now, the music was all he needed. It was all he'd ever needed.

*

Ro stared at her micro, waiting for news from Micah, and tried to ignore the throbbing in her ankle. The makeshift splint Jem had made helped, but she could feel the swollen flesh pressing against the bandages. She watched the breath rise and fall in his chest. How could he be so brilliant and his brother so ordinary?

She glanced at Barre, his long dreads swaying in time to music only he could hear. At least he was out of the way. The micro beeped and she shifted her attention back to what she hoped would be good news from Micah. The lights in the bridge dimmed. Gripping the micro in one hand, she levered herself up to standing with the other, pulling on the command console and blinked up at the lights. That shouldn't happen. The AI had been disabled and only she had access to the autonomics through her micro.

Ro accessed her session of Jem's interface program. If the AI had woken up again, there was no predicting what it might do. She scanned the status. Environmental systems were all online, unchanged, with no sign of the SIREN code running. "This doesn't make any sense," she said, blinking up at the lights.

The door slid open. Micah wrestled a large box onto the bridge. "Nice of someone to come and help me."

"What?" Ro turned to him. "Sorry. What do you have?"

"Battlefield med-kits and rations. Enough for a small strike force. Should last us months." He shrugged. "My father never does things by half-measures."

Barre headed over to where Micah stood and took the box. "I've seen these before," he said. "Not fancy, but they'll do the job."

"You're welcome," Micah said.

"Yeah. Thanks." Barre had already set the box down next to his brother and was rifling through it. "Antibiotics and suture glue. You can fix almost anything with this stuff."

"What's our water situation?" Ro asked. The ration bars tasted like asteroid dust and had a texture to match, but they would keep them going. The battlefield ones even had a jolt of caffeine added.

"I don't know about the ship's recycling plant, but we have plenty of water in my lab." Micah shrugged before she could say anything. "We need it more than the plants do."

"I need some clean water to flush Jem's wound."

Maybe Barre wasn't as useless as Ro figured. "Anything in there to stabilize my ankle?"

"Cast tape. Here." He tossed a roll to her. She had to set her micro down to catch it.

"Great. Thanks," she said, glaring at him. "A little help here?"

Barre stared her down. "Water, Jem, and then you. It's called triage."

Her cheeks burned and she looked down at her hands.

"Water. I'm on it," Micah said as he slipped from the bridge.

Ro watched him leave, her eyebrows crinkling together. Micah was barely recognizable without a snarky comment, push back, or an argument. She slid back to the floor near Jem. "Anything I can do to help?" she asked. Like anyone on a space station, she'd done her basic emergency training, but it was nowhere near what the Durbins must have taught their sons.

Barre knelt by his brother, completely ignoring her. "This is probably going to hurt."

"You couldn't lie?" Jem said, his lips crooking into a small smile.

"Do Mom or Dad ever?"

"No."

Ro strained to hear Jem's soft voice and then looked away, feeling like she was eavesdropping on something she had no right to know.

Barre snapped on the sterile gloves from the med-kit and leaned over Jem's head. "Good thing you don't keep dreads like me."

Ro winced as Barre pressed down on Jem's skull. A small trickle of new blood traveled down his forehead.

"Hang on, I need more light."

"I'll see what I can do," Ro said, grabbing for her micro. Before she could access the environmental subroutines, Barre looked up and away, his eyes unfocused. The lights brightened so slowly, she initially thought she'd imagined it.

Barre turned back to Jem. "That's better."

"Wait." Ro frowned, looking from her quiet micro to the lights and back again. "Wait. You did that. How the hell did you do that?"

"What? The lights?"

"Yes! The lights!" If she could, she would have taken him by his shirt and shaken him. "How did you ... if you'd triggered the AI ..." Fear burned a cold wave through her chest. He could have gotten them all killed, just like she'd almost done. Ro swallowed hard.

"My neural." Barre turned back to Jem as if it was that simple.

All the warmth drained out of her face. "You can directly talk with the ship?" Maybe she needed both brothers, after all.

"Not talk. Not exactly. Not in words."

Now she definitely wanted to shake him.

"You can do that with your music?" Jem asked. "Wow. That's, that's seismic!"

"I guess." Barre busied himself lining up the supplies he needed to close up Jem's head wound. "How many fingers?"

Ro placed her hand on his arm. "I need you to tell me exactly what you did," she said, slowly, and carefully.

He shook her off. "Not part of the triage."

The door opened and Micah walked in with two containers of water and a roll of some thin, translucent fabric. Ro sat back and watched Barre take care of his brother. He carefully flushed the wound and patted it dry with sterile gauze. Antibiotics were next, then fresh gauze to protect it. He wound a strip of the fabric Micah brought around Jem's head to keep the bandages in place. Barre had precise hands—the hands of a surgeon or a musician.

And the mind that guided those hands—that mind could control the ship's computer without triggering the defense mechanisms that Ro had tripped. She would have time to be jealous of him and ashamed of her assumptions later.

"Is some of that water for drinking?" Barre asked.

"Yes," Micah said. "We won't have to ration for some time."

"Good. Give Jem small sips until he's finished about a half liter."

Micah raised one eyebrow at Ro and she shrugged. Barre knew more about medical than the two of them put together. If he wanted to give them orders, she figured he was entitled.

He turned back to his brother as Micah came over with the water. "Stick out your tongue."

"Barre, no. I need to stay awake. What if Ro needs my help?"

"What we need is a real scanner, a full sick bay, and a cold suit. What we have is me and the sedative I'm going to force into you if you don't open your mouth."

"You're just like her, you know. It's why you two always fight."

"Shut up and stick out your tongue." When Jem had swallowed the tablet, Barre dragged over a med kit to Ro. "Your turn. Jem did a decent job with what he had, but this will be better."

"How long will he be out?"

"His brain needs to rest," Barre said, shrugging. "If he's lucky, it's only a concussion."

A chill walked up and down Ro's spine. "And if he's not?"

He held her gaze with his dark, intense eyes. "Can you get us back?"

Ro glanced back at Jem and Micah and then up at the unfamiliar star field. She swallowed the reassuring lie she knew he wanted, the answer even she wanted to believe and found, instead, the uncomfortable truth. "I don't know."

Nodding, he turned his steady hands to her broken ankle. Gone was the kid who would rather disappear in his own head than talk to you. Now, he had his mother's confidence and some of her arrogance, too.

He was gentle, at least, as he unwrapped Jem's temporary

splint. Free from its constraint, her ankle throbbed in time with her pulse, each beat bringing a fresh wave of pain. Ro winced. The bottom third of her lower leg was mottled purple and swollen. "Without a scanner, I can't tell you anything specific about the break." He ran his hands up and down her leg. Ro bit her lip to keep from crying out. "I don't think it's displaced, but it's definitely broken."

"I already figured that part out, Doc."

He frowned at her. "Don't call me that."

"Can you stabilize it? Enough so I can walk?"

"It's better if you don't."

"Not one of the choices we have."

"You're risking permanent damage." Barre shrugged. "But it's your choice. The cast tape has time-release anesthetic woven in to the fabric. It's meant to keep soldiers going after battlefield injuries. Should work for your ankle."

"Good." The sooner she could get moving, the sooner she could troubleshoot the AI without the pain distracting her. The sooner she could figure out just what Barre could do that she couldn't.

"You think? Not if you want the bone to knit."

"Not at the top of my priority list. Just wrap me up."

"Aye, aye, Captain."

"Don't call me that," Ro whispered, as he unrolled the bandage and shook it in the air to activate it. If he heard her, he didn't react. The wrap went on her leg cool. She gasped and stiffened as Barre coiled it around her ankle in repeated figures of eight, but within moments, a warm numbness spread upward. Her tense muscles relaxed as the pain retreated.

"You need to give the cast wrap a few minutes to harden

completely. Then you should be able to bear weight."

"Excellent."

"Pain is not your enemy, Ro. If you don't feel it, you're likely to add to the damage. And as far as the fracture is concerned, too much stress will just delay true healing."

All true and all irrelevant if she couldn't get them home. "I appreciate your concern."

"But you're going to do what you want anyway."

So they understood one another. "Pretty much."

"Jem's asleep. Now what?" Micah set the water container aside and stood up.

Ro exhaled as her ankle faded from her awareness. "The essentials. Food. Water. Assess the ship's systems so we know what we have to work with."

"And how does finding out where we are and calling for help fit in?" Barre asked.

"This is my version of triage. Can you leave Jem?"

He glanced over at his brother and chewed his lower lip before turning back and nodding.

"Good. I need you to find our other drone. It's somewhere on the ship and having both will make life easier. Micah—go figure out if we have working heads and water reclamation." If not, they would have to set up a field latrine.

"And you?" Micah asked.

"Me?" Ro pulled herself upright and set her foot down carefully before letting her weight settle. As Barre promised, there was no pain, only a distant sense of pressure and a kind of spongy emptiness that just felt wrong. "I'm going to see how much I can link to without waking our homicidal AI." She stared at Barre until he looked away. "And when you get back with that drone, you and I are having a talk, music-boy."

Micah and Barre left without another word and Ro wondered how long that would last. She hobbled over to the little utility robot in the far corner of the bridge and put it up on a console. At least this was something she knew she could fix. Its primitive programming capabilities meant it had serious limitations in autonomy, but it also meant very little could go wrong. She paired her micro with it and quickly turned off discoverability. Unfortunately, that meant she couldn't just use it to find its companion, but that was a small price to pay against the possibility of it pinging the ship's AI.

But maybe she could use the drones in another way. Back on Daedalus, they formed a network that functioned as the arms and legs of the station's AI. Each individual drone only had a small broadcasting signal, but linked, they were able to cover the whole station. She only had two. But she also had four micros and maybe, just maybe a way to get them all to play nicely with the ship's communications array. At least long enough to get a fix on the nearest ansible and send out a distress call.

Chapter 23

BARRE WASN'T SURE what he expected when he handed Ro the drone, but her disinterested grunt as she set it aside wasn't it. Her long hair shading her face, she barely looked up from tapping on her micro with one hand and tweaking something on the first drone with her other. He watched her coordinate her two hands in different rhythms for a few minutes. She'd have made a hell of a drummer.

The door slid open and Micah stepped onto the bridge, mimicking his father's confident stride. This was the most time Barre had spent with him since he showed up on Daedalus. He wondered how else Micah was like the infamous senator.

"We have functioning heads. As far as the reclamation, it should work." Micah shrugged. "But these types of systems were notoriously inefficient, and the ship is close to forty years old."

Ro didn't respond, didn't even move when Micah walked up to her.

"So, what other busy work do you have for us?" he asked, his voice light, but his gaze locked on her with a laser's focus.

She glanced up at the two of them as if surprised to see them there. "You." She pointed at Barre. "Don't go anywhere."

He glanced down at his sleeping brother. "Yeah. No problem." Jem's color still wasn't great, but at least there was no fresh blood on the bandages. That had to be a good sign.

Ro reached for the second drone.

"Care to let us mere mortals know what you're doing?" Micah asked.

She blinked up at him, not seeming to register the sarcasm. "I need your micros. All of them. Even Jem's."

All Barre's music lived on the small device. Everything he'd collected across planets and systems and cultures and all the pieces he'd composed. "Why?"

Slapping the cover back on the second drone she sighed. "Setting up an ad hoc."

"Um, what?"

Ro pushed the hair back from her face. At this point, Jem would have been rolling his eyes.

"I'm using all the transmitting power in the drones and the micros to link up directly with the ship's comm array. With a strong enough signal, we can trigger the antenna's repeater function."

"That's assuming someone's listening for us," Barre said. A pang of unfamiliar guilt hit him. Their parents would be insane with worry and they would probably blame him. He curled his hands into fists.

She fixed him with a steely look. "A ship abandoned for forty years breaks free of a space station with four kids on board. You don't think they'll be listening for us?"

"And what if the wrong people hear us?" Micah asked, his gaze fixed on Ro.

"What choice do we have?" she answered.

Barre glanced from Ro to Micah, frowning. What were they talking about?

Micah handed over his micro and Jem's. Barre dragged his out of a deep pocket. Ro had no idea what she was asking. Barre gripped the small machine tightly. She held out her hand.

"Fine," he said. "Do you need me to unlock it?"

She blinked up at him. "Oh, sure, that'd be easier."

Easier than what? He drew his pass-code across the screen and toggled it open. "Will it work?" he asked, finally passing it to her.

"It should."

"Like the AI was supposed to work?" Micah said.

Ro winced. "Doing my best, here."

"Fine. If we're going to do this thing, is there anything I can do to help?"

"No. But he can." Again Ro pointed at Barre.

"I'm thinking you want the other Durbin kid." Jem still slept, but fitfully, his eyes shifting rapidly beneath his thin lids, as if he knew they were talking about him.

"You're the one who can sing to the ship, right?"

"Not quite," Barre said.

"You accessed the computer and it didn't freak out. Before I send out this pulse, I need you to do it again." Her green eyes didn't blink as she stared up at him. "Whatever I did triggered the ship's defenses. I don't know about you, but I like air and I like breathing it. If your music can keep the AI happy, we might just live through this."

"You've got to be kidding," Micah said.

Barre drew his eyebrows together. "No, it makes a kind of

strange sense. You said the SIREN code was broken. It's like the AI has brain damage. And neuroscientists have known for a long time that alternative inputs can help organize motor outputs in brain diseases. Before the diaspora, on Earth they used to use music to get patients with Parkinson's moving."

The two of them stared at him and Barre fought the urge to turn away.

"Parents. Doctors. Remember?" After a burst of excitement, anger and resentment burned through him. Why were they so surprised? "I may not be a genius like Jem, but I'm not an idiot."

Ro hobbled over to him and placed her hands on his shoulders. "Hey, I never said that."

He shook her off. "You didn't have to."

She looked away.

"Sorry, I—" Micah started.

"Don't sweat it," Barre said. It wasn't like he didn't get the same shit from everyone, once they met his parents and his brother. He gathered his loose dreads in a tail and tied two of the outer lengths around them. "What do you need me to do?"

"I'm going to trigger a multi-band, multi-directional pulse. Then we're going to listen for an answer. Even with you distracting the computer, it's a risk." She looked back at Jem. "But it's the only option we have. It's not like someone is going to just stumble across us out here."

If they were somewhere off the main jump paths, that would never happen. "I vote yes."

Micah snorted. "Not sure Ro cares what we think, but for what it's worth, I'm with you."

"Just so you know," Barre said. "I'm not even sure how I connected before. All I wanted was to turn down the lights."

"Well, you're going to have to do a little more than that," Ro said. "What other kind of commands can you send through your neural?"

"Pretty much anything you can do with the heads-up, I guess." Her attention and focus made him squirm. "It's just simpler for me to think in music, so I started by programming a bunch of macros using rhythms and notes instead of gestures or words. It scaled up from there."

She was staring at him, open mouthed. "When we get back to Daedalus, I want you to show me, okay?"

"Yeah, whatever." It didn't seem that radical to him and he doubted she would be able to use it, not unless she had perfect pitch and rhythm. "I guess I could just send a ton of commands, all at once."

"Then we risk flooding the AI. No telling what it would do." Ro pursed her lips and dragged her hands through her hair. It fell in smooth waves around her face. "Wait. If I give you a program, can you translate and transmit it?"

Barre scratched at the stubble of his beard. "What kind of program?"

"Something that would occupy the computer without sending it into threat mode." Ro tapped on her micro in a staccato beat. "Let me see what I have already written."

"Sensor calibration," Micah said. "It's routine enough and uses up lots of processor cycles."

"That should work." Ro tapped some more before holding up her micro for Barre to see. "If you can parse these commands in music-speak, or whatever it is you do, the computer should let me sneak out my comm pulse."

Barre scanned the code. He might not be any sort of

programming savant like his brother, but he knew the basics. This seemed pretty standard.

"Here." Ro handed him his micro. "I'll just need it back before we execute."

He shook his head. "This is what I do. It's all in here," he said, tapping his forehead.

Ro raised her eyebrows. "Okay."

Unspoken was the skepticism. No surprise there and he didn't bother explaining. It was easier to just show them. Accessing his neural, he set its small internal memory to record and started translating Ro's code into a melody.

It was a strange music, full of wandering notes and short, choppy lines. But it was meant for one listener only and as far as Barre knew, AIs weren't programmed for art appreciation. He captured the "song" and turned off the recording before focusing back on the bridge where Ro and Micah stood watching him. "Ready."

"That's it? Don't you need to error check it or something?" Micah said.

"No."

"Good," Ro said. "I'm ready, too. On my mark." She set her micro down, completing a lopsided circle on the floor with the other three and the two drones. Crouching down, she let her hand just hover over her micro. "Three."

Barre set the music to trigger with a nod.

"Two."

He lifted his chin and held his breath. The timing had to be perfect.

"One."

Ro locked her gaze on his face.

"Go!"

Barre dropped his chin and let the odd song flood through his neural, broadcasting out toward the ship. Ro's hand swiped across her screen and she sat back, waiting.

Micah hooked his arm around a stanchion. Music swirling through his mind, Barre glanced around the bridge looking for a place to brace against, just in case.

Chapter 24

NOMI STOOD WAITING outside Mendez's office, her energy and her attention still back in the communications room. The staff couldn't work any faster whether she was there or not, but it didn't make her feel any better about being called to command again. Her right foot tapped against the hard floor. When Mendez's assistant glanced up at her, frowning, Nomi forced her body to be still. She looked down at her micro for the hundredth time in about ten minutes.

"You may join the meeting, now," the guard said, her blank expression and stiff posture giving nothing away.

Mendez's door opened and Nomi stepped through into a chaos of raised voices. Halting just inside the doorway, she did a quick headcount before anyone noticed her. Senator Corwin Rotherwood loomed over the commander's desk, his finger pointing at Mendez, his face flushed a deep crimson. The Doctors Durbin—Kristoff and Leta—sat against the right hand wall, rigid, leaning forward, their chairs close enough to touch, though their bodies didn't. Alain Maldonado leaned against the far left wall, his face half turned from Mendez, his arms folded across his chest.

Rotherwood's shout drowned out the commander's reply and Leta Durbin's clipped outrage.

"Find that ship, Mendez!"

The commander folded her hands across her chest. The muscles in her jaw bunched and released. "Sit down, Senator."

Maldonado swiveled his head around to Nomi, his expression blank. She stepped away from him, her back hitting the closed door behind her.

Spinning on his heel, Rotherwood turned and confronted her in three strides. "Where is that ship?" He stood so close she could count the beads of sweat collecting on his upper lip. "Where is my son?"

Leta Durbin shifted her disapproval Rotherwood's way before turning to Nomi. "I have a son on that ship, too, Senator."

"Sons," Kristoff Durbin corrected, before leaning back in his chair, his face stiff and unreadable.

Both of them? That made four on board, somewhere, anywhere in the universe. Nomi didn't remember the Durbins' kids' names, but she'd seen them around the station in the few weeks she'd been posted there. What were they doing working with Ro?

"Please tell us what you have discovered, Ensign," Mendez said, her steady voice betraying none of the tension so plain in the cords at her neck and the tightness in her shoulders.

Five sets of eyes turned to her and Nomi cleared her throat before standing at attention. "Sir, the array is back on line. We are performing a partial, emergency calibration in order to send out a series of interrupted ansible carrier waves. If they're able to listen, they'll hear us and respond."

The chorus of outrage started again.

"Is that the best you can do? You have ships and pilots. Where's the rescue mission? Rotherwood thundered at her, his pointing finger millimeters from her chest. Nomi held her ground. Surely Mendez wouldn't allow him to assault her. And if he so much as tried, Nomi would happily break his hand.

"We expect a full investigation and an accounting of your security failings. This should not have happened, Commander," Leta Durbin said, her sharp voice cutting through Rotherwood's resonant and well-practiced anger.

"Barre has just recovered from a serious illness. He needs to be evaluated, given these new circumstances. His life is in your hands." Kristoff Durbin spoke quietly.

The only person silent in the room was Maldonado. Nomi studied him, looking for Ro's features in the closed, suspicious face. They shared those odd, changeable eyes, hazel, brown, or green depending on the way the light hit them. His hair was a few millimeters of blond fuzz cut close to his scalp. Unlike her father's harsh features, Ro had a delicate cast to her nose, a slight upturn of her eyes, thinner lips, but Nomi would recognize the same challenge in the Maldonado stance anywhere.

Mendez ignored them all, focusing only on Nomi. "When will you be ready to send out your signal?" The commander rubbed her bloodshot eyes and pinched the bridge of her nose as the senator and the Durbins finally fell silent.

Nomi lifted her micro. "If you'll allow me?"

"By all means," Mendez said.

She linked with her comms console and checked on the progress of her team. They had ansible coverage through about ten percent of the network and widely distributed. They would keep working at pulling more satellites online, but given the urgency, Nomi needed to start transmitting now. "This isn't a perfect solution, Commander, but it's the best we can do in the time window."

"Understood."

"You understand once we start making noise, it will effectively drown out any other ansible traffic."

"Proceed, Ensign," Mendez said, her expression hard.

The senator glared down at her. "That ship is your number one priority. Find it."

Mendez ignored him. Nomi decided she would do the same. She checked the transmission protocol one more time before sending the pulsed signal out in a repeating loop in all directions. If Ro were listening, she would hear it. Best case scenario, she'd be able to track the signal back to its source. More likely, she'd at least be able to latch onto the nearest ansible and orient from there. Nomi wouldn't let herself think of the worst case.

"How long before we know where they are?" Kristoff Durbin asked. His voice, if not gentle, at least didn't accuse her of anything.

She met his gaze. "There is no way of knowing, Dr. Durbin. All we can do is to keep transmitting and wait for them to find us."

"If Ro wants to find you," Alain Maldonado said. "She has a ship. She could be anywhere by now."

Nomi frowned and turned away from him. Of course Ro wanted to find her way back.

"Maldonado, Nakamura, get back to your stations. Everyone else, return to your quarters."

"Mendez, we will not let you sideline us. Our children are at risk." Senator Rotherwood glanced at the Durbins, suddenly seeking to be their ally.

Leta Durbin gestured to her husband. He nodded and stood. From the side, her angular cheekbones looked sculpted from dark marble. "We will be in the infirmary, if you need us," she said, ignoring Rotherwood. They left without looking back.

The senator stomped from the commander's office.

Nomi turned to leave. Maldonado brushed past, pushing her against the door frame. She glared at him, rubbing her shoulder.

"Keep me informed," Mendez said.

"Sir." Nomi strode from the office, her boots clicking against the floor. The signal was broadcasting. There wasn't much more she could do in the comm center, but she didn't want to be alone in her quarters either. Her stomach growled and Nomi realized she hadn't eaten since before her normal shift began, nearly twelve hours ago.

She turned left from command toward the commissary. The hallways were still as empty as they were at the start of her grave-yard shift. She hoped the commissary was considered essential.

Angry voices drifted down the corridor and Nomi froze.

"This is your fault," Senator Rotherwood said.

"I did what you told me to do," Maldonado answered.

Nomi pressed back against the corridor.

"Do you have any idea what's going to happen when my associates find out the ship is gone?"

"They can't have gone far. All they have is interstitial drive."

"For your daughter's sake, you'd better hope we find them first."

Cold slithered though her and settled in the pit of her stomach. She retreated back down the corridor, no longer hungry anymore.

Chapter 25

RO SAT CROSS-LEGGED on the floor, leaning against the command console. At least with bunk padding now spread out on the floor, it was a little more comfortable. Micah had argued to relocate to the lab because of the access to water, but Barre refused to let his brother be moved. As much as she would have liked more room to work, Ro had to agree with him.

No one said anything about it, but they kept looking to her to make the final decisions. She hadn't expected to feel so uncomfortable about anything in her life. It gave her a pang of sympathy for Mendez.

"Anything?" Micah asked.

"Not yet." Ro had to alternate between transmitting and listening, the ship's primitive ansible unable to achieve full duplex. "Barre?"

"All quiet."

He seemed to have gotten the computer's higher cognitive functions to stay asleep. She remembered a holo reproduction of an image from old India of a snake charmer. Barre was her AI charmer.

So far, so good. Everything had been set to automatic, with a link back through her micro if anyone responded to their signal.

Micah yawned and apologized. Now that the adrenaline rush had worn off, Ro realized just how exhausted she was, too.

"We need to get some rest. This could be a long haul."

"We should set a watch rotation," Micah said.

He was right. And she should be the one to take the first watch. "Three hour shifts?"

Barre and Micah nodded. "One, two, three." She pointed at herself, then Barre, then Micah.

Micah stretched out on a pad across the room. "I don't suppose you can tickle the AI to turn the lights down?"

"And would you like room service and a wake-up call with that?" Ro asked.

"What, no chocolates on my pillow?" Barre asked.

The three of them burst out laughing, a sound as much terror as amusement. When they wound down, all three out of breath, they shared a wry smile. "Sweet dreams," Ro said. Micah closed his eyes without another word. Barre glanced at Jem and slid his sleeping pad closer to his brother. "I'll wake you if anything changes," she said.

"I'd feel a lot more comfortable if he was back on Daedalus."

Ro sighed. "I know."

Silence rang the room, interrupted by the soft rhythm of their breathing. Ro had never shared a room with anyone before. It was both comforting and disconcerting to realize she wasn't alone. She yawned and scrubbed at her eyes. It still hurt to put weight on her ankle, but she needed to stay awake, so she stood, leaning on the console to take some stress off it.

Hobbling over to her makeshift network, Ro carefully lifted

her micro to eye level, making sure it didn't lose connectivity with the other pieces of the ad-hoc. Toggling split screen mode, she watched the ansible signals transmit and recede. It was as hypnotic as the rhythmic in-and-out breath of her companions, or the cycling of a tide. Her head bobbed sharply and she startled herself back to full wakefulness.

"Crap." Ro eyed the pile of supplies Micah had brought from the hold. Tubes of battlefield-boost lay beside the food bars. One of those would keep a corpse awake. She wasn't sure it was worth paying the cost later, especially when a little pain might do the trick just as well. Wincing, she leaned all her weight onto her left leg. An electric spike rammed through her ankle and up her calf and she wasn't sleepy anymore.

Watching the transmissions wouldn't make someone hear them any faster. Ro wiped her micro clean and returned the whole screen to sleep mode. Something should get its rest. "Ro, you've spent way too much time with machines," she whispered. If only she could have made a connection with the AI. That would have been something.

Ro stroked the surface of the command console, thinking of what could have been. "We could have made quite the team," she said.

A rumble moved through the ship. Ro stiffened, her hand rigid on the console. The emergency lights splashed red shadows across the cockpit.

"Intruder alert, sector nine."

"Shit, what did you do?" Micah shouted, fighting to be heard over the computer's impassive voice. He bolted upright and blinked, looking around the bridge.

"Intruder alert, sector nine. Enemy craft bearing one-six-seven mark ten. Time to engagement T minus eight minutes."

"I didn't do anything!" Ro said, quickly snatching her hand away from the console. "Maybe someone heard us."

"Or maybe the ship is trying out a new way to kill us."

"Ro?" Barre stood between her and the still-sleeping Jem, frowning.

"Hang on," Ro said, reaching for her micro. If there were someone out there trying to respond to their signal, why didn't the comm system let her know?

"Ro?" Barre repeated.

She shot him a warning look. "I'm on it."

"Intruder alert, sector nine."

The lines of code scrolled across her micro in a blur as she scanned for any evidence of an incoming transmission.

"Time to engagement T minus seven minutes."

Shit. What the hell was the ship going to do this time?

"Ro!" Barre slammed his hand against the nearest console with a sound that reverberated through the bridge, over the AIs metronomic warnings.

"What?" Ro and Micah answered simultaneously.

Barre frowned, his eyebrows pulling together. "I'm not sure, but I think the ship is trying to talk to me."

*

Barre's head buzzed with a strange music. It drowned out the computer's monotone voice and somehow blended with the random chaos of the strobe lights to form coherent themes and melodies.

Trying to listen and talk at the same time, Barre felt as if his own mind was playing out of phase. He opened his mouth and couldn't find words. "I don't understand," he said, but he wasn't sure if he was speaking to Ro and Micah or the ship. The music rolled through him, overpowering all of his senses. It was all he could hear, but all he could see, taste, smell, or touch, too. The bridge and the ship itself receded, becoming bright notes and musical phrases, strange but recognizable.

"Please, I don't understand," he cried, but the plea never sounded outside his own head. It reverberated inside, a discordant counterpoint to the ship's song. Something hit his face with the impact of a cymbal strike. The music cut off mid-note and Barre could feel the blood surging through him, the heat rising through his chest, the pressure of red lights against his eyes.

Ro stood close enough for him to see the fear in her dilated eyes and the pulse racing at her throat. Barre lifted his hand to touch the side of his face.

"I'm sorry," she said. "I didn't know what else to do."

Barre blinked at her, trying to re-orient himself to the ordinary sensory world.

"Time to engagement, T minus six minutes."

"I don't understand," Barre said again. It was like the chorus of a song, familiar, catchy, strangely comforting.

"Well, you'd better figure it out. You may be the only one who can," Micah said. "I'd like to live past the next six minutes."

Had he only been lost in the symphony for a minute? "I think —I think the AI just figured out a whole language based on my musical interface."

Ro looked down at her micro. "I can't access anything, now."

"So, what's it saying?" Micah asked. He appeared as calm as ever, his expression giving little away. But Barre could see past the polished look at the tension rippling in Micah's jaw and in the tightness of his shoulders.

"It was too much." Even the memory of the music sent waves of vertigo through him. He leaned onto a console, waiting for his head to clear.

"The clock is ticking and we're sitting ducks out here."

"Barre, you have to try," Ro said.

His heart started to pound again, a metronome set to too high a speed. "You don't understand. It's too much. All in my head. I can't. I can't."

"Time to engagement, T minus five minutes."

"Please." Ro looked up at him, her eyes a too-bright green, before glancing down at Jem.

What would his genius little brother do? He certainly wouldn't curl up in the corner and whine. Barre looked around the bridge, avoiding eye contact with Ro or Micah. What would Jem do? Ro's weird pile of electronics lay on the floor, his micro part of the circle.

With a simple thought, he paired his neural with the tiny computer and set it to external speaker. Triggering playback mode, he pushed the ship's music through it, blasting the bridge.

Outside the resonance of his own skull, the music was still as strange and as alien, but not as overwhelming. Barre could listen without being swept away in a tide of incomprehensible emotion. The AI had taken elements from every sound the ship could make and created scales that didn't exist in any musical idiom Barre had ever studied. It had its own odd beauty.

"What the hell does it mean?" Micah said, wincing, his hands clasped over his ears.

Even Ro looked vaguely ill, her face taking on a greenish cast in the red lights. Barre turned the volume down, but kept his focus on the music. Even though it had seemed to last forever in his head, it was just a few lines, repeated over and over with just slight variations. If the ship learned everything it knew about music from him, then there had to be some kind of meaning in it.

"Engagement in T minus four minutes."

"I know, I know," he said. "Tell me something useful, damn it."

Ro placed her hand on his arm. The warmth startled him, as did the concern in her normally icy gaze. "You said the AI took your musical commands and created its own language."

Barre nodded.

"Then listen and tell us if you recognize anything."

"It's not that easy."

"I know. But you have to try."

Barre set the music to loop slowly. It distorted the sound, making it even less melodic and more eerie. How was he going to make sense of this? Something was coming at them. Given his luck, it wouldn't be a convenient rescue ship. He didn't much care about what happened to him. It wasn't like he had a whole lot waiting for him back on Daedalus, but he owed it to Jem.

He sunk to the floor, sitting cross-legged, eyes closed, focusing not on the individual noises the AI co-opted for notes, but on the phrases, the pauses, the way the music made him feel. That's how he always interacted with new music and this was the newest of the new.

The distractions of the emergency lights and Ro and Micah's fear kept pulling him away. Barre took a deep breath and shut off the external speaker. The only way to do this would be to let the music fill him up again, hoping he could ride the wave this time instead of drown.

The concerns of the derelict ship and their possibly unwelcome company faded. But before he could trigger the recording, new melodies spilled into him. He held his breath, straining to listen with his whole body. Woven into the barrage of sound, something seemed familiar. He traced the line of a descant, high, wordless, yet filled with defiance and despair. Barre recognized the emotions he had poured into his last composition. "Yes, yes." He smiled and played the refrain back to the AI.

It echoed back to him, distorted, but unmistakable, with a new refrain added. This one made his arms break out in goose bumps. He understood the sound of fear and composed a flute solo in his head, a thin wail. The computer added the line to its composition. Anger. Desperation. Fear.

A melody that he always thought of as the sound of Daedalus Station flitted through his mind. He played it for the AI, hoping it meant "home." The music fell silent. His heart beat a wild rhythm.

Barre was no programming genius like Jem or Ro. It wasn't like he could wrest control of the ship from its damaged computer. All he could do was play. He played his fear for his brother and Ro's reckless competence. He didn't know Micah well enough to add him to the mix, but he figured that wouldn't matter. It would have to be enough.

For himself, he repeated the main melody from his own score. *I'm like you. I'm broken, but I want to survive.*

"Please."

*

"I'm in!" Ro shouted, as her micro displayed a schematic of the ship's ansible controls.

"Engagement in T minus three minutes."

"Yeah, yeah, I know," she muttered to herself, frantically accessing the unfamiliar interface. "Who the hell are you?" Every ansible had a unique designation. If it tried to hail them, there should be some sort of electronic fingerprint. No fingerprint meant no registration, which meant nothing good for them. A drifting craft would be fair salvage, with or without people on board. Unless they could get it under control, they would be at the mercy of anyone who stumbled across them.

A legitimate salver might consider them crew instead of cargo, but a legitimate salver would have hailed them and identified themselves. She scrolled through the comm logs, frantically looking for anything that would look like a signal. The tiny blip was so small, she nearly missed it against the background cosmic noise. She isolated it, blew it up, and ran it through an interpreter.

"Come on, come on, tell us who the hell you are."

A small speaker crackled to life, startling a squeak out of Ro.

"Transport three two seven, this is the Commonwealth vessel Hephaestus. Acknowledge."

This was military, not a salver, or worse a marauding chop shop. With any luck, they would be back on Daedalus inside of a few hours. She wrote a quick program to send an auto-reply with their identification, but before she could transmit, a packet of music drowned out the recorded comm message and nearly burst Ro's eardrums.

"Warning: Emergency burn in ten seconds."

Her micro screen blanked out. "What? Barre? What the hell is it doing?"

"Ten"

"I have no idea, but I'd hold on if I were you!"

"Nine."

"Can you stop it?"

"Eight."

"I don't know."

"Seven."

"Shit," Micah said, and stretched out flat on the bunk padding.

"Six."

"It's not listening to me," Barre said, looking over at Jem.

"Five."

"Shit. Get low," Ro warned, scrambling for her own cushion.

"Four."

"Three."

The AIs voice continued its implacable countdown.

"Two."

"One."

The giant hand that pressed down on Ro was no gentler than when the ship first blasted free of Daedalus. But at least now, she was ready for it. The massively increased weight of her body seemed to crush her spine into the bridge floor as if the old, worn cushions were only a molecule thick. All the air squeezed out of her lungs and Ro struggled to breathe, wondering where they would end up or if any of them would survive.

Chapter 26

Nomi dressed quickly and left her too-empty quarters in search of coffee. Was it yesterday she and Ro were supposed to meet for breakfast? At least it was well before shift change and, other than the mess hall chef, the room was empty. He handed her a hot cup. Nomi took it, grateful she didn't have to speak to anyone. She slumped into the chair nearest the door and took a sip, grimacing at the bitterness. Micah never did get her that coffee he promised.

Did he know that his father and Ro's had their own interest in the ship?

Her micro buzzed. "Nakamura, report to the commander." It was a relief to have something to do with the worry that spun through her odd, restless dreams last night. Leaving the still steaming coffee, Nomi sprinted across the quiet station to command.

Silent guards let her into Mendez's office. An unfamiliar man sat in the chair the senator had occupied yesterday. She looked up at Mendez, trying not to let her confusion show. The commander had clearly not slept well either, given her rumpled uniform and the dark smudges beneath her eyes.

"Sir!" she said, standing at attention, deliberately not looking at the visitor.

"Ensign Nakamura, you are being reassigned to the Commonwealth ship Hephaestus."

Nomi's head jerked upwards. "Sir?"

"You will join their search and retrieval mission as the representative of Daedalus Station."

She swallowed the lump in her throat. Reassigned? Retrieval? What about rescue? "Sir, have we heard from the ship?"

"Our sensors detected the transport last night." The man's voice rumbled through the office.

Nomi forced herself to stand still, her attention fixed on her commander, even as the blood surged painfully through her chest. She wanted to interrogate the man. Why were they calling this a retrieval? Her throat tightened. What about Ro and the others?

"But she fled before we could salvage her."

What did he mean by fled? Was Ro actually flying the ship?

"Commander Targill, our priority is with her passengers," Mendez said.

Out of the corner of her eye, Nomi watched the man lean forward and stand.

"Of course, we will make every effort to secure your people." He towered over both her and Mendez, making the room feel significantly smaller. "But that ship is a danger to shipping lanes. As is your little homing beacon."

Mendez's eyes narrowed slightly. She turned to Nomi. "Ensign, kill the transmission."

Her mouth fell open. If they were alone, she might have dared to argue, but Targill was the real deal—a Commonwealth Military lifer with the posture and the stripes to prove it. He kept his silver hair in a severe brush cut and an ugly burn scar puckered the skin along his right temple. Nomi turned away from the cold appraisal in his blue eyes and back to Mendez. "Yes, sir."

She pulled out her micro and, offering up a silent apology to Ro, stopped the signal. Even with the crew working around the clock, it would still take time for the resumption of anything resembling normal communications. She should be there with them and helping to contact Ro.

"We leave in fifteen minutes." Targill turned on his heel, a motion as precise and economical as the rest of him, and strode out of Mendez's office.

"Ensign," Mendez said.

Nomi blinked and turned back to the commander.

"This is a temporary posting. You are being attached to the Hephaestus at my request."

Mendez had already made that clear. Nomi stared at her, wondering what she wasn't saying.

"Dismissed."

"Yes, sir."

She walked back to her quarters in a daze, packed spare clothes and her toiletries, and headed to where Hephaestus docked. A bored crewman escorted her aboard the sleek cruiser and to an excruciatingly small cabin along the ship's port side. "Mess hall directly opposite to starboard. Report to comms when you're settled. Pair your micro to the ship's AI for a map."

Barely wide enough for Nomi to walk through with her bag,

the cabin had sleeping berths for two. She hoped her roommate had a sense of humor. Her stomach rumbled and she remembered she hadn't eaten yet today. After shoehorning her bag into the square storage locker set into the wall beside the foot of the empty top bunk, Nomi went to find the mess hall.

Immaculately uniformed crew walked the narrow corridor with purpose. None of them even glanced her way. Alarm bells sounded. Targill wasn't kidding when he said fifteen minutes.

"Liftoff in five minutes. Stations." The AI's voice was clipped, efficient, like everything else she'd seen on board so far. In the mess hall, Nomi experienced a sense of deja vu. Just like on Daedalus, it stood nearly empty. One man, his tall frame stooping slightly, thrust a spill-proof mug under a spigot. If that was coffee, she'd almost forgive Mendez for placing her here.

Grabbing one of the lightweight mugs, she joined the man by the dispensers. "I'm Ensign Nakam ..." She trailed off as the man turned, his hazel-green eyes the one piece of familiar she would have happily lived without.

Alain Maldonado.

How did he get here? And did Commander Mendez know?

"Hello Konomi," he said.

"Ensign Nakamura," she snapped in return.

He held her gaze for several uncomfortable seconds before leaving the mess. Hephaestus's engines roared to life.

*

As suddenly as the burn began, it ended, leaving Barre light-headed and a little nauseated. He sat up, waiting for his head and stomach to settle. At least the ship hadn't put them in free-fall.

That would have been messy.

"Everyone still in one piece?" Ro asked, climbing to her feet.

"A few microns thinner, I think," Micah said, as he stood and stretched out his back. Barre cringed at the multiple pops he could hear halfway across the room.

"How's Jem?" Ro asked.

Barre scooted over to check his brother's pulse. Slow, but regular, the same as his breathing. "No change." It wasn't a good sign. He was going to have to wake him soon and get him to drink some more, or he'd have to rummage through the medi-kit for an IV setup.

"Any ideas as to why we just ran away from potential help?" Ro put the question to the room, but Barre knew she was mainly asking him.

"I didn't do anything," Barre said. They had to believe he wanted to be rescued, at least for his brother's sake.

Micah stared him down. "Maybe it's time you did," he said.

Barre's shoulders tightened. "What do you mean by that?"

"You spend your life trying not to take up any space. Well, you're the only one who seems to be able to talk to this crazy ship. Figure something out."

"I'm not the one who got us here," he snapped back. "That would be my brilliant brother and Ro." A faint music played through his head. "Not now," he muttered.

"And if you don't stop whining and get to work, we're going to be stuck here." Jem's voice barely registered over the odd melody, but it got them all to shut up.

"Hey," Barre said, leaning over and checking his brother's vital signs again.

"Can you open your eyes?"

"Not unless you want me to vomit."

"Oh." The dizziness didn't bode well for the state of Jem's brain.

"So, if you're the genius, what do you think we should do?" Micah asked, ignoring Ro. She glared at him but kept silent. Barre shook his head. They were quite the team.

"Figure it out. But do it fast." Jem's voice trailed off and Barre thought he'd lost consciousness again. "I can't help you. I can't make my eyes work right."

"Fuck," Barre swore. Kneeling over his injured brother, he carefully peeled back one eyelid and then the other. Without a penlight, he had no way of checking how his pupils reacted, but his right eye was dilated nearly all the way. The left side looked pretty normal.

He swallowed hard and sat back on his heels. "Jem's right," he said, staring at his brother. He knew Ro and Micah were watching him. "We don't have a lot of time. I think he has a bleed in his head." He squeezed his eyes shut for a moment. "I've done everything I can for him."

"Not everything." Ro stood behind him and squeezed his shoulder. "Come on. Let's see if we can get through to the ship again."

"What about me?" Micah said.

Barre stood up and bit back his sarcastic reply.

"Once we get control over the ship, we're going to have to figure out how to crew it with just the three of us. Don't worry. You'll be plenty busy then. For now, keep an eye on Jem."

Barre reluctantly shifted away from his brother's side as Micah sat down beside him.

He looked up at Barre and gave a half-smile. "Hey, it's okay. I got this."

*

Ro turned to Barre and tapped the side of her head. "What do you hear in there?"

They were adrift again, and again, nothing in the star field looked familiar. Maybe if they could access navigation, they might be able to at least figure out where they were. Though if the ship went off on another random burn, it wouldn't much help to know where they'd been.

He shifted his attention between her and his brother.

"Barre?"

He moved closer to her. "I know. I'm sorry."

"So, anything?" Ro kept her voice casual. Maybe Jem would have understood how much it hurt to admit she needed help.

"Just a kind of background noise. Like someone humming to themselves."

Pulling her eyebrows together, she studied Barre. He was so completely different from his brother. When she worked with Jem, she could almost hear the thoughts whirring in his head. His brain always raced ahead of his ability to explain himself. And he was always thinking. Barre seemed causal to the point of disinterest or disdain.

"Background noise? What do you think it's doing?" She'd figured the AI was pretty heavily damaged and about as conscious as Jem was. But what if she was wrong?

"How the hell should I know?" Barre glanced around the bridge, his gaze lingering on the damaged forward screen and the unfamiliar stars. "It could be doing anything."

"Well, we know it doesn't want me sending any signals. What about getting into the informational archives? Navigation? Star charts?"

"And how do you expect me to do that?"

"I don't know. Ask it? Sing it to sleep?" Ro couldn't help laughing at the absurdity of this. All her hacking skills and she needed a musician to access the AI.

"Nursery rhymes are not my specialty," Barre said, his mouth turning up into a reluctant smile.

"What's the music like? I mean, do you think the AI is out of fight-or-flight mode?" It seemed odd to describe a computer in those terms, but that's literally what it was doing before.

Barre tapped the side of his head. "Here, listen."

The music poured from his micro. Repetitive and hypnotic, it was oddly soothing. It did remind Ro of her habit of humming to herself as she worked. "What do you think would happen if we fed it back to the AI?"

"Why?"

"Kind of like 'We hear you and we want to get to work, too.'"

"I can try, but it might not trust me anymore. The last time I played something, you did an end-run around it."

Ro glanced around the remnants of the ruined bridge, wondering again what had happened there decades before. There was no sign of weapons fire anywhere else on the ship. "I think it's worth the risk, Barre. We have to find some way of getting it to trust us. At least now we know people are searching. It would be nice if we could help them find us."

"We should probably brace ourselves." Barre glanced over at Micah and he nodded.

Ro limped over to the nav station and wedged herself between it and the wall. Barre did the same over at comms. Micah set his back against a console and threw his feet over Jem's legs.

"Okay," Barre said. "Three, two, one, now." The music faded from the small speaker in his micro and he looked up, unfocusing his eyes. Seconds ticked past in an uncomfortable silence. She wanted to ask Barre what he was doing and how the AI was responding, but she didn't dare break his concentration. It gave her a greater appreciation of Jem's patience when he worked with her.

The bridge work lights remained steady as Ro stared up at them, half daring them to turn red and flash their warning. She gripped the edges of the console so hard her hands went numb and still nothing happened.

"I think it understood. Look." Barre pointed behind her at the console she leaned against.

Ro turned, shaking out her hands, and looked down, her breath catching in her throat. The few lights not melted in the nav station winked at her. Slowly, she reached for her micro.

"Do you think that's a smart move?" Barre asked.

She paused, giving his worry serious consideration. The old Ro wouldn't have done that. "I think I'd rather find out now if the AI freaks out then when our military friends come back."

Barre's gaze flicking back to check on his brother before returning to her. "Okay. I'll keep the feedback going."

Ro set the micro down on the console and wiped her sweaty palms on her pants. Three other lives depended on her making the right decisions. Four, if you counted the AI. It had a kind of personality, and certainly a degree of self-awareness and self-preservation, too, by the looks of things. She wondered what Dauber and May would have thought if they were here.

If the AI saw any systems integration as a threat, maybe she could just get into the files and not try for any overrides. It would be a start, anyway. "Okay, baby. Here we go," she murmured, and paired her micro to the autonomics. "I'm not trying to hurt you. I just want to figure out where we are."

She didn't care if Micah and Barre heard her talking to the computer. It was her version of humming and maybe the AI would understand her, at least on some level. The lights remained steady. Ro closed her eyes briefly before she triggered Jem's interface edits. "This is my music."

Barre stepped closer to her. "No change in the song."

Ro lifted her hands and triggered the commands for file access. The display blanked out.

"Still no change," Barre said.

The virtual screen filled with rapidly scrolling text and Ro had to stop herself from jumping up and down and shouting. They were in. Her heart pounded painfully as if she had been starved of oxygen. "Barre?"

"Five by five."

Ro winced, hearing the echo of Nomi's voice and her bright laugh. If she ever wanted to see the woman again, she had to focus. "I'm going to look for anything navigation related. Nav logs. Star charts, if I can find them, okay?"

"Agreed," Micah said.

"Good to go," Barre answered.

She was tempted to look for an ansible map, but the ship was forty years out of date. Star charts didn't change all that much in a few decades, but the ansible network had.

The files were a mess. It looked like something had eaten its way through the computer's memory, leaving random nonsense strings behind. More than half of the data were simply missing. Of the files she could find intact entries for, many registered as having zero size.

No wonder the AI had problems.

Zipping through the directory almost as fast as the display could scroll, Ro found little of any use. A few intact files, she toggled for copying to her micro, but didn't dare stop to examine anything for fear the AI would decide to shut her out. At the end of her scan, she had less than a dozen useful files. And nothing labeled with a helpful 'star chart' or 'you are here' designation. She backed out of the file system carefully and decoupled her micro before glancing back at Barre.

"Good job."

Ro snorted. He wouldn't have said that if he knew how little she recovered. Grabbing her micro, she sat back down. The pain in her leg was a distant thing—too easily ignored. Barre had warned her about that. She studied the recovered files. None of their names gave much of a clue to their contents. Some would be a challenge to open.

She started with the basics. The format of plain old text files hadn't changed all that much in forty years. Glancing through them, she found antenna calibration logs, crew rotation schedules, and supplies lists. Ro closed the files and frowned, studying the list again. A few looked like they might be log entries, but playing the old recordings would take a bit of finesse. She glanced back at Barre and then frowned, looking away.

"What's wrong?"

"Nothing." Ro opened a basic audio compiler and slid one of the recordings towards it. The expected file error message flickered in red. Just once, she'd like the easy way to work the first time.

"You probably have to re-encode that to play it." Barre looked over her shoulder and shrugged when Ro stared back at him.

"Give me your micro."

He handed it over.

"Here. Make it work." She bumped the audio logs to him and went searching through the database files from her own micro, discomfort twisting her stomach into knots. Everything she learned about dealing with other people, she'd learned from her father. She tinkered with the awkward databases, keeping part of her attention on Barre.

Static-filled audio crackled through the bridge.

"... *fried the personality sub-* ... . *Lieutenant Murray* ... *every scan she* ... *self-healing virus* ... *damn thing* ... *tates every time we* ... *boot.*"

The recording stopped.

"I can try to clean it up a bit. But there's not a lot left. Sorry."

"I remember studying about that in school." Micah's voice startled her.

"About what?" Barre asked.

"During the war. The anti-Commonwealth forces developed viruses that targeted AIs. Figured out a way to sneak them in ansible packets. They burned out a ton of computers before Commonwealth programmers figured out how to stop it."

Well, that explained the damage to the computer. But it still didn't tell them what happened to the bridge. "Barre, go through every single log. See if there's anything in them we can use."

"What are you going to do?"

"Make sure when the AI wakes all the way up, we don't also resurrect the virus."

Chapter 27

Nomi winced as her coffee overfilled, scalding her hand. Leaving the steaming cup at the coffee station, she grabbed a cup of ice water and submerged the burn in it. "Baka tare," she muttered, falling back on the old Japanese curse words she learned as a child from her great-grandmother. She wasn't sure if she were referring to herself or Alain Maldonado, though they both would qualify as utter idiots.

Nomi frowned. The cold water numbed her fingers, dulling the pain. If it got any worse, she would have to find Medical and get some analgesic. She slammed a top on the coffee, and headed to comms, the throbbing in her hand a living reminder of Maldonado's presence.

Silent crew members gave her cautious nods. The door to the communications room opened and it looked like a clone of the station's. Nomi exhaled. Thank the cosmos for small favors. As she walked into the softly lit workspace, the four staff there turned to look at her. She had to force herself not to retreat.

"Ensign Konomi Nakamura, from Daedalus, reporting for

duty." Not that they didn't know who she was or where she'd been assigned from.

A tall, ebony-skinned woman pushed back from the main console, and stood. She had the stripes for lieutenant on her immaculately creased blue-and-black uniform. Everything about her was angular, from the line of her skull revealed beneath her shaved head to her sharp cheekbones and lanky limbs. "Welcome aboard. I'm Lieutenant Odoyo. Take position three and relieve Jenkins. I assume you're familiar with executing a search pattern?" She lifted a single eyebrow in a high arch and stared down at Nomi. This was a woman used to using her height to intimidate.

Nomi stood at attention. "Yes, sir." Her voice echoed in the close room and she thought she sounded like some eager recruit. Odoyo's lips twitched into a brief smile.

Jenkins, another ensign, vacated his station, giving her a curious glance. She sat down and slipped the headset over her ears as the still-warm seat quickly molded to her body. It took her a few minutes to orient to the display. Daedalus Station was a relatively fixed point in space. Messages came in from all directions, but converged on their array.

In a moving ship, they had to anticipate and account for the variance. It was hard enough to hit a big stationary target when your transmitter shifted and much harder when both ends of the transmission were mobile.

Nomi's world narrowed down to the pitch and volume of raw ansible signals—her own calibration shots, sent back to her, and relevant network traffic. It was a strange kind of music and she usually found the work soothing, especially during the late-night shift on Daedalus when traffic was sparse in their little pocket of the universe.

Here, surrounded by strangers, Nomi tensed. No one knew for sure if Ro was in control of the ship or even if she was alive. She squeezed her eyes shut briefly, thinking of her. Ro's intensity softened when she slept, giving her face a vulnerability that she would probably hate. When her blond hair had spilled across the pillow, all Nomi had wanted was to let its soft silk slip through her fingers. Sighing, she focused her attention back on the display.

A hand dropped on her shoulder and Nomi jolted upright in the chair. Jenkins stood beside her, grinning broadly.

"You have to pace yourself out here," the thick-set man said, running his hand over his scalp. "Called your name three times."

Nomi shrugged, suddenly aware of the tension in her shoulders and the back of her neck.

"We just do two hour shifts on this kind of job. Two shifts of two on, two off. Otherwise you lose your edge and miss signals."

She pushed the chair away from the console and stood, stretching. Jenkins plopped down in the chair and grabbed the headset.

In search of some real food and more coffee, Nomi headed back to the mess. Filled tables and loud conversations made the room ring with noise. After the focused quiet of comms, Nomi wasn't in the mood for company, but there wasn't a place to sit in her cramped quarters. Sighing, she threaded her way through the room to an empty chair at a corner table. Two crew members leaned close to one another, deep in a very intense conversation.

They waved her into the free seat and turned back to a discussion of some arcane point in fluid dynamics. Shaking her head, she set down her tray. Engineers. She ate quickly, suddenly nostalgic for her lonely night shifts and missing Ro.

Ro had to be all right. The engineer was just too smart and too stubborn not to be. Flipping through her micro's display, Nomi checked for any messages from her family. Anything sent to Daedalus would follow her here as soon as they hit the range of the nearest ansible. Her brother had sent her his latest vid.

She paused, her hand hovering over the waiting message.

If the Hephaestus was searching for Ro in this sector, they must have some reasonable suspicion the ship hadn't traveled all that far. And Ro had hacked into Nomi's micro. She looked up at the two engineers still in intense discussion at the table and smiled, bending forward to compose a message. With any luck—though she was starting to think it was all planning with Ro—that message would find its way through a few ansible pings straight to her micro. Even the thought of Maldonado on board Hephaestus couldn't sour her mood.

*

Ro sat cross-legged on the acceleration mat, staring down at her micro. Her lank hair swung forward and she tucked it behind her ears, trying not to think of how good a shower would feel. What could she possibly have that would detect and disinfect a forty-year-old virus? And if she were even able to string some program together, how would the AI react?

"Here. You need this."

Micah stood over her looking just as neat and as composed as if he were headed into a news conference with his father. Then she looked at his eyes and the dark circles that bruised the skin beneath them. They hadn't had more than a few hours of broken sleep and ration bars in too many hours.

He handed her another bar and a drinking bulb full of water.

"Thank you." Ro would never have thought to make sure they were all eating and drinking. So who really was the self-centered one?

Nibbling on the ration bar was like chewing on lightly salted and sweetened insulation. She'd be ready to abandon ship even to the most crooked salver after a few more meals like this one. *Focus, Ro, focus.* She dug through her programming tool box again. Whatever she put together, it had to be old school and dead simple. Any complex code seemed to make the AI choke and then lock itself into threat mode.

She set down her micro and pushed herself to standing. Walking around gave her a chance to stretch her spine and roll her shoulders.

"If it helps," Micah said, "I remember the virus targeted the personality subroutines. It left the basic ship's functions intact, so the crews never knew what hit them until it was too late and the AI would basically go crazy. A lot of them just self-destructed, or crashed into other ships."

Ro glared at him.

"My mom and I were both history buffs. I think she always wanted me to follow in my dad's footsteps." He looked off into the distance, seeing something far beyond the ship or even the stars in the display. "At least until everything went to shit for him. For all of us."

"I'm sorry."

"I'm not." He met her gaze straight on, an unfamiliar anger burning in his eyes. "I need some air."

She watched as he strode out of the bridge, his long legs

moving quickly. Sighing, she returned to her makeshift base of operations, a half-eaten ration bar waiting beside her micro. So the virus spared the autonomic centers of the computer's brain. Well, Ro knew she could access the environmentals, no problem. And Dauber and May's SIREN code just curled around that basic machine language, much the same way a human cerebral cortex wound around the older reptilian brain structures and integrated with them.

Introducing something through the environmentals could work, should work. Though that code was even older than the SIREN programming, it was still the building block of her micro and every other piece of machinery in use today, from the ansibles to the current generation of AIs.

She opened her toolbox and snapped together a bunch of basic debugging and anti-virus tools into something that should be able to scan the computer for anything that didn't belong. "Barre?"

The lanky musician glanced up at her from where he'd been sitting at Jem's side.

"If I wrote a small auto-run command, could you translate it into your music?"

He squeezed Jem's hand before joining her across the room. "Show me what you've got."

She quickly coded the program and slid her micro over to him.

"Hang on." He looked up and away, triggering the neural, and hummed quietly to himself as Ro drummed her fingers on her knee.

Come on, come on, she urged him silently, annoyed because he just looked like he was daydreaming. It was probably what she looked like when she was coding.

"Got it," Barre said suddenly, startling her. "Here."

The program spooled into her micro as a small sound file. She saw where he'd left a hook for her to attach her scan and her estimation of him went up a few more notches. "You're a lot better at this than I thought."

Barre glanced at her sharply, then twisted his lips into a wry smile. "I get that a lot." He paused. "Or I would, if anyone cared about what I did."

Her father's usual tact, right out of her mouth. "Sorry, that's not what I meant."

"I know."

"Time to get this going." She frowned, looking around the bridge. Micah still hadn't returned. He didn't need to be there, but she didn't want him wandering around the ship if it reacted with another wild burn. She buzzed his micro. "Micah—let me know when you're secure. We're ready to start the scan."

"I'm fine. Go."

Family shit wasn't anything she could help him with. "Barre?"

"Ready."

"Here we go," Ro said. She keyed the musical shell, her diagnostics wrapped within it. It was the best she could do. When she glanced at Barre, his intense brown eyes were filled with doubts. "Will you monitor the AI?"

"Already on it."

If anything changed, it might give them some advance warning. Unless the AI decided to act first and sing later. Either way, if the ship spooked and ran again, their chances of rescue diminished from remote to likely impossible. She risked a brief glance at Jem before returning to stare at the code scrolling on her micro. The minutes passed. Nothing happened. Ro squeezed her fists so tightly, her short fingernails left deep indents in both palms.

What if she chose wrong? What if the scan itself triggered a defensive response? What if the AI was just too damaged to completely resurrect itself? "Barre?"

He shook his head, the 'not now' message perfectly clear. It only increased the cold tide of nausea in her stomach. An alarm squawked through the micro's small speaker and Ro jerked her head. A sharp pain stabbed her lip where she bit it. "Shit."

"What's wrong?" Barre asked, his voice tight, breathless.

She studied the error messages piling up in a separate window from the scrolling diagnostic code. Closing her eyes briefly, she offered up a prayer to the programming gods in general and to Dauber and May in particular.

When she opened her eyes again to look at the error messages, she decided there had to be a special place in hell for whoever had constructed the virus that downed the AI. Much of the virus had attacked one specific part of the personality subroutine—the decision making algorithms. The code in the error-checking and hierarchical-reasoning centers looked like Swiss cheese.

"Huh." That didn't make a lot of sense. Everything should have been clean after she ran the patches and overrode the damage with fresh source code. Unless her tinkering had reactivated the virus as well. That made things more interesting in ways she didn't need right now. "Keep listening to our friend, here. If the song changes, tell me right away." She didn't even wait for Barre's acknowledgment, but hunched over her micro, her hair falling forward, shutting out the rest of the bridge.

"Where are you hiding?" Ro slowed down the seemingly endless stream of error messages, looking for patterns. She could spend hours disinfecting each sector, one by one, but she suspected that way would trap her in an endless recursive loop.

If Micah was right and the virus had been originally deployed in ansible packets, Ro would have to pick her way through the comms architecture for clues and hope that the AI wouldn't have another freak out.

"Okay, baby, hold still, I'm just taking a look."

Carefully picking her way through the computer's basic architecture, she identified the communications subroutines. Ro wiped her sweaty hands on her pant legs before tweaking the display again, this time looking for the corresponding errors for this part of the code. A self-resurrecting virus had to set its hooks in the registry but it also had to hide somewhere so it would reinitialize after every boot. The blasted thing covered its tracks well. She couldn't believe she hadn't noticed any sign of it.

A slow process, but Ro would have to track each error back to its source for clues. If only Jem could help. It would take too long to train Micah or Barre on what to look for.

She paused and looked up from her micro, her hair swinging away from her face, and blinked in the suddenly bright room. Could it be that simple?

"All quiet," Barre said. "Anything?"

"Maybe," Ro answered and returned to the blinking display. She went back into the file system, searching for the hidden caches of old ansible messages that had to be there. It was the only thing that made sense. "All I have to do is find the virus, figure out how to extract it, run a fresh set of scans, and then convince the system to reboot. All without trying to kill us all or self-destruct."

Barre barked out a strangled laugh.

"Easy, right?" She set her search parameters to look through all the hidden, temp, and system files. "I know you're in there," she muttered. The micro beeped once and a list of suspect ansible files blinked on the display. "Ha! Knew it." The system kept a hidden backup for ansible traffic. The poor bastards. Every time they thought they cleared the system and rebooted, the message would trigger as new and reinfect the AI.

She paused, frowning at the file list.

"What are you waiting for?" Barre asked.

The question was, how sophisticated was the virus? If she were coding something like this, Ro would have added a fail-safe against direct extraction. Her stomach knotted up, a combination of the ration bars, fatigue, and paranoia.

"Ro?"

"I'm on it," she said, her hands trembling as she manually purged the suspect files. A minute crawled by and then another without any kind of response from the AI. It didn't calm her stomach down one bit. "Rescanning now," she said. This time, she set the diagnostics to obliterate any questionable files and to quarantine the damaged sectors.

The micro beeped again, and Ro jumped, nearly fumbling the device. She clutched it tightly as her pulse slowed down to something approaching normal. She did it. No, she corrected herself, looking up at Barre, they'd done it.

"Now, can you convince our patient to reboot?" She forced a light tone in her voice as a cold sweat chilled her arms.

"I think so." Barre had that faraway look in his gaze again.

She shivered.

The seconds crawled by as she sat, unable to do anything but imagine scenario after scenario that ended with the damaged ship crashing them into an asteroid or flying them into a star or through an unstable worm hole.

There was nothing more Ro could do now, except wait and trust in Barre to work his musical magic.

"Done," he said.

Her hands shook as she set the SIREN source code to deploy once more. While the patches ran, she stood and stretched, her whole body stiff from hunching over her micro for far too long. Her eyes felt gritty and dry and she'd probably trade the ship and her accidental crew mates for a hot shower and a real meal.

"She's coming back on line," Barre said.

"She?"

He shrugged. "The voice feels feminine."

"Incoming ansible transmission. Text only. Stand by."

Ro turned quickly toward the sound and slammed her hip into the comms console.

"Holy shit, it worked!" Barre shouted.

The door to the bridge slid open and Micah raced inside, breathing quickly, his face red.

The AI's voice did have a definitely feminine timbre to it. Still a synthesized voice, but it had a lot less hesitation and clipping than before. Ro exhaled, letting her shoulders relax. They did it. They really did it.

"Ansible transmission complete. Downloading now."

Downloading? Ro looked down at the comms console, but the display was dark and not likely to ever work again, given the burn scars across it. The main forward display still showed the unfamiliar stars.

"Hey. Look," Barre said, pointing to her micro. He glanced down at it, shook his head, and looked up. "It's for you."

She frowned, her eyebrows drawing together. "What?" He leaned over to pick it up and handed it to her. Shrugging at the absurdity of getting ansible traffic when she didn't even know where in the cosmos she was, she looked at the display. The pulse pounded in her ears and the soft sounds of the bridge disappeared. A short, plain text message spooled over and over across the small screen, but Ro saw a delicate, round face, framed by smooth back hair, eyes filled with laughter and curiosity and a wholly undeserved, unexpected kindness.

Nomi.

Chapter 28

"SON OF A BITCH," Micah said, staring at Ro. "What the hell's your father doing there?"

Ro stood, her hands on her waist. "Well, it's certainly not rescuing me. I'll give you one guess."

Micah knew someone would come after them for their cargo. Part of him hoped it would have been his father. That way he could confront the bastard himself.

"Look, I have as many family issues as the next guy." Barre glanced at each of them before shrugging. "But we have to get Jem to a real med-fac. That ship can't be too far away. Send a new signal. Tell Nomi to trace it back to us."

At least Barre had a family to have issues with. Micah just had the senator. Sometimes it was easier to think of him as that than his father.

"It's not that simple, Barre," Ro said. She ran her fingers through the tangles in her hair. "I still don't know how the AI will react."

The cargo hold full of illegal weapons under counterfeit diplomatic seal was enough evidence to send someone to prison for a long and unhappy life sentence. Micah needed to make sure that someone wasn't going to be him.

"It is simple." Barre looked at his injured brother and back to Ro. "If we do nothing, there's a good chance we'll all die." A muscle jumped in his jaw. "That Jem will die."

"And if we can't get control of the ship?" Ro asked. "Then what?"

Barre squared his shoulders. "I'm not going to let that happen."

Micah wasn't sure if he meant the ship, or his brother.

Ro tapped her fingers across her micro's display, her lips pressed together. "If we get boarded, it would be best if we didn't have a bittergreen farm on board."

Part of him knew it would come to this. At least he'd be able to save his data. "Barre, I could use your help."

"I don't want to leave Jem again."

"I'll watch him." Ro gestured down to her makeshift cast. "I'm not running anywhere fast."

Barre followed Micah out of the bridge. Was this strange reluctance about his brother or about the bittergreen?

"Look," he said, as they stepped inside Micah's shared lab space. "I'm in no place to judge, but dealing this stuff is stupid. The last thing we need is to get into a bittergreen turf war. If it's you versus the cartel, well, I know nothing is going to save you— not your charm, not your father's political connections, nothing."

Micah stopped short and Barre nearly bumped into him. "Is that what you think? That I'm a dealer?" He held back a laugh and it emerged as a strangled snort. He walked through his field-airlock and into his living laboratory. "We need to toss the plants and break down the trays, the hangers, and the light stands. We can let the ship recycle the biomass. As for the equipment, it's standard hydroponics. Not unusual to find on this class ship." He turned to face the airlock again.

"Wait, where are you going?"

"I need to encrypt the remaining data to my micro, then eliminate any breadcrumbs."

It just about killed Micah to trash a lab full of healthy, thriving plants. Damn it, but he was so close. If he'd had another few weeks for this crop to set its flowers, then he could have collected the pollen and waited for the seed heads to form. But they didn't have weeks. It wasn't Ro's fault. Even if she hadn't been messing with the AI, he wouldn't have had the time he needed.

Following his instructions, Barre tore the leggy plants from their perfectly controlled environment. Turning his back on the little biosphere he'd set up, Micah started to collect any equipment that might betray the work he'd been doing. The notes and files would be next.

It was easier to just start cleaning and breaking down the assay hardware than brood on the loss. A thorough wiping with ethyl alcohol and formalin would obliterate any evidence of biologicals. Once the bittergreen was disposed of, the rest of the contents of his lab shouldn't raise suspicions, given Mendez's approval and his registered course load. He could try again.

Barre emerged through the now useless airlock with a large tub filled with dejected looking bittergreen. The lab had the abandoned look of old storage. "Thank you." Micah set the nozzles to spray a fine mist of his decontamination mixture. "There's what looks like a working recycler in the mess. We can try it. If it doesn't run, we can just jettison the stuff, I suppose."

Barre shared his rueful smile. "Seems like a huge waste."

"Not worth the risk. Come on." The decon cycle would be done by the time they finished with the bittergreen and he could dismantle the rest of the hydroponics setup. Then it would be done and far more of a waste than Barre would ever know.

*

Nomi nearly fell out of her seat when her micro buzzed for an incoming text.

<u>Sorry about breakfast. I guess I owe you one.</u>

She blinked back tears and glanced around the crowded mess hall, making sure nobody noticed, before staring down at the small display. A blinking dot replaced the words. Nomi's heart knocked against her chest as the transmission continued.

<u>Likely more than one. Had some static here, but we're mostly five by five now. Could use a tow home, but can't id where we are.</u>

What did the "mostly" refer to? She nibbled on the edge of her lower lip, a thousand questions for Ro bubbling through her mind, but with the vagaries of ship-to-ship ansible communication, she'd have to make do with this disjointed, asynchronous conversation.

Ro was alive. She wanted to jump up and shout, but this wasn't the time or place.

<u>Don't trust my father. Stay away from him! Promise me.</u>

It was sweet that Ro was trying to protect her, but Nomi needed to keep an eye on him for both their sakes.

<u>Going to send out another broadcast if we can. Keep an ear</u>

out for us. We're counting on you. Over.

She stared at her micro for a moment more, even though she knew that was the end of the transmission. At least they had this ansible version of a message-in-a-bottle. If Ro were here, she'd probably be able to track her own message back using a piece of wire and an empty cup.

Now that was an interesting thought. Nomi drew her eyebrows together. It might be possible to track the ansible path it had taken, even if the ship had moved since. If nothing else, it would narrow down the search area.

She rested her fingers back on the small virtual input. What should she write back? How long would it take for Ro to get her response? And more importantly, how could she use Hephaestus's resources to sniff out the message path without raising questions? One thing at a time. She smiled and started writing.

Her table mates stood to leave. She glanced at the big clock in the mess. It was still nearly an hour until she could report to comms for her next shift. If she showed early, she'd have some explaining to do. Pushing back from the table, Nomi tossed her tray into the recycler, and wondered how she was going to kill the next forty-two minutes. She opened the ship's schematics, looking for a common space. Even on a ship this small, there had to be somewhere for the crew to blow off steam. A twenty minute run would clear her mind and still leave enough time for a cleansing cycle. Then she and her uniform would be ready for duty again.

"Nakamura!"

Nomi stiffened. Alain Maldonado's deep voice reverberated in the corridor. She glanced quickly fore and aft, but for the moment, they were alone. She turned to him, holding herself in a ready stance, though she wasn't sure what she was getting ready for. He stepped closer.

"Maldonado," she acknowledged, standing her ground and staring up into his face.

"I'm not stupid," he said, his eyes, the same shape and color as Ro's, filled with suspicion.

"Sir?" Her mouth dried. Despite his poor service record, he did outrank her and she knew it would be better if she didn't antagonize him.

He took a step closer. "She may be the better hacker now, but much of what she knows, she learned from me."

Maldonado's eyes were bloodshot and, judging by the stubble, he hadn't cleaned up since Ro blasted off with the ship. To anyone else, he might even look the part of the worried father.

"Shall I tell Targill that I intercepted an encrypted tunneled transmission?"

The warmth leached from Nomi's face. Maldonado backed her against a cabin door. The hard, smooth surface pressed into her spine and transmitted its chill through her uniform. Goosebumps broke out along her arms.

"A transmission I traced back to your micro?"

The ship had a small crew, but surely someone had to come down this hallway. And then what? It wasn't as if she had any allies on Hephaestus. Even if she did, what could she tell them without incriminating herself?

"What do you want?" She hated that her voice shook. She hated the flash of triumph that lit his eyes.

"The same as you. To find that ship."

"What about Ro? Don't you care about your own daughter?"

Loud footsteps echoed from down the corridor. Maldonado turned to lean against the wall beside the cabin door. Anyone coming would just see two station-mates having a quiet conversation.

"If you're worried about her, know this. Her best path to safety is to get off that ship as soon as possible. Better I should be the one to extract her than some others with a vested interest in it."

He must be talking about Rotherwood. What did they want with the ship? It couldn't just be the bittergreen. Sure, there was money in it, but to risk going against the military or to challenge the cartel? That was pure crazy. "What's on the ship, Maldonado?"

He leaned forward until his face was centimeters from hers. She shook in silent fury. Ro's words echoed in her mind: *Don't trust my father. Stay away from him! Promise me.*

"Trust me. Some questions are dangerous to ask."

His breath heated the skin on her face. Nomi stiffened her spine and glared at him. Maldonado likely outweighed her by thirty-five kilos, most of it muscle, but there were ways to fight against much stronger and larger opponents. If he touched her, she would hurt him, superior officer or no.

"I'm counting on you, Konomi. Her life is in your hands."

For now, she forced herself to keep still. Let him think she had backed down. Let him think she was afraid of him.

She watched him walk down the corridor and shivered.

She was afraid. Not for herself, but for Ro.

Chapter 29

Ro looked up as Micah and Barre came back to the bridge. "All set?"

Micah nodded as Barre hurried to check on his brother.

It wasn't as if she was totally useless, but Barre was the one with medical training.

"Whatever you're going to do, you need to do now," he said. "Jem's not going to just get better on his own."

"I know. I'm not stupid," she said. "And I'm worried about him, too." It would be better for all of them if she could just establish full control of the damned ship and fly Jem back to Daedalus. Then they wouldn't risk getting tangled up with the military or have to worry about the cargo. She glanced at Micah, but he wouldn't meet her gaze.

"Okay. I suggest we do a systems check and make sure we have access to all the ship's functions before we do anything."

Micah did turn to her then and raised a single eyebrow. "Wow. The new and improved Ro."

"You're an idiot," she said. But he was right and it wasn't only because of Jem. Nothing in this whole excursion had turned out the way she'd planned. If she was being honest with herself, she hadn't planned any of it. She surveyed her unintentional crew, not sure she would have managed this far without them.

Micah opened his mouth to reply, but Ro cut him off. "Fine. I'm an idiot. But this is what this idiot wants to do." She started tapping on her micro. "I'm going to set up a system-wide diagnostic, section by section, starting with communications all the way through sensors."

"Why don't you just ask her?" Barre said, flicking his gaze between something in the distance only he could see and the rest of them on the bridge.

"Huh?"

"The AI. She's awake and listening to us."

As much as Ro worked with complex computer systems, she rarely assigned them gender. "And does 'she' have a name?"

Barre's eye defocused again for a moment. "Well, the ship's name was Halcyone, so that should do for the AI as well."

Micah snorted. "Halcyone? Really? The avatar of calm winds and smooth sailing?" He laughed until he started coughing, the sound like a high-pitched bark.

"Yeah, I get it. Irony. Here, take a drink." She passed a water bulb his way before turning to face one of the AI's speakers. "Okay. Halcyone, we need to perform a systems check."

"Please state authorization for system level access."

The voice seemed smug and more than a little resentful. Ro always knew that programming AIs with strong personalities had been a mistake. "Maldonado, Ro, Daedalus Station, engineering." Her idents were coded into her micro, which was still connected to the computer.

"Access denied."

"Stupid machine," she muttered, and turned to her micro and the diagnostic hack she had started to set up.

"No, wait," Barre said.

"Excuse me?"

"Just a minute. Just wait." He tapped the side of his temple where his neural had been inserted. "I have another idea."

With enough time she knew she could brute-force her way in, but she paused, her hands stilled. Maybe this was the new and improved Ro. Certainly her father wouldn't recognize her anymore.

"Try it now," Barre said.

She frowned at him, but he didn't explain. "Okay, I'll bite. Halcyone, initiate systems-level diagnostic, authorization Maldonado, Ro, engineer, Daedalus station."

Soft tones played through the bridge—a brief fanfare that did sound a little like a command. The room fell silent. Ro gave it another minute before shrugging and turning to her micro.

The AI played the fanfare back, slightly shifted in tone and speed.

"Maldonado, Ro, proceed."

"Nice," Micah said.

"How'd you do that?" Ro asked.

Barre took a step back and Ro realized how harsh her tone had been.

"I figured she listened to music before, so I set up a translation algorithm on my neural, and had it push the result through the speakers."

"So now what?"

"What do you mean? Just run your diagnostic, or whatever you need to do."

"And it all goes through you?"

"Well, through the algorithm."

"Which conveniently is located on your neural."

Barre glanced back at his brother. "We're wasting time."

"Fine." Ro clenched her teeth. For now, they didn't have much choice, but she was certain there had to be a way to establish primary control over the AI. She blew her breath out in a rush and rolled her shoulders. "Halcyone, run communications diagnostic."

A brief flurry of notes filled the bridge and faded away. "Communications functioning at 92%. Dead sectors report available. Select verbal or visual display."

"Visual. Pass it through to my micro."

One tone echoed through the air. "Report complete."

Ro frowned at Barre before focusing on the AI. "Halcyone, run diagnostics for the following systems in order. Life support, navigation, propulsion: interstitial drive, propulsion: jump drive, sensors: internal, sensors: external. Push visual reports only. Verbal status every five minutes. Acknowledge."

The instrumental piece played longer this time before the slightly hesitant voice returned. "Diagnostics running. Life support in progress. 40% complete."

She wanted to wipe the smug smile off Barre's face. "This is likely to take a little time." She held up her hand to keep him from snapping at her. "I know, we don't have unlimited time, but I also can't see putting Jem in more danger."

He glared at her, before turning away. "Fine."

"We should probably get some rest. I'll babysit the diagnostics for a bit."

Shrugging, Micah flopped down on one of the acceleration

mats. Barre curled up near Jem without another word.

Ro sat leaning her back against a console and cracked her stiff neck before picking up her micro. The virus had left behind some damage in comms. Nothing critical, nothing that should prevent them sending out a broadcast, but little on this ship worked the way it should.

A chime reverberated through the bridge. "Life support functioning at 76%. Within acceptable parameters for minimal crew. Proceeding to navigation."

That was better than she expected, given the age of the ship. She scrolled though the extended report. Air and water reserves looked good. The scrubbers had a few thousand hours of life left before they needed to be replaced. That surprised Ro. The ship must not have been in active service for long.

The mystery of the bridge nagged at her. There was no sign of forced entry or external combat. It looked like someone's attempt to destroy all the consoles from inside the bridge itself.

Ro navigated her way back to the files they nabbed earlier. They had more audio files to play. Maybe some of them held clues. She tossed the most recent of the files over to Barre's micro and waited as his conversion and enhancement program churned. The crackle of static burst through the quiet bridge.

"Shit!" Barre bolted upright and banged his head on the underside of one of the consoles. "You could have asked."

"Same old Ro," Micah said, rubbing his eyes.

She glared at both of them, trying to think of the perfect comeback when a babble of voices blared from Barre's micro.

"... *not responding! Interstitial engines off ... collision course.*"

Another burst of static turned everything to gibberish.

"... *locked me out, Captain ... . day, mayday, mayday, this is transport vessel ....*"

"*Jesus, Merryweather is down. Halcyone's gone crazy.*"

The collision alarms in the background of the recording echoed through the bridge and sent chills down Ro's spine.

"*Abandon ship! Get to the life ...*"

The crackle of an energy weapon discharging was no different today than forty years ago. Ro flinched, imagining the panicked shooting, the chaos, as the ship hurtled closer and closer to the asteroid.

"*Harris! Stand down! ... going to get us all ...* "

"*... want to die,*" came the high-pitched reply. Ro filled in the "I don't" that she knew had to be missing.

More weapons fire burst through the bridge and the recording stopped.

"Shit." Barre's face had turned ashen.

"Well," Ro said, trying to keep her voice level, "now we know what trashed the bridge."

"Poor bastards," Micah said.

"Do you think any of them made it?" Barre asked, standing and looking around with wide eyes.

"I don't know," Ro said. "The ship landed pretty much intact, so someone had to have gotten control before the crash."

"Someone or something?" Micah asked.

That was a good question. "Someone cleaned up in here." She surveyed the damage. "At least the bodies."

"That's a lovely image, thanks," Barre said, grimacing.

Ro looked up at her companions and all the warmth leached out of her face. The AI could have killed them all. Ro could have killed them all.

"Navigation report complete."

Halcyone's flat voice filled the bridge. "Interstitial engines functioning at thirty-seven percent. Radiation levels in engineering eighteen percent above ALARA."

As Low As Reasonably Achievable was never a fixed target. Those levels were probably solid for nuke tech forty years ago. They were high compared to a modern ship. They'd have to monitor it if they were going to be aboard for any length of time or if she had to work directly in the engineering compartment. The radiation would only be a problem if the AI didn't actively kill them in some other way first.

"So now what?" Micah said. Ro figured he wasn't talking about the nav report.

Barre took a step closer to her. "We call for help."

She wanted to find a way to argue with him. This was her project, her freedom, her ticket out of dead-end Daedalus. She looked down at Jem, watching his chest rise and fall in a slow, shallow rhythm. Blinking her eyes clear, she looked away.

"Jump drive off line. Worm hole mapping functions off line."

"Ro—we have to call for help," Barre repeated, his deep voice thick with worry.

"I know." The memory of the doomed crew's conversation echoed around them in the silence. "Can you keep the AI from going all fight or flight? Because otherwise, I'm not putting a peep through the ansible." Without navigation, if the AI spooked again, they could end up within spitting distance of Daedalus and never know it.

Barre didn't answer.

Micah tapped his fingers across a melted console.

"Internal sensors fully functional." The AI continued through its diagnostic, oblivious to the undercurrents of emotion in the bridge.

"Barre?" Ro asked.

"Send your signal. I'll manage Halcyone."

Part of her had to bite back the question she wanted to ask: *Are you sure?* Of course he wasn't sure. It was a forty-odd-year-old half-demented AI, hauling around a ship that should have been consigned to the scrapyard decades ago. Hell, if he were sure, she wouldn't trust him.

"Okay, then. Time to make some noise."

Chapter 30

Nᴏᴍɪ sᴡᴇᴘᴛ ɪɴᴛᴏ comms, the click of her boot heels and her rapid footfalls the only outward sign of her anger. As soon as she relieved Jenkins, her focus lasered back to finding Ro. She slid her micro under the console, resting it on her thighs as she dug into the program Ro had left her.

"Ensign Nakamura?"

Nomi froze, her hands jerking from the micro and slamming into the underside of the comms console.

Lieutenant Odoyo stood behind her, leaning over Nomi's chair. "A word, please."

She swallowed hard. The other staff glanced her way briefly before returning to their silent work. Odoyo stepped back. "Follow me."

Swallowing hard, Nomi palmed her micro and slid it back into the pocket of her tunic before pushing away from her borrowed work station. "Yes, sir." Her voice wavered.

Odoyo led her into a small alcove on the far side of the communications room. The door sealed behind her and she stood at attention, hands still at her sides, eyes front, waiting for the lieutenant to lay into her. The sound wouldn't leave this room, but transparent walls let everyone know exactly who was being dressed down.

"Something wrong with our interface?" Odoyo's voice was dangerously calm. Her still, composed face gave nothing away, but her dark-eyed stare made Nomi want to crawl under a desk.

"No, sir."

"Then explain yourself."

Nomi met Odoyo's gaze with her own, hoping it seemed as direct. Standing in a confined space in the shadow of this imposing woman, Nomi regretted her impulse to channel Ro quite so fully. "I had an idea that might allow us to narrow down the ship's location to a single ansible sector."

Odoyo leaned forward and waited.

Even as Nomi's discomfort increased, she was impressed by the lieutenant's ability to intimidate with the slightest of motions. The silence lengthened as she considered how much to tell the lieutenant.

"I received a private communication from Rosalen Maldonado, sir. I believe I can trace its path back through the ansible network and find the satellite that first pinged it. However, I didn't want to use resources already allocated through Hephaestus until I had the chance to test my theory."

"A private communication."

Her cheeks heated up again. "Yes, sir."

Odoyo held out her hand and waited.

Nomi clenched her jaw and reached for her micro, unlocking it before handing it over to the lieutenant.

The woman scanned it slowly, as if the message were pages long instead of a few short lines. Her lips pressed together briefly. "Her father. Alain Maldonado."

"Yes, sir," Nomi said.

"So presumably, she knows you're aboard."

Nomi blinked at the change in subject. "Yes, sir."

Odoyo handed Nomi her micro. She reached for it, a tiny tremor betraying her eagerness to get it and her only link to Ro back.

"Upload what you have to a virtual machine on Hephaestus's network. I'll reallocate half the consoles to your search."

Nomi rocked back on her heels, nearly stepping out of position.

"If you succeed, we will consider your security breach simply a matter of misplaced enthusiasm for duty."

Odoyo didn't have to tell her what would happen if this didn't work.

"Dismissed."

Nomi saluted and spun on her heel before fleeing the overly exposed room. By the time she'd returned to her console, everyone in the room had stopped their work to stare at her. Some were openly curious. Others, she would have sworn, were a little disappointed. She set her micro down on the console and paired it with the ship's AI.

"Interesting," a quiet voice said from beside her.

Nomi swiveled in her chair and stared up at Jenkins, confused. Two hours hadn't nearly passed. "I thought you were off shift."

"Odoyo pulled all of us back to see if we could piggyback on what you're doing."

"Oh." Nomi scanned the comms center. Every work station had several crew crammed into it.

"As soon as you tell us where to listen, there won't be a micron of that sector we can't cover."

Now if she failed, she would fail spectacularly and publicly. And succeed or fail, Maldonado would certainly find out what she'd been trying. Nomi pulled her hands through her short hair.

"Okay. Since you're standing there, you may as well help."

"You're the boss, Nakamura."

"Can you pull up a list of ansible node-idents?"

"Sure," Jenkins said, "But you're going to drown in data."

"How about just the sector headers?"

"Easy."

"Can you display them in 3-d map mode? But only the sector headers." The first ansibles didn't have the ping-back and error correction they had now and messages used to get increasingly garbled in transit. Nomi remembered playing "ansible" as a child. No matter what message they started with, it always ended in gibberish and peals of laughter.

Jenkins leaned over and manipulated what looked like a web of stars strung across the reaches of space until ansible clusters collapsed in on themselves, a short string of alphanumeric characters next to each one.

"Good. Thank you." Nomi turned to her familiar micro, now controlling a small virtual machine through Hephaestus. The interface looked just like it had when Ro's message first pinged through, but her little program was now supported by the full processing speed and power of the ship's AI.

Nomi sifted through the utilities on her micro, looking for a basic code parser. If she could isolate the headers and the appended idents, she should be able to track back to the ansible that had originally routed Ro's message.

It didn't take long for the AI to spit out a reverse chronological list of sectors the message had bounced through. That was too easy. Wouldn't Ro have deliberately masked the idents or randomized the path somehow? Nomi shook her head, infected by Alain Maldonado's mistrust and paranoia.

"What have you got?" Jenkins asked, breaking through her distracted thoughts.

"Give me a minute." Nomi stared at the disarticulated message, isolating the content from the context. "Here. Can you map them?"

"Got it."

Nomi tapped her fingers against the console as she stared at the map, willing the random strings of numbers and letters to resolve into a coherent path.

"Done."

A sector on the upper left side of the display brightened. The map zoomed in and re-centered. The light stuttered several times before rotating and shifting again. Nomi blinked and the display stabilized, showing a drunkard's walk between a half dozen ansibles. Smiling, she traced it back to the first stop and touched her index finger to a single node. It zoomed in again, automatically. "There!" she said. Her map propagated to every console in comms. The room burst into a frenzy of activity.

"Ro, we're coming to find you," she whispered.

*

Micah paced in the small clear area in front of the bridge door as Ro and Barre sat with their heads nearly touching, bent over a single micro, his dark dreads mingling with her light hair. He hated having nothing useful to do. It reminded him too much of the hours he spent waiting while his mother lay dying.

All he could think of now was how his father had betrayed them all.

A bright burst of static crackled through the bridge.

"Ow!"

"Shit!"

Ro and Barre swore, each rubbing their forehead from where they had banged into one another.

"We have an incoming transmission!" Ro said.

Micah stopped pacing and grabbed onto a handhold set into the wall. Even with Barre to pacify the crazy AI, he wasn't going to trust that it wouldn't jump them to cosmos knows where just for spite.

The engines rumbled beneath him. Micah gripped the handhold harder.

"Barre!" Ro shouted.

"I'm on it."

More of his discordant music filled the bridge, merging with the static, changing it from white noise to something at the edge of Micah's perception. It scratched down his spine like a jagged fingernail. The drone of the interstitial engines added an angry whine to the symphony.

As the ship shook, Micah let go and slid to the floor and clasped his hands over his ears. If they were going to die out here, at least he could shut out the noise. If they were going to die out here, then he was no longer responsible for his father.

The thought brought him a strange mixture of relief and regret.

The bridge fell silent and still, the absence of sound a new kind of pressure against Micah's skull.

Barre jumped up and punched the air. "Yes!"

"... ship Hephaestus. Hold your position. We are en route to your last established ansible coordinates."

The message ended. Micah swept his gaze across the bridge, not sure he could risk believing in the possibility of rescue. Ro stared into the ruined forward screen, her eyes narrowed, her lips pursed. A huge grin stretched across Barre's face.

The deep voice boomed through the bridge again. "Transport vessel Halcyone, this is the Commonwealth ship Hephaestus. Hold your position. We are en route to your last established ansible coordinates."

All three of them waited, not wanting to break the spell the looped message cast. When it started its third repeat, Ro turned to Barre. "Tell the idiot AI we're not deaf."

Barre smirked at her before staring off into space for a minute, doing his music thing.

"I'm going to reply." She glanced at each of them. "Anyone have any problem with that?"

"Hell no," Barre said.

Micah shook his head. If they could transmit, then some new possibilities presented themselves.

"Commonwealth ship Hephaestus, this is Ro Maldonado on transport vessel Halcyone. We are currently adrift. Navigation is non-functional. All other systems stable. There are a total of four crew members aboard. One in need of urgent medical assist. We await your arrival. Maldonado out."

"Any idea how long it will take for them to get here?" Barre asked, looking down at his unconscious brother.

"No way of knowing how many ansible hops the message will

take. Without current star charts, I can't establish our position. We have to make sure this ship stays put and hope Hephaestus has good navigators."

For Jem's sake, Micah hoped they'd find them soon. And for his own, he just needed enough time to send his own message.

He turned to Ro, trying for an expression that mingled hope and relief. She was the one he had to convince. "Are we done with the homicidal-AI-murders-the-crew part of our adventure?"

She smirked, shaking her head.

Micah smiled back. At least the Rotherwood charm hadn't failed him.

"Yes, I think that portion of our program may be over."

He let his shoulders settle. "If you don't need me here, I should double check the lab. Make sure I didn't forget anything before the folks with the big guns show up."

"We're okay here. I'll buzz you if anything changes."

"Thank you." Micah didn't even look up as he grabbed his micro and left the bridge. He quashed the unexpected and unwelcome pang of guilt that followed and hurried to his former lab.

Now that Ro and Barre had done all the heavy lifting, it was a matter of pairing his micro directly to the ship's communication array without them finding out. He might not be the coding guru that Ro was, but in his years of playing dreadnaught and shuttle with the cartel, he picked up a few tricks.

Besides, Ro wouldn't be looking for him and if he sent simple text with diplomatic headers, it wouldn't use enough bandwidth for her to notice.

Setting up the comms program would be the easy part.

Figuring out how to make sure his father didn't slip out of the net again was another matter. He typed a very careful message.

Chapter 31

Nomi's roommate brushed past her as she stumbled out of her temporary quarters in search of coffee. The short, red-haired woman mumbled something incoherent before collapsing in the lower bunk without bothering to peel off her uniform. Nomi felt a pang of sympathy for third-shifters everywhere.

Clutching her filled mug, she wove her way through the crowded mess, looking for an empty seat. The one advantage to third-shift was the quiet.

"Nakamura!"

She stopped short and swore as hot coffee sloshed onto her fingers from the lid she'd failed to tighten down.

"Over here!"

Jenkins stood and waved from across the room. He pointed to an open seat. Nomi shook the coffee from her hand and joined him. "Any word?" she asked.

"We'll find out soon enough."

Their reassigned shift was set to start in twenty minutes. Jenkins frowned and Nomi felt the back of her neck prickle in warning. A shadow fell over her.

"Good morning, Konomi."

Maldonado's voice sent cold shivers down her spine. She forced herself to pick up her mug and take a slow drink. "Chief Engineer," she said, keeping her voice neutral.

Jenkins frowned and tried to catch her gaze.

"I hear you are the person to thank for establishing contact with my daughter." He placed a hand on her shoulder. Anyone observing them would see it as a friendly gesture. Nomi knew better.

The coffee soured in her stomach.

She reached up and covered his hand with her own and squeezed across his knuckles just hard enough to warn. He lifted his hand from her and stepped back. Smiling, she stood up and gestured to Jenkins. "Well, then I guess we have some work to do."

Maldonado stepped in behind them and followed them from the mess hall. "Commander Targill has given me permission to observe in comms."

"It must be quite a relief to know your daughter is safe," Jenkins said.

"Yes, that ship took off with something very dear to me."

That was an interesting way to phrase it. Nomi wished she could risk looking back at Maldonado. Well, whatever it was, it certainly wasn't Ro. What could possibly be on an abandoned ship worth risking your own daughter for?

The door to comms opened onto a scene of quiet chaos. Odoyo's normally impeccable uniform was rumpled and her eyes were red. "Briefing in one, people," she said, her low voice cutting through the din of scattered conversations.

"Let's make this quick," Odoyo said, rubbing her hand over

her head. "Good work, last night." She nodded at the third-shift crew, still here, running on adrenaline, caffeine, and curiosity. "Hephaestus is closing in on the ansible coordinates where the message originated. The good news is since the ship has remained in the same sector as Daedalus, we don't think it has jump capability. The bad news is we've had to make the trip on interstitial or risk jumping past it."

Nomi's pulse sped up. She had to make contact before the ship arrived.

"Time is of the essence, people. We know at least one of them is injured."

Nomi must have made a questioning noise, because Odoyo held up her hand.

"We don't know who and we don't know how serious. We sent a reply asking for clarification, but haven't received a response. Keep your ears sharp. Any information may make the difference for someone's survival here. Dismissed."

The third-shift officers made way for the first-shift crew. Nomi followed Jenkins to what she was starting to think of as her station and got down to a routine she could have done in her sleep. Except she was listening for Ro and anything involving Rosalen Maldonado seemed to turn into anything but routine.

She could feel the intensity of the elder Maldonado's stare from across the room. As much as she wanted him gone, at least when he was here, he couldn't be snooping into her transmissions. Time flew by as they swept the area around their destination with long range sensors. Other comms personnel listened for passed traffic though the ansibles closest to Hephaestus. Expectant silence filled the room. Nomi wanted to pace, but this wasn't Daedalus and she wasn't alone in comms.

"Need a break?" Jenkins asked.

Nomi rubbed her eyes and removed the headset. "Can you cover me for five?"

"Sure."

Her neck cracked as she stretched first to the right and to the left. She used the movement to find Maldonado. He was talking to Odoyo, his back toward her. Nomi signed off her console, grabbed her micro, and walked from comms. At the door, she risked another look back, but Maldonado hadn't turned. She sagged against the corridor as the door closed and wiped her damp hands on her uniform tunic before taking out her micro.

She typed quickly.

<u>Your father is after something on the ship. Be careful.</u>

Sending it was an act of faith, or at least a race. And even if she did get the warning before Hephaestus got there, what was Ro going to do about it? Nomi straightened her uniform and slipped back into comms.

Maldonado stared at her all the way to her console.

*

Ro wrinkled her nose. A shower would be her first priority, even before she let them examine her ankle. Then maybe something to eat that wasn't an emergency ration bar. She'd even be happy to drink whatever crappy coffee they served on Hephaestus if she could enjoy it with Nomi. But thinking of her slender, dark-haired friend led to her father and the threat he posed, both to Nomi and to the rest of them.

"How do we know Targill can be trusted?" she asked.

Barre looked up from where he sat next to Jem. "What are

you talking about?"

Ro pressed her lips together.

"Look," Barre said, "I'm probably the wrong person to be saying this, but they're here to rescue us, right?"

That part was true enough. But it wasn't the entire truth.

"Ro." Micah stared at her. "You need to tell him."

She glared back and remained silent.

"He deserves to know," Micah said.

"Know what?" Barre asked, his voice a dangerous low rumble.

"Fine. You may as well, it seems like everyone else does." She shrugged off Micah's smirk. "Easier if I can show you." Ro stood up and tested the stability of her cast. The pain was still a distant, small annoyance behind a cool numbness that circled her leg from lower calf to foot. "Come on."

Barre hesitated by Jem's side.

"If you want to know, follow me."

Micah stood up to leave with them.

"You, stay with Jem and monitor comms."

"Aye, aye, Captain." Micah saluted her and sat down next to Jem.

"Fuck you," she said, stomping from the bridge, her cast making satisfying thumps against the floor. Either Barre was behind her or not, but she wasn't going to look back or wait for him.

"Slow down, Ro, you're going to hurt yourself."

Even through the anesthesia, she could feel the pressure against her ankle. She stopped and waited as Barre stepped alongside her.

"I'm sorry," she said.

"What's going on here?"

Ro led him to the storage bay. "You really want to know? There. See for yourself."

*

Micah checked his micro for the thousandth time. No response could mean a few things, but the consequences of each were decidedly different. The diplomatic headers he used could have been terminated, at which point his message would have been rejected at the first ansible. A setback, but potentially not catastrophic. Or the message was delivered but his father could have gotten to Hephaestus's commander, which meant Micah was screwed. Or the ansible network was skipping either his message or Targill's reply like a stone across water and he just had to keep waiting.

At least Halcyone hadn't flipped out over it. The bridge was silent except for the soft sounds of Jem's breathing, barely noticeable over the ship's air handling. He sat down next to the injured boy and didn't like what he saw. Gray circles pouched beneath his closed eyes. The skin on his lips had cracked.

He tore off a piece of his salvaged row cover and soaked it in water. Dripping it over Jem's lips, Micah was relieved to see the boy open his mouth and swallow. He repeated the ritual over and over: Dip, drip, watch.

"Barre?" Jem voice rasped through the bridge. "Barre, I really have to pee."

"It's Micah."

"Where's my brother?" His eyes shifted rapidly back and forth under his closed lids and his breathing quickened.

"He's fine." Micah placed his hand flat on Jem's narrow chest. "It's okay. I can help you."

"I can't keep my eyes open or I'll hurl."

"It's okay," Micah repeated. He had helped his mother like this, at the end, when his father could barely stand to be in the same room as her. Micah helped the nurses and the aides, and then after a while, just did everything for her himself.

But Jem wasn't dying. He couldn't be. He was just a kid.

"Do you need help with your pants?"

"No, but I can't stand."

Micah brought over a beaker. "Okay, you can use this." He guided Jem's hand to the empty vessel. "I'm turning away so you can have some privacy. Just call me if you need anything."

"Thank you."

The familiar, pungent odor of urine brought back his mother's sick room: Vials and tubes of medication lined up in neat rows. The beeping monitors. The intrusive needles.

"Micah?"

"I'm here."

"Can you take the beaker? I'm sorry. I think I spilled."

"No problem, kiddo. I got it covered."

He pulled on gloves from his father's plundered supplies and cleaned up the small puddle on the floor. Jem's urine was dark and cloudy, further signs of dehydration. He'd have to let Barre know. "Do you think you can drink some more?"

But Jem had fallen back asleep, his breathing slow and regular.

His micro vibrated as he tucked the used row cover, the half-full beaker, and his gloves on the far side of the bridge for disposal.

<u>These are serious charges. We will require proof before proceeding.</u>

Between the forged seals and Jem's recording, he could give Targill all the proof he wanted. Let's see his father politic his way out of this one.

<u>Proof in return for immunity, a place at uni, and full-adult status.</u>

Ro would have to make her own arrangements. The senator was the bigger fish here, the one he could dangle in front of Targill and get the biggest concessions. For now, he had done everything he could for Jem and for his mother's memory.

Chapter 32

THEY WALKED BACK to the bridge in silence, Ro simmering in anger over her father. Barre hadn't said a single word since she showed him the weapons cache.

"I didn't know what was inside. I swear it." But even after she found out, even after she understood that her father had manipulated her all along, she still kept working on the ship. She hated how he twisted her around so easily.

"Anything?" she asked Micah, as the door slid open.

"Nothing from Hephaestus," he said, before turning to Barre. "Jem was awake. I gave him some water. Helped him pee."

"Thank you," Barre said, hurrying over to his brother.

Micah looked away.

"So now you know. Does it change anything?" Ro asked.

"No. Not for us." Barre sat next to Jem and squeezed his hand. "Do what you have to do about your father. I don't care as long as my brother gets help."

Ro stared at the floor, letting her hair cover her face.

"Halcyone, this is Hephaestus. We are in ansible range and holding our current position. Do you copy?"

It took Ro a few precious seconds to realize what they meant. She gripped the edges of the nearest console searching for even the slightest vibration that might mean the ship was preparing to flee again.

Barre met her gaze. She tapped her index finger against her forehead. He looked off into the distance, listening to the AI's internal music.

"Nothing. Quiet," Barre said.

Ro exhaled heavily. "Hephaestus, this is Halcyone. We continue to be adrift, but life-support and critical systems are stable. We require immediate medical assist for one crew member with suspected head trauma." It was probably a stretch to call themselves crew, but they had become one over the past few days. 'Stowaways' didn't really fit. Neither did 'passengers'. "Advise you hold position. The AI has reacted unpredictably to the presence of another ship."

The three of them waited. Even within a single ansible's range, there would be a certain amount of latency. Just how much would give Ro some idea of how far apart the ships were.

"We noticed. Are your air locks functioning?"

"Hephaestus, stand by, please." Ro grabbed her micro and scanned through the systems reports. Nothing mentioned external damage, but that relied on the sensors reporting accurately. "Micah, can you take a look at the main airlock?"

"We're towing a big section of the temporary corridor, but we didn't see any sign of damage when we looked earlier."

"Hephaestus, you'll have to hack away some of the station we're pulling, but it appears intact."

The pauses between messages had shortened. She hoped they knew what they were doing.

"Stand by, Halcyone. We have a medic on the way."

"You should have them look at your ankle, Ro," Barre said.

"Not a priority."

He fell silent again, glancing at his brother. "What are you going to tell them about the weapons?"

What was she going to tell them? She picked at a piece of ragged cuticle on her thumb with her index finger. "I haven't figured that out yet."

"I have."

Ro and Barre turned to Micah. He stood in front of the main view screen staring at them.

"I made a trade. My father and the weapons for my freedom."

Heat traveled from Ro's stomach, up through her throat and face. Clenching her fists, she lurched toward him. "You what?"

Barre stepped in front of her and held her by her shoulders as she struggled. "Wait. Listen to what he has to say."

"Why the fuck are you taking his side?"

"Because what's in our hold is illegal as hell and we're the ones sitting on it. Are you that stupid? We have the weapons. We stole a ship. Do you have any idea what this looks like?"

Ro stopped trying to push aside a solid wall of Barre and let out a pent up breath in a large sigh.

"Are we good?" Barre asked.

"Fine," she snapped, looking past him at Micah. He hadn't moved.

"I'm sorry. I didn't have any choice. Once they find that shit here, they'll search every micron of this ship and no matter how well I cleaned up, they'll find evidence of the bittergreen."

"The hell you didn't have a choice!" Ro crossed her arms and turned her back to Micah, afraid of what she might do if she had to keep looking at him. "Like father, like son, Rotherwood."

I'm not anything like my father," he said, in a low, dangerous growl. "I thought you would understand."

The door to the bridge opened and closed. Ro turned to the empty space where Micah had been standing. "Fuck."

"Let him go."

"Halcyone, this is skimmer alpha-niner. We can see your airlock. Attempting to dock."

Pulling herself up to her full height, Ro decided she would damned well act the part of Captain, at least until they came to arrest her. "Skimmer alpha-niner, we are standing by."

"So really, how screwed are we?" Barre asked.

"We?" Ro laughed. "Not we. Me. You were technically a stowaway. I'm the one who stole the ship." And took the weapons. A deep clang reverberated through the ship. "Ah, our company's here. Shall we escort them to the bridge?"

Barre glanced at Jem, frowning.

"Never mind. Stay with him. I got this."

"Are you sure?"

Ro wasn't sure of much, except that Jem needed to get medical help. "Yeah." She made a futile effort to look less like she'd been in the same clothes for three days and more like the captain of a ship. Lifting her chin, she strode out to meet the skimmer crew.

At the airlock, she paused and took a deep breath. She got them all this far, she could take the next step. Peering through the porthole, she saw the shadow of the skimmer flush against the transport ship. She placed her hand against the door controls. At least Jem would be okay. A deep thunk reverberated through the corridor, a sound she could hear and feel as the crew on the other side of the lock mated their port to Halcyone's.

She studied the readout, keeping her eye on the cycling lights —green for a good seal, red for you're screwed. She looked up for the AI's pickup. "Barre?"

"What's up, Cap?"

It didn't bother her quite as much to hear him call her that now. "Keep your ears tuned for any signs that our friend is getting agitated, okay?"

"Will do. All quiet right now."

The airlock lights fixed on steady green. Ro let her breath out in a long, slow whistle. Relief mingled with a prickle of fear as the skimmer's port door unlocked. The hatch opened with excruciating slowness. Two survival-suited figures stood back to back in the tiny airlock proper. One held a supplies bag. Both were armed. A coil of dread curled around her stomach.

The seconds ticked by as the skimmer's door dialed shut and Halcyone checked the pressurization before starting to open the transport ship's side. Green lights flashed in the airlock and both of the crew members from Hephaestus flipped up their visors.

Alert bells rang through the corridor.

"Airlock door opening. Prepare for arrivals."

The two crew nodded, saying something to one another she couldn't hear. One of them looked up. Ro couldn't swallow the dry lump in her throat.

Her father stood in the airlock staring back at her. A loud clunk broke her paralysis and Ro slapped her hand on the airlock controls to abort. The hiss of air taunted her. She was too late.

He strode aboard Halcyone and stood, towering over her.

She shivered, looking down at his sidearm.

"Hello, Rosalen. I've been concerned about you."

Concerned about what she might have done with his cargo, was probably more accurate. She ignored him and turned to the medic. "We have an injured boy on the bridge. Follow me."

"And you need some care as well," the medic said, ignoring the tension he must have sensed between them.

"I'm stable. Jem is not." She pivoted on her heel and headed away from the airlock, her back tingling, imagining the potential of weapons trained on her.

"I'll need to examine everyone on board."

"Jem first," she insisted, as the bridge doors hissed open.

Barre stood and Ro envied the look of relief in his eyes.

"Over here," he said.

The medic picked his way across the detritus strewn about the bridge. As he knelt beside Jem, Barre leaned in and started throwing medical terms at him. A tightness pulled across her chest. Barre's face perfectly captured the expressions she'd seen in Jem's so often. Ro wondered why she'd never noticed that before.

Ro's father stood in front of the door, facing in. Did he think she planned to escape? He met her gaze and strode through the bridge as if he owned it. She stood her ground, refusing to look away.

"I found your toys. Nice trick with the seals. Your handiwork or the senator's?"

He raised his eyebrows. "You've changed since I saw you last."

"You haven't."

"Touché," he said, giving her a mock bow. "Good work, here, by the way."

"Don't think you can walk in here and steal my ship."

"Your ship?" He laughed and both Barre and the medic looked up at him, frowning. They lowered their voices to intense whispers. "What about my cargo?"

"I think you'll find the cargo already claimed," she said. Maybe Micah had done her a favor after all.

He gripped her arm with the force and bite of a vice. "Whatever you think you've done, you're dangerously mistaken."

Ro gripped his restraining arm with her free hand. "If you don't let go right now, I'm going to require the medic's help. Urgently."

Her father opened his hand and she tumbled away from him, rubbing her arm, hoping the bruising wouldn't be that bad this time.

The medic broke into their uncomfortable silence. "I'm going to transport this young man back to Hephaestus. Once I get him transferred to our sick bay, I'll come back for the two of you. You've done the best you could with him, given your resources. Your parents trained you well."

"Is he going to be okay?" Barre's voice cracked. Ro looked away from the pleading in his eyes.

"We'll do our best." He pulled a small, square packet from his bag. It unfolded into a backboard. "Maldonado, a little help here?"

"No," Barre said. The medic shot him a sharp look. "He's my brother."

Her father shrugged and stayed at Ro's side. She shifted a step away from him as Barre stabilized Jem's head and shoulders and helped roll him to the side so the medic could slip the board beneath him. With practiced efficiency, he got Jem secured in the strapping until he looked like an insect trussed in a spider's web.

The medic stood, flipped a switch on his belt pack, and the backboard rose to hover at his waist height. "Even with the gurney, I can take one more back with me. Do you want the honors?"

Barre stared helplessly at Jem and then back to Ro. She closed her eyes, steeling herself for being alone with her father.

"Take Jem first," Barre said. "I started this trip with Ro. I think I should end it with her."

She snapped her head around. What was he doing?

The medic shrugged. "I'll let you know when I'm on my way back. Both of you can take the next trip."

Barre watched the medic tow his brother out the door and into the hallway, his hands in tight fists. She owed him and the worst part was she didn't know why. He should have saved himself. It's what she would have done.

Chapter 33

"HALCYONE, THIS IS Commander Targill of the Commonwealth Ship Hephaestus. The skimmer will return shortly. All souls aboard will be transferred here immediately. If you are able, assist Chief Engineer Maldonado in preparing the vessel for towing."

Ro triggered her response, refusing to look at her father. "Commander Targill, request permission to stay aboard Halcyone until we return to Daedalus." The seductive call of a shower and a real meal would have to wait until she figured out what her father was up to.

"Request denied. You and the other children will be dropped off on Daedalus Station en route to a military repair depot."

Her father snickered and she glared at him. There were no children here, only her crew.

"You didn't think they'd let you keep it, did you?" her father asked.

"You son of a bitch. You set me up. This is my ship. It was nothing but a glorified storage hold before I got her to fly."

"Really?" His laughter filled the bridge. "And who do you

think did all the work on the infrastructure? No, my dear Rosalen, this is my ship. It's always been mine. I just needed you for its final touches."

"Ro?" Barre said, his low voice cutting through the tension. "I don't understand."

"You should have gone with your brother," Maldonado said.

"No. We all leave together or we all stay together."

A lifetime of painful lessons made Ro an expert at reading even the subtlest of her father's signs. His body betrayed his fury in dozens of small ways, from the tight-lipped smile to the ripple of muscle across his shoulders, to the slight cock of his head as he examined Barre as if he were just another engineering problem to solve.

"I think you should wait at the airlock, son. I really do."

Barre's hands clenched and unclenched. "You have no jurisdiction over me. I'm a civilian and I'm sure as hell not your son." He kept his gaze locked on Maldonado's and stepped forward.

"Barre, don't!" Ro warned.

He glowered at her father, unable to see the hard-calloused hand reaching casually towards his holstered weapon. But Ro couldn't look away. A coldness gnawed its way into her gut. He couldn't shoot Barre. He'd never get away with it. Targill wouldn't let him. But Targill wasn't here and if she didn't do something, Barre would be dead and dragging on her conscience like a storm drogue.

Ro stared at her father's arm as if the weight of her fear could stop its relentless movement. Then her feet moved and she steered herself between the gun and Barre, never lifting her gaze from its deadly metallic shine.

"Out of the way." His gun arm lifted. She raised her head to stare him in the eyes. He swept the gun across the small space that separated the two of them. Ro heard the crunch of the metal against her shoulder before she crumpled, flung across the room by the power in his muscular arm. A sharp cry rang out, her own, familiar voice echoing in pain.

Barre screamed out her name.

The smallest sound caught at her fading consciousness—a whisper of air that she knew was important, even if she couldn't think of why. She heard her name again, but this time in Micah's voice. An energy bolt crackled through the bridge. The sizzle of burning hair and flesh assaulted her sinuses. And then she remembered that soft sound and what it signified: the whoosh of the bridge doors opening and closing again.

A giant's hand pressed down on her battered shoulder, wrenching another scream from her sore throat. The floor growled beneath her. Everything went black.

*

In the darkness, the burn seemed to go on and on. Barre's arm lay twisted beneath him at an awkward angle and he wished it would just go ahead and break already. If he still had two functioning arms when the crazy ship stopped again, he was going to strangle Maldonado. If anything had happened to Micah or Ro, he'd kill him, broken arm or no.

He couldn't even draw a full enough breath to shout for either of them. Halcyone was pulling at least three or four gees. It wasn't a huge hardship when you were in an acceleration couch or even lying flat on a beaten down old cushion. But Halcyone hadn't waited for them. She just bolted again and doused every source of light on the bridge in the process.

At least Jem was safe.

Barre could have been safe. But if he'd gone with his brother, he would have been heading back to Daedalus and mandatory rehab.

He triggered his neural and opened up a link to Halcyone. A burst of chaotic, discordant sound reverberated through him. His stomach roiled. Bile flooded his mouth and leaked through his clenched teeth. Pain roared across the connection in raw arpeggios he was powerless to silence.

The pounding in his head and the screaming in his shoulder became part of the song, amplified by the AI's panic until Barre couldn't separate his fear from her fear. He could feel his body's pointless struggle against the gee forces, but it seemed a distant thing.

He breathed out a silent prayer. *Please. Please. Please.* His neural blazed, burning like a distant star in a corner of his mind as the music kept pouring through. *Please. Please. Please.* The rhythm of his cries added a soft counterpoint to Halcyone's furious song. The AI paused to listen, a nanosecond of blessed silence that Barre sank into, his body trembling. *Please. I can't. It's too much.*

A single note echoed in the emptiness. Barre took a shaky breath. When the high bell-like sound died away, another overlapped it. Again and again the note pealed through his mind. A cry or warning, he didn't know which. The pressure against his body eased just enough so he could roll away from where his arm had gotten pinned beneath him.

He sent a silent thank you to the AI. Its brooding quiet filled his mind.

The ship continued to accelerate. He lay panting on the floor of the bridge, his cheek pressed against the floor. The sour reek of his own bile nearly made him retch again.

Stop. You've got to stop. He sent a few tentative notes, wincing in anticipation. The same notes whistled back at him, matching his volume and intensity. The pressure against his chest softened. The growling engines slowed to a high pitched whine. Barre groaned as the blood flowed back into his arm, the sting of pins and needles traveling the length from shoulder to hand.

A sharp cry came from the far side of the bridge followed by a dull thump. "Ro? Are you all right?"

The bridge door hissed open and closed. Barre blinked furiously against the darkness. "Damn it, I can't see!"

Red emergency lights cast muddy shadows across the consoles. He pulled himself up to standing and scanned the room. There was no sign of Maldonado or Micah. He swallowed hard against a lump in his throat. "Ro, where are you?"

A groan came from someplace behind him. He scrambled over to the sound, cursing as he banged his shin on the base of the command chair. Ro lay crumpled on the ground, unmoving, her cheek dripping blood. "Shit."

He knelt beside her and checked her pulse—rapid, but steady. A roll of Micah's row cover lay at his feet and he tore off a length, folded it into a thick bandage, and pressed firmly against the cut on Ro's face.

"No!" she cried out, batting wildly at his arm.

"Shh, Ro, it's okay. It's me. Barre." He kept even pressure on her cheekbone as he spoke.

Her eyes snapped open and she stared at him, blinking in

confusion for several seconds. "Barre." She grabbed his arm in both of her hands. "Where is he?" Her voice shook and he didn't have to ask who she was talking about.

"Gone."

Ro winced. "He shot Micah."

"I know." The smell of burnt hair still hung in the air. "I think he took his body."

"We're going to die here." She turned her head away from him. "And it's all my fault."

Barre let the blood-stained cloth drop from his hand. A chill slithered down his spine. "Are you just going to lie down and die for him?"

"You don't understand." Her voice was flat, dull.

"The hell I don't." Barre wiped his hands against his pants and stood. "You can stay here, but if he wants us dead, I'm damned well going to make him work for it."

"You don't understand," Ro repeated. "He has an army's worth of weapons."

Barre listened to the quiet humming of the AI in his head. "But we have the ship."

*

You weren't supposed to be nauseated when you were dead. Strange logic, but it made sense to Micah. Therefore, he realized, he had to be alive. Something tugged on his ankles and his body lurched forward. His head bounced on the floor and pain arced across his forehead and along the top of his skull. The cooked-meat smell of his own flesh made his stomach heave, but there was nothing left to empty.

He tried to shout, but the sound came out as a low groan. The jerky motion stopped and his legs thudded to the ground. A shadow fell over his body.

"Your father thought he could burn me, but now I have his cargo and his son."

Alain Maldonado stared down at him. Memory flooded through Micah and he flinched. The bastard shot him. He reached his hand towards his forehead. Pain knifed through his arm as Maldonado kicked him.

"I can't risk you getting an infection."

"But you shot me." This conversation made no sense and it wasn't just because Micah happened to be lying on the floor after being dragged halfway across Halcyone's corridors with a burn wound across his skull.

"You surprised me." He reached an arm down toward him. "Get up."

Micah grasped the hand on automatic pilot and gasped as Maldonado jerked him to his feet.

"Move," he said, the ugly weapon sitting too comfortably in his large hand.

The blood drained from Micah's head and the corridor spun around him. He sagged against the wall, fighting the dry heaves, half expecting to hear the whine of Maldonado's gun.

"Get inside," he said.

Micah risked opening his eyes. The corridor wavered, but didn't spin.

"After you." Maldonado gestured toward the open doorway that led into the storage bay. And the weapons.

"Where's Ro?" Micah asked, limping across the threshold.

Maldonado pointed to an unopened crate set against the far

wall. "Sit."

He couldn't have shot his own daughter. He couldn't have. Micah struggled to remember what had happened on the bridge. Everything fell apart. Maldonado was here and he had the weapons. And if Ro and Barre were dead, he had the ship, too.

Maldonado rummaged through the opened crates, humming to himself. He walked back to Micah and dumped a bundle of medical supplies at his feet. "Clean yourself up and make sure you do a good job."

He glanced down at the sterile gloves, cleanser, and antibiotic-laced bandages and figured Maldonado really did want him alive. "This would go a lot easier if you helped."

The man's steady gaze never left his face.

Micah swallowed hard and bent over to pick up the supplies. Maldonado hadn't given him anything for anesthesia. He snapped the gloves on and leaned over, squirting the cleanser over his head. It stung almost as bad as getting shot had and Micah had to bite down on his lower lip to keep from passing out again. He sat there panting as the liquid blazed a path through his burns and dripped off his face onto the floor. Blood, skin, and bits of hair pooled at his feet.

It was good he had nothing left in his stomach to hurl. Micah probed his forehead, wincing at the tenderness. If he survived this, he'd have one hell of a scar to talk about. The wound stretched from the center of his eyebrow across his forehead and disappeared into his hairline. His hands shook when he thought of how close the burn came to taking his eye.

He snapped off several small segments of bandage and one at a time pressed their adhesive ends to his forehead, moving from his eyebrow up. It wouldn't look pretty, but it would keep the wound clean. "Now what?"

Without any change to his watchful expression, Maldonado stepped close and pressed the barrel of his gun against the fresh bandage and twisted. A bright hot lance of agony tore a scream from him. "Has anyone told you how like your father you are? It's irritating."

The man pulled away and the pain ebbed to a manageable throbbing. Micah trembled on the crate, his breath coming in ragged gasps, staring at Maldonado, his eyes wide.

"And speaking of your father ..."

Micah blinked, trying to follow this odd, nearly one-sided conversation and getting mental whiplash.

Maldonado holstered his gun and pulled out a micro. "We're going to send him a little message. It would be in your best interest to cooperate, Micah."

Micah blinked slowly, understanding things about Ro he'd rather not have.

"Hello, Corwin. I've found our missing shipment. As well as some lost lambs. In fact, I have one of them right here with me." He turned the micro to face Micah. "Say hello to your father." The threat in Maldonado's voice was unmistakable.

"Hello, father," Micah said, keeping his tone as flat as possible, never moving his gaze from Maldonado.

He shot him a foul look and turned the micro back to himself. "As you can see, he's a little worse for the wear. A small misunderstanding. I know how unreasonably fond you are of the boy."

The only person Corwin Rotherwood was fond of would be Corwin Rotherwood. By some happy accident, Micah looked enough like him that he was useful to the senator's image.

"I think it would be in your best interest to relinquish any claim to our cargo. Maldonado, out."

"And if he refuses?"

"I think you know the answer to that question, Micah."

So they both understood the situation.

Chapter 34

NOMI PAUSED TO straighten out where her uniform had creased during her short off-shift rest before knocking on Targill's door.

It slid open noiselessly and he watched her from behind his massive desk. "Sit."

The hard stools bolted into the floor and Targill's large, open desk spoke of a ruthless efficiency, a utilitarian ideal, just like the commander, himself. She sat. "Sir?"

"Our medic transported one of your compatriots on board. Jeremy Durbin."

Disappointment warred with relief inside her. "What's his condition?"

"Preliminary assessment indicates serious head trauma."

Poor Jem.

"How well do you know Micah Rotherwood?"

She blinked. "I'm sorry?"

"Micah Rotherwood. The senator's son. You are aware he's on the ship as well."

"Yes, sir." Was this about the bittergreen? "He's a civilian, sir. Other than a brief interaction with him in the mess back on

Daedalus, I have had no contact with him." Nomi pressed her feet into the floor to keep from fidgeting.

Targill tapped on his desk with his index finger. The integrated display winked out before she could see what he was looking at. "Well then, what can you tell me about Alain Maldonado?"

"Sir?" Her voice emerged high and squeaky.

"Alain Maldonado. Chief Engineer of Daedalus Station. I assume you know him."

"Yes, sir." She wondered what he already knew. "I haven't had the opportunity to interact with him much on the station, either."

He leaned forward, the silver in his buzz cut hair catching the overhead light. "But?"

"He has a scattered resume. A pattern of short postings, going back nearly twenty years." She tried to stick with what would be publicly available, but it was clear he expected something more. "It's curious that he hasn't moved up in rank."

"And?"

Nomi frowned. This wasn't anything he couldn't get through Maldonado's service record or even through Mendez, so why was he asking her? "Ro Maldonado is my friend." Her face heated up, but she didn't look away from Targill. "She believes her father cannot be trusted."

Targill steepled his long fingers beneath his chin. "What do you think?"

"Why are you asking me, sir?" Nomi cringed inwardly at how whiny she sounded. "I mean no disrespect, but there are far more senior staff members than me on Daedalus."

Leaning back in his chair, he nodded, his expression more

curious than annoyed. "But you're here. And I think you know more than your precise answers indicate. "

She closed her eyes briefly, calling up an image of Maldonado's anger. "He wants the ship. Or rather something on the ship." Looking up, she met Targill's gaze directly, without hesitation. "And that something doesn't include Ro. I believe she's in danger."

He fell silent as Nomi struggled not to fidget in the hard chair.

"Ensign."

"Sir?"

"For what it's worth," he said, "I agree with you."

He spun his micro around and projected an image from their forward view screen on the gleaming surface of his desk. Halcyone hung in space, pitted and battered. A skimmer disengaged and moved away, getting larger as it came closer to Hephaestus. Nomi glanced at Targill, but his face remained impassive and he flicked his gaze back to the image.

"This will make it clearer."

He waved at the micro and the image jumped, winked out, and started again. This time, the skimmer was much further from the derelict ship.

"Sir?"

"Watch."

Halcyone vanished.

"Ro!" Nomi cried out, leaning forward to peer at the empty field of stars filling up the neat cube on Targill's desk. A harsh metallic taste flooded her mouth and she struggled to catch her breath. "I don't understand." Looking away from the commander and the space where the ship had been, she blinked back tears.

"Maldonado elected to remain behind when the medic returned to Hephaestus."

She clasped her trembling hands together.

"Thank you, Ensign." He wiped the images clean.

The door opened and she walked out into the corridor, her stomach churning. What was on that ship?

Gripping her micro in shaking hands, Nomi composed a terse message for Ro. <u>Be careful. We know who's on the ship with you. Need a new ping to track.</u>

She needed answers and there was only one person who could give them to her. Nomi ran all the way to sick bay, dodging crew members and mumbling apologies. She burst into a bright room full of intense and well-orchestrated activity. Jem lay pale and still on a treatment plinth, the insectoid form of the portable scanner looming over him.

A technician brushed past her and she tugged on his arm. "Is he going to be okay? When can I talk to him?"

"Get the hell out of the way before I report you to the commander."

She retreated to the walk-in area at the front of the room, refusing to leave Jem, not when he was her only link to Ro.

"Prep him. We have to evacuate the blood."

Nomi stood up, her heart pounding. "Please, is he going to be okay?" she repeated. The doctor and her staff moved around Jem like a single organism, swarming the small boy, hiding him from sight. She turned toward the door, tears making her vision blur.

All she could do now was wait and hope Jem recovered and that he could tell her something of value. She turned and strode back to comms.

If Odoyo had slept there, Nomi couldn't tell. She'd never seen the woman outside of the softly lit, cramped space. A fresh uniform hugged her lanky body and she prowled the space behind the consoles coordinating the search efforts with a quiet efficiency.

"You're not on shift, Ensign."

"I know. I need to do something." Nomi stared directly at the lieutenant hoping she wouldn't toss her out of comms. "Please."

She jerked her chin across the room to an empty console. "Take a sector and set up a sweep. We know they don't have jump capacity. There's a limited distance they could have traveled, even at max interstitial."

Even so, it represented a lot of ground to cover. *Damn it, Ro, answer me.* Nomi's micro remained mute and staring at it wasn't going to make it ping. She sank into the console chair and plugged in the headset. They would never just stumble on Halcyone, but what else could she do?

*

Ro grabbed Barre's hand and snatched the make-shift bandage from him. "You have no idea what he's like."

He sat back on his heels. "Suit yourself. Keep the pressure on. It's a deep one. You must have sliced your cheek open on the sharp edge."

"He gets what he wants." And even if he wanted her alive, she couldn't think of what use he'd have for Barre. The singed meat smell of the bridge turned her stomach.

"And what about you?"

Ro scowled up at Barre.

"What do you want?"

"Why do you care? What I wanted got us all in this mess. I got Jem hurt and nearly got you killed." She swallowed back a sob. And probably got Micah killed.

Barre gripped her arms with his powerful hands.

She winced at the pressure where her father struck her with the gun. "Let go of me," she said, forcing her voice to stay level. Alain Maldonado had given her plenty of practice at pushing pain and emotion aside.

He released her and stood, watching her. "What's wrong with you?"

There would be a fresh bruise on her arm—another in a long line of bruises and threats. Ro spent her whole life finding small ways to defy her father that wouldn't end up with her getting too badly hurt. She folded her arms and cradled her head on her bent knees. It wasn't fair. Finally, she thought she could take something from him after the years of losing everything and everyone she cared about.

A few bars of music trilled through the bridge. Ro lifted up her head. Barre stood across the room, staring out at the star field. "What are you doing?"

"Why do you care?" he said, turning away from her.

Ro figured she deserved that.

"Fine," he said. "I'm asking the AI to send out a mayday. They found us once, maybe they'll find us again."

"Space is big," Ro said, shrugging. "But hey, knock yourself out." For all she knew, her father was working with Targill and Hephaestus knew exactly where they were.

"It's better than drowning in self-pity."

She lowered her head back down.

Barre's footsteps echoed in the bridge. His shadow fell over her. "Look, I understand."

"Do you? Really?" Ro stared up at him. "Let me tell you about my father. Alain Maldonado is a nasty, vindictive man. He drove my mother away not long after I was born and raised me out of spite. I learned early on not to get attached to anyone or anything because every time I did, he would move us. For the past few years, I've been doing everything I could to figure out how to get away from him." She glanced around the bridge. "This was the closest I came."

Harsh, mocking laughter filled the room. "You've got to be kidding. That all you've got?"

Heat rose from her chest through her throat. Ro stood and glared into Barre's eyes, her arm folded across her chest. "How dare you?" She took a step forward.

He stepped back. "Well, that's better."

"Fuck you. Who do you think you are?"

"Right now, your only friend."

Her body sagged. She looked down at the floor and at the cast Barre had so carefully wrapped around her ankle.

He set his hands gently on her shoulders. All she could feel was their warmth. "Look, I get it. I do. It's why Jem smuggled me on this ship in the first place."

"I'm sorry," she said, unable to meet his gaze. His music. Her freedom. Micah's retribution. Her father wasn't the only threat they faced, or the most urgent. He was just the closest. "You're right." She tucked her hair behind her ears. Taking a deep breath, she triggered the AI. "Halcyone, locate Maldonado, Alain."

"Ident unknown."

He must not have paired his micro with the ship. "Okay, then. Halcyone, identify and locate all unique individuals on this vessel."

"Maldonado, Rosalen—bridge. Durbin, Bernard—bridge."

"Bernard?"

"Family name. Jem couldn't pronounce it when he was little."

"Unknown individual—aft storage compartment."

That had to be her father. "Halcyone," she said, "identify unknown individual as ..."

The AI interrupted her. "Rotherwood, Michael—aft storage compartment."

Barre squeezed her shoulders and Ro yelped, the flare of pain as unexpected as the flash of triumph that shocked through her. She threw her arms around him in a fierce hug before her cheeks flooded with heat and she jumped back.

"Halcyone," Barre said, smiling broadly, "tag unknown individual as Maldonado, Alain. Confirm occupants in aft storage compartment."

"Maldonado, Alain, and Rotherwood, Michael."

"Now what?" Ro asked. "It's not like we can storm the place. He's the one with all the actual weapons."

"Well, I don't want to wait here for him to come back and pick us off."

"I can ghost us and we can play hide and go seek. And Halcyone can keep us updated if he moves." Ro pulled out her micro and paused. They were in this together. "What do you think?"

"Do it and let's get out of here."

"You got it." She looked at the view screen. "Can you set the comms to loop our distress call?"

Barre flicked his awareness to somewhere inside his musical brain. "Done."

"I'm never going to be able to do that, am I?"

"Nope."

Her lips twisted into a wry smile. "Okay. Done. Let's go."

The door didn't respond.

"Halcyone, unseal bridge door," she said, frowning.

"Bridge door damaged, non-functional."

"Shit."

"Halcyone, assess damage," Barre said.

"Energy weapon discharge. Door sensors malfunction. Manual backup inoperable."

"Son of a bitch, he sealed us in."

Barre examined the seam where the doors met. "Melted it shut is more like it. Now what?"

"He can't take my ship." She straightened up to her full height and she still didn't make it up to Barre's shoulders. "So how can we make his life more difficult?"

"Without hurting Micah in the process."

"He thinks we're trapped in here, helpless."

"Well, he is right about the trapped part."

She'd sell her micro for a laser cutter or even one of the stacks of guns in that storage bay. The door wouldn't be the only obstacle she'd want to use it on. "We have to be patient. Keep Halcyone monitoring him. My father works alone. He'll stash Micah somewhere he won't have to babysit him. Once he's on his own, we'll have more options."

"What does he want, Ro?"

"We're just collateral damage. The weapons and supplies in those crates are worth a fortune. I'm not even sure he wants the ship past getting the goods delivered."

"And Halcyone can't jump, so he's not going to do the delivering."

Ro paced the small area between the view screen and the nav console. "He's got to send out a signal. He must be planning to rendezvous with the buyer out here."

"And Halcyone just made things easier for him."

"But you and I," she said, smiling, "we're going to make them a lot harder."

Chapter 35

"So which of you realized the seals were fake, you or Ro?" Maldonado asked.

"Ro."

"That's my girl," he said, smiling.

Micah couldn't figure the man out. There seemed to be genuine admiration, but he also watched him wallop her with the end of his gun. At least his own father was a self-centered bastard all the time.

He rummaged through the already opened containers.

Micah measured the distance between where he sat and the cargo bay door. Then he looked up at Maldonado. Even if he didn't feel like crap and the room would stop spinning, he could never make it to the door. Maldonado's weapon would always beat out Micah's legs.

"Ah, that will work." Maldonado stood up, palming something small. "My buyer will have to accept a certain amount of necessary loss." He strode over to Micah. "Hold out your hands."

He lifted his chin to stare the chief engineer in the eyes. "Why?"

"Because if you don't, I'll just knock you out and when you wake up, you'll be confined in these anyway." He tossed security cuffs in his hand.

Micah held his arms out while Maldonado secured them around his wrists. A second pair fastened his ankles together.

"Thank you," Maldonado said.

"I think I like it better when you don't bother being polite."

Maldonado laughed and engaged the restraints. They tightened down just enough to make contact with his hands and feet. Micah tried to wriggle his fingers and a jolt of electricity shocked through them.

"Effective for emergency situations. Sensitive to acceleration and they titrate the punishment accordingly, so it's best if you stay put."

Micah should have told Commander Mendez about the weapons when he had the chance. Resting his arms carefully in his lap, he closed his eyes, and leaned back against the wall. How had he gotten here? Even if he traced the entire line of circumstances that led from a different storage bay to this one, he couldn't make sense of it all.

A low-level buzzing startled him. Micah stared down at the restraints but it wasn't coming from them. It was his stupid micro and he couldn't get to it, even if Maldonado wasn't in the room. The buzzing got louder. Maldonado looked up from the stack of sealed cartons.

"I'll get that," he said.

Micah kept his hands very still as Maldonado pulled his micro from his front pocket. "Clever. Text only uses so much less bandwidth and the messages get passed fairly quickly through the ansible network. Must have been Ro's idea."

It could only be Targill or Ro. Micah seriously doubted it would be his father. He studied Maldonado, hoping to see some clue in his expression, but the engineer just looked down at the message, a slight smile twitching his lips.

"Oh, I have underestimated you, Micah. Does your father have any idea?"

Shit. That meant it was Targill. Micah shook his head.

"No. Of course he doesn't. Why would he? You're his golden child."

"You're wrong." Micah's fingers curled partly closed until the shock made him jump.

"If you'd have told me about your deal, we could have saved a little time. But in any case, thank you for tossing your father in the path of the afterburners."

Maldonado turned toward the door.

"Now what?" Micah asked.

"Now I get paid for my troubles and I figure out if I have a use for you." He slipped Micah's micro in his pocket.

Micah stared across the room and then down at his restraints. The doors might as well have been on the other side of a wormhole.

*

The lights burned through Jem's closed lids. He hated when Barre screwed around with the environmentals, especially when he wanted to sleep in. He tried to put his arm across his face, but it wouldn't budge. "Hey, cut it out." All he heard was a muffled cry.

"Welcome back, Jeremy."

The deep and unfamiliar voice came from his right side. He couldn't turn his head to see. Jeremy? No one called him Jeremy —not even his parents. Jem squinted and the brightness seared his vision. "Can you turn down the damned lights?" His voice emerged as a hoarse croak. The lights dialed back. The scrape of a chair moving against the floor hurt his ears. He focused on the white coated figure beside his bed just as he noticed the familiar beeping of monitoring equipment. Sick bay? How did he get here?

A gentle hand peeled back his eyelids one at a time. Jem steeled himself for the light pen that followed. "What's the last thing you remember, Jeremy?"

"Jem."

"Excuse me?"

"It's Jem. And the last thing I remember?" He frowned. Images fell through his mind in a tumble: Finding Barre sprawled unconscious across his bed. Sick bay on Daedalus. The ship. The ship! Ro! "Where's Ro?" He struggled to lift his head but nothing moved. A distant thrum of pain beat against his eyes.

"Easy, there. You're on Hephaestus. And you've just come out of surgery."

"What?" He shifted his gaze back and forth trying to see as much of the room as he could. Smaller and more compact than sick bay on Daedalus, it had the spartan feel of a ship. He didn't see Ro, Micah, or his brother. "Where is everyone? Are they okay?" Ro's ankle probably didn't need a whole lot of attention. That was good.

"It will take a day or so before your brain unscrambles, I'm afraid. Until then, we can push something through your line to help you rest."

More sleeping was the last thing he wanted. "Can you just tell my brother I'm awake?"

"Your brother?"

"Yeah. Barre. Barre Durbin."

"I'm afraid you're the only one we evacuated before the ship disappeared."

Jem heard the whine of his own cardiac alarm as his pulse raced.

"Get him sedated!"

"No!" he shouted, trying to free himself from the restraints.

"I need his pressure down. Now!"

A stream of warmth slithered through his arm, spreading an enforced calm that took away the fear and the pain, but not a terrible sense of loss. "Please. I need ... talk to ... Barre." As he floated away on the chemically induced quiet, something kept irritating him. Like the remembered space from a lost tooth, he kept poking at what was missing. Ro. Something about Ro and Hephaestus. And a message.

The medic leaned forward, checking his vital signs, as if they'd be any different by the monitor. Jem smirked. His folks did that, too.

"Easy there, Jem. You need to rest your brain. Head trauma is serious stuff."

The sounds of the medical bay blended together into a kind of distant music. He wondered if he could capture it on his micro for Barre. No, that wouldn't work. His micro was probably still on Halcyone's bridge with Ro.

The melody incorporated a soft voice, speaking with punctuated urgency. "Is he awake? Can I talk to him?"

"Ensign, I've already told you, we need to keep him sedated. When he's out of the immediate post-surgical phase, we'll re-evaluate."

"Please, he's our only link to Halcyone! I need to—"

"Nakamura, if you don't leave my sick bay, I'll call security to escort you out."

Jem blinked slowly, trying to sort out why that name seemed important. The floating feeling make it hard to pull it together. "Wait," he said, his voice a ghost of a whisper. "Nomi."

The voices by the door got louder and more agitated. "Wait! Nomi!" The words were only distinct in his own head. But after a lifetime in and around medical wards, he knew how to get their attention. Jem smirked, took as deep a breath as he could, and held it.

Pressure built up in his chest and against his throat. He wanted to cough. His body struggled between thinking he was drowning and wanting to wrap itself in the soft, muzzy blanket of the drugs. His pulse pounded in his ears. Why weren't the alarms going off? His lungs burned. This wasn't going to work. He should just let go and breathe.

He had to breathe.

His head throbbed in time to his pulse—a slow thud, thud, thud. A distant, uncaring part of him wondered how high his carbon dioxide levels would have to rise before the monitors started screaming. Would they trigger before his body relented and reached for the cool bliss of air?

The whine of a siren pierced his foggy brain.

"Damn it, the kid's crashing!"

In the instant before Jem was sure his lungs would burst, he huffed out the breath he'd been holding and drew in fresh oxygen, sweeter than anything he'd ever tasted. He panted for a minute, then smiled up at the circle of concerned faces watching him. "Hey, it worked."

The doc who'd been caring for him frowned, his eyebrows drawing together as he studied Jem.

He held the man's gaze with a direct stare. "I need to talk to Nomi." It would have been a lot better if his voice hadn't cracked, but he figured he got his point across.

"Well, I guess this means you're going to live."

Jem would have shrugged if he could have moved anything but his eyes.

"I wouldn't have wanted to be the one to tell your parents otherwise."

"Please. If you arrest Nomi, I'm just going to have to hold my breath again." He smiled again. "Let me talk to her. It's not like I can do a whole lot else. And I promise I'll rest after."

The doctor studied Jem for what felt like a long time before he nodded and turned to the door. "Let her go."

"Thank you," Nomi said.

"You have five minutes."

She sat in the stool the doctor vacated, shifting closer to the bed.

"Hey. You going to be okay?" she asked, her gaze shifting between his face and the bandages on his head he couldn't see.

"So they tell me." Not being able to turn his head or shrug was worse than having an itch in the center of his back he couldn't scratch. "Do you think you can get them to turn off the restraint field?"

"Given that you saved me from being tossed in the brig? Doubtful."

The sedative smoothed over all his earlier urgency now that she was sitting with him.

"Jem?"

"Huh?" It would feel so good to sleep again.

"They're going to drag me away from here in about three minutes." She leaned forward, her dark eyes shining. "I'm worried about Ro. Can you help me find her?"

Adrenaline washed through him and his drooping eyelids snapped open fully. "Halcyone. Where's the ship? Where are they?"

"I don't know. And Ro's father is on board." Her dark eyebrows drew together. "Jem, we know he's after something on that ship. Do you know what it is?"

"The weapons." Jem coughed, wincing as his head throbbed.

"That's it, Nakamura." The doctor leaned over him and pushed another dose of warm fluffies into his line.

"You've got to stop him," Jem mumbled. His thoughts spun off into softness, but he had to tell her. Had to. They were together. Maldonado and the senator. "... Rother ... Rother-wood." A welcome darkness folded around him like the cushion of an acceleration pad.

*

"Anything yet?"

"No." Two blips represented Micah and her father on the schematic of the ship. Only one was moving. She bit her lip trying not to worry about Micah. Halcyone wouldn't be monitoring him if he weren't alive, but she didn't trust the decades-old internal sensors to report much beyond basic life-signs. They had to get out of here. "How's our signal?"

"Five by five, but Ro, he's bound to be able to hear it, too."

That couldn't be helped. Unless her father physically damaged the transmitter, he couldn't prevent their SOS either, or the private message she sent to Nomi. No, he would keep the transmitter working, not willing to risk his ability to contact potential buyers. "Let's hope Hephaestus gets our message before anyone else does." Her stealth program traveled through the same ansible channels as the distress call, but it used so much less bandwidth, there was a decent chance it would reach Nomi before Barre's signal got picked up.

A movement across her micro's display caught her attention. "He's on the move!"

Barre scrambled over to where she sat, her micro perched on her knee. He split his attention between the screen and the bridge doors.

Ro watched the small blip of light pulse along the ship's corridor moving toward its nose and the bridge. She reached over and grasped Barre's hand. He squeezed hers back, gently. His hands had thick calluses but his long, large fingers were surprisingly delicate.

"Well, it's not like he can sneak up on us," Barre said quietly.

"Then why are we whispering?" she asked, the corner of her mouth curving upwards. "He already knows we're in here."

He smiled back at her.

The bobbing light came closer. Ro gave Barre's hand another squeeze, grabbed her micro, and stood. "Not going down without a fight. You with me?"

"Hell, yeah," Barre said, and jumped up beside her, his dreadlocks swaying around his head. "How about we welcome him back with this?" He picked up a piece of twisted metal the length of his arm and hefted it at shoulder height.

Brute force against state of the art energy weapons. Shit. Well, it was better than huddling on the floor waiting to watch her father shoot her friend. Looking into his grim face, she smiled, feeling the cut on her cheek split open.

"What?" He lowered his improvised weapon.

She laughed. This was crazy. She'd made every mistake in the cosmos, put all these people at risk for her damned ego, and the image of Barre standing there, all fierce and heroic reduced her to helpless giggles. "I'm sorry," she gasped, struggling to get herself back under control. "It's not funny. It's not."

Barre set the metal down on the floor and cupped her shoulders. "It's going to be all right. We'll get out of this."

"Jem is lucky to have you," Ro said, the wild energy slipping away, leaving her terribly tired and spent. "Okay, Daddy dear, where the fuck are you?" She glanced down at her micro. "Barre," she said, disbelieving both the AI's tracking and her own eyes.

"What?"

She blinked several times, staring at the map. "He's gone to engineering."

"What?" he repeated, frowning at her.

"Look." She handed him her micro.

"Halcyone," he said, his gaze frozen on the display. "Locate Maldonado, Alain."

"Engineering bay."

Barre picked her up and swung her in a complete circle, laughing, his dreads flying around his head.

"Hey, watch the shoulder!"

He set her down and sobered. "You know it's just a reprieve, right?"

"Yes. We have to get out of here."

"Got any ideas?"

Micah was sitting in a room full of ways to blast through that door. Ro paced the bridge. They could see him there, but that was about it. If Halcyone had been a modern ship, she'd be able to get a full audio/video feed to and from practically anywhere, but there wasn't much of anything to hack into. Outside of some museum, the communications devices they'd used back when this ship was built didn't even exist. Her damned micro had more sheer computing power than the machine that ran Halcyone's autonomic subsystems.

Ro tapped her finger across the ubiquitous little device. It should still be paired to Micah's through her ad hoc program. "Yeah, I guess I do have an idea." It only took her a few minutes to initiate a direct connection to his micro. She paused before she said anything and checked on her father's location. Still moving through engineering.

"What are you waiting for?" Barre asked.

But what if he wasn't? "What if my father's ghosting and he's still in the storage bay with Micah?" He had to know she'd be trying to track him.

"Why would he do that?"

"I don't know." Ro wanted to scream, but that wasn't going to help. Underestimating her father was a bad idea, especially when he seemed to have all the advantages. "Wait. Give me a minute." She reconfigured the link to stream its audio and video feed through to her micro. "Huh."

"What?"

"Nothing. Look." She set it to display in holo mode and the two of them stared at a dark rectangle. It didn't make any sense.

"Can you clean it up?" Barre asked, squinting at the display.

"There's no image. Nothing."

"Malfunction?"

She double checked her program parameters and sent a silent ping to the device. It returned the ping-back almost instantly. "Nothing wrong with the micro or the signal." But something was wrong. She could feel it in the pit of her stomach.

A loud thump echoed through the bridge from the micro's small speaker. It was followed by a string of curses in her father's voice.

Chapter 36

"Shit! shut it down, Ro!" Barre shouted, leaping to his feet.

"But Halcyone pings him in engineering. I don't understand."

"It doesn't matter where he's supposed to be. Shut it down." Barre couldn't understand how someone as smart as Ro could be so slow and stupid when it came to her father. "What if he does what you did in reverse?"

"So what. So he knows we're listening to him. It's not like he doesn't know where we are."

True enough, but he didn't want to give Maldonado any reason to head back here anytime soon. He sat beside her and watched the empty video feed. "So now what?"

"We listen."

Well, he could do that. Barre threw part of his attention to Halcyone, listening for her music. That, more than anything, told him about the state of the ship. Ro could study her sensors and diagnostics.

A crackle of static burst through Ro's micro as a discordant blare of sound blasted Barre's mind. Clasping his hands over his ears didn't do anything to quiet the internal music. Ro would have to deal with whatever came through the micro. He focused on settling his breath to a hypnotic and regular rhythm, feeding it back to the AI. Ro was right—it was a lullaby of sorts. In a lot of ways, the AI reacted like a frightened child.

He had no idea how long he spent working to soothe Halcyone, but the music finally softened. Barre let out a long, whistling breath.

Crouching in front of him, Ro stared into his eyes, her own narrowed, her eyebrows pulled together. "What is it?"

"I'm not sure. But Halcyone doesn't like it. What have you got?"

Ro leaned over her micro and moved her hands too rapidly over its surface for him to follow. "He is in engineering."

"How do you know?"

"Because he's hacking directly into the antenna array." She swore methodically in the quiet of the bridge.

"But who is he sending a signal to?"

"How the hell should I know?" Twin bright spots of red burned in the middle of her cheeks.

Barre only got the slightest of warnings, a bugling fanfare that repeated in his ears, before the rumble of engines shook the bridge.

*

Micah fumed long after Maldonado strode out of the cargo bay. The damned restraints were effective, he had to give him that. After getting shocked a few times, Micah didn't even breathe too deeply, for fear he would trigger them again. The hard surface of the packing crate pressed into his backside, but trying to shift would only bring new punishment from the cuffs around both his wrists and his ankles.

Whoever invented them should be slowly roasted in a skimmer's afterburners.

If Ro didn't kill her father, Micah would.

He pressed his lips together in a frown. She could be dead, along with Barre. And if Micah couldn't find a way out of here, Maldonado would kill him as soon as he was no longer useful.

A vibration shook the hold. Micah grabbed for the crate beneath him and was rewarded with a lance of fresh pain through his hands. "What the hell?" The rumble of engines shook the crate. "Oh, no. Oh, shit."

The floor lurched beneath him, throwing Micah down, agony curling him into the fetal position.

"No, no, no!" he muttered, struggling to relax his arms and legs.

*

"Shut it down, Barre! You have to shut it down!" Ro's heart beat wildly as she dove for the meager protection of the worn down acceleration mats.

Barre glanced around the bridge with wide eyes before following her example. "I can't. I don't know how!"

"We can't let the damned ship do another burn or they'll never find us."

Barre tilted his head to the side and frowned. "It's not Halcyone this time. It's something your father is doing."

"How the hell do you know that?"

"Here, listen." Barre patched the AIs song through Ro's

micro. The alien music, high pitched and frantic, pounded through the bridge. "She's terrified."

"Damn it!" He couldn't have her ship. "We have to stop him. Can you get the AI to help us?"

"Right now, I'm doing all I can to keep her from shaking us to pieces."

The ship shuddered beneath them as if the AI and Ro's father were playing a giant game of tug of war. Ro sat up and wedged herself in the corner where the navigation and comms consoles butted up against one another.

"What are you doing?"

"Don't know yet," she said. "Keep singing to the ship. I'll see what I can do from my end." The vibration set up a painful resonance of sound across the bridge. Barre winced and she could only imagine what it must be like hearing it from the inside, too.

Ro cleared all the running programs from her micro and concentrated on finding a way in again. A violent jolt banged the back of her head against the console and she swore. If her father managed to wrest control of the engines, she wouldn't have time to get flat, and the gee forces would twist her into a knot. "Come on, girl, we're a team. You know me. I'm not going to hurt you."

The bridge shook too much for her to use the more efficient 3-d interface and she struggled to input the commands she wanted. A shudder tipped her sideways and nearly set her micro flying from her hands. "Barre, you've got to calm the ship down!"

He lay on his back, hands clawing the thin mat, his lips pressed into a thin line.

The engines whined, a piercing sound that seemed to shiver through her spine and bore into her head. The pitch slowly climbed, drowning out Barre's reply, if he gave her one. "Damn it, Halcyone, I'm trying to help you. Let me in," she whispered, frantically tapping in commands through her micro.

Without warning, the ship canted, rolling Barre off the cushion and pressing Ro into the nav console. Then Halcyone lurched back to level. Silence rang through the bridge.

"What in the cosmos just happened?"

Barre sat up, dazed, blood trickling down his lower lip. His dark skin shined with sweat. "I don't think we'll hold together if she does that again."

Ro rubbed her sore shoulder and blinked up at the forward view screen. "Look, we're still here."

Barre pressed his thumb to his lip to stop the bleeding. "She stood her ground."

And her father lost this time.

"Now what?"

"Our turn," she said. "Can you get Halcyone to let us access the rad sensors in engineering?"

"Isn't that your department?"

"I'm not asking you to run a hack. Just do your AI charmer routine and ask for manual override. For calibration or maintenance—I don't care how you manage it. Besides, the AI likes you better than me." Another time or place it would have hurt to admit that.

"What are you going to do?"

She stared out across the bridge as if she could see through the doors to the damage her father had caused. "If you can get control over the sensors, I'm going to figure out how to initiate a radiation lock-down and trap the bastard in engineering."

"Turnabout."

"Yup," she said. "Give him enough problems to deal with that he won't have the time to try that again."

"Can you? I mean, won't he just be able to break your hack?"

Ro stared Barre right in the eyes and lifted her chin. "I'm better than he is." And for the first time in her life, she knew it was true.

*

Micah groaned, his head slamming against a crate, igniting a fresh burst of pain, a throbbing counterpoint to the lightning bolts thrumming at his wrists and ankles. He blinked, panting as the ship stilled, and risked a glance at his hands. The restraints held him snugly and his skin was unmarked.

"Son of a bitch," he said, growling. He had to get the damned things off. Moving as slowly as he could, Micah wriggled himself back into sitting, gritting his teeth against a new barrage of shocks. Something this brutal should at least leave marks.

The edge of the crate pressed into his spine, its top littered somewhere through the cargo bay. He twisted his head to look inside. Stacks of energy rifles lay in their protective cushioning, their brushed metallic sheen gleaming dangerously in the dim light. He glanced at the door and back at the weapons, his hands twitching weakly in his lap.

It was only pain, right?

All he had to do was reach up and he could grab the rifle. Easy. He stared at his hands. *Move, damn you.* His fingers trembled and invisible fire ringed his wrist again.

No wonder Maldonado left him in a damned arsenal. Sadistic bastard. Micah swallowed the howl of fury in his chest and sat shaking, blinking back tears. It was only fucking pain. Just pain.

His mother had lived with it and more for months, never crying out even during those final, terrible days when he had to turn her every hour, the agony of moving replacing the agony of staying still.

He panted, drawing as much air into his lungs as he could. Sitting here trussed like a turkey and waiting to die wasn't on his bucket list. Getting his hands around Maldonado's throat was.

"Any time now, Micah," he muttered. Sweat beaded across his forehead and his upper lip. "Count of three." He took another gulp of air. "One, two, three." Clenching his jaw, Micah twisted and reached up into the crate, howling as his arms exploded in agony. He stared at his hands, making sure he kept his grip on the rifle, since all feedback from his nerves had been replaced by wave after wave of fire.

The weapon slid from his fingers and tumbled into his lap. Micah sat panting, his mind refusing to believe he still had hands.

He didn't know how long it took before the nerves stopped firing their brutal message. The rifle lay beneath his touch, smooth and cold. If Maldonado stepped through that door right now, Micah wasn't sure he could even pick it up and shoot. He couldn't stop the laugh that shook through him, moving his hands and sending small jolts through the cuff. It was only pain.

Pure reflex made him grip the barrel. He flicked the safety off. His finger tightened over the firing mechanism. Before he could change his mind, he pressed the trigger and sent a bolt of blue sizzling against the ankle restraints, melting them to useless slag. The rifle rolled out of shaking fingers that refused to listen to him. The heat that melted part of his shoes to his feet barely registered on his abused nerves. His whole body trembled. If the gun had been pointed at his brain, Micah would have gladly fired the weapon, just to make the punishment finally stop.

It took a long time before he realized his legs were free.

The laughter that ripped out of him sounded like something from the throat of an animal.

He moved his feet, welcoming a pain that he'd earned and understood. Its throbbing counterpoint made his wrists easier to bear, somehow. Blinking in surprised relief, he picked up the rifle, lurched to standing, and hobbled across the cargo bay.

The trip to the bridge was a nightmare. Every step jogged the rifle in his grip, causing him to squeeze his hands. Each shock shook through him before the last one had fully faded. Micah gritted his teeth and kept going, imagining all the places he'd clamp the cuffs on Maldonado's body.

He stared at the half melted bridge door for several minutes trying to force his pain-wracked mind to make some sense of it. It had to be Maldonado's handiwork. He'd even torched the emergency manual release. That meant someone had to be alive in there. His heart thumped with wild hope.

Shouting would only waste time. The doors were vacuum rated. Even if he wanted to risk his hands, the butt of the rifle would disintegrate before he made any sort of dent in its surface. He only hoped that whoever was still alive wasn't standing by the door.

"It's only pain," he whispered and lifted the gun to shoulder height, resting the butt against his chest. Flickers of invisible fire circled his wrists and coursed up and down his arms. Ignoring what his mind kept screaming, he dialed the weapon to maximum and its narrowest beam. "Only pain."

Squinting his eyes to focus on the center seam of the door, Micah fired, howling his defiance as the metal glowed red. Using the rifle like a laser scalpel, he cut through Maldonado's improvised weld until he couldn't differentiate between the heat from the gun and the punishment from the restraints.

The door smoked and the stink of burning polymers irritated his nose and mouth. The rifle's pulse stuttered and failed. He let it slip from his abused fingers to clatter on the floor at his feet. A widening crack of light split the doors open. Micah tumbled over the threshold.

Ro stood in front of him, her mouth open, her eyes wide circles of green.

"Permission to enter the bridge, Captain." His voice croaked from his aching throat.

"What took you so long?"

Micah shrugged and immediately regretted it. His vision narrowed to a dim tunnel, with Ro's shining hair the only illumination in it. "Got tied up," he whispered, before even the small slice of brightness vanished to a pinprick.

Voices echoed from far away as he swayed, blinking, trying to figure out why he felt so strange.

"Help me get the cuffs off him."

"Shit! They're live."

"Only pain," he mumbled, or thought he did. But it felt like someone else's pain, or at least pain he didn't have to care about anymore. Micah sank into a welcoming darkness. The burning in his arms didn't follow.

Chapter 37

BARRE DRAGGED MICAH to one of the mats. His nose wrinkled at the acrid stink of burning plastic and flesh. Ro stood over them as Barre knelt at Micah's side trying to figure out what was more important—the electrified cuffs or the plasma burns on his feet.

He glanced at the ruin of Micah's feet and his stomach lurched. Definitely the burns.

"Is he going to be okay?" Ro asked, her green eyes wide.

Triage now. Answers later. "He's going into shock. I need to set up an IV and give him something for pain. Get the box of medical supplies."

Ro dragged it over.

Good, at least she'd be able to follow simple commands. He rummaged through the supplies and found at least the bare bones of what he needed—a conscious sedation kit, fluids, and a wound care set up. Barre slid on the sterile gloves and picked up the IV injection gun with shaking hands. He had only ever done this in a sim before.

It was supposed to be idiot-proof. Anyone could pull the spring-loaded trigger somewhere near a vein and the tiny needle would seat itself. Easy. He rolled up Micah's sleeve, careful not to touch the restraints. Once had been quite enough. He set the injector against the inside of Micah's elbow and triggered it. The IV gun sprayed a cool mist of topical numbing agent. The needle deployed almost immediately after. Micah didn't even flinch. Barre wondered who had bandaged his head and why.

Ro made a sound between a squeak and a gasp. Barre looked up and smirked. "Smart girl like you afraid of a little needle?"

She gave him the finger before folding her arms across her chest. "What next?"

"The cuffs and his feet."

She made a sour face.

"I'll take the feet. Can you handle the cuffs?"

"At least I won't pass out if I get zapped by the cuffs," she said, glancing quickly at Micah's blistered feet and swallowing hard.

The inside of Micah's hands had mild burns from where he'd gripped the rifle, but nothing compared to what the feet were going to look like. He attached the medicated saline to the tiny catheter sticking out of Micah's arm. Short of full anesthesia, which would take his parents and a real sick bay, this was the best Barre could do. It would have to be enough.

He grabbed the suture kit and sat by Micah's feet. Running the full burn treatment sim hadn't included the smell, but he vividly remembered the soldier his parents made him examine who had later died from his wounds. He shuddered and focused on Micah. The remnants of his low boots looked as if they'd fused with the inside of his ankles. What the hell had he done? He peered closer and reached for the long handled tweezers. Barre carefully picked out a thin piece of curved blue metal about three centimeters long. "Ro, does this look like the same crap the wrist cuffs are made of?"

She scooted closer, keeping her eyes averted from his feet. "Son of a bitch."

"That's what I thought." Barre's estimation of Micah's resolve rose way, way up. He met Ro's gaze with his until she turned away, her face pale. "Your father did this."

"I know."

They didn't have a whole lot of time. Maldonado would get impatient with his lack of progress controlling the AI. He'd come for his daughter. She had value to him. Clearly Micah did too, or he wouldn't have restrained him and kept him alive. Barre knew he had nothing Maldonado could possibly want.

Ro swore softly and methodically as she worked. Barre switched the tweezers for a pair of laser cutters, glad for the pain meds that would keep Micah sleeping. A metallic snick echoed in the bridge. "Got it!" Ro cried and flung the cuffs across the room.

"I got this. Get your lock-down running before he comes back for you." Barre turned back to the problem of Micah and his injuries. The battlefield kits were state of the art. At least the senator didn't skimp. If he had gotten cheap knock-offs, Micah would have lost his feet for sure. It was also a good thing the standard issue station boots were made of a basic polymer similar to body armor. Barre mixed up the antibiotic-laced enzymes that would dissolve the manufactured composites and leave the damaged flesh alone.

"Sorry, buddy," he said. Even through the sedation, it would hurt. "Ro?"

"Hmm?"

"You might want to cover your ears."

*

The scream that ripped through the bridge raised goose bumps up and down Ro's arms. Bile gathered in her throat, tasting of the mingled stench of burned plastic, flesh, and something oily and noxious she couldn't even name.

"Fuck, Barre, what are you doing to him?" She whirled around, terrified of what she'd see.

"Trying to save his god damned feet. Now shut up and let me work."

Ro swallowed hard, and breathing through her mouth, turned back to her micro. There was nothing she could do for Micah that Barre couldn't do better and more safely. "Halcyone, locate Maldonado, Alain," she whispered, not wanting to break Barre's concentration.

"Engineering."

So he was still wrestling with the ship. She pulled up the AI's schematics and found her way into the rad sensors subroutines. Barre had done his work. Manual overrides were enabled. A combination of changing ALARA settings and tweaking the sensors should trigger a lock-down. If nothing else, it would buy them some time. She found the rad safety officer's interface. ALARA was a moving target. Even forty years ago, they understood that. And what was 'as low as reasonably achievable' differed on a military mission versus a civilian one. It was all about acceptable losses.

She'd like to dump her father in a radiation waste facility and consider him an acceptable loss.

Halcyone didn't even hum as Ro tinkered with radiation sensors. The trick would be to slide the ALARA settings down to something approximating the slightly elevated levels actually present in engineering. Then she could dial up the sensor readings. "Just a safety exercise, nothing to worry about," she murmured to the AI, before closing the subroutine.

"Hack that, daddy-o," she said.

The blare of the rad alarm whooped through the ship. "Warning, radiation leak in engineering. Radiation twenty-six percent above ALARA and climbing."

"Thank you, Halcyone." Ro smirked, imagining her father's expression about now. He'd be attempting to dig through the computer, trying to figure out if this was her doing, but he couldn't be certain and he'd have to check the levels manually. It only took a few minutes before the AI sounded another alarm.

"Radiation levels in engineering thirty-three percent above ALARA. Initiating emergency lock down and containment. All personnel in engineering must proceed to indicated decon chambers."

"Good girl," Ro said. That would keep him busy. Even if he did figure out it was her hack, he'd have a tough time convincing Halcyone to stand down.

"Rosalen."

Even though she expected it, his voice emerging from her micro jolted her. "Hello, Father. Safe and secure?"

"I know you did this, Rosalen. Clever. Very clever."

"You taught me well," she said, her jaw tight, her right eyelid twitching.

"Perhaps I've miscalculated," he said. "You have done nicely, but now it's time to put our disagreements behind us."

Cold coiled in the pit of her belly. "What do you want?"

"Control over the AI."

He was brutally direct. Some things never changed. She rested her head in her hands. "And if I help you?"

"Then your companions will have safe passage."

Her cooperation for their lives. Why wasn't she surprised? She tugged her fingers through her long, tangled hair. "I don't believe you." The weariness in her voice was a thing with weight.

Approaching footsteps made her look up. Barre sat beside her, stripped off his gloves, and placed a hand on her arm. Ro put her hand on his and squeezed. She waited, counting the seconds for her father's response. Based on long, bitter experience, it would be either a threat or a bribe. She was betting on threat.

"Rosalen, I'm giving you a chance because you're my child. We both know you can't lock me in here forever. And if my business associates think you are my adversary, I won't be able to protect you."

Ro bowed her head. Parents were supposed to protect their children. It wasn't something open for negotiation.

Barre kept his silence, waiting with her.

"I need to consult with my crew." She glanced at Barre. He nodded.

"Don't go away, Father."

Barre smirked as she muted his response. Whatever it was, it wouldn't be pretty.

"How's Micah?"

"Asleep. His feet are pretty messed up. I sealed them with antiseptic goo, but he's going to need skin grafts."

That meant getting back to Daedalus somehow, and before her father's 'associates' showed up.

Barre frowned. "How long do you think before he gets out of

engineering?"

"Not sure. Depends on how cooperative Halcyone is feeling."

"I might be able to do something about that." Barre's dark eyes shone. "Can you carry a tune?"

"I guess."

Frowning, he shifted his gaze from her to her micro. "Never mind. Here, record this."

A few trilling notes from his device created a brief fanfare in the bridge.

"It'll let Halcyone know you're authorized."

"That's different," Ro said, smiling as she imagined her father trying to hack that password.

"Will that buy us some more time?"

"Hell, yeah. It's brilliant."

Barre smiled before turning away to try and hide the flush on his cheeks. She knew what it felt like to be systematically squashed for being good at what she loved.

"Okay, then. We need to figure out how to ping Hephaestus. Even if Halcyone's jump drive were on line, without maps, we're just so much floating space junk."

"Any word from Nomi?"

Ro ducked her head, staring at her micro. "No."

"Intruder alert, sector two."

"Hey, there's our ride." Talk about perfect timing. "Halcyone, put it on screen and magnify."

The broken image of the star field remained unchanged.

Barre smirked and played the fanfare.

She nodded her thanks and repeated the command. The screen blanked out for a brief flicker. When it brightened again, the image shifted so quickly, Ro got queasy and had to look away.

"Intruder alert, sectors two and nine. Time to intercept, three minutes."

"What?" Ro scanned the screen. A single moving blip at its center moved in and out of the jagged crack that split it into two discontinuous images. "Halcyone, display both ships with trajectories."

Another nauseating shift and her perspective changed. Two vessels streamed towards them at nearly identical bearings from either side.

"Time to intercept, two minutes, thirty seconds."

"Shit," Barre said softly. "Which one is Hephaestus?"

Ro's mouth dried and she swallowed hard. "What if neither of them are?" She pulled out her micro and reestablished comms to her father. "Who did you contact?"

"Rosalen, give me access to the AI."

"Who. Did. You. Contact." Ro pushed the words out between gritted teeth.

"Time to intercept, two minutes."

"They'll be expecting a greeting. I think you'd better rethink your current course of action."

"And if I don't?"

"They'll cripple the ship and take the cargo. My way will leave us with money and freedom. What will your way accomplish?"

"Fuck you." Ro cut him off again.

"Time to intercept, one minute, thirty seconds."

"Barre?"

"Can we hail them and bluff?"

"I don't think so."

"We have to run."

Time seemed to slow down and speed up at the same time. They couldn't jump and they couldn't outrun anything in this ship. Halcyone was a cargo vessel, retrofitted to transport troops. Their shields would hold against an asteroid hit or a near miss, but not against modern weapons fire. Hell, even if they had weapons, she wouldn't trust them not to tear themselves apart.

"Time to intercept, one minute."

She glanced at the ruined bridge doors. They would never seal again. "Grab Micah. Come on!" She ran towards the corridor without looking back, a countdown starting in her head. "Hurry!" Ro led them into the storage bay that had been Micah's lab.

Barre grunted as he set Micah down on the floor. He didn't stir.

"Halcyone, seal the doors in this compartment." Engineering was already taken care of, and if not, her father would experience a very nasty decompression. "Vent atmosphere from unsealed compartments and one third of our plasma. Shut down all but emergency lights." She hoped Barre didn't get motion sick. "Take inertial stabilizers off line and roll the ship twenty degrees to port."

Halcyone fell eerily quiet. The soft breath of life support, the nearly imperceptible hum of the stabilizers, and the high-pitched whine of the lights that Ro had become accustomed to were all silent. She was sure Barre would be able to hear her wild heartbeat.

"What about life signs?" Barre asked. "Can you mask our signatures?"

"I think so." Her fingers flying across the micro's input, Ro tweaked her ghost program. It wouldn't hold up to scrutiny, but it was the best she could do. It would have to work.

"Time to intercept, zero seconds."

She looked into Barre's wide eyes, knowing hers were just as frightened. "We've got company."

Chapter 38

"ENSIGN NAKAMURA, REPORT to the bridge."

Nomi smiled grimly. She was already on her way there. At least now she didn't need to find a reason for them to let her talk to the commander. Sprinting hard the rest of the way, she was out of breath by the time she got to the doorway. The doors hissed open.

The bridge was a model of quiet efficiency. Soft task lighting cocooned each work station in a cone of brightness and every bridge officer sat focused at task.

She stepped up to Targill's command station. "Ensign Nakamura, reporting, sir."

He turned his intense blue-eyed regard to her and it took all her will power not to retreat. "Take primary comms," he said.

"Yes, sir," she said, blinking in confusion. The woman sitting at comms handed over her headset before vacating the chair. The routine of settling in kept her thoughts from spinning into a whirlwind. Sweat beaded at her forehead.

Targill's voice vibrated through her headset. "We're tracking an unknown, unmarked ship in this sector."

Nomi's heartbeat thumped in an erratic rhythm. The ship's signature brightened on her display. Nothing traveling that fast could be a forty-year-old wreck.

"We're extrapolating its trajectory in relation to Halcyone's last known position."

What could he possibly want her to do that Hephaestus's own comms officer couldn't do with more skill?

"You will have the entire ship's array at your disposal, Ensign. Find a way to contact Rosalen Maldonado."

"Yes, sir," she said, pairing her micro directly to the vastly more powerful ship's antenna array. "Sir?"

"Ensign?"

"The cargo, sir, Jem told me. It's weapons." She hoped Ro would understand. "Micah Rotherwood may be part of the conspiracy." Targill didn't answer. At least she'd passed on the message. Now she needed to warn Ro or at least to find her before the other ship did.

Nomi narrowed her focus to the micro and Ro's tunneling program. The ship's transmitter should be able to directly hit most of the ansibles in this sector. One of them had to be close enough to one-hop a message right to Ro.

We're coming. Hold tight. Rogue ship also searching.

She paused for a moment before adding something for Barre.

Jem's in recovery.

No matter what happened next, if it had been her brother, she would have wanted to know. Nomi set the message to loop every five seconds as they streamed toward wherever the enemy ship was heading.

She sank into the high-backed chair and focused on any ping-back from the ansibles she could see directly. The soft murmur of orders and acknowledgments formed a background hum that comforted her. All these people, all the resources of the ship, were trying to find Ro.

The routine of ping, search, and check for reply became hypnotic. She had to blink away every few cycles to stay sharp. Part of her console screen showed the rogue ship and Nomi's gaze flicked toward it. Navigation mapped its trajectory, updating its course on a moment to moment basis, but there was nothing she could do to help. Ro was smart. Ro was resourceful. She was going to be okay.

An alarm blared through the bridge, obliterating the soft sounds of their routines. Nomi jerked upright in her seat as the lights flashed red.

"Target acquired. Engagement in ninety seconds." The AI's steady voice cut through the alarm.

Nomi blinked at the display. Two lights pulsed on the screen. One hung motionless in the field of stars.

"Battle stations," Targill ordered, his voice just as emotionless as the computer's.

"Shields stable."

"Weapons ready, Commander."

"Tactical ready."

The voices of the bridge crew seemed to come from everywhere, moving through her headset and the overhead comms in a strange echo.

"We have visual confirmation on Halcyone!"

"Magnify and display," Targill said.

Nomi looked up and gasped. Plasma vented from the ship in a thin milky stream that obscured the stars behind it. The wreck drifted, nearly invisible but for emergency marker lights and the glowing plasma. "No, no, it can't be," Nomi whispered, a heaviness lodging itself in her throat.

"Life support is offline. Engines are cold."

"Bring us around between Halcyone and the target."

Targill's voice was so calm.

"Scan for life signs when in range."

How could he be so calm? Nomi couldn't tear her gaze from the crippled ship. Ro's ship. She couldn't breathe. She couldn't swallow. Tears made her vision waver and Nomi swiped them away, forcing herself to stare at their target. "Die you sons of bitches," she whispered.

"Tactical, fire a warning shot."

Light crackled at the bottom of the view screen and arced toward the ship. Hephaestus rocked with return fire.

"Shield integrity at ninety-eight percent." The implacable voice of Hephaestus's AI kept a running counterpoint to the murmur of commands across the bridge.

"Comms, hail them."

Nomi jerked upright in her seat. She was comms now. With impossibly steady hands, she opened a line-of-sight channel for the commander.

"This is Commonwealth Vessel Hephaestus," Targill said. "Cease fire immediately and identify yourself."

She split her attention between her console screen and the commander. Another volley hit them and bounced off their shields.

"Shields holding."

"Halcyone in range. No life signs aboard."

The words seared themselves into her brain and Nomi cried out, her pain cutting through the bridge chatter like a plasma knife through polymer.

Targill kept giving orders as if the report and her reaction never happened. "Tactical, target comms and propulsion. I want that ship crippled."

"Aye, aye, sir," answered a chorus of voices from around her.

Crippled? They deserved to be obliterated. An ache settled in her chest as she stared back at the drifting, broken Halcyone. "I'm so sorry, Ro," she whispered. It wasn't fair. She barely got the chance to know her before the cosmos snatched her away. It wasn't fair. Nomi curled her hands into tight fists.

Hephaestus shook under a barrage of torpedoes. The red lights ringing the bridge stuttered before stabilizing.

"Evasive maneuvers!" Targill shouted.

Nomi gripped the armrests as the ship shuddered under the sudden acceleration. Her stomach fluttered until the stabilizers compensated.

"Shield integrity at seventy-six percent and falling."

The AI sounded positively cheerful, as if it were announcing local time or distance to a wormhole nexus.

"Helm, come about. Divert power from the rear to the forward shields. Plot a collision course."

"Yes, sir."

Nomi's hands shook to match the tremor in the helm officer's voice. She glanced at Targill, but his face remained utterly impassive. Only his roving gaze betrayed any of the tension he had to be feeling.

The rogue ship stood its ground and fired volley after volley.

"Shields holding."

"Increase speed twenty percent."

"Yes, sir."

The bridge vibrated ever so slightly as Hephaestus accelerated.

Their target switched to plasma cannons and the main screen flared out under the fierce impact.

"Increase speed another twenty percent."

"Aye, aye."

Nomi blinked as the screen refreshed. The ship bloomed huge in front of them. Her breath caught in her throat. Hephaestus zoomed out and rescaled. It was still too close.

"Fire all weapons."

"They're pulling away, sir."

"Calculate intercept course and pursue."

"Aye, aye, Commander."

Halcyone receded in the distance as they pursued the attacker. Nomi kept her gaze on it as long as she could until it dwindled down to a pinprick of light at the edge of her display.

*

The ships disappeared in a flash of weapons fire so intense it washed out the forward display. By the time the sensors had accommodated, there was nothing but empty space where the two vessels had been. "Well, there goes our ride." Ro slid to the floor, her whole body shaking, helpless to stop the laughter that echoed back to her, harsh and distorted.

"Ro, it's okay. We're safe."

Tears blurred her vision and she couldn't catch her breath. She was some desperate, wild animal, howling her mingled anger and fear to the empty cosmos. A hand pressed against the small of her back, warm, human, and reassuring.

"Ro. You did it. We're still here. It's okay."

She gulped in stale air and hiccupped several times as her breathing settled.

Barre hummed the soft fanfare he had written to access Halcyone, and the sound resonated through her bones. "Halcyone, bring life support and the stabilizers back on line. Right the ship. Set lighting to diurnal, daytime mode."

The room brightened and the barest of vibrations sent a tremor through the floor.

"Seal inner compartments. Assess and report atmosphere status."

Ro let Barre run through the ship's systems, comforted by his quiet competence. So this was what it was like to trust someone.

"Life support functioning at twenty-three percent. Crew advised not to leave sealed areas without backup oxygen."

That left them trapped here for the time being. At least she'd effectively trapped her father as well. Barre was a warm presence at her back and part of her wanted to just lie there and let someone else take charge. But that wouldn't be fair to him or to Micah. Ro might have dragged them into this on her own, but she wasn't alone anymore.

She took one more deep, steadying breath and pushed herself off the floor. "Thank you," she said. Barre lifted an eyebrow. "How's Micah?"

"I'll live," he said, his voice hoarse.

Ro swallowed in sympathy, her throat raw. "Good to know," she answered, barely able to look him in the eye.

Turning to her, he frowned. "Where is that fucker?"

"Stuck. In engineering," Barre answered. "Thanks to Ro."

She ducked her head and let her hair fall to cover her face.

Micah grunted, levering himself upright with his arms and looked down at his bandaged feet. "And where the hell are my shoes?"

"Melted. With several layers of skin," Barre said.

Micah's face paled and he lay back down, closing his eyes. "I didn't really need to know that."

"I wouldn't stress those bandages."

"You got it, Doc."

Ro's lips quirked into a brief smile as Barre accepted his defacto title.

"Someone mind telling me why we're in here?" Micah gestured to the disorganized, dismantled lab space. "And what happened while I was in brain orbit?"

"Quick version?"

"Sure."

Ro ticked off the major points on the fingers of her right hand. "My father's under radiation quarantine in engineering. Two ships intercepted us and probably blasted each other out of the cosmos while we played dead. We're still drifting and have no idea where we are. The hold is still full of weapons any number of parties are after. You need to be transported to a real medical facility after your action-hero impersonation." She ran out of fingers. "Oh, and Jem was evacuated to Hephaestus before everything went to shit. Any questions?"

He took a minute to digest all that before shaking his head. "So what do we do now?"

"Well, there's nothing we could do in the bridge that we can't access here. And I don't think it's a good idea to move you." She checked in with Barre and he nodded. "I know we have to be relatively close to Daedalus." Without star charts, it would be virtually impossible to navigate anywhere and stumbling around trying random burns in interstitial space was not Ro's idea of a good time. If they only had the damned star charts.

Her micro buzzed and Ro nearly let it crash to the floor. Her knees buckled and she grabbed the wall for support.

"What's wrong?" Barre asked.

She shook her head and reread the multiple copies of Nomi's scrolling message. Hephaestus had been one of those ships. The blood drained from her face. She turned to Barre and stared at him, her eyes burning with tears that refused to fall. He took her micro from her white fingers.

"No," he said. "We don't know. We can't know. Not for sure."

"Know what?" Micah asked, his gaze jumping from Ro to Barre and back again.

Barre kept his lips pressed together, still staring down at the message.

Ro collapsed to the floor, pressing her hands against her legs to keep them from trembling. "One of those ships was Hephaestus."

"Oh," Micah said.

The cargo bay fell silent. She closed her eyes, thinking of Nomi's gentle smile and her persistent kindness in the face of Ro's abrasiveness.

"We have to get back to Daedalus," Micah said.

"No," Barre said. "What if they need our help?"

It wasn't possible. There wasn't even enough debris left from the battle to register on their sensors.

"Look, if Hephaestus survived, they'll limp back to Daedalus. We can't stay here," Micah said. "Besides, our fathers have to pay for what they did, Ro."

Neither Jem nor Nomi would have been on that ship if it weren't for her. Ro slumped, her hair hanging lank and dull in her face.

"Barre, help me up," Micah said.

Ro ignored the shuffling across the room and Micah's sharp intake of breath. Two sets of feet intruded in her narrow view, one booted, the other bandaged. She looked up.

"We have to find a way back to Daedalus," Micah repeated, his face pale, but his gaze clear and steady.

"Tell us what you need us to do," Barre said, his voice hoarse, his skin grayed out, the circles beneath his eyes dark and shiny.

What she wanted to do was collapse and never get up again. There were not enough apologies in the world to ease the bruising in her heart or to soften Barre's grief, but if he could function, so could she.

A wet, dark stain spread across one of Micah's insteps. "Sit down, you idiot," she said. "And you." She turned her face to Barre. "You should know better."

Barre reached out his free hand and she let him help her up. Looking into his face, she made a silent promise to answer both Jem's loss and Nomi's, no matter what it took. She uncoupled a chair from its floor bolts and dragged it over to Micah.

"Sit."

He collapsed into the seat, trembling with relief.

"You need to keep them elevated." Barre pulled over a crate.

"But they don't hurt."

Ro looked down at her own foot, still blessedly numb in its cast. "That's not an advantage, you idiot."

"Warning. Unauthorized launch attempt. Emergency pod S-seven."

351

"Shit." Ro winced, reluctant to see the evidence of her stupidity, but they had to know. "Halcyone, show pod S-seven on ship's schematic, heads up display."

With vision-blurring speed, Halcyone zoomed through the ship, centering its point of view on engineering. Ro silently cursed her father.

"Warning. Unauthorized launch. Emergency pod S-seven."

"I'm sorry. I fucked up." She forgot to disable them, but who in their right mind would voluntarily cram themselves into one of the old-style life-pods unless they were desperate? Basically a kind of soaring airlock and without navigation or propulsion other than the initial thrust they got from their launch, the pods were slow, cramped and inefficient. Wincing, she looked up into Barre's and Micah's eyes, searching for the anger or condemnation she deserved.

"Halcyone, can you get a fix on it?" Barre asked.

"Affirmative."

He grimaced and triggered the authorization fanfare. "Track emergency pod S-seven."

"Course zero one three, mark twenty. Speed nominal."

"Where the hell is he going?" Ro said, more wondering than asking. "He wouldn't leave his precious cargo behind unless he had some plan to get control of it." The pods were barely big enough for a person, and Halcyone would have let them know if he'd been able to break the radiation lock-down and get to the cache. No, the guns were still on the ship. He had to be planning on retrieving them somehow. If they followed him, they could be limping right into a trap.

"He knows we're dead in the water," Micah said. "Hell, all he has to do is come back with a ship and declare salvage."

"Over my dead body," Ro said, glaring at him.

Micah glared back. "He'd probably be okay with those terms."

She knew he was right, on all counts. They had to move.

"Do you think he has charts?" Barre asked, staring at the little blip moving away from Halcyone.

"It doesn't matter. It's too risky," Ro said.

"Then what's our next move?" Micah said.

This would take Barre working on all frequencies. She looked into his grief-lined face. "We have to get control of the engines and navigation. With the wild burns this thing's made, it's a minor miracle we haven't plowed into an asteroid already."

He blinked, staring at her. "She did that once already."

Ro shivered, the echo of the lost transmission in her mind, the ghosts of the long dead crew, another helpless cargo just as they were now. "Wait." She shivered again, but this time a flare of excitement burned down her spine. "Wait. I think—" Barre and Micah both stared at her, hope and fear in their nearly identical expressions. Ignoring them, she leaped to her feet and wiped the micro's display clear.

"Halcyone, display current position."

Everything fell away from Ro—her grief and guilt, her responsibility for Barre and Micah, her father's latest betrayal—everything except the miniature star field and one tiny blinking light. "Access specifics of our last burn. Acceleration, direction, and distance." She held her breath, waiting, wondering just how badly Halcyone's memory and personality subroutines had been damaged. The silence in the cargo bay pressed down on her. *Come on, come on.*

"Burn data acquired."

She let out her breath in a relieved sigh. "Halcyone, calculate trajectory of last burn and display. Extrapolate the inverse course. Display overlay on current map. Zoom and recenter as needed."

She heard a gasp from behind her as the AI drew a dotted line from their current position to a second blinking dot. Just a few centimeters on the hologram—it seemed so impossibly close. With maddening precision, she asked the damaged computer to map out their crazy course in reverse, each leg representing a jagged line of a random flight.

"Here, sit." Barre slipped a chair behind her and pressed down on her shoulders. Her knees wobbly, she fell into the chair, panting as if she'd run a race.

The three of them looked up at the map and their way home.

Chapter 39

BARRE STARED AT the final blinking light that represented Daedalus station and swallowed, hard. Even the possibility of returning ignited a fierce pain in his chest. How could he go back without Jem?

"Barre, I need you to normalize the rad sensors in engineering."

He looked at Ro, the words making little sense.

"Otherwise the fail-safes won't let us calculate a burn."

Losing Jem was a raw wound, one he knew Ro and even Micah shared. But going back meant facing his parents—facing his own failure to keep his little brother safe.

A heavy hand settled on his shoulder and he turned to see Micah standing beside him.

"You did everything possible for him. No one could have done any more."

"I should have kept him here." Or he could have gone with him to Hephaestus. Then they would both be dead and he wouldn't have to drown in this terrible guilt.

"People we love die. Even when we do everything right. It's

not your fault." Barre tried to look away, but Micah's gaze trapped him, his blue eyes clouded with pain.

"Sit down. Your feet need to be re-bandaged, but all our supplies are on the bridge." Barre figured the anesthetic wouldn't hold for very long—not against the nerve damage from his burns.

"Look, I know what it's like to lose someone. If you need to talk, I'm here." Micah squeezed his shoulder before shuffling back to his seat.

He turned to Ro. She stood, her slim body rigid, staring at the little cube of space that glowed above her micro. "I'm going to work on calculating a single course back to Daedalus. The faster we get back there, the faster they can go after my father."

There was no guarantee the ship would even let them fire the engines, but he knew they had to try. Barre watched as Ro added a notation to the map, along with the time stamp of when Maldonado had stolen the life-pod and its last known course and speed. Even Barre knew the chances of finding him were slim to none, but he wasn't going to puncture Ro's happy little bubble-of-revenge fantasy.

Composing the strange melodies that communicated directly with the AI didn't distract him from Jem's death, but it let him pour his grief into something outside himself. Halcyone may have been a construct created out of logical code, but he knew the ship understood loss and regret.

As he released his musical program into the AI's awareness, he heard an answering coda; his pain played back to him.

"Radiation levels in engineering eighteen percent above ALARA. Within acceptable limits for crew safety. Lock-down lifted."

Ro glanced back at him and nodded her thanks. "Okay, people. Here's the plan." Micah scooted over to the display. "I have a course plotted. It should bring us in far orbit around Daedalus. If we have Halcyone go for maximum acceleration, we'll need to get back to the bridge and use the mats."

"How deep of a burn are you thinking of?" Barre asked. Even with the mats, it would be rough on Micah.

"Five gees."

"Not possible." If they had modern acceleration couches, maybe. Even then, he wouldn't risk Micah's feet, not unless they didn't have any other choice.

Ro glanced between him and Micah. Barre could just about see the code spinning in her mind. "Ro, it won't help us if we kill ourselves getting there. And it won't find your father any faster."

"Recalculate the burn at three," Micah said.

Barre frowned. It was still over the limit he was comfortable with, especially given the condition of the ship.

"Do it. My father has some questions to answer."

Ro returned to her micro's display. "Okay. Atmosphere is back to minimal safe levels in the ship. I have the parameters set. Ready to roll?"

He walked over to where Micah sat and bent down to pick him up. "Let's go."

"You're not carrying me," he said, scooting back.

"How do you think you got here in the first place?"

"Fine. Push the damned chair."

The more he could focus on Micah and his injuries and the upcoming burn, the less Barre had to think about Jem or his parents and how they would react. They would blame him. It didn't matter.

"Get settled as best you can," Barre said, shoving Micah's chair into the bridge. "At three gees, even with padding, it's still going to be a rough trip."

Micah tumbled out of the chair and onto his mat. Barre gritted his teeth and pulled Jem's over to give Micah's feet extra padding.

"Thanks, man."

He looked away, not trusting his voice.

"Ready?" Ro asked.

Barre looked away and lay down on his own mat.

"Barre?" Ro called his name softly.

He rolled his head toward her.

"Thank you." Her face burned scarlet all the way up to her scalp. "For everything. We wouldn't ... I wouldn't have gotten this far without you."

"Let's get out of here," Barre said. "We all have responsibilities back on Daedalus."

Ro nodded, her expression tight. "I'll toss the course data to your micro. Can you set a musical trigger for the burn?"

He should have thought of that. "Yeah, no problem." It took less than a minute for him to set up his auto-run to hook onto her program. "All set. Get yourself secured."

She scrambled to her mat. "Set."

Taking a series of deep breaths, Barre triggered Ro's navigation program through his neural. The engines growled beneath him. He forced his tense muscles to relax. Even expecting it, even lying as symmetrically as possible, he nearly panicked when the burn started and his weight suddenly tripled. The pressure squeezed down and his spine seemed to grind against the hard floor. The pad could have been tempered steel for all it cushioned him.

But no matter how much his own body complained, Micah would fare much, much worse. The pressure would stress the already damaged capillaries in his feet that were oozing plasma through the burned skin. He wished he'd taken the time to re-bandage him before. But it was too late now and all Barre could do was struggle to force air into his squeezed lungs and hope that Ro knew what the hell she was doing.

The burn seemed to go on and on. What if their commands had triggered another fight-or-flight response from Halcyone? What if the acceleration never stopped, not until Halcyone's fuel ran out and the fusion drive died, leaving the silent ship to drift in space, carrying three battered corpses?

Then his own parents would be long dead and Jem's memory lost as well. There was something oddly comforting in that thought.

Silence blanketed the bridge. *So this is what deafness feels like,* he thought, a floating calm carrying him along in its wake. No noise. No music. No need to do anything. It wasn't just his mind that floated, but his body felt strangely light. He could breathe. The enormous fist that had pinned him down had disappeared so suddenly, he gasped. The return of the ragged sound of his own breathing seemed like a wheezing metronome. Barre blinked, reveling in the sensation of his chest rising and falling easily. A groan pulled his attention outward.

"Micah?"

"Shit. My feet. They're bleeding again."

Barre pushed himself to sitting, shaking his head to clear it of his lightheaded confusion. "Ro? Where are we?"

Her laughter—a bright sound, but to Barre's trained ears,

edged with fear—filled the bridge. "Ground zero. Look."

For the first time since Jem smuggled him aboard the broken ship, the view screen showed a familiar constellation. The small asteroid that had been home for the past year twinkled in the distance with its evening lights. "Now what?" he asked, though no one but Ro and Micah could hear him.

"Wait until we're line of sight with their antenna array and send a message directly to Mendez," Ro said.

"We need to get Micah to sick bay." Which meant his parents. He scrambled over to him and shook his head at the mess of his feet. "At least I can re-seal these wounds, for now."

"Intruder alert. Ship bearing zero-zero-seven-mark-three. Time to engagement thirty-seven seconds."

"Shit!" Ro shouted.

Barre winced as a blast of defiant sound pierced through him.

The ship's engines rumbled.

Red lights washed over the melted consoles.

He crouched over Micah, stabilizing him.

"Halcyone, this is—"

"Ro! Ro can you hear me?"

"No! We can't make another burn like this!" Micah said.

"Wait! Nomi?" Ro's voice cracked.

"Hephaestus." Barre stared up at the ship displayed on the cracked screen as if he could see his brother somewhere inside it.

"Halcyone, stand down," Ro shouted.

The engines continued to growl. Barre sent a furious arpeggio of sound through his neural toward the ship. "Don't you dare," he warned, as the music surged around him. "This is home." Jem was home. The song he composed swelled and filled the bridge, too. "Don't you dare," he said again.

The engines stilled. Barre let the music falter and sat back smiling as Ro and Micah stared at him in stunned silence.

*

Hephaestus's orderly bridge erupted in an explosion of sound until Targill bellowed, "Silence!"

"Ro," Nomi whispered, staring up at the view screen, tears blurring her sight of the definitely not-adrift Halcyone, her face hurting from smiling so hard. The bridge reassembled into its usual quiet efficiency. Targill stood.

"Open a channel. Let's try that again."

Nomi blinked the wetness from her eyes.

"Comms?"

She jolted upright. "Aye, Commander. Channel open."

"Halcyone, this is Hephaestus. What is your status?"

"Hephaestus, this is Halcyone. We are five by five. Repeat, five by five. All systems stable."

Hearing Ro's confident voice set her heart pounding.

"We have skimmers standing by to escort you to Daedalus station. Do any of you require medical assistance to evacuate?"

"Thank you, Hephaestus. Please stand by."

Commander Targill stood and every eye on the bridge turned to him. He cocked his head at the view screen and lifted a single eyebrow. Nomi blinked and her mouth fell open. Targill drummed his fingers on the arm of his command chair.

"Halcyone, we will send a skimmer to repatriate Alain Maldonado to the crew."

"Alain Maldonado is no longer on board this ship, Commander. Halcyone out."

The channel snapped shut from Ro's end, feedback from Nomi's headset squealing through her ears. What the hell was that all about? She glanced up at Targill to find his deep-set eyes staring at hers.

"Open a secure channel to Commander Mendez. I'll take it privately," Targill said, his voice very calm and controlled.

Nomi swallowed hard before turning to her console and contacting Daedalus.

*

"What?" Ro asked, meeting the nearly identical and stunned expressions on Micah and Barre's faces.

Micah got control of himself first. "You just dismissed the commander of a Commonwealth ship, Ro."

"Yes. Yes, I did." A smile stretched across her face. "We started this and we're going to finish it. On our own terms." She glanced at each of them in turn. "You with me?"

Barre laughed, a deep booming sound that reverberated through the bridge.

"Hell, yeah," Micah said.

"Good." Ro took a quick peek at the view screen at the larger, newer ship. "If he moves, let me know." She turned to her micro and tuned the comms interface to Daedalus's frequency. "Daedalus station, this is Rosalen Maldonado aboard Halcyone. Request a secure channel to Commander Mendez."

"Stand by, Halcyone." The man's voice sounded bored, as if ships returned from the dead with missing crew members every day.

The seconds stretched out into minutes. Ro turned to Micah and Barre, frowning. What the hell was taking so long?

"Miss Maldonado, you've had quite a ride, I understand."

Ro looked into Micah's eyes. He nodded.

"Commander Mendez, we advise that you place Senator Rotherwood under guard immediately." Her words came out in a pressured rush.

"This young woman is clearly deranged, Commander."

Fuck. So much for their secured line.

Micah's eyes widened and his already pale face turned an icy gray.

"Where is he?" the senator shouted. "I demand to speak with my son."

"Rosalen," Mendez said, "there are some very concerned parents here who would like to hear from their children."

Ro stiffened at Mendez's use of her given name and struggled to keep her voice calm. Barre squeezed her shoulder. "Commander, we have evidence on board Halcyone that implicates the senator in the forgery of diplomatic seals and arms trading."

"Barre, what is happening up there? How did Jem get injured?"

So the Doctors Durbin were there too. Hephaestus must have gotten to Daedalus before they did.

Barre kept silent.

"I swear if she's done something to Micah—"

"Shut up, Father," Micah said, softly, the pain and exhaustion in his voice mirrored in his slumping shoulders and deep frown lines across his forehead. "We have the weapons and we have the seals. We have audio of you and Ro's father conspiring together. It's over."

"Maldonado?" Mendez's sharp voice pulled Ro to attention. The patronizing tone had vanished.

"Our hold is full of contraband, Commander."

"I protest these baseless insinuations. That my own son would support them speaks to some kind of brain washing or threat." The elder Rotherwood's voice filled the comm link and the bridge with smooth, polished denials.

Micah spat out a curse and would have strode out of the bridge if it weren't for his damaged feet. Ro winced in sympathy and wished she could cut off the line and shut the bastard up.

"Maldonado," Mendez interrupted, "maintain your orbit. Our skimmers are en route to tow you in."

"You will, of course begin proceedings against this Maldonado girl."

Ro gritted her teeth. How far did the conspiracy go? What if they took control of Halcyone and made the evidence vanish? Micah gripped the chair, his knuckles turning white. Barre paced the bridge, his brows drawn low over his eyes.

"Sergeant, please escort the senator to his quarters," Mendez said, and Ro could well imagine the cold look she turned Rotherwood's way. "I think, under these circumstances, it would be best if we kept you in protective custody, Senator."

Ro exhaled heavily. "Holding orbit, sir."

A furious roar distorted through the comm link. "Keep your hands off me!" the senator shouted.

"Take cover!" someone yelled.

More shouts followed the twang of energy weapons discharge.

Micah jumped to his feet. Barre tried to wrestle him back down and they both ended up on the floor in a pile.

"Commander! Commander!" Ro cried out.

"Daedalus—medical emergency, command," Leta Durbin's voice cut through the confusion. "Code gamma. Two men down. Repeat, two men down."

The comm link shut down abruptly and the silence in the bridge was broken only by their harsh breathing.

"What's code gamma?" Ro asked, keeping her voice to a strained whisper.

Barre scrambled off Micah and hauled him back into the chair.

"Weapons fire, thermal, or chemical burns," Barre answered, his voice shaking.

"What the hell's going on?" Micah asked. He leaned forward and stared at the station in the cracked view screen.

Ro shivered and folded her arms across her chest. "I don't know." She joined him, looking straight ahead and gasped as two skimmers rose from the station hangar. "There's our welcoming committee."

"You think?" Micah said, continuing to stare ahead, without blinking, not bothering to track their escorts.

Ro dropped her head in her hands. "I don't know what to think anymore."

Chapter 40

Micah sat, his eyes squeezed shut, hands gripping the arms of the chair to keep from moving as Barre re-bandaged his feet. He didn't need Ro's startled gasp to tell him how bad it looked. The coppery tang of the bloody bandages mingled with the sickly sweetness of infection.

"I know you probably don't want to hear this now, but the pain is a good sign. It means the burn didn't damage the nerves in your dermis."

"Thanks," Micah muttered through his clenched jaw. He knew Barre was being as gentle as possible and that once his feet were covered again, some of the pain would ease. And if they weren't being thrown into the brig, real treatment was just moments away. He opened his eyes. "Anything?"

"No," Ro answered. "They're not answering our comms."

A crackle of an incoming message startled them all. "Halcyone, this is security detail alpha one and two. Please match speed and vector. Acknowledge."

They glanced at one another for a moment before Ro shrugged.

Barre did his musical communion with the AI and Ro set the ship in motion.

"Security detail alpha one and two, this is Halcyone," she said. "Matching speed and vector."

"Stand by for tow deployment."

Two jolts rocked the ship in quick succession. Micah gripped the edge of his chair, but the ship didn't even twitch.

"Tow lines deployed, Halcyone. See you ground-side."

"Thank you, security," Ro said. "Please be advised we have an injured party on board who will need transport assistance."

Micah envied Barre and Ro's smooth choreography as the ship glided down in the wake of the two skimmers. Automatic docking clamps pulled them in with barely a bump. The ship's engines faded. They were home. He blinked and glanced around the bridge. They hadn't even been gone a full solar week.

"Come on. Let's greet our 'escorts' at the airlock, shall we?" Ro held herself straight and tall, every centimeter a captain, despite the dark smudges beneath her eyes, her lank hair, and the worn and dirty clothes.

"Aye, aye, Cap," Micah said, summoning a smile from somewhere for her.

She smirked. "Barre, would you kindly escort our engineer-slash-botanist?"

"After you," Barre said.

"No, Doc, after you."

Barre shoved Micah's chair toward the ruined door.

"I think she's confused," Micah said in a stage whisper. "Something about the captain going down with the ship. Should we tell her we've already landed?"

Ro swatted him on his head as they passed her.

They watched as pressure-suited crew attached a new temporary umbilical to the external hatch.

"What do you think? Are we under arrest?" Micah asked.

"Probably not 'we'," Ro said, her face expressionless.

Two of the station crew stood in the airlock, side arms prominent, but holstered. Micah glanced at Ro. She stared straight ahead, her body at parade rest, but he could read the tension in her shoulders.

"Barre, open the lock," she said.

A soft hiss escaped from the door as he broke the seal. The round door swung inward silently on enormous hinges. Two bridge officers nodded to them. "Commander Mendez has requested your presence in her office." Neither made a move for their weapons. That seemed a promising sign.

"Micah Rotherwood needs medical assistance. He has serious burns on both of his feet and a head wound that needs looking after."

The taller man turned and waved. "We have transport available. Medical staff will meet him at the commander's office."

Well, that was that. He looked up at Barre. "Hey, Doc, thanks for everything."

He glanced down at Micah's feet. "You're crazy, man. You know that?"

A medic ran through the open airlock with a transport chair and helped Micah scoot over into it. At least it moved more smoothly than the one they'd been using. Barre and Ro fell in beside him and the three of them followed their escorts to command.

They must have made a strange parade, but the corridors were fairly deserted. It wasn't unusual for mid-shift on the sparsely populated station, but still Micah felt uneasy. He glanced at Barre. At least he'd expected the Doctors Durbin to meet them, if only to triage his injuries.

What a fucked up mess all their families were.

Silent guards led them to Mendez's office. Their escorts peeled off and took positions at either side of the door. Even the transporter left. Barre pushed the chair over the threshold.

The acrid scent of burning synthetics triggered a cough deep in Micah's chest and made his eyes water. "What the hell?" He glanced up into the fierce gaze of Commander Mendez. "Sorry, sir."

"Ms. Maldonado. Mr. Durbin. Mr. Rotherwood." She made eye contact with each of them before indicating two additional seats.

"Commander. I don't understand. What's going on?" Ro asked, looking around the burn-scarred walls and floor, her eyes wide. Micah followed her gaze and found a small drying pool of blood by the door. He swallowed the lump in his throat.

Mendez's micro buzzed softly. "I need to ask for your patience. I only want to go over this once."

Micah frowned as the door chime sounded.

"Enter!" Mendez said sharply, and hit the door release.

"Barre!" Jem's squeal filled the office. Barre turned, his mouth falling open as Jem was wheeled in a chair twin to Micah's. Half of his head was shaved even closer than Jem usually wore it and a z-shaped scar traversed the bald area.

Barre's face grayed and he grabbed onto the back of Micah's chair to keep from hitting the ground. "Jem!" He stepped over to his brother and knelt at his side, his dreadlocks falling to cover his face as his shoulders shook.

Micah looked away, embarrassed. At least someone would have a happy reunion.

He glanced at Ro to share the irony. Her mouth open, she stepped back slowly until she hit the wall behind her. Micah followed her gaze across the room and met Nomi's smiling face.

Well, shit, he thought, *where's my happy ending?*

Mendez cleared her throat and everyone snapped their attention to her. "Commander Targill, thank you for your assistance."

A large man crowded the room. Targill stood nearly a head taller than Barre and his silver hair gleamed in the soft light. When he turned, Micah shivered at the cold, calculating blue gaze that flickered over his face and dismissed him. It traveled on to take in the damage to the room and the blood on the floor. This was the man he'd tried to make a deal with. If he'd have seen him in action first, he wouldn't have bothered.

Silent officers glided in with extra chairs for Targill and Nomi. She scooted hers next to Ro.

Mendez leaned on the edge of her desk in front of the six of them and cleared her throat again. "Thank you for your patience," she said. "Your father is under guard in the med bay. He killed one of my security officers and then shot himself. Unfortunately for him, not fatally."

Micah slumped against the back of his chair, trying to make sense of her words, and failing.

"Even without your evidence, he will be tried for this crime." Her mouth hardened to a thin line.

There were ways to wriggle out of nearly anything if you had the money and power of his father's "friends," but this was the murder of a Commonwealth officer recorded through an impartial AI and duly witnessed.

"Ms. Maldonado."

Ro snapped to attention and Nomi's hand slipped from hers.

"Where is my chief engineer?"

"Sir, I have no idea."

Mendez frowned and leaned forward.

"He was able to escape from Halcyone in a life-pod. We have his last known position and bearing but were unable to follow him."

"Escape? Explain."

Micah read her reluctance in the tremor that shook her hands and the tension in the set of her shoulders. She glanced at his face, then down to his bandaged feet. The new dressings were already beginning to seep through.

Ro stared straight ahead and spoke tonelessly as if she were reading a lab report. "Commander, Chief Engineer Maldonado struck me, shot Micah, sealed Barre and me in the ship's bridge, and imprisoned and tortured Micah with illegal restraints." The room fell utterly silent. "Micah sustained significant burns on his feet escaping from said restraints and freeing us from the bridge."

"Continue," Mendez said, her arms folded across her chest.

"We trapped the chief engineer in engineering. He somehow escaped to the life-pods and was able to flee the ship."

Micah wanted Ro to stop, to break down and cry, to show her rage or her frustration, but she sat locked in a painful stillness he didn't have a clue how to shatter. Nomi lifted a tentative hand toward her. Ro shuddered and looked up at Mendez. Nomi looked away, her hand falling back into her lap.

"Continue."

"You'll find the cache of weapons, field rations, medic

supplies, and the shock restraints in Halcyone's hold. Enough to start a small war," Ro kept talking in that same emotionless voice. "They were packed under diplomatic seal. Very well forged diplomatic seals."

Mendez still didn't say anything.

Ro fell silent as well. Micah caught Barre's gaze and frowned back at him.

"Commander Mendez," Micah said, drawing all the eyes in the room. He sat up as straight and with as much dignity as the transport chair would allow. "Are we under arrest?"

"No, Mr. Rotherwood. Is there a reason you should be?"

Micah exhaled slowly. They could search the ship and maybe they'd find some evidence of bittergreen, but nothing that tied him to the plant. Certainly not intent to distribute, which was as much a move of utmost stupidity, given the cartel, as it was against the Commonwealth codes.

"Then are we free to go?"

Mendez frowned and studied each of them in turn. "I'm releasing all of you to medical. When our doctors pronounce you fit, you may return to your quarters."

Out of the corner of his eye, he saw Ro slump against her chair back. "What about Halcyone?" she asked softly.

The door chime sounded and Mendez hit the release. A swarm of medical staff wove through the chairs and pulled him and Jem away before he could hear if Mendez answered Ro's question.

*

Jem squeezed Barre's hand. "I'm glad you're not dead. It would have been really awkward to tell Mom and Dad."

"Right back at you, kid," Barre said. "Hey, I got this." Out in the corridor, he grabbed the transport chair and wrested it from the orderly's hands.

The motion jerked Jem side to side and he was overcome by a wave of dizziness. He shut his eyes, but that didn't stop the heaving in his stomach or the throbbing that started in his head. "Barre?"

"What's up?"

"Can you go easy, okay?"

"Sure. Everything all right?"

"Yeah. No problem." He'd tried to use his micro on Hephaestus, but every time he focused in on the display, the same terrible chaos would overwhelm his brain. If he couldn't see, he couldn't program and if he couldn't program, Jem didn't know what he was going to do. He turned his face away so Barre couldn't see tears gathering in his eyes.

The ride to medical was worse than getting off Hephaestus, not only because of the increasing nausea, but because he knew his parents would be waiting. They would blame Barre, but Jem knew it was his fault.

Barre patted his shoulder and Jem knew he would do it all again, just the same way, even if he knew how it would turn out.

*

Nomi walked Ro to medical, waiting for Jem and Micah to be transported first. She watched her limp, favoring the left leg in its cracking cast. "Do you need a ride?"

"I can manage."

She was quiet, pulled inward. Something had happened in the hours between the time her father came aboard and the return to Daedalus—something more than the bruises she could see on Ro's face. For the thousandth time, Nomi cursed Alain Maldonado and his selfish paranoia.

Ro seemed to sense Nomi's unease and she turned to her, a half smile on her face. "I'll be fine after a shower and some real food."

"And coffee?"

The smile widened. "Most definitely coffee."

Nomi squeezed Ro's hand at the door to the sick bay. "Come find me when you're done here, okay?"

Ro squeezed back, but her gaze looked past Nomi's. "I will," she said. Her green eyes shifted and focused again. "Thank you."

"For what?" Nomi laughed. "You rescued yourselves." She should have known Ro would figure out a way.

"Knowing you were looking for me—" Ro paused, her face flushed. "It helped. It was important. That we weren't—that I wasn't alone."

Nomi ducked her head.

"I promise. I'll find you," Ro said.

She felt Ro's gaze follow her as she walked the length of the corridor back to her quarters.

Chapter 41

THEY HUSTLED MICAH from the transport chair to a medi-bed and pulled the privacy screens down. Dr. Kristoff Durbin stared down at him, frowning, his thick, graying brows nearly masking the ice blue of his eyes.

"Tell me," he said, as he turned his hands front to back under the sanitizer and slipped into the waiting gloves.

He shrugged, trying to avoid the full horror of what Maldonado had done to him. "I had to get free. There was a blaster handy. I used it."

"Cutter," he said, holding out his right hand. A silent, gloved tech placed the thin laser-augmented blade in his sterile palm. "This won't be pleasant. Do you want a sedative?"

Micah bit his lower lip to keep from laughing. Not pleasant. Right. "No, thank you, sir." No. He wanted to be fully awake and owning the pain and anger for the time he could confront his father. "Just get it over with." He lay back and folded his arm across his eyes.

"Huh," Dr. Durbin said.

That was not exactly what Micah wanted to hear.

"Barre dress this?"

"Yes, sir." He wanted to add something to push back against the slightly nasal, superior tone in Durbin's voice.

"He did a good job."

Micah smirked at the grudging praise. It was too bad Barre couldn't hear him.

"Hold very still."

The pain echoed the blast burn, but it wasn't the insidious torture of the shocks. He gritted his teeth and let it sear through him as Durbin sliced the bandages off.

"I'm afraid we're going to have to cut your pants as well."

At this point, they could probably get up and walk away on their own. "Knock yourself out, Doc." No, that was Barre. "Doctor Durbin."

Competent hands turned him and tugged the fabric away as Durbin opened the trouser seams. The technician covered him with a warm blanket.

"Thank you," Micah said.

"You're a very lucky man, Mr. Rotherwood. Another few seconds on the trigger and you might well have lost your feet. Without the field bandages, the infection would have spread to your vascular system and would likely have killed you."

Lucky wasn't how Micah would have put it.

"Normally, we'd start rebuilding your feet with artificial skin implants right away, but we're going to have to do this in stages."

Micah levered himself up, leaning on his arms, careful not to look down at his feet. "How long?"

Durbin blinked. "Until the lesions are fully healed?"

"Until I can walk."

"Sorry, son, but you're going to be off those feet for at least several weeks."

He stiffened. "Don't call me that."

"Apologies." Durbin gave a small, formal bow.

"Accepted."

"We need to clean out the wounds and deal with the infection first."

"Do what you have to." Micah lay back again. "Where is my father?"

"Set up the ultrasonic unit in here," Durbin ordered, ignoring the question.

The isolation curtain shifted and the hushed sounds of medical orders, conversations, and beeping machines drifted into his cubicle. The technician returned with a tubing kit and quickly assembled it as Durbin waited.

"Doctor Durbin. Where is he?"

Durbin sighed. "In the isolation bay."

"I want to see him."

"That's up to the commander."

"Like hell it is. He's still my father. I'm his next of kin. Trust me, I've been down the medical road before. I know what I'm allowed."

Durbin closed his eyes briefly. When he opened them, he nodded. "Let me clean and seal the tissue first. Then I'll arrange for you to see him."

"Fine."

"Hold still."

Durbin pulled the wand over and gestured to the technician to turn the unit on. A high-pitched hum filled the room and

Micah wondered if Barre would be able to tell him what note it sang. He stiffened as the device played over his feet, but other than a strange pulling sensation, it barely hurt.

"The sealant has antibiotics and analgesics in a time release matrix. It's not pleasant when it touches the damaged nerves, but it will ease. Are you ready?"

"Just get on with it," Micah said, nearly snarling with impatience. In the end, he regretted not asking for that sedative, but he wasn't going to tell Durbin that. "My father. Take me. Now."

Durbin frowned down at him. "I'm concerned—"

Micah swung his newly bandaged legs over the side of the bed. "Doctor, I will be seeing my father now. With or without your help."

The Doctor narrowed his eyes.

The blood throbbed in his feet, and the pain nearly made Micah retch, but he focused on his breathing, keeping Dr. Durbin's face in his receding line of sight.

"All right," he said softly. He motioned the technician over. "Bring us a transport chair. I'll escort him." Turning to Micah, he frowned again. He could tell by the deep lines in his forehead that it was a well-practiced expression. "Your father is in critical condition. You have five minutes."

"Fine." Durbin stabilized his legs and helped him scoot over to the chair. Micah tucked the blanket under him and sat up stiffly as the doctor pushed him out of the treatment bay and to the shaded isolation area on the far side of medical.

Two armed guards stood at attention on either side of the closed ward.

"If he's that critical, what do they think he's going to do?"

Durbin didn't answer. He cycled the two of them through the airlock.

Micah drew his breath in sharply. His father lay on a medi-bed, intubated, and on life support. The soft beeping of monitors and the whoosh of air forced in and out of his unresponsive lungs were the only sounds in the sterile room.

Swearing quietly, he maneuvered the chair out of Durbin's hold and toward his father. Half of his head was covered in surgical drapes. "What happened?" His voice was hardly louder than the life support equipment.

"He wrestled a weapon from one of the officers. The man got shot in the scuffle. The senator shot himself in the head." Durbin could have been giving any bland medical report.

Micah struggled to find a single memory of the man where he wasn't selling something to someone. Even when his mother lay dying, he hadn't had the balls to show her some honest grief.

He leaned forward and laughter shook through him until he couldn't breathe and tears streamed down his face. Durbin placed a heavy hand on his shoulder. Micah shrugged it off. "Can he hear me?"

"Probably."

"Good." Micah pulled his chair closer and bent his head close to his father's intact ear. "You son of a bitch. Selfish to the end. You didn't even leave me anything to trade you for. But hey, your perfect face will look just fine at the funeral. Well played, Senator. Well played."

"Micah," Durbin said.

He cut him off. "I'm done here." The senator would live or die, but it didn't matter anymore. His father had been gone a long time. It just took Micah until now to accept it.

*

Ro watched Micah disappear into a treatment bay and turned to the triage nurse. "My ankle needs to be re-cast. Then you're going to clear me to return to duty."

He stared her down. "Trust me. If I can throw you out of medical, I will."

She gritted her teeth, knowing of all of them, her injuries were likely the most inconsequential. "How are Micah and Jem?"

He consulted his micro. "Stable and Serious. Turn your head." He cleaned the split on her cheek and ran a scanner over the cast. "Give me five minutes."

"Fine."

In his competent hands, the laser cutter seamed the broken cast in seconds. Exposed to the air and free of the anesthetic wrap, her ankle throbbed in time to her heartbeat.

"I'm going to infuse a bone stimulant along with the pain-killer. Minimal walking once I put the stabilizer on."

She nodded, watching him prepare the tiny device. He affixed it to her ankle, bridging the fracture, before wrapping her lower leg in a device as much external scaffolding as cast.

Ro lurched her way to her quarters and stood at the door, her heart pounding. For once, she didn't have to consider where her father was or what his mood would be. Taking a steadying breath, she triggered the door and strode inside. Dirty cups and dishes filled the sink and overflowed onto the counter. Snarling a curse, she snatched one of her father's cups and hurled it across the room. It crashed against the wall with a satisfying crunch.

It took three full cycles before Ro felt her hair got clean enough. The clothes couldn't be salvaged and she shoved them in the recycler. Wearing a pressed, fresh basic work uniform, Ro headed back to command, struggling to hold onto a fragile sense of control.

The two senior officers guarding the commander's office nodded and passed her request through to Mendez. The door opened. "Come!" Mendez's sharp voice rang out.

In the brief time she'd spent in medical, the staff had been busy. The only sign of the violence that had scarred the room was a jagged line carved across the far wall. The blood had been cleaned off and the floor smoothed back to its unblemished shine. Mendez, too, seemed untouched by the conflict, until she turned and Ro saw the dark bruises beneath her deep-set black eyes.

"You are not your father."

She winced. How true was it? Maybe Nomi could tell her, because she didn't know anymore.

Mendez drew her micro out and gestured toward Ro. Frowning, she pulled her own device from its pocket. The file Mendez sent blinked at her. Emancipation papers. Signed and witnessed.

Her knees trembled and she grabbed at a chair to hold her balance.

"There is the matter of compensation."

Ro's shoulders slumped. They had done a fuck-load of damage when Halcyone blasted free of the station. She had no idea what kind of resources her father had, but she supposed they belonged to her now. It would be better to pay reparations with it than to use it any other way.

"I don't suppose it matters, but I regret the damage my actions have caused." She paused. "Commander, about Halcyone —" Ro hadn't ever wanted anything in her life as much as she wanted that ship. Her ship. The ship she woke from the dead.

"The transport Halcyone has had a salvage claim registered on her by the commander of Hephaestus."

"She's not salvage!" She leaned forward. "She was under my command!"

Mendez raised her eyebrows and Ro fell silent, feeling the blood pulse in her ears.

"That's technically true, Ms. Maldonado. And it's also technically true that her designation is officially registered to a long dissolved private corporation, not the Commonwealth of Planets."

"Oh." Ro could hardly breathe. Would Mendez support her claim?

"But we have yet to settle on compensation."

Her breath eased out of her in a sigh. It would likely take her a lifetime on Daedalus to finish paying for the destruction.

"Rather than a lump sum of credits, would you accept a free-and-clear deed to the ship?"

She stood, blinking. "What?"

"Halcyone. Is she just compensation for your losses and your testimony at the weapons trial?"

Tears blurred her vision, turning Mendez's uniform into a sparkle of silver glints on gray. "Yes," she said. "Yes."

Ro walked through the corridors in a daze, seeing only the lines of the ship. It was battered and scarred, like her. Crew members and station personnel greeted her by name. She didn't think that many people had even known who she was.

At Nomi's quarters, she paused, her hand hovering near the chime. The door slid open and Nomi stood in off-duty casual, a short floral kimono wrapped over slim leggings. Ro glanced down at her gray and silver uniform and wondered if she were actually on duty or not and what it meant for her position on Daedalus that Mendez had given her the ship.

"So, do you actually want to come in?" Nomi said, a gentle smile curving her lips.

"Oh, sorry." Ro took the offered hand and stepped over the threshold. Her blunt, squared off nails contrasted with Nomi's soft skin and smooth fingertips.

"I decided to go with the traditional—tea rather than coffee. Is that okay?" Nomi led her to the sofa. The low table in front was set with a stark, geometric teapot and matching cups, all in a bright glossy white. Steam rose from the teapot and a woody, aromatic scent filled the small space.

"Sure," Ro said, and sat. Nomi sat beside her, poured each cup half full, and handed her one. The fluted squared-off shape fit easily in her hands.

"Thank you."

"The set belonged to my grandmother. She would have liked you."

"Why? Was she blunt and unsocialized, too?"

Nomi laughed. "Well, maybe a little. She was well known for speaking her mind. Not a traditional or desirable trait in the history of Japanese culture, but I adored her."

Ro glanced around the room at all the reminders of Nomi's family and wondered what it would be like to feel connected like that. "You're lucky." She took a sip from the hot tea and set the cup down. "I never want to see my father again."

"Do you think he's still drifting out there?" Nomi gestured up, as if they could see the field of empty stars that surrounded Daedalus.

"I think he's too vindictive to be dead." Ro jumped up and paced the living room area.

Nomi set her tea down and stood, blocking Ro's path. She reached up to cup Ro's face, her thumb gently tracing beneath the suture line across her cheek, just below her left eye. Ro stiffened and Nomi let her hands drop.

"I'm sorry," Ro said, staring into Nomi's disappointed eyes. "I don't think I know how to do this."

"Am I that scary?" Nomi asked.

"No. It's just—" Her father had used her need for companionship as a threat and all those years of fear didn't vanish with him. "I'm sorry. I want—" She didn't know what she wanted, but she didn't want to lose Nomi and her gentleness. "Wait! I have something to show you!"

"I'm not going anywhere," Nomi answered, laughing. "I live here."

Ro sank back onto the sofa and dug out her micro. "Look!" Waking up the screen, she showed her the emancipation papers. "I'm free to go to Uni. Free to leave. To do anything!"

"Congratulations, Ro." Nomi handed her back the micro, her face still, her voice flat. "Where will you go?"

Ro wanted to chase the sadness from Nomi's eyes. "That's not even the best part." Her pulse sped up. Slowly, she reached out to clasp both of Nomi's hands in hers, her body moving on automatic pilot. Part of her brain froze, repeating a terrified

384

mantra. *What am I doing? What am I doing?* She swallowed the fear.

"Halcyone is mine. I can keep her." She looked into Nomi's dark eyes, wanting to see her shared excitement. "I can ... We can go anywhere."

Nomi's eyebrows met in the center of her forehead. Ro wanted to smooth the lines away.

"I don't understand."

"Come with me," Ro whispered, before she could take the words back. She straightened her spine and lifted one hand to touch Nomi's cheek. It was smooth against the roughened skin of her palm. Her hand shook, but her father wasn't here and he no longer had control over her or her choices. "Come with me," she repeated, her voice gaining strength.

Nomi pressed her hand over Ro's before standing and stepping back. "You could stay here. Daedalus is going to need an engineer."

"I can't." Ro winced, unable to meet Nomi's gaze.

"He's not here anymore. There's nothing to run away from."

But her father was still here. He'd dragged her to Daedalus just like he'd dragged her from one posting to another her whole life. "Come with me, Nomi." She stood, afraid to close the distance between them. "Halcyone needs a comms officer."

Nomi smiled sadly and looked around her quarters at the photos crowding the walls. Ro followed her gaze, settling on her graduation picture, a hologram of Nomi, standing between her beaming parents, all three of them with their arms entwined. "I have a responsibility. To them. To Daedalus Station. And obligations to honor." She reached for Ro, gathering her in her arms.

Ro stiffened against the taller woman and forced herself to

breathe. Her head nestled easily against Nomi's shoulder.

"You are not your father," she said. "You don't have to make his mistakes."

"No, I'm perfectly capable of making my own," Ro said, her tears soaking into the soft fabric of Nomi's kimono.

Chapter 42

WALKING INTO THEIR quarters, Barre felt like he had stepped into someone else's past. With a distant, observer's eye, he watched their parents fuss over Jem. His mother gathered him in her arms as if he were a baby and carried him from the transport chair to the living room.

"There's nothing wrong with my legs, Mother," Jem complained.

"You should be in medical," she said, depositing him onto the sofa.

Jem glanced up at his father for support. He stood by the chair, his arms folded. "Look, you said it yourself; they did everything they could on Hephaestus. And I'll be more comfortable here anyway."

His father nodded.

"None of this would have happened if you hadn't interfered in your brother's affairs." The set of his mother's expression had always said anger to him, but when Barre met her gaze now, he recognized the fear.

"You didn't give me a choice!" Jem cried, glaring up at her, his body trembling.

Barre sat next to his brother and took his hand. "We all have choices." If he hadn't made some monumentally stupid ones, things might have ended up differently. He glanced up at both of his parents. His father met his gaze briefly, a flash of pain moving across his face. They had made their own choices as well. And here they all were, trapped at the intersection of them all.

"Barre, you need help. Your father and I have made our decision."

"You can't!" Jem cried. "You don't understand!"

Barre squeezed Jem's hand and stood. "But I do." He squared his shoulders and faced his mother and father. "I did some stupid shit, but I'm okay now. I know what I need to do."

"Barre, no!" Jem shouted.

"I don't have a place in your world, but I have a place in my own." He thought he saw a flicker of pain pass through his father's expression, but it was gone before he could be sure, replaced by his usual stoic frown. "I'm not asking for anything you don't want anyway." They would have their orderly life and their genius child to continue the family legacy. Barre would no longer be their problem to fix.

The play of emotions across his mother's face told Barre everything he could ever hope to understand. He walked over to her and took her cold hands in his, leaned down and kissed her cheek. "You have what you need. This is what I need," he said, softly.

His father gave him a huge spine-cracking hug. It was the kind of touch Barre hadn't remembered getting from him since he was younger than Jem.

"Please, don't go," Jem said, his voice thick, his eyes shining.

He knelt by his brother's side. "Look, you know there's nothing for me here. And don't worry; I'll only be as far as your micro."

A wild look of fear flitted across Jem's face before he threw his arms around Barre's neck. "I want to hear all the music you make, okay?"

"You got it, kiddo."

"Where will you go?" his mother asked, her voice raspy, tuneless.

"My emancipation petition will be lodged with Commander Mendez," Barre answered. "I think it's best for everyone if you sign it without protest."

No one said a word as he slipped into his old bedroom and packed a small bag. He looked around at the music and instruments he had collected over a lifetime. Stroking his hands across a replica of an old style twelve-string guitar, he listened until the echoes and harmonics faded away before leaving it all behind him.

*

Ro walked blindly through the station until she found herself at Halcyone's airlock. The silence of the temporary corridor only increased the emptiness she felt inside. She rested her head against the dulled metal of the hull. The ship or Nomi. She couldn't have both.

"Halcyone, unseal the outer door."

Nothing happened. She tried triggering the release through her micro, but it wouldn't pair with the AI. Was she under quarantine? Had Targill disputed her claim? Ro's mouth dried. She'd walked away from Nomi. If she had also lost Halcyone, then there was nowhere she belonged. She swore and slammed her hand against the hull, wincing at the pain that traveled up the length of her arm.

"Here. Let me try."

Ro whirled around. Barre stood blocking her way in the umbilical, a bag thrown across one wide shoulder. He whistled a brief fanfare and waved his arm toward the lock. "All yours."

She glared at him before turning back to the ship. "Halcyone, unseal the outer door." The airlock cycled and it sprung open with an audible pop. "What are you doing here?"

"Same as you, I'd bet."

His tone seemed casual, but even Ro's untrained, unmusical ear heard a kindred sadness in it. He stepped into the lock with her and shut the outer door. Ro triggered the inner door to open. Her shoulders relaxed as she returned to her ship. Her ship. Relief flooded through her. "How did you know I'd be here?"

"I didn't. Not for sure. But I figured whoever claimed her was going to need me."

"You are going to have to teach me to do that."

"What? And put myself out of a job?"

She stopped and Barre bumped into her. Slowly turning around, she confronted him. "Are you asking to stay on the ship?"

He clutched his bag to his chest and stepped back. "Would you let me if I did?"

"She's officially mine, now," Ro said. "In all her damaged glory."

The wild hope that lit Barre's eyes was also something she recognized.

"But she's going to need work. This isn't a holiday cruise."

He laughed, a deep, hearty sound that filled the corridor. "Not like our last trip, then?"

Her laughter joined his. A familiar melody played through Halcyone's speakers in harmony with them. "I guess she approves."

Barre shrugged.

Ro smoothed down her uniform tunic and stuck out her hand. Barre shook it, a huge smile breaking across his face. "Well, then, welcome aboard, Doc." Halcyone was going to need everything both of them could give before she was fully functional again. "Time to get to work."

"My pleasure, Captain."

She smiled a small, private smile and strode toward the bridge.

* * *

Acknowledgments

Two years ago, I had this crazy idea about a derelict space ship, its AI damaged in a long ago war, and a group of teens who inadvertently wake it up. This novel developed from that image, from brainstorming sessions with my husband, Neil, and with my SFWG critique buddies, as well as from many hours of daydreaming.

I owe a debt of gratitude to my dream-team—the talented and hard-working writers who critiqued draft versions of the story, including Lisa DiDio, R.J. Blain, A.J. Dyer, Chris Howard (yes, the same talented Chris Howard who created the cover art that graces this novel), Mike Reeves-McMillan, Susan Spann, and DL Keur.

Thank you to Erin M. Hartshorn, K.M. Frontain, Heather Webb, Janet Taylor, DeAnn Smith, April Brown, Mehdi Piloor, Emily Winch, Elaina Newton, Melodee Engle, and Lorena Lombardo who gave me important and helpful feedback on the opening chapters when I feared I had lost my perspective.

And to Lynn Viehl, Nathan Lowell, Wen Spencer, and Jeff Carver: Thank you for your encouragement and your support. It means the world (and beyond) to me.

~LJ, June 2014

About the Author

LJ Cohen is the writing persona of Lisa Janice Cohen, poet, novelist, blogger, local food enthusiast, Doctor Who fan, and relentless optimist. Lisa lives just outside of Boston with her family, two dogs (only one of which actually ever listens to her) and the occasional international student. When not doing battle with a stubborn Jack Russell Terrier mix, Lisa can be found working on the next novel, which often looks a lot like daydreaming.

Connect with LJ online:

Homepage: http://www.ljcohen.net/
Blog: http://ljcbluemuse.blogspot.com/
Newsletter:
http://www.ljcohen.net/mailinglist/mail.cgi/list/bluemusings
Facebook: http://www.facebook.com/ljcohen
Twitter: @lisajanicecohen
Tumblr: http://www.ljcohen.tumblr.com
Google+: https://www.google.com/+LisaCohen
email LJ: lisa@ljcohen.net

Want to read more?

Sign up for Blue Musings, an occasional email newsletter complete with free, original, short fiction offered in a variety of drm-free formats. (www.ljcohen.net/contact.html)

Other titles by LJ Cohen: (available in all eBook and trade paperback formats)
THE BETWEEN
FUTURE TENSE
STRANGER WORLDS THAN THESE (short story collection)
TIME AND TITHE (January 2015)

Edited by LJ Cohen:
PEN-ULTIMATE: A Speculative Fiction Anthology